A MODERN CANDIDE

By
Richard A. Uhlig Sr.

Copyright © 2013 Richard A. Uhlig Sr.
All rights reserved.
ISBN: 1489571043
ISBN 13: 9781489571045

Dedicated to my Uncle Cecil,
a man and storyteller
of great ebullience.

*To a great Sis-in-law, Doris;
hope you enjoy it.
Love,
Dick*

Chapter 1
MOTHER

Harkerville, Kansas

At 6:30 AM, the coffee klatch gathers at Mom's Café on Main Street. Farmers in bib overalls, plaid shirts, ball caps, and manure-caked boots, fresh from chores, garrulous, gossipy, congregate around two large tables near the kitchen. About 6:45 AM sleepy-eyed merchants in leisure suits and Stetson hats stumble in, eager for a jaw-loosening, sunup jolt of roasted mud. Toss a quarter in the bowl and you can sip coffee and flap-jaw right up to lunchtime. Gray-headed, Khaki-clad, knit-shirted retirees take up seats at the counter and in the booths along the wall. The grumble of male voices intensifies as coffee flows. Amicable *hell yes* and *you're damn right* punctuate the chatter. They talk about the weather, politics, ballgames, and the cost of fertilizer. "Hey, did you see on the news where…"

Dead spots happen when sudden insights or profound confusions grip the whole. During a lull, Kent Mullins asked: "Does anybody know where flies go in the winter?"

"Why, they hibernate, don't they?"

"Nah, they fly south."

"They burrow underground."

"Hey, Charlie. Where do flies go in the winter?"

"Florida?"

"They hide in attics where it's warm."

Leona, the waitress, a grainy alto in a din of baritones, piped, "A fly in the house at Christmas is good luck."

"They come and go with the seasons."

"They're worst in August."

People in this prairie hamlet knew Kent Mullins as the kid who went around asking questions. Kent pumped people for answers because he desperately wanted to know things and he couldn't read very well, hardly at all. Whenever he stared at the printed page, letters of the alphabet twisted into hieroglyphics and words ran together like raindrops on the windshield of a speeding car. His brain flat-out refused to make sense of written symbols. When Kent, a likable good-natured kid, wanted to know something, he'd just ask people. And most Harkervillians gave considered and thoughtful answers to his many questions.

Concerned about her son's intellectual development, Mrs. Mullins dragged Kent to a variety of specialists: neurologists, psychologists, and ophthalmologists. He underwent blood tests, brain wave test, draw-a-man test, arrange the blocks test, and tell-a-story-from-the-pictures test. Finally, a specialist in a big city told Kent's mom, "Your son suffers from *dyslearnia*. It's a rare condition, the afflicted learn only by listening. The written word means very little to them."

"Can you help my son?"

The specialist shook his head grimly. "There is no known treatment for this condition."

Some people thought Kent eccentric, for after graduating high school at age twenty-one he still went around town politely interrogating people. If Kent were eccentric, he could afford to be. Kent was a millionaire.

Kent's mother, a strikingly tall, affable woman became a millionaire when a trucker driving a flatbed loaded three-high with half-ton hay bales slammed on the brakes to avoid hitting a yellow cat crossing the highway a mile north of town. Hay bales rumbled off the truck in an avalanche, two of them crashing down on Kent's dad's red Honda Prelude like giant anvils dropped from the sky. The hay bales flattened the Honda and smashed Mr. Mullins' face all over the steering wheel, killing him instantly. The funeral was closed-casket.

Kent's mother happened upon the accident on her way home from a Domestic Science Club meeting where she'd taken pictures for the club's yearbook. She had the good sense to snap shots of the accident with her new digital camera. Armed with her photos she sued the feedlot that owned the truck and the hay bales. Normally, a person isn't worth much in an injury case if they're dead. But when the jury saw the pictures of Mr. Mullins' head smashed all over the dented-in steering wheel and his mangled body covered in blood and hay, and when they saw Kent and his mother sitting there in the courtroom in an ocean of tears, they awarded Mrs. Mullins two million dollars.

The next year, Kent's mom died from an overdose of bagworm poison that destroyed her red and white blood cells. She hated those wormy-critters that chewed up her evergreens and rolled themselves into ugly little sleeping bags that dangled vulgarly from the mutilated branches. In a desperate attempt to save her doomed trees, she sprayed every Spruce, Juniper, and Boxwood in the yard eight times. That was seven times too many. For good measure, she sprayed the trees once more, straight from the little amber bottles, undiluted. A massive overdose. Some weeks later, her blood cells began dying. Kent watched in horror as his mother shriveled up and wasted away like a piece of forgotten fruit in the back of the refrigerator. She died painlessly with Kent, Father Donley, and Dr. Jenkins at her bedside.

Being an only child, Kent suddenly found himself abandoned, awed by the injustices and mysteries of a strange and unrevealing world--an orphan who couldn't read, who had a burning desire to know things, an orphan with three million dollars. The two million his mother got from the hay bale accident, plus five hundred thousand from his dad's life insurance, and another five hundred thousand from his mother's life insurance.

The night of his mother's funeral, Kent dreamt he was standing on the loading platform of a railway station like in those old movies: passengers rushing to the trains, a locomotive spewing steam into the air, a conductor in a black uniform shouting, "All aboard," and Kent's mom waving good-bye to Kent from an opened coach window.

"Why do you have go?" Kent cried running along side the moving coach.

"I don't have much choice. This the D-train."

"Where is it going?"

"I got my fingers crossed."

Kent ran faster to keep up with the outbound train. "I'll miss you."

She leaned out the window, tears streaking her face. "I'll miss you, too, sweetie."

Kent sat upright in bed and rubbed his eyes. Outside his bedroom window the morning sun crept over the horizon, reddening the sky. *What exactly is death? Why does it frighten me so? What really happens when someone dies? Who could I ask about death?*

Chapter 2
FATHER DONLEY

Most people slave away day in and day out to earn a living, to pay the rent, to keep their heads above water, but millionaires can do whatever they please. They can sleep late. Play golf any day of the week. Go skiing. Hang out at health clubs. Run for political office. Take warm-water cruises on luxury liners manned by impoverished third world refugees. Kent didn't do any of these. Instead, he dedicated his life to finding answers to difficult and puzzling questions. The questions foremost on his mind concerned death.

Kent decided to ask Leona, the sixty year-old, chain-smoking, crinkled-faced waitress at Mom's Café about death. He placed great value in Leona's opinions because she always told him straight out what she thought, and what she thought was usually what other people in Harkerville thought, the pulse of the working class. He recalled her terse reply when he once asked for her opinion about there being life on Mars. Leona spat in a breath laced with tobacco and coffee, "Who gives a shit about Mars."

Kent sauntered into Mom's Café at lunchtime. Finding it impossible to make eye contact with Leona as she flittered table-to-table with her sloshing coffee pot, Kent slipped into an empty booth and waited. When Leona finally waltzed over, Kent asked, "Leona, what do you think really happens when someone dies?"

She jabbed the coffee pot at him. "I don't have time to bullshit, it's lunchtime. You wanta eat or not?"

Kent ordered a cheeseburger with fries. Lunch at Mom's Café was an everyday town meeting. Weather talk. Back slapping. Country music blaring. Hamburgers sizzling in onions. The clinking of dishes melded with the buzz of small talk. While stirring a glob of ketchup with a fry, Kent got an idea. Why not direct his questions on death to the professionals of

Harkerville, those not preoccupied with the demands of everyday living, learned men who had studied and reflected on difficult subjects. He decided to get two views on death: the religious and the scientific.

※

The red brick rectory squatted like a satellite beside the church, also red brick all the way up to the cone-shaped cupola. Kent knocked lightly on the rectory's door, waited, and then knocked again with more vigor. Father Donley finally opened the door, his white collar loosened around his neck, his shirt half-pulled out of his black britches, his hair in disarray, his wizened face squinting severely at Kent as if he had intentionally interrupted Father's afternoon reverie of smoke and drink.

"I'd like to ask you some questions, Father."

"Does it have to be today? Oh well, since you're here come on in."

The dimly lit parlor smelled of cigar smoke, old furniture, and old books. Kent like most of his fellow parishioners knew Father Donley preferred to spend his leisure hours in the company of his old friend, Jack Daniels. Father eyed his visitor almost contemptuously. "You know, it's come to my attention that you're still grieving. I never see you a Mass or morning prayers anymore. People say you've become a gloomy recluse."

Kent shrugged. "I suppose I'll always be grieving some."

Father dipped his head, pointing to the couch by the front window. "Sit down, my boy. I realize losing both parents within such a short time span was a terrible shock. But let me reassure you, your mother was a good Catholic woman and your father a fine man. They're in God's hands now and that's all you really need to know."

Kent nervously clasped his hands together as he sat. "I just don't understand death. It's on my mind constantly."

Father's forehead wrinkled, and he growled from deep in his windpipe. "Don't think about it. Your parents were given the rites and good Catholic funerals. And I understand they left you well endowed, which reminds me," he suddenly spoke in a softer tone, "have you given any thought to our parish fund?"

"To be honest I can't think about anything but death. It keeps me awake nights."

"Get over it, you won't see them again until Judgment Day."

"You don't understand, it's not just that, I mean it's not so much that I'm grieving, it's just…well, I don't understand death. Anybody's death. I want to know what death is. Why does it have to happen?"

Father shook his head wearily. "Have you read the passages from the Order of Christian Funerals?"

"I had someone read them to me. Frankly, they didn't make much sense. They seem to evade the question of death."

Although Kent couldn't read, as a youth he had no trouble memorizing and reciting his catechism once it was read to him. In Sunday school he was the one asking impertinent questions, like "How do you know God exists? A talking snake, c'mon, I don't buy it. A parrot maybe? How did Noah get all those animals onto one boat?"

Father glanced at his cigar smoldering in an ashtray across the room beside his drink. "I don't want you dwelling on this. Just be a good Catholic, say your Hail Mary's, and attend Mass. Don't worry about things like death."

Father Donley was getting agitated, his face reddening, his lips thinning. Talking with Father was a little like talking with the marble sculpture of St. Peter perched in the apse of the church's sanctuary, a stern countenance, glazed eyes peering weightily downward, and nothing registering. At confession, whenever Kent looked into Father's scowling, leonine face through the crosshatches of the confessional booth, he felt as if he were standing at the tollgate to Purgatory. He always confessed something banal, like oversleeping or shooting rubber bands at the neighbor's cat. He feared if he ever confessed a real sin to Father Donley, the floor of the confession booth would drop open and he'd plummet straight into hell.

Father cleared his throat and managed a fleeting smile for the young parishioner sitting on his couch. "I'm glad we had this talk. I pray you got some good out of it." Before Kent could get off the couch, Father had the front door open. "We'll talk again, my boy. And please give the parish fund some thought."

As Kent walked out of the rectory, his thoughts turned to the new preacher in town who started up a church in an old abandoned grocery store on Walnut Street. It wasn't much of church, only a dozen or so members, but Kent had heard this preacher was friendly and outgoing. Maybe he should ask him about death. What Father didn't know wouldn't hurt him.

Chapter 3
REVEREND HIBBERBLAST

Reverend Hibberblast found religion in the Salem County Jail on a warm July evening. Lying on a hard bunk, contemplating a bleak future, this being his third arrest for drunkenness and spousal abuse, he glanced through the iron bars at the television in the jail corridor. There Bobby Haggett, handsome, well groomed, impeccably attired in an Italian silk suit, a TV evangelist, waved a floppy Bible in cadence with his rising and falling pathos-choked voice. "If you are burdened by sin or sickness, brother; if you have fallen into temptation; if your life has become one misfortune after another; then come to the Lord. Let Jesus carry your burdens. Let Him shine a redeeming light into the dark hollows of your soul. Yes, brother. He will lift you up. Free you from the pain and shame of sin. He will cast out the devil. Heal your body. Renew your soul. Come brother, behold the power!"

Hibberblast sat up on the bunk, his eyes raining tears, his heart singing, and his soul rejoicing. "Come brother," commanded the evangelist. "Come down to the altar and be anointed with the love and the power of the Lord. And you brothers and sisters out there in television land, lay your hands upon your TV set and pray along with me."

Hibberblast stretched his arms through the bars as far as he could, his hands grasping.

The next morning at the arraignment, Hibberblast's battered wife shuffled into the courtroom with two small children in hand. She looked at her husband in astonishment, his normally booze-red eyes were clear and vibrant, the perpetual scorn in his face replaced by a smile. On bent knee before the judge and his children, Hibberblast promised this wife, "I'll never drink again, dear, never carouse and never touch you except with loving caresses. I'm going to become a man of God."

The judge peered over his spectacles suspiciously at the groveling defendant, askance rather than mercy in his countenance. Mrs. Hibberblast looked up at the judge with teary, ecchymotic eyes. "Please, your honor, for my sake and the children's give him another chance."

The judge's eyes narrowed and he spoke sternly to the defendant. "If I see you in my courtroom one more time, it'll be three strikes and out. You understand?"

Hibberblast spoke softly and humbly. "I do, your honor."

All charges dropped, Mrs. Hibberblast headed out of the courtroom with her repentant husband in tow.

"Praise the Lord! Praise the Lord!" Hibberblast shouted from the courthouse steps.

The next morning, his eyes tightly closed, Hibberblast blindly tossed a dart at the Rand McNally Road Atlas thumb tacked to the wall of the family's crudely furnished, two-room urban apartment. The dart stuck in a tiny dot in the middle of the USA, a place called Harkerville.

"Come on, we're moving today," Hibberblast announced to his family as he stood in his underwear, staring at the map, his exposed skin a rainbow of tattoos.

"Where are we going," Mrs. Hibberblast asked.

"To a land flowing with milk and honey. A place called Harkerville. That's where I'll start my ministry. With a little patience and hard work, I'll someday wear a silk suit and preach on TV, and we'll be rich just like Bobby Haggett."

"Where will you get the money to start your ministry?"

"We'll sell your wedding ring and the diamond necklace you inherited."

Mrs. Hibberblast bristled. "That was my great grandmother's necklace, a keepsake."

Hibberblast put his arm his wife and squeezed her gently to his chest, while slipping the ring from her finger. "We have to sacrifice for the Lord, for the ministry." He looked heavenward. "Our reward will be seven times seven times seventy."

In less than a week, Reverend Hibberblast opened his *The Gospel of the True Living God Church* in an abandoned grocery store in Harkerville, the first six months rent-free for cleaning up the place. At a garage sale he bought a JESUS SAVES neon sign and hung it out front. Sunday services swung, guitars twanged, a karaoke blared, and from the pulpit Hibberblast praised the Lord, blasted the devil, and drummed for money. So loud was the music, so rollicking the services that the JESUS SAVES sign jiggled precariously above the door, causing passersby to cross to the other side of the street. Town folks came to call the church, "The Shaking Grocery Store Church."

The reverend went about his ecclesiastical duties in a black suit, a white collar, and with a brass crucifix dangling from his neck. His grinning face and contagious affability earned him the reputation of being a nice guy. But beneath his Andy Griffith exterior blazed an Elmer Gantry fire.

Kent climbed out of his car at the supermarket and spotted Reverend Hibberblast lugging a sack of groceries across the parking lot. He recognized the reverend from his picture on the flyers floating around town inviting people to *The Gospel of the True Living God Church*. A stout man with straight dark hair, a bald spot, a strong nose and chin, and intense brown eyes, Hibberblast strolled over to a beat-up, dented-in, rusted-out red and white El Dorado coupe de Ville, a fugitive from the scrap yard. A tattoo of a naked girl with red flowing hair graced the reverend's right forearm wrapped around a sack of groceries. The redhead danced whenever the muscles in his arm contracted.

"Reverend," Kent called out, running across the parking lot, "may I ask you some questions about death?"

Hibberblast turned and faced the young man, his brows raised. "Are you ill?"

"Nah, I'm just curious about what death is and what happens when someone dies?"

Hibberblast shifted the sack of groceries to his other arm. "It all depends. Are you saved?"

Kent eyed the reverend closely. "I'm not concerned about me. I'm speaking of death in general terms."

The reverend tossed his groceries into the back seat of his Cadillac. "Well, you should be concerned about your soul." He shoved one of his flyers at Kent. "Listen, why don't you come around to Sunday services. I'll get you right with the Lord."

Kent took the flyer and said politely, "I think I already am."

"Oh, yeah?"

"I'm Catholic."

The reverend crawled into his heap and fished in his pocket for his car keys. "Well, I've nothing against Catholics per say, 'cept they don't read their Bibles much and they tend to play with idols."

Kent leaned on the car door. "Just what is death anyway?"

The reverend thought for minute and smiled warily at Kent. "It's nothing to be afraid of, son, that is, if you're saved. Think of it as a trip.

A one way trip to an eternal fiery Hell, or to the eternal bliss and joy of Heaven. It's up to you where you go."

The reverend turned the key in the ignition and the El Dorado shook like a wino with the jitters. Kent stepped back. The reverend leaned out the window. "I'm worried about your soul, boy. Don't throw away eternal life. Sunday, the old grocery store." With a burp of black smoke the El Dorado lunged like a wounded animal out into the street.

Chapter 4
CLEO

Not satisfied with the religious views he'd garnered on death, Kent set out to get a scientific perspective on the subject. He'd ask his old biology teacher, Mr. Hoover, about death. In high school, Hoover took a keen interest in Kent's inability to recognize letters and words and tutored him after school, not only about biology, but also about life in general. To bolster Kent's self-confidence, Hoover put him in charge of the biology department's pickled pig fetus collection. Although retired with a bad heart, Hoover without a doubt was still the most scientific mind in Harkerville.

When Kent rang the doorbell at the Hoover house, Mrs. Hoover opened the door and peered out through the screen. She looked more gray and bent than he remembered her.

"Hello, Mrs. Hoover. Is Mr. Hoover home?"

"Oh, it's you. Haven't seen you since your mother's funeral. How have you been?"

Kent smiled. "Just fine, Mrs. Hoover. I was wondering if I could speak with Mr. Hoover?"

"He's not here, he's in the hospital."

"Nothing serious, I hope."

She looked a little shaken. "It's his heart. Thought when he got that special new pacemaker, he'd get better. And here he is short of breath again. Poor man. Listen, why don't you go by the hospital and see him."

"Are you sure?"

"He'd be delighted to see you."

"Okay, I think I will. You take care now."

While driving to the hospital, Kent thought about his old girlfriend, the nurse, Cleo. They had had an intense, passionate relationship that ended abruptly. The thought of running into her again made Kent a little nervous.

Generally, girls weren't attracted to Kent. He wasn't an awe-inspiring physical specimen: slumped shouldered, small chin, a caved-in chest that to him looked like the Grand Canyon, and unruly hair that never looked groomed no matter how much gel and conditioner he used. He did have a marvelous smile that allowed him to make friends easily, but it had never gotten him into the sack with anyone, until Cleo.

In high school, Kent secretly admired the cute blond cheerleader, Cleo. She hung with a clique that hobnobbed with jocks, making her as inaccessible to Kent as the latest *Playboy* centerfold. Two ships sailing different seas. She was a coed celebrity, and he was Kent Mullins, the kid who asked questions. Although the same age as Kent, Cleo graduated high school three years ahead of him. It takes a little longer when you can't read. The year he finally graduated high school, he bumped into her at a movie concession. They bumped hard and Cleo's coke spilled down the front of his trousers. "Oh, I'm so sorry," she apologized.

"It's all right, don't worry about it." Kent thought that was the end of it and settled into a seat in the back of theater where he fanned his wet trousers with his hand. The lady seated across the aisle stared suspiciously at him. Then came Cleo with a lace hanky and sat down beside him.

"Please, let me help. I feel terrible about getting your pants all wet."

"Really, that's not necessary."

"I'm a nurse, I know best. There. How's that?"

"Terrific."

Watching Cleo blot the wet spots on Kent's pants must have further upset the lady across the aisle. She got up and returned with the manager who escorted Kent and Cleo out of the theater. They went to Mom's Cafe for cokes and fries.

Settled snugly in a booth at the back of the cafe, Kent leaned his elbows on the Formica tabletop and smiled at Cleo. "That was pretty lousy of that manager to throw us out of the movie."

"Maybe not. Otherwise we wouldn't be sitting here talking to each another."

"Hey, you're right. Everything happens for the best, that's what my mom used to say. So you're a nurse, huh?"

"First year out of training. I work at the hospital. It's just wonderful, fighting disease and helping people. Just yesterday I helped Dr. Jenkins removed an appendix. It had almost burst."

"Is that bad?"

"Terrible. The little girl might have died of infection."

"What kind of infection?"

"Bacterial of course. There are dangerous bacteria everywhere. Even right here on this table. On your hands even. That's why we scrub up before surgery."

Kent stared at his hands. "I see."

Cleo asked, "What do you do?"

Kent shrugged. "Well, nothing much. I guess I do whatever I want, like going to movies, talking with people, asking questions."

"I remember you were always asking questions in high school?"

Kent said sheepishly, "Yeah, I can't read."

Cleo cracked a smile. "That's all right. We all have difficulties. I had an uncle who was blind. And a cousin who couldn't talk until she was twelve years-old." Cleo giggled. "Now she never shuts up. Listen, anytime you'd like me to read to you, I'd be happy to."

"That's nice. Say would you like to go to movie sometime."

Cleo reached across the table and gently rubbed her thumb over Kent's hand. "If we don't get kicked out. Friday night?"

"It's a date."

Old Hoover had taught his biology students that the desire to have sex was due to DNA, those twisted-up molecules inside our cells that determine everything about us: the color of our eyes, how tall we'll be, and whether we'll become serial killers or presidents or both. According to Hoover, sex was nothing more than DNA acting out its chemistry. Those corkscrew genes have one purpose, Hoover told his students, to reproduce themselves. He explained that DNA lived on generation after generation, only as long as there were sex and babies. He claimed DNA's lust for immortality was the driving force behind history.

Cleo taught Kent things about sex old Hoover hadn't mentioned in biology class. Like the tongue was a sex organ. She taught him French love, Italian love, and the international conjugal. He learned to do it upside down, backwards, and perpendicular. In bed, Cleo was an Olympian. A gold medalist. Kent was a mere bronze and could hardly keep up with his beautiful blonde girlfriend with firm medium-size breasts and exquisite creamy satin skin. But he loved trying.

One morning after a long lovemaking session, Kent lay exhausted on his bed. Cleo had already dressed and left for work. Kent stared up at the ceiling and asked himself, why had this voluptuous woman fallen in love with a skinny nerd like me? The answer jumped out at him as vividly as if his mother had read it to him. He was a millionaire. Was she in love with his money? He never told her he was a millionaire. Maybe it was his new Mercedes that tipped her off, but it was C180 not a 600SL. He recalled that Cleo's uncle was the Mercedes dealer in Kansas City where he bought the car. Did her uncle tell Cleo that Kent was a millionaire?

On a sultry July afternoon, stretched out on a blanket at the Harkerville Lake, his stomach bulging with Kentucky Fried Chicken, Kent rolled over and looked into Cleo's sparkling eyes. The wind tossed loose strands of hair across her face.

She brushed back her hair, smiled at him, and in a low voice asked, "When are you going to make an honest woman of me? We've been an item for sometime."

Kent had to know if she really loved him or if she was just looking for marriage followed by a quick divorce and years of alimony.

He rose up on an elbow. "I can't get married just yet. I lost all my money at the casinos and dog races."

Startled by Kent's revelation, Cleo shot up from the blanket. "You're joking?"

"Do you know anyone who wants to buy a Mercedes? I need to unload it to pay the taxes on my house."

The blood siphoned from Cleo's face and shock filled her eyes. "You mean you're really broke?"

"Broke as a bum." Cleo headed for the car. He picked up the blanket and followed her. "I guess I could find a job somewhere."

In the car, Cleo stared into the rearview mirror and brushed her hair with vicious strokes. Her lips blanched with anger. "What kind of job?"

"I'm not really qualified for much of anything."

"Then you are a bum. No money. No job."

He slid across the seat and put his arm around her. "It's not that bad, baby."

She shoved his arm away. "Keep your hands to yourself and take me home."

Cleo was crying when she got out of the car. "It isn't fair," she sobbed, "I never want to see you again!"

Kent thought his question had been answered.

Some people claim breaking up is harder on the girl than the boy. Kent wouldn't agree. It had been over a year now and he still craved the touch of Cleo's skin, the moist sweetness of her lips, and her Olympian bedroom performances.

Kent parked his Mercedes in the visitor's lot of the Harkerville Hospital and leaned his head back against the headrest. What would he say to Cleo if he bumped into her? A lot had happened since they broke up. Cleo married Larry Lakes, president of Green Pasture Fertilizer and Pesticide. Several months later, a judge sent Larry to prison for polluting the water in Harkerville with pesticides. Cleo divorced Larry shortly after the gavel fell. Larry went bankrupt and there wasn't any alimony.

Kent climbed out of his Mercedes determined to stay focused on the business at hand--death. If he ran into Cleo, well, he'd just be nice and polite.

The hospital was a dinky one-story bone factory. The nurse at the nurse's desk busily counted out pills into little plastic cups. Kent rubbed his eyes and took a second look. Cleo! She still looked beautiful. Kent's heart flip-flopped.

"Hello, Cleo."

She looked up at him, hurt showing in those extraordinary eyes that gleamed like gems above the arches of her cheekbones. "What are you doing here?"

"Uh, I-I came to see Hoover."

Her left eyebrow rose. "You've been driving a brand new Mercedes every year. You never was broke, were you?"

"Well, I…uh…I wanted to explain…but you said you never wanted to see me again."

"I didn't mean it. Anyway, Mr. Hoover is in room 127."

"How's he doing?"

She shrugged casually. "Not so good. His heart's getting weaker."

Kent leaned across the desk drawn by the magnetic attraction of Cleo's glittering blue eyes. When she put her hand on his, he trembled all over. The flame still flickered, but he wasn't going to stoke it. He was here about death. With a great effort Kent pulled his hand away.

Chapter 5
HOOVER

Kent headed down the hospital corridor past rooms where TV's played and patients moved about, their spindly legs and bony butts exposed by short, flowered gowns unabashedly opened in the back. In room 110, Millie Davis shouted at her husband, Ervin, who'd been dead ten years, something about the cistern going dry. Across the hallway, Father Donley mumbled the sacrament of Last Rites over old Bill Parker. The antiseptic smell of the place reminded Kent of his fifth grade tonsillectomy.

Kent peered into room 127 at Hoover stretched out on his bed with a green oxygen tube in his nose, his dentures in a plastic cup beside him, and wires stuck to his chest leading to a heart monitor. The toothless open mouth, the closed eyes, and sunken cheeks gave a cadaverous appearance to Kent's old mentor.

Kent stepped quietly into the room and cleared his throat. Hoover's eyes opened. "Kent, is that you?"

"Yes sir, it's me." Kent suddenly felt guilty. How could he ask a dying man about death? He wished he hadn't come. "How are you feeling, sir?"

Hoover raised his head, nodded, and with a gasping chuckle said, "Like a pickled pig fetus. Come on, what's on your mind? I can tell when something's bothering you."

Kent looked at the little spikes on the heart monitor all jumbled and irregular. Hoover rallied, his eyes brightening, a hint of a smile on his face. "Don't hide anything from me," he exhorted, wagging a finger. "We were always open and honest with each other."

That the old man seemed pleased to see him heartened Kent. He recalled that day in biology class when Hoover, dissecting a frog, suddenly straightened, his eyes wide with wonder, his whole body trembling with excitement. A scalpel fell form his hand, and he pounded the dissection table and shouted, "Man is animal! We're all animals! Everybody."

That day was the defining moment of Hoover's long career. After all those years of cutting up little animals and comparing their insides, and all that experience and knowledge smoldering subliminally in his brain, his "Man is Animal Theory" suddenly erupted. All day his voice boomed through the halls of Harkerville High, "Man is an animal! We're all animals! We're all the same on the inside!"

When the Harkerville school board unanimously resolved that Hoover's "Man is an Animal Theory" could not be taught in the school system, Hoover ignored them. Everyday, he told his students they were animals, even after the school board demoted him to teaching mathematics. Even when the ministerial alliance paraded in front of the school brandishing "WE ARE NOT ANIMALS" signs, Hoover would not relent. Kent remembered the day Hoover threw open the second story window of his math class, looked down at the parading mob and gave them the "finger."

Hoover looked at his former student, an avuncular grin on his face. "You know I didn't flunk you in biology because you were honest. You asked questions that, well, they were questions others took for granted or didn't think to ask. I can't tell you how often you caught me off guard. If I had flunked you and I could have, you'd never graduated, you realize that?"

"Yes sir, I do."

"So, better tell me what's on your mind. I haven't had an intellectual challenge since you graduated."

Kent spoke slowly, "I'd like to know about death. What actually happens when someone dies?"

"Death! You hit on an appropriate topic there. I've been giving that a lot of thought lately. You see my heart muscles are weak and…" Kent listened intently while Hoover chronicled his medical history: three heart attacks, bypass surgery, stents, an artificial valve, a pacemaker, abnormal beats, blood thinners, then a new bigger and better pacemaker, a variety of high-powered drugs, and now this oxygen tube in his nose. "I blame the damn school board for my heart attacks, the bastards. All at once Hoover's eyes turned milky and he began panting, the paleness returning to his face.

"Are you okay, sir?"

"A little short of air," Hoover gasped. "Would ask the nurse to turn my oxygen up."

Kent nodded and rushed up the corridor to the nurses' desk where Cleo sat peeling an orange. "Cleo, Hoover wants more oxygen. He doesn't look so good."

"Sure." Cleo grabbed Hoover's chart and started down the corridor. Kent followed her. She stopped and turned to Kent. "You know I just can't get over you lying to me about your Mercedes and being broke and all."

Kent shook his head. "If I hadn't, we probably gotten married, then divorced, and you'd be living off alimony."

Cleo resumed her fast-paced walk. "That's not fair. We were getting along pretty good."

"Yeah, until you thought I was broke."

"A girl has to make sure her man can support her." She stopped at Hoover's room. "You wait out here."

Kent watched Cleo hurry into Hoover's room. It suddenly dawned on him that what she said made perfect sense. He recalled Hoover telling his biology students that all boys think about is getting their penises into the moist cul-de-sac of the feminine body. Those were his exact words, the moist cul-de-sac being the vagina. Forced into this thought and behavior mode by hormones ordered up by their DNA, boys, according to Hoover, function primarily as sperm donors. Girls on the other hand make families, because that's what their DNA wants them to do. Hoover claimed it was up to the female of the species to sort out from all those horny boys which ones would make dependable mates, loving parents, and good providers. The whole boy-girl saga was due to DNA wanting to be immortal. Cleo had walked out on Kent because she was sorting out, following the dictates of her DNA. He couldn't blame her for not wanting to marry a bum.

A loud beeping noise, shrill like a fire alarm came from Hoover's room. Another nurse raced by Kent shouting "Code Blue!" Dr. Jenkins came slumping down the hallway in a crumpled gray suit, a stethoscope slung over his shoulder, a look of grave concern on his face. Kent followed him into Hoover's room, where Hoover lay sprawled on the bed, his head arched back, his mouth agape, and Cleo bent over him, pushing up and down on his chest.

"He flat-lined while I was turning up his oxygen," Cleo explained.

The doctor and nurses continued to shove on Hoover's chest, put a bag over his face, stuck needles in him, shot him up with drugs, and shocked him with electrical paddles that caused his body to jerk and sent spirals of odious smoke into the air. The hectic activity went on for fifteen minutes, the medical team working frantically.

Finally, Dr. Jenkins stepped back from the bed and said grimly, "It's no use. He's gone."

Kent asked, "You mean he's dead?"

Dr. Jenkins nodded. "Afraid so. Cardiac arrest."

"But his arms are jumping."

Dr. Jenkins looked at Kent. "It's just his pacemaker stimulating his pectoral muscles, the arms will stop jerking when the batteries in his pacemaker run down." He turned to Cleo. "You can call the chaplain." With that Dr. Jenkins tossed his stethoscope over his shoulder and shuffled out of the room.

Chapter 6
INTERNECINE

The nurses yanked the bed sheets out from under Hoover's body and stuffed them into a green bag along with his hospital gown. The dead pundit lay naked on the bed, arms flapping, a white hernia support clinging to his left groin, and his eyes staring inertly at the ceiling. After covering the body with a clean sheet the nurses headed to the desk to summon the chaplain and the undertaker.

Frozen in the doorway, Kent watched the sheet move eerily up and down as Hoover's arms jerked with each firing of his pacemaker. Kent had never stared death in the face like this before. His mother had faded away slowly, almost peacefully. He didn't see his dad after the fatal hay bale accident, the funeral being closed-casket. He stumbled out into the hallway, frightened, shocked, and confused.

Several minutes later, Reverend Hibberblast, chaplain for the religiously unaffiliated, came puttering down the corridor, Bible in his hand. He smiled at Kent and stepped reverently into Hoover's room. When he saw the sheet wagging up and down, he tossed open his Bible, threw back the sheet, placed his hand on Hoover's head, and cried, "The soul is re-entering the body! Rise up and live again, brother. I command you, rise up!"

Kent watched from the doorway as Reverend Hibberblast danced around the bed, waving his Bible, his bronze crucifix bouncing on his chest, and him shouting for old Hoover to get going.

A dark shadow fell across the doorway. Father Donley in black priestly attire, his nostrils flaring, face furrowing, implacable dark eyes glaring at the goings-on, pushed Kent aside and stepped into the room. Fresh from Bill Parker's Last Rites, Father had come face to face with the latest mutant of the Protestant Reformation, the Shaking Grocery Store Church heretic. Kent thought he heard hackles crinkling under Father's collar. When Father saw Hoover's arms flopping, he must have thought Hibberblast had actually brought the old skeptic back to life--a shameless desecration of the dead. Even though Hoover was a hell-bound unbeliever, Father intervened.

"Stop that, you idiot! What do you think you're doing?"

Rev. Hibberblast glared at the priest. "What am I doing! What are you doing here? This one belongs to me." Hibberblast laid his Bible on Hoover's chest, passed his hands over the body, and commanded the corpse, "Rise up. Walk upon the earth again, ye who has seen the other side."

Father Donley's face turned blood red, much as it does when he has too much Jack Daniels. He chanted in imperfect Latin, *"Tu domine, adjuabius me. Idiota, visne aliquid de illo facere?"*

Hibberblast's eyes narrowed. "Don't give me any of that Latin bullshit. I've got a resurrection going here."

Father stepped up to the bed and the two clerics faced off over Hoover's body like cage fighters at center ring. Hoover's arms flopped feebly now. Father Donley jabbed his crucifix at the heretic. Hibberblast jabbed his crucifix at the priest. Around the bed, came Father, head down, charging like a linebacker.

Hibberblast sidestepped the priest and hurled affronts. "Ransomer of the dead. Indulgence monger. Blind guide."

Kent stepped back from the door, his head bent in contemplation. Death seemed more mysterious than ever. He needed answers.

Father Donley had Hibberblast in a headlock and the two men of the cloth tumbled across the room, kicking, scratching, and grunting.

Father growled, "Had enough, tergiversator?"

"Idolater," Hibberblast countered and drove his fist into the priest's paunch. The air went out of Father like a burst balloon. Hibberblast, an ex-bar fighter, gouged his thumbs into the priest's eyes. Father groped blindly about the room throwing wild haymakers and left jabs. Hibberblast whopped him on the head with a stainless steel bedpan and then helped the wobbly priest into a chair. Father's gouged eyes spun like lemons in a slot machine. Hoover's arms stopped flopping.

Kent turned and walked away down the hall. *Who can I ask about death now that Hoover is gone?*

Chapter 7
TOMMY TENNYSON

Hoover's obituary, all too brief for a man so brilliant, for a man who caused such a commotion in the school system, for a man who meant so much to so many students, simply stated he was born, taught school 40 years, and was survived by his wife--as if 40 years were a Popsicle on the hot August pavement. Emerson Funeral Home overflowed with Hoover's friends and his ex-students. After the graveside ceremony, Kent took Mrs. Hoover by the arm and walked over to the undertaker's limousine. She looked at Kent and smiled. "He thought the world of you."

"He was my all time favorite teacher."

Mrs. Hoover hugged Kent. When he turned to walk away, he noticed Cleo standing near the limousine in a black dress, blotting her eyes with a lace hanky, a small black hat with an upturned veil askew on her head.

"Hi, Cleo."

"I have a message for you."

Kent smiled. "Oh, from who?"

"Hoover."

Kent looked startled. "What are you talking about?"

She stepped closer and spoke in a soft voice. "That evening at the hospital, while I was adjusting his oxygen, just before he flat-lined, he grabbed my hand and whispered, 'Tommy Tennyson. Tell Kent to ask Tommy.' Those were his last words. What do you suppose it means?"

Kent scratched his head. "Tommy Tennyson? Well, he lived down from street from me, but I didn't know him very well. Nobody did."

"Wasn't he the weirdo with the humongous ears?"

"Yeah, everybody made fun of him. But he's the smartest person around these parts. I hear he's a full-fledged professor." Kent took a quick breath. "That's it. Hoover knew if anyone could answer my questions about death, Tommy could."

Tommy Tennyson had graduated Harkerville High valedictorian, a perfect 4.0, all solid subjects, no shops or rinky-dink. Despite his academic successes, his passage through the Harkerville school system hadn't been pleasant. Kids teased Tommy unmercifully because his huge ears stuck out from his head like the broad leaves of an exotic jungle plant. "Dumbo" and "monkey-boy," they called him. Whenever Tommy talked or chewed food his crooked jaw twisted upward to the right and one eye would open and the other close, thus the nickname, "Popeye." In class, kids shot paper wads at Tommy's ears, put chewing gum in his seat, and flipped him off whenever he looked their way.

In the restroom, they'd shove Tommy's face in the toilet and flush it to watch his ears flutter in the turbulence. In the fifth-grade, Tommy's classmates chased him down after school and took off all his clothes. He ran home naked, in December, in the snow. Everybody threw rocks at Tommy. At recess, all the kids punched him. Tommy never complained; he'd just grunt and double over.

In junior high, he hid out in the library whenever he could. He read everything. His only friends were characters in books and those he imagined. By high school, he had mastered the art of camouflage. Caps with flaps and long hair concealed his huge ears. A doctor's note kept him out of gym. To avoid the crush, he came early and stayed late. He hung out in laboratories and hid in nooks, stairwells, and restroom stalls.

Tommy scored the highest SAT grades in the history of Harkerville,, and Midwest University gave him a full academic scholarship. Graduating college with honors, he went on to graduate school. Phi Beta Kappa. Ph.D. in physiology and biochemistry. A faculty appointment. Professor Tennyson never returned to Harkerville.

Early Saturday morning, Kent telephoned Cleo. "I hope you don't mind my calling, considering our break up and all."

"You know," Cleo said softly, "I'm glad you called. It's silly the way we've been avoiding each other."

"That's exactly how I feel. Say, I'm going to Midwest University this morning, would you like to go along?"

"Sure," Cleo replied without hesitation. "Going to the ball game?"

"No. I want to find Tommy Tennyson and ask him some questions."

"Whatever. I can be ready in half an hour."

Kent showered, shaved, put on a pair of jeans, a Polo shirt, and sprinkled on some Old Spice. On his way out of the house he grabbed a windbreaker. Cleo was waiting on her front porch when he pulled up at exactly ten o'clock. She wore trim black slacks and an embroidered vest with gold spangles over a wool sweater, her hair in a pageboy. She greeted him with a smile, slid into the front seat, threaded her arm through his, and murmured, "Good morning."

Kent frowned. "You know, I feel terrible about Hoover."

Her index finger touched his lips. "Don't say a thing. Let's just let today be one of the best days of our lives."

At the Dairy Queen drive-through, they picked up two coffees. Driving across the desolate prairie without caffeine could be risky; the flat, hypnotic, colorless autumn Kansas landscape had lulled many a red-eyed traveler into permanent sleep.

At the four corners stop light, Kent turned north and a lump formed in his throat as they sped by the site of his father's hay-bale accident. With his Styrofoam coffee cup secure in the cup holder and the Mercedes on cruise control, Kent slid his arm around Cleo, his fingers gliding through rasps of golden hair to the nape of her neck. Her skin was special.

Forty-five miles of undulating grassland dotted with cattle and cross-hatched by gravel roads and rain-carved gullies separated Harkerville from Midwest University. Like a magic carpet, Kent's Mercedes floated smoothly over the café au lait prairie at eighty-five miles an hour. Cleo closed her eyes and emitted little snoring sounds. Kent sipped coffee to stay alert.

Chapter 8
FOOTBALL SATURDAY

It was football Saturday at Midwest University. Cars and purple-painted vans decked with bobcat emblems crammed the streets. Some of the people on the streets had purple-painted faces; others wore purple and white sweatshirts and jackets adorned with snarling cats. If religion is the opium of the masses, football is their beer. When the Bobcats win, everyone is happy, comforted by the fact the universe is unfolding as it should. With a Bobcat defeat, people argue, sue each other, and divorce papers get filed. God forbid a losing season.

Kent's Mercedes inched along the crowded, maple-lined streets of Midwest's campus, where an armada of John Deere tractors towed crepe paper floats manned by long-legged girls in short shorts, shivering in the cold and waving to an enthusiastic throng of gridiron fans.

"Are we here already?" Cleo asked, stretching. "I'm thirsty."

Following a Taco Bell drive-through for a Diet Pepsi, Kent drove across campus to the four-story, gray-brown limestone Science Building with *Chance Favors the Prepared Mind* etched in the stone above the double doorway. Kent parked his Mercedes in front of the building, handed Cleo a ballpoint pen, and asked her to write down Tommy Tennyson's name in large letters on piece of paper.

"I shouldn't be long," Kent promised, getting out of the car with his slip of paper.

Cleo slurped on her diet drink. "Take your time, honey."

Walking up to the Science Building Kent listened to the sound of drums from across the campus, the distant blare of trumpets, and the strident cries of thousands of football fans as the Bobcats took to the field.

Rome cheering her gladiators. Kent wondered if Tommy Tennyson would remember him.

Inside the deserted Science Building, beams of sunlight from gothic arched windows crisscrossed the foyer like the scantlings and girders of some ghostly edifice. Kent studied the registry in the foyer trying to match the name on the piece of paper in his hand with a name on the registry. After several minutes, he thought he had a match, the two capital T's were the key; Tommy Tennyson's office was three lines up, the third floor in the chemistry department. Surely, he would find Tommy in the chemistry lab. In high school, Tommy always hid out in laboratories. He never went to ball games.

The chemistry department smelled like paint thinner and bananas. Rows of blacktop worktables cluttered with gleaming Pyrex glassware reminded Kent of old Hoover's science class. Charts and graphs with squiggly lines adorned the walls. Kent walked to the back of the lab and identified what looked like a set of "T's" on the door, Tommy Tennyson's office no doubt.

Before Kent could knock, the door flew open and Tommy strode out of his office in preppy white pants and a purple jacket with snarling bobcats front and back. Tommy's ears were small and perfectly shaped. A thick, well-groomed beard hid his crooked jaw. Kent took a second look.

"Hey, Tommy, is that you?"

Tommy turned and looked at Kent, the expression on his face going from causal regard to surprise to revulsion. He resumed walking. "I'm in a hurry. The game is starting."

Kent followed Tommy through the chemistry lab. "Don't you remember me? I'm Kent Mullins from Harkerville."

Pain and incomprehension showed in Tommy's eyes as his pace quickened. "What do you want?"

"I'd like to ask you some questions."

"About what?" Tommy headed for the stairwell.

"About the modern scientific explanation of death." To keep up with Tommy, Kent did double time down the hall. "Hey, what happened to your ears? They look great."

Tommy stopped, whirled, an icy look on his face. "My ears are no concern of yours. Do you understand, no concern?" His voice had a razor's edge.

"I didn't mean to offend you, I only meant...." Tommy headed speedily down the stairwell. Kent followed full tilt, two risers at a time. "Gee, I'm sorry, Tommy."

In the foyer, Tommy stopped, his cross-eyed stare riveted on Kent. "You know, I'd like to talk to you too. Come back to my office upstairs after the ball game. Say around eleven tonight. I'll leave the doors to the building unlocked. We can talk all you want. Maybe about old times, huh?"

Tommy rushed out of the building and galloped urgently up the street like an ungulate pursued by hungry lions. Kent couldn't believe that Tommy Tennyson was actually going to a football game.

The six thousand cars jamming the streets a short time ago, now crammed the stadium parking lot. The crowd noise rose and fell with the Bobcats' fortunes. Kent drove to the center of town where the streets were deserted and everything locked up. Ubiquitous bobcats with saber-tooth fangs bedecked store windows, doors, lampposts, and every unadorned, vertical surface in sight.

"What'll we do until eleven o'clock?" Cleo asked.

They exchanged glances. She gently took his hand and laced his fingers with hers. He put the Mercedes in park and slid closer. Her lips were warm and soft.

The only available motel room in town was cheap and dumpy. Walking through the door, they kissed, embraced, and off came the gold-spangled vest and sweater, her bra, his jeans, her slacks. Under the sheets, his hands melted into a creamy satin heaven. Together they curled, two heads, eight limbs; their conjoined bodies rocking with exquisite energy. A passionate frown knitted her brow. "Oh. Oh. Oh, Kent!" Through the flimsy motel room walls came the distant roar of the multitude. The Bobcats had scored.

Kent caught his breath. Then standing up, she against the wall, they made love again. And again in the shower. After more than a year of abstinence, three orgasms were not enough, but it's all he had.

Exhausted, sweat-soaked, they lay on that cot of a bed in that dumpy motel room and watched *Painting By Number* on the educational channel, an Alaskan brown bear eating a salmon. Before the painting was finished they fell asleep. Several hours later, Kent awakened to Standard Deviant's Beginner's Spanish, yo *estoy muy bien, gracias*. He flipped off the TV and glanced at the wall clock, big hand, little hand—analog, yippee! Digital clocks were undecipherable to Kent, nonsense. In thirty minutes, he'd meet with Tommy. Cleo slept like a stone, her little snores the only sign of life.

Kent dressed and placed his car keys on the small bedside table in case Cleo for some reason would need the car before he returned.

Chapter 9
TOMMY'S RAGE

Kent zipped up his windbreaker, gently closed the door behind him, and headed out into the night for his appointment with Tommy. He hurried across the motel's parking lot, down the street, and into a park. He followed a deserted, well-trodden path through the arched walkway of a bell tower, his breath a ghostly mist in the cool night air. Questions bounced around inside his head. Was he falling in love with Cleo? What was love? Was making love, love? He glanced at the luminous spear-shaped hands of his glow-in-the-dark Timex. Almost eleven o'clock. He'd think about love later. Right now, he had to get his mind back on death.

From the knob of the campus he listened to the sounds of post-game revelry: the beat of rap, car horns, sirens, shrieks of laughter—a beer bacchanalia. Win or lose, Bobcat fans celebrate on game night. The sounds of merrymaking pursued him right up to the double brass doors of the Science Building, which were unlocked just as Tommy had promised. Kent stepped inside and the huge doors swooshed closed behind him. A heavy silence fell over the darkened foyer as if a thick velvet curtain had dropped from the ceiling.

Kent's footsteps echoed cavernously from the walls. The glazed eyes of Darwin, Newton, and Linnaeus peered down at him from their exalted positions among the marble scrollwork. It was like walking through a mausoleum. Halfway up the stairwell, a sudden heaviness in his chest and an uneasiness of mind halted his ascent. In the darkness, he clung to the iron railing and listened to the immense emptiness around him. After a few deep breaths, he felt better, straightened, and trudged upward to the third floor.

The chemistry laboratory was darker yet, the shades pulled, the only light a faint glow from Tommy's office at the back. He groped along the blacktopped worktables until his hand upset a rack of Pyrex tubes that clashed like cymbals.

"It's me. Kent Mullins. Are you here, Tommy?"

Tommy appeared out nowhere, his long white lab coat luminous in the dark. Kent nearly jumped out of his shoes. Tommy spoke in a deep voice barely above a whisper, "I hope I didn't startle you."

Kent steadied his quivering legs. "No, uh-uh, not at all."

In the dark, Tommy appeared more full-bodied and robust than Kent remembered him. That beard and those smaller ears made him look almost normal.

"I should explain about the ears." Tommy plucked his perfectly shaped left ear from the side of his head. "Soft plastic."

Holding the artificial ear in his opened hand, Tommy grinned, his face uneven and surly. Kent's eyes adjusted to the dark and he stared first at the ear in Tommy's hand and then at the projecting nubbin of skin on Tommy's head where the ear had attached. A small hole in the nubbin went straight inside Tommy's head.

"I had reduction surgery on my ears, but it wasn't successful. The wounds became infected. Gangrene set in. Do you have any idea what that's like?"

Kent shrugged. "Painful, huh?"

"It's hell. They had to remove both my ears. I ended up with prosthetic ones."

"They really look nice. Can you hear okay?"

Tommy spat, "I hear fine." He jammed the plastic ear into his coat pocket. "I'm a different Tommy Tennyson than you knew back in Harkerville. Vitamins, steroids, and daily workouts have given me the strength and manhood I lacked. I can bench press two hundred pounds."

"Wow! That's really great, Tommy. But what I'm here to ask about is death. Exactly what happens when…"

"I'm not the wimp I was back in high school."

"I can see that, you really look great."

Tommy's eyes narrowed. "You know what it's like to get hit in the belly fifty times a day? To have people call you Dumbo? Of course, you don't. I was a freak of nature to you. An E.T." Tommy's lips grew thin, his nostrils widen. He was a one-eared pit bull tearing at the fence.

Kent glanced at the door to the outer hall, a good fifty feet away. He cleared his throat. "That was a long time ago."

Tommy stepped closer, his face screwed up to the right, one eye searing Kent, the other looking errantly away. He backed Kent into a worktable.

"You and the others thought you were pretty cool, didn't you. Beating up on old Tommy. Throwing rocks at him. Thought you were hot shit, didn't you!"

Kent smiled, the muscles in his jaw quivering. "I only threw a couple rocks. And I didn't hit you as much as the others."

"Psychological trauma like mine isn't easily erased. I've spent years trying to forget Harkerville! And it all came back when you walked in here today."

"Come on, just because you were a … "

"A what," Tommy shouted. "A freak? A circus sideshow? Come on, what was I?"

"You were just a funny looking kid." Kent clutched the edge of a worktable and leaned away as Tommy pressed closer.

"A funny looking kid. Pshaw! You have no idea, you bastard."

Kent's stomach tightened into a knot and his heart beat erratically. "Hey, you've got to get over this."

Tommy's eyes blazed with vengeance. "There are some things you never get over, like having your childhood stolen. Plastic surgery doesn't repair emotional scars. They require something retributive. Something like a bloodletting!"

Tommy grabbed a Pyrex flask by its long neck and smashed it on the tabletop, the glass shattering with a sharp metallic ring. He was now a brawling drunk wielding a broken beer bottle. He raised the jagged flask above his head.

Kent's eyes grew big as half-dollars. "You're crazy. Put that down!"

Tommy snarled. "No reason to talk about death when you can experience it first hand."

Tommy lunged, thrusting the makeshift weapon at Kent's neck. Kent grabbed Tommy's wrists and fell back on the worktable, shards at his throat, the mad professor bearing down on him.

"Stop it, Tommy. You don't know what you're doing!"

"I'm going to rip open your jugular and watch you bleed to death. That's what I'm doing."

Tommy had great strength in his arms, but the adrenaline in Kent's blood served as an equalizer, two men locked in a death struggle atop the worktable--arm wrestlers in suspended animation, the jagged edges of the flask only millimeters from Kent's jugular vein.

Seconds seemed hours. Tommy bored down relentlessly, his one-eared, lopsided face growing hideous, his hot breath lashing Kent's face.

Kent's arms trembled and sharp glass scratched the skin of his throat. He couldn't hold out much longer. He needed an edge, something to give him the advantage, and he needed it now. He recalled Tommy saying, *Psychological trauma like mine isn't easily erased.* Yes, that's it. A psychological advantage. Once a wimp, always a wimp.

Kent's eyes narrowed, his voice deepened. "I'm really going to kick your ass when I get up from here. I'll mop the floor with your ugly face. Then I'll flush your face in the toilet, Dumbo."

It was working. He detected a slight release in Tommy's arms. A little trash-talk should do it. "I'm gonna make you eat those fuckin' plastic ears of yours. When I get through with you, you'll need a transplant team to put you back together."

The jagged-edged flask shook in Tommy's hand. Kent squeezed tighter on Tommy's wrists. *Come on. Cut off the circulation.* Defeat showed in Tommy's eyes. His hand opened and the flask fell, just missing Kent's vulnerable neck and splintering on the tabletop. Kent hands went to Tommy's throat, and he squeezed until Tommy's eyes bulged. He let go and Tommy crumpled to the floor. Triumphantly, Kent gazed down at the crazed professor.

"Get up, Tommy."

Tommy's face sagged as he rose. Kent punched him in the belly. Nostalgic. Tommy grunted and fell back to the floor.

"Please, don't hit me again," Tommy begged, his hideous countenance replaced by a fawning, glazed look. "I don't know what came over me."

Chapter 10
THE POISON

"That was attempted murder," Kent shouted angrily at his defeated assailant sprawled on the floor. "You could be in big trouble."

"I'm sorry, honest I am," Tommy whined. "Seeing you today released all those old repressed frustrations of mine." Tears streaked Tommy's face as he rattled on like a man facing the gallows. "I didn't mean for this to happen, I must have gone crazy, it just happened, really, I'm sorry, it just happened that's all, please…"

"Shut up."

"You're not going to turn me in to the police, are you?"

In a strange way, Kent understood how Tommy felt. He had experienced some of the same frustrations growing up. He took Tommy's hand and yanked him onto his feet. "Listen, you tell me the latest scientific information on death and I'll forget the whole thing. And put your ear back on. You look really weird with one ear."

"It's a deal." Tommy stuck the plastic ear onto its nubbin and swung open his office door. With a sweep of his hand he motioned Kent to enter.

Kent sat down in a chair across from Tommy's desk and drew a deep breath. All of Tommy's smoldering, pent-up childhood resentment had exploded today like an overheated pressure cooker. Thank god it was out of his system now.

Tommy set a beaker of water on a hot plate. "How about some tea?"

"Sure, why not."

Kent glanced at the computer and microscope on Tommy's credenza. Stacks of scientific journals and piles of papers cluttered the professor's desk. Tommy's diplomas and awards decorated an entire wall of his office. In the far corner, a human skeleton dangled from the ceiling on a hook. Old Hoover must have been proud of his former student.

Tommy sat down on the edge of his desk and shook his head as if clearing away cobwebs. "I can't explain my behavior. I've a great position here at the university. I wouldn't jeopardize it for anything. I just can't believe I lost control like that. I'm truly sorry."

"Maybe you should get some counseling."

"Great idea. I'll look into that."

Kent glanced at his watch. "Tommy, I'm concerned about death. I don't understand it. I need some answers."

Tommy nodded. "I'll do my best to help you."

As the water in the beaker bubbled and steamed, Kent told Tommy about Hoover dying suddenly in the hospital and how it had frightened him, and that lately he'd been unable to think about anything but death.

Tommy smiled pleasantly. "Memento mori."

"What?"

"Hoover's death reminded you of your own mortality. Perhaps, Kent, you should be concerned about life, not death. Life is much more interesting. And we know more about it."

Kent shook his head. "But it's dying that frightens me. We live only a short time, but death is for eternity."

Tommy took an amber bottle from a shelf and emptied its contents into the beaker of boiling water and stirred the brew with a glass rod. With a folded towel, he picked up the beaker from the hot plate and poured the steaming green concoction into two white porcelain cups. He handed one of the cups to Kent. "Green tea," he said, "it's not only salubrious, but good tasting. Antioxidant, you know."

"Thanks."

"Look around you, Kent. Death is everywhere." Tommy took a ballpoint from the pocket of his lab coat. "This pen is dead." He tapped the pen on the desktop. "This desk is dead, although at one time the wood was alive. The majority of everything around us is dead. This building and the stones that make it up are all dead. The cars parked out there on the street are dead. The universe itself is made up almost entirely of dead things. The miracle of it all is this bit of life on this small planet. It's improbable. It's rare. And it's worth studying and talking about."

Kent felt confused. He wanted to talk about death and Tommy seemed to be talking around it. This was Kent's show and he was determined they were going to talk about death. "Look, I'd like some straight answers to simple questions. Okay."

"Shoot."

"What is death?"

"The absence of life."

"What happens after death?"

"First rigor mortis sets in and then...."

Kent looked irritably at Tommy. "I know that. I know dead bodies rot and all that. But what else happens?"

Tommy twirled his left ear on its nubbin as he thought. Finally, he said, "What you're asking can't be described scientifically. It's more in the religious field."

Kent frowned and bit his lower lip. He wasn't going to let Tommy wiggle out of this. He slammed his fist on the desktop. "Damn it, I know all about Purgatory and the Pearly Gates. What I want are some scientific answers."

"Drink your tea and relax. I suppose you want to know if the personality survives death, and, if it does, what happens to it."

Kent perked up. "Yeah. That's the kind of stuff I'm interested in."

"All the information we have on that comes from out-of-body experiences. And that's all anecdotal, unverifiable, and subjective."

Kent walked over to the dangling skeleton, wondering how to tell a man skeleton from a woman skeleton? He held the skeleton's bony hand and flexed the bones of the index finger backwards as if torturing the scrawny specimen. He could tell it made Tommy nervous. *Put a little fear in the wimp and maybe he'll come up with some decent answers.* The finger bone snapped in two.

Tommy jumped.

"Tell me Tommy, what is the soul, scientifically speaking?"

"It's simply the same as personality or consciousness."

Kent held up the broken finger. "Hold it. When a person is dead, aren't they unconscious?"

Tommy asked, "Is consciousness then switched off when someone dies?"

Kent tossed the broken finger bone onto Tommy's desk. "I'll ask the questions. Is it?"

"Good question. As a biochemist and physiologist I can tell you that consciousness comes down to reverberating neuronal circuits." Tommy then launched into a lecture about cell membranes, ions, and the electrical activity of the brain. He used big, scientific words Kent didn't know.

"Wait a minute," Kent interrupted "Are you saying consciousness or soul is nothing more than electricity flowing around inside the brain?"

Tommy chuckled. "That's sort of right. When those circuits are shut off, when the voltage drops to zero, that's death. The legal definition of death is a flat brain wave test. Which simply means there is no electrical activity in the brain."

Kent sipped his tea; it had a tangy almond flavor. Tommy was inscrutable. Only a short time ago, he was a raving, bloodthirsty ghoul trying to kill Kent, and now a rational scientist answering Kent's questions as best he could. That's childhood trauma for you. Kent wondered if Cleo was still sleeping back at the motel. It was getting late, after midnight. He decided to sum up the death discussion.

"You're saying death occurs when the lights go out in the brain, when it's zero voltage and everything is darkness."

Tommy shrugged. "Not entirely."

"What do you mean?"

Tommy walked over to the window and looked out at the starry sky, his hands clasped behind his back. A contemplative silence ensued.

Eventually, Tommy turned and looked at Kent. "Everything that goes on in our heads during life, all our mental activities, every thought, every idea, every wish, well, they may exist forever in the form of radiating brain waves. Like light emitted from the sun."

"Light?"

"Yes, light waves travel essentially uninhibited from the sun into outer space, bumping into planets, bouncing off, and continuing forever. As do radio waves from a broadcast tower. Our brain waves are electromagnetic waves just like light and radio waves. Some scientists believe that all our brain activity, our personalities, our every thought, even our emotions radiate forever through space."

"Wow," Kent erupted, "that's unbelievable."

"It's an interesting hypothesis," Tommy agreed, "in some ways, it's as interesting as the 'oscillating universe hypothesis of eternal life.'"

"The what?"

"It's also called the *Omega Point Hypothesis*."

Kent had to know about this. Tommy settled into his swivel chair and Kent leaned forward, his elbows on the desk, teacup clasped in his hands. This was going to be a magnificent night of talk and green tea.

Tommy tirelessly explained the oscillating universe hypothesis in detail, using a lot of terms Kent didn't fully comprehend. However, as the night wore on, Kent got the gist of the theory. The universe, according to Tommy, started in an explosion called the Big Bang. The universe, it seems, is still in the throes of that explosion, still expanding. The theory states that eventually gravity will slow the expansion down, and the universe will start contracting. Everything that existed and passed away will reappear. Kent's mom, dad, and old Hoover would come back to life. Only everything will be in reverse, like a video rewinding. Kent would start out a millionaire and end up a kid with *dyslearnia*. It'd be worth it, he thought, to get mom and dad back.

Kent asked, "Do you think it could really happen?"

Tommy refilled Kent's cup from the beaker. "Like I told you, it's just a hypothesis."

Kent rubbed his forehead. All this interesting talk had given him a headache. He glanced at the red glow in the window. The sun coming up. They had talked all night. He had to get back. Cleo would be worried. Kent stood and extended his hand. "Thanks for the information, Tommy."

"It's Doctor Tennyson to you," Tommy said, a sardonic tone to his voice. He picked up the beaker, swooshed the green liquid around, and held it up it to the light. He laughed, a crazy, cackling sound. "You like asking questions, you always have. You're in hurry to know all things, as if time were running out."

"Why are you laughing?"

Tommy's voice hardened into a deep monotone. "Because time is running out for you." He shoved the beaker under Kent's nose. "That wasn't green tea you were sipping all night. It's a deadly poison."

Kent eyed Tommy for some hint of a joke. "Come on, stop kidding. You are kidding, aren't you?"

"Didn't you notice that I didn't drink any? In a year, give or take a few months, you'll be dead, unless…"

Kent's face turned a deep red and his hands balled into fists. "Unless what?"

"Unless you find the antidote."

Kent gave Tommy a hard shove and the beaker fell from his hands, shattering on the floor, the carpet soaking up the deadly brew. Tommy howled hysterically.

Kent seized him by the collar. "Damn you. Why?"

"Why? You have to ask why after you and those other Harkerville rats robbed me of my childhood, gave me the biggest inferiority complex in history. I've never had a date? I'm a virgin. My life is totally unfulfilled. But at long last, I'm revenged."

Kent's head throbbed like an abscessed tooth. He let go of Tommy and backed away. Sweat rolled off Kent's face, his limbs trembled; he could feel the poison draining away his strength. "I'm dying right now!"

Tommy straightened his collar. "Don't be stupid. You won't feel anything tonight but a transient headache. The poison goes directly to your bone marrow and is stored there. It will activate in a year or so, depending on your metabolism, and then, without warning, it'll attack your nervous system. You'll know when it happens. First come violent headaches, then nausea and vomiting, and finally you'll grow weak and lapse into coma. It'll be a slow, miserable death."

Kent staggered over to the door. "I'm going to the police."

"Go ahead. The poison's undetectable in the body, and I'll deny everything. In fact, I'll tell the police you broke in here and assaulted me, that you harbor some crazy childhood grudge against me. Your fingerprints are all over the place. You'll spend the last days of your life in jail."

Kent drew back his arm.

Tommy held up his hands. "You hit me and I'll call the police. If you hire some thugs to intimidate me, if you lift so much as a finger against me, you'll never get the antidote. And I'm the only who knows the formula." Tommy tapped his forehead with his index finger. "I keep it here inside my head."

Kent's arm fell limply to his side. "Okay, how much do you want? I've got lot's of money."

"Keep your money. You'll have to earn the antidote."

Kent leaned against the door, his head throbbing and spinning. Tommy plopped into his chair, swung his feet onto his desk and grinned.

Chapter 11
A HOMOPRAGMATIC TRUTH

Tommy swung his feet back onto the floor, leaned back, and looked up at his pale, confused, inquisitive visitor. "You've always asked questions. But your questions are relatively unimportant. At the rate you're going, you'll never come up with anything meaningful. What is beauty? What's happiness? What's love? There are a lot of those. Philosophers through the ages have pondered these questions. But no one has ever come up with…" Tommy stood up and his voice thundered, "…a **HOMOPRAGMATIC TRUTH!**"

Kent fell into a chair. Tommy was crazy, but crazy or not, he was in control.

Tommy spoke slowly, "Listen carefully to me, your life depends on it. You bring me a *homopragmatic truth* and I'll give you the antidote."

"W-w-what is this 'homo' thing?"

Tommy walked over to the door. "It's the dream of every academic, every philosopher, every human being who ever held a noble thought in their head. A *homopragmatic truth* transcends time and place. It's Tao, Zen, and the Holy Grail rolled into one." Tommy lowered his voice. "A *homopragmatic truth* is a truth so compelling it can bring about its own existence. It's more than knowledge. More than culture." Tommy spread his arms. "It's more than anything. Knowing a *homopragmatic truth* and the effect of knowing it become one and the same. Such a truth forever changes the knower."

Kent took a weary breath. "I don't get it."

"You'll recognize it when you see it."

"I will?"

"Yes, because a *homopragmatic truth* dominates the mind of the beholder to the exclusion of all else. It is a piece of knowledge so enlightening, so brimming with veracity, so eye-opening, so all encompassing that once you possess it, your life is forever changed and nothing will ever be the same again."

"I'm sorry, I really don't know what you're talking about."

"You better know. Your life depends on it. Perhaps, you should start by asking the question?"

"What question?"

Tommy grinned a lopsided ear-to-ear grin. "The question to which the answer is a *homopragmatic truth*. You like asking questions. Get busy." Tommy's mood was buoyant; he seemed to be basking in the power he held over Kent, the power of life and death.

"I need more to go on," Kent complained.

Tommy turned the doorknob and pushed open the door. "Sorry, that's all there is. You see, in the entire history of humankind, no one has ever come up with a *homopragmatic truth*. It's your turn to try. You'll have to excuse me, it's Sunday morning and I've got to get ready for church."

"Church! You just poisoned me and you're going to church?"

"The dean expects all the faculty to attend religious services at least once a week."

Kent watched Tommy walk out the door. He looked down at the broken glass on the floor and across the room to the skeleton dangling from the ceiling. He was a poisoned man with only a year to live. *I'm going to die.*

It took several minutes for Kent to marshal the strength to heave himself out of the chair. Once up, he stumbled over to the window, opened it, and inhaled the crisp morning air. Below, walking across the green carpet of the campus was Tommy, his white coat fluttering in the breeze and gleaming in the morning sun.

Kent shouted out the window, "I'll find your fucking truth, you… you poisoner. Hey everyone. Tommy Tennyson has plastic ears."

Kent walked slowly back towards the motel. His head felt as if storm troopers were goose-stepping across his brain. Transient headache, hell--his skull was splitting open. A year to live, to find the antidote--where does one look for a *homopragmatic truth*?

On the sidewalk he passed a young man with mussed hair and the smell of stale beer, his loose shirt flapping in the morning breeze, and on his face the gnawed look of one who had just survived some disaster. Kent's face was etched with the angst of a man facing a terminal disaster. The campus around him lay in ruins, the aftermath of a football war. Beer cans like spent artillery shells cluttered the ground. Tattered purple banners fluttered in the wind, the battle-torn flags of a gridiron army. Whitewash epithets streaked sidewalks and store windows. People in Sunday clothes drove by frat houses festooned in toilet paper. Church bells rang.

Where's my Mercedes?

Kent scoured the motel parking lot for his car. *My car's disappeared.* The motel room was unlocked but Cleo wasn't there. Kent took a deep breath and glanced at his watch. She probably went out for breakfast.

Kent flopped down on the lumpy bed and went over the events of this horrible, tragic night with Tommy Tennyson. Nothing made sense. Unable to relax, he flipped on the TV, a ballgame pre-show, Lions versus Packers. Television voices made his eyelids heavy and his headache waned as the storm troopers bivouacked. He hoped Cleo would be back soon. He needed to talk to some one. *For God's sake, I've just been poisoned! A piece of knowledge so enlightening, so brimming with veracity, so...* he fell asleep.

Cleo shook his shoulders, her blue eyes beaming down at him from her cheerleader-pretty face.

Kent rubbed his eyes. "What time is it?"

"Almost five."

"I've slept all day?"

Cleo said in a casual tone, "I have some bad news."

Kent sat up, supporting his head with his hands. "Wait until you hear mine."

Cleo motioned with her head. "Come on, we'll talk over food. I'm starving for some Chinese."

In the motel parking lot, Kent looked around for his Mercedes. Cleo walked over to a beat-up, faded blue Ford from another era and opened the door on the driver's side.

Kent peeked inside at the ragged upholstery. "This is not my car!"

"I know. It's a loaner. Get in and I'll tell you all about it."

Reluctantly, Kent got in. Cleo drove them to a Chinese restaurant in a nearby shopping mall. She threw the Ford into park, dug around in her purse, and handed Kent his Mercedes' hood ornament.

Kent fingered the hood ornament. "What happened?"

"A small accident, fender bender. We'll talk while we eat."

In the dungeon darkness of the Chinese restaurant, Kent stubbed his toe on a three-foot ceramic Buddha. A waitress in a dragon kimono led them to a table near the tropical fish tank, the only source of light in the place. The waitress couldn't speak English but smiled pleasantly. Luckily, the menus were number coded. Cleo read the menu to Kent, and he selected number nine, the almond chicken. Cleo got number 20, the flaming beef delight.

While waiting on the food, Cleo announced, "I ran into the warden's Lexus. No big deal."

"Warden. What warden?"

"The warden at State Prison. He was backing out when I drove in."

"Prison?"

"Of course. Where else would you find a warden?"

"What were you doing at a prison?"

Kent's almond chicken came microwave quick, steaming.

"I went to see Larry," she explained.

"Larry who?"

"Larry Lakes, my ex."

"Where's my Mercedes?"

"In the body shop. It's nothing. I told Larry about us. I thought it only fair that he know."

Kent couldn't eat. He nervously rapped his fingertips on the table. He wanted to go home, go to bed, and wake up from a bad dream. The waitress shuffled over with the Cleo's flaming delight. Kent wondered if they put lighter fluid on the beef to get it to burn like that.

Kent stopped tapping and stared at Cleo. "Look, you and I, well, we aren't exactly, you know, in a permanent relationship. You know what I mean?"

Cleo dipped an egg roll in hot mustard. "Give it a chance. We've only been back together a couple of days."

Kent glanced at his Timex. "How long did you say?"

Cleo looked at her watch. "Thirty-four hours to be exact. Larry said he was going to kill you. But he's all talk. Wouldn't hurt a flea. Anyway, he won't get out of prison for another eight years."

Kent's voice broke. "He'll be seven years too late. I've been poisoned."

Cleo reached across the table with her chopsticks and sampled Kent's almond chicken. "It's not that bad."

"Not the food. Tommy poisoned me."

"You're joking," she said with a full mouth.

While she chopsticked her beef delight, Kent told her about Tommy trying to kill him with a broken flask and later poisoning him with deadly tea. "I'll be dead in a year, give or take a few months, that is if I don't come up with a *homopragmatic truth*. Will you help me, Cleo?"

Cleo smiled. "First thing tomorrow morning I'm taking you to Dr. Jenkins and have some tests run."

Kent shook his head. "Tommy said the poison is undetectable."

"Tommy's a nutcase. We'll leave this in Dr. Jenkin's hands, whatever he advises, that's what we'll do. Now pass the soy. Would you like me to read your fortune cookie to you?"

"No."

Chapter 12
IT'S A DILEMMA

Seated in a small exam room in the doctor's office, Cleo thumbed through a *Better Homes and Garden* while Kent twirled his thumbs. "Dr. Jenkins is always late," she informed Kent. "The poor man works night and day." She had no more finished saying that when Dr. Jenkins opened the door and slumped into the room. He sat down heavily on the exam table with some papers in his hand.

The doctor cleared his throat and said to Kent, "Your tests were all normal. The toxicology studies showed no foreign substances in your blood."

"Yeah, but Tommy said the poison is undetectable."

"Humh...well, these tests were done using the most up-to-date technology."

Cleo asked, "Are you sure everything is all right, doctor?"

"It's a dilemma," the doctor admitted, his tired eyes moving from Kent to Cleo and back to Kent. "If Tommy is lying and you go ahead and find this truth thing, whatever, and get the antidote, you're not really out anything. On the other hand, if he's telling the truth, you darn well better get the antidote."

Kent nodded stiffly. "In other words, I have no choice but to find a *homopragmatic truth.*"

Dr. Jenkins shrugged his shoulders and made a thin-lipped smile. "Better safe than sorry."

When the doctor walked out of the room, Kent looked at Cleo with both sadness and determination in his eyes. "I'm going to find it. I don't know how, but I'm going to find a *homopragmatic truth,* even if I have to travel to the ends of the earth."

Cleo clasped his hand in hers. "I'll help you."

Chapter 13
LARRY LAKES

A hundred miles from Harkerville, behind hoary concrete walls topped with rolls of razor wire Larry Lakes, Cleo's ex, lay in his bunk at State Prison trying to exert some control over the twitching of his left foot. He tried to quiet his foot by thinking about quieting it, which only made it twitch more. Afraid to make any sound lest he awaken Eugene, his sex-crazed cellmate, he stared in silent mystification at his unruly foot. He was Eugene's punk, and Eugene was getting rich in cigarettes, reefers, and low grade snow because everyone in this hellhole wanted a piece of Larry's young ass. And Eugene sold it anywhere and everywhere, even to a couple of guards for extra servings in the mess hall.

Earlier in the day, when Cleo visited Larry and told him about her renewed relationship with Kent Mullins, Larry's Irish face flushed, his lips curled, and his fingers ripped at the wire screen that separates prisoner from visitor—that separates prisoner from the world. "I didn't divorce you, bitch! You divorced me."

Larry became so rambunctious the guards had to physically subdue him and drag him away. "I'll kill the bastard! Mark my word, Cleo, I'll get that motherfucker."

Before coming to State Prison, Larry never used such obscenities. Being sodomized every day had taken its toll on him. And that was only half of it. Thanks to the warden, Larry had been assigned the most dangerous job in the prison—mop-man for the T and A unit, the house of maniacs. Daily, he ran the gauntlet with his mop, and one day a maniac would get him, just as they had gotten all the other mop-men. Short of a lethal injection, mopping the floors of the T and A unit was the surest cure for recidivism.

After Larry calmed down, the guards sent him out to the yard, where Eugene waited for him—Eugene with his tattoos, his muscular arms, his greasy forelocks, and his connections. Head down, Larry slouched over to this master. Eugene patted his ass.

"How did it go, man?"

Larry shrugged.

Eugene lit a cigarette. "Women, they're the shits, man. Listen, I got a bull I supply with grass. It's only a matter of time I'll get you off that mopping job."

Larry shrugged.

"Listen man, I got two guys comin' to play. Go on back to the cell, and we'll meet there." Larry turned and Eugene kicked him in the behind. "Don't go wanderin' off. These is payin' customers."

Larry, Eugene, and the Boys, went the song that Silky, a toothless black man in the adjacent cell, sang as Eugene and the two paying customers gang-banged Larry.

> *The boys came to play and to give Eugene his pay.*
>
> *They came to fuck poor Larry and be on their way.*
>
> *Two packs of camels, a little song, empty out, and get along.*
>
> *They fucked poor Larry up and down, they fucked him all around.*
>
> *Good old Larry, the punk, the queen, the clown.*

Larry gripped the mattress with both hands as he absorbed hard thrusting into the two major orifices of his body. Why me, he asked himself? Why me for getting Eugene as a cell mate? Why me for getting raped every fuckin' day? And for two lousy packs of Camels. And I don't even smoke. Why me when I was on the top of the world?

That evening, Larry paced in his cell and daydreamed of revenge. Of driving a lead pipe through Eugene's head. Of drowning a certain banker back home in a bucket of pesticide. Of torturing Cleo's boyfriend with killer bees.

"Stop pacing and get up in your fucking bunk," Eugene ordered.

Larry climbed slowly into his bunk. "You'll get yours."

"What, man?"

"I couldn't remember. Did you get yours today?"

"Hell yes, man. I always get mine. Now go to sleep before I kick your fucking ass."

Why me? Why me when I was on top of the world?

Chapter 14
GREEN PASTURE

A right-brain, left-brain switching problem had plagued Larry Lakes during his formative years. When his left-brain was in charge, Larry displayed extraordinary analytical skills, top of the class in math, unbelievably good with computers, first prize at the school's science fair. Then unpredictably, uncontrollably, he'd switch to right brain, and all he wanted to do was sing, dance, and play the ukulele. When in left-brain mode, Larry became downhearted, gloomy and withdrawn, his world a film noir black and white. When right brain, Larry was happy, robust, and extroverted, his world bright with colors, alive with melody. There seemed to be no middle ground.

Then one glorious day in his junior year at high school his brain shifted right and stayed there. Larry's grades plummeted. He was no longer a math whiz or computer savant, but he was happy. He flunked out of high school, found a job, sang in the church choir, and got involved in community affairs. Yes, right brain Larry was very happy.

In great demand as a vocalist for funerals and weddings, Larry enjoyed the limelight, being out front like a Rhinestone Cowboy. He often gave talks to Harkerville's civic organizations and local clubs, talks about being a good citizen, about being for good and against bad. People came away from his talks empty, but un-offended. He was the clown at the county fair. The emcee for the Jaycees. Magician for the pre-school Halloween party. Singer, dancer, speechmaker, and local actor, Larry developed his entertainment skills while practicing the most quintessential of the laissez-faire arts—he sold used cars.

He advertised his clunkers on local TV in a clown suit, playing his ukulele. Even though Larry was a local celeb, Cleo, the beautiful ex-cheerleader nurse he long admired, turned him down for dates, apparently following the dictates of her DNA, a used-car salesman having little potential for enriching the gene pool.

One day it happened, as Larry always knew it would. Ed Jones the local banker, Bob Teasley a real estate man, and Marvin Farrell of Farrell Truck Lines, all stock holders and officers in Green Pasture Fertilizer and Pesticide, asked Larry to take the corporate reins as president and CEO of Green Pasture. Never once did Larry ask *why me?* He knew why. He had been a true believer in the American Way, a civic-minded extrovert who had fought his way to the top, singing, dancing, and giving talks. *Why not me?*

"What do I do as president?" Larry asked the laconic banker, Mr. Jones.

"P.R.," Jones told him. "Just keep giving those little talks of yours."

"What subject should I speak on?"

"Umm...speak on growth."

"Good idea," Larry said. "What could be more free enterprise than growth, especially for a fertilizer company?"

Larry gave his talks about growth wherever farmers gathered, at implement dealerships, in basements of country churches, and after hours in public libraries. Speaking to farmers was like rehearsing, no applause, dead-pan stares, and a severe case of "punch line recognition deficiency." More often than not, the farmers walked out before he finished his talk, and he'd end up speaking to librarians, implement salesmen, and church custodians.

Larry learned an invaluable lesson. If you want farmers to listen, feed them. And don't bother to wear a clown suit; they won't appreciate it. And don't feed them too quickly, dish out the main course in increments or they'll leave as soon as the food's gone. Set out the dessert where they can see it, but don't serve it until the talk is finished.

Speaking at the Harkerville CO-OP, Larry looked out at that sea of phlegmatic feeding faces and saw the beautiful Cleo sitting at a table, listening demurely and smiling sedately, her blue eyes gleaming like polished gems. She'd developed an abiding interest in growth and in the new young chief executive of Green Pasture. Whenever Larry gave a talk, she was there gazing up at him intently, apparently following the dictates of her DNA. Larry had become a comet soaring through the firmament of corporate success, and Cleo was ready to hitch her wagon. The touch of Cleo's skin and the taste of her lips exhilarated Larry.

Having dumped her lover Kent Mullins, Cleo married the up-and-coming Larry, and he sang at their wedding. Larry's faith in free enterprise had paid off; he was president of Green Pasture, married to the beautiful Cleo, and he was the most sought after speaker and singer in Harkerville. For a high school drop out in right-brain mode, it was life at the zenith.

There wasn't much for Larry to do as president of Green Pasture other than sign papers put on his desk by banker Jones. One day he asked Jones, "What are all these papers?"

"Various things."

One morning, Larry read one of the papers. It didn't make much sense to him, just a lot legal mumble jumble and lines to fill out like on a tax form. Larry dutifully signed the papers.

He asked banker Jones, "How's our business doing?"

"Great. Just keep giving those little talks of yours."

"I will. Growth is important."

"Growth?"

"Yes, farmers like growth."

Jones shoved more papers at Larry. "Sign with this pen, please."

Larry often wondered but never asked why he had to sign papers with special pens. He didn't know the pens and the ink in them were several years old, nor did he pay any attention to the dates on the papers. When the State Department of Health investigated Green Pasture, they concluded that Larry had authorized and was responsible for a dozen substandard pesticide tanks that leaked tons of poisonous chemicals into the Harkerville water supply. Signed documents showed that Larry personally made the decision not to place the tanks on concrete basins as the law requires, which would have prevented much of the leakage and contamination. Green Pasture Fertilizer and Pesticide had poisoned the city's water, the ground water, and the local river. Those documents and memos signed by Larry completely cleared the other corporate officers of any wrongdoing.

Larry told the jury, "But I wasn't president of Green Pasture when all this happened." They didn't believe him. Signatures in old ink are prima facie.

"This happens to big executives sometimes," banker Jones explained to Larry. "Take in on the chin, do your time, and when you get out Green Pasture will be waiting for you. Remember, white-collar crime is different. For executives like you, prison is just a country club without golf carts. You'll be playing Ping-Pong and reading the 'One Hundred Greatest Books.' Time'll fly."

⁂

While visiting her grandmother, the 11 year-old niece of the warden of State Prison swam every day that summer in the Harkerville public swimming pool. The problem was the little girl sucked in huge amounts of polluted water, because she swam with her snorkel almost completely submerged.

Her daily intake of water was more than that of a large, thirsty adult. Her body reeked of pesticide when she was embalmed. That's why Larry was never assigned to the white-collar section of State Prison. By order of the warden, Larry descended into the hellhole of the regular prison right along with the hustlers, rapists, and murderers from the socially and economically deprived inner city law-of-the-jungle ghettos.

Eugene spotted Larry's potential right off. For ten cartons of Camels, guard Chico Morales moved Larry into Eugene's cell. It took two days of merciless beatings to turn Larry into a punk.

Chapter 15

DOCTOR VU

Dr. Pho Ven Vu, a portly Vietnamese immigrant, strolled into the Office of the Department of Corrections waving a Green Card and a completed application for the position of prison doctor. Penal authorities were overjoyed. Better he than no doctor at all. Treating the ills of goons and scumbags wasn't a highly sought-after position by physicians, and Vu's application was the only one on file. Vu had excellent training and wartime surgical experience in Viet Nam. Although he couldn't speak English, Vu had learned to communicate with Americans using gestures, frowns, smiles, and mime-cues of various kinds. When he was desperate for an interpreter, his niece in Corpus Christi was just a phone call away. The warden hired him on the spot.

Vu became the first doctor in state history to document the vast abnormal neurological and psychological disorders in the state prison population. It was a fruitless effort, though, because Doctor Vu wrote down his observations in Vietnamese, which no one in the Department of Corrections could read.

Vu overtaxed the prison's small pharmacy, prescribing therapeutic doses of antidepressants, anticonvulsants, anti-psychotics, and little green pills that not only prevented erection, but also stopped prisoner lusting. The pharmacy aid working blindly under Doctor Vu's supervision called the little green pills *anti-Viagra*. The prisoners called them "snake charmers" and spit them out.

Confident that his astute observations of mentally ill and brain-disordered prisoners would someday become an invaluable and unparalleled contribution to Medicine and the American Justice System, Dr. Vu diligently studied his English grammar book so that one day he could publish his results.

Each morning, he yammered at the warden in Vietnamese, "You know, a lot of these prisoners are crazy and brain damaged."

The warden always nodded and answered, "Good morning to you, too, doctor."

One day, Doctor Vu asked the warden if he could visit the T and A unit. The initials T and A stood for "Treatment and Adjustment," a euphemism of high degree. The prisoners there were all dangerous maniacs, and Dr. Vu was anxious to see if they fit into his evolving theory of brain-disordered criminality. Fortunately, Vu's niece, Veronica, a long-necked Asian beauty who moved with the grace and charm of a Montessori alumnus, and who had mastered both the language and lifestyle of her adopted country, was visiting her uncle and translated his request into English.

"Sure, I'll show him the maniacs," the warden said, "first thing tomorrow morning."

⁂

Working within a protective wire enclosure called the "Shark Cage," T and A guards used closed-circuit television to keep watch on the sixteen maniacs housed in individual 4 x 8 cells. Four corridors, each with four individual cells, radiated like spokes from the broad expanse of concrete that encircled the shark cage. The cells were staggered so that the maniacs could not see each other. In the center of the shark cage, a staircase spiraled up to a trap door in the roof. If the maniacs ever broke out of their cells, the guards were to escape up the staircase onto the roof, locking the trapdoor behind them. On the roof was a red button, which when pushed would release a paralyzing nerve gas into the interior of the T and A.

The maniacs called the guards inside the shark cage "Tweedy Birds."

All a maniac could see of the outside world from his tiny compartment were the floor and wall of a dank corridor and a TV camera peering down at him from the ceiling. Each cell had a small drain hole and a stainless steel stool and sink. The maniacs slept on special rubbery mattresses that were impossible to tear or shred. With no television or radio, they lived out their lives in a scummy Platonic cave world of shadows and faceless voices--the most stringent form of sensory deprivation short of being trapped under tons of earthquake rubble. A maniac left his cell only when he croaked. Even then, he was handcuffed before being carted off to the morgue.

Twelve armed and padded attack guards called "Bears" escorted the warden and Doctor Vu into the T and A. Once the warden and Vu were safely inside the shark cage, the bears backed out of the building and locked the steel door behind them. Dr. Vu felt uneasy in this grim enclosure of wire inside a building of iron bars and concrete. He and the warden stood behind the Tweedy Birds and watched the TV monitors. Wearing button-less drab prison garb that looked like pajamas, each maniac sat silently in his cell on his rubbery mattress, hands folded, head bowed, sixteen praying statues.

An hour passed and nothing changed. Boring, thought Vu, glad he had gone to medical school instead of becoming a prison guard. Another hour passed and still nothing. The warden sipped coffee and flipped through the pages of a *PEOPLE* magazine. At ten o'clock, the maniacs showed signs of restlessness. Some paced, others peered out through the bars expectantly. Still others ran their hands back and forth along the bars as if performing some ritual.

With the slightest of noise, the steel door to the T and A creaked opened and Larry Lakes stepped gingerly into the unit with a bucket of soapy water and a mop. His eyes darted warily like those of a pet store mouse dropped into the snake terrarium at feeding time. His left foot taped uncontrollably against the concrete floor. He jumped when the steel door clanged shut behind him.

One of the maniacs detected Larry's shadow and made an eerie animal-like sound. Then the whole place erupted in shouting and feet stomping like at a high school pep rally. The daily game of "get the mop-man" was about to begin. So far, Larry had had a winning mop strategy. Mopping down one side of a corridor then up the other side, he stayed exactly in the center just out of reach of clutching hands. There was a lot of mop grabbing, but the soapy braids were too slippery for the maniacs to hang on to. He always began in corridor Q, because the prisoners there were the most dangerous, all psychopathic killers. Best to get Q over with first.

Olgesby occupied the first cell on corridor Q. An ex-butcher who caught his wife in bed with the exterminator man, Olgesby chopped them both up with a meat cleaver and ran them through the sausage machine, hair, bone, and all. After a year at State Prison, he went nuts with reactive homophobia, stole a knife while on kitchen duty and went fag hunting. He stabbed two inmates to death, cut off their testicles, and ate them. That qualified him as a maniac. He had slowed down over the years and wasn't much of threat to the mop-man, except he had become a shit-thrower. Larry mopped right past cell number one before the old butcher could get his hands through the bars.

Across the corridor in cell number two, waited the maniac Tool, in whose hands any object, no matter how trivial, became a lethal weapon. In the throes of winter, Tool had stabbed a man to death with an icicle and bludgeoned another with a frozen newspaper. He had murdered a policeman with a screwdriver, decapitated his neighbor with a Swiss Army knife, strangled his sister with a shoestring, and electrocuted a defecating cellmate by touching the bare ends of a lamp cord to the stainless steel toilet. Adept at picking locks, Tool had escaped from three other institutions before being transferred to the T and A. Although his hands were extremely quick, he had short arms, useless for tripping up a wary mop-man like Larry. Tool eyed the wire handle on the mop bucket as Larry sloshed down the corridor.

Cell number 3 housed the infamous Hot Dog Jenkins, State Prison's number one killer--more kills than a World War II fighter ace. His neck-wrenching hands had dispatched victims of every sort: clergy, cops, salesmen, prostitutes, bartenders, janitors, anyone unfortunate enough to agitate his raw and ever exposed sensibilities. During his long tenure at State Prison, he killed two guards and four inmates--two of them mop-men. He was what prosecutors call a mad dog killer, and there were no vaccination for his kind of rabies. His close-set simian eyes followed Larry as he glided down the corridor swinging his mop like a hockey stick. Hot Dog was in no hurry. Sooner or later.

The last prisoner on Q corridor was Willie, a six-foot ten-inch black arsonist, with arms as long as his legs. During his incendiary career, he torched over twenty buildings, burning up eight people and sending dozens more to hospitals. He ended up in the T and A unit after setting fire to the prison laundry and two cellblocks. Gentlest of all the maniacs on corridor Q, he was a danger to the mop man because of his long arms. Willie waited, coiled like a viper.

Larry splashed by Willie's cell in a whirl of suds, pirouetted, and started back up the corridor, mopping the opposite side. Willie struck like a whip, his right arm lashing out through the bars nearly halfway across the corridor. Larry thought he had enough room to get by, but the middle finger of Willie's outstretched hand hooked a loop of Larry's shoestring. Larry stumbled and his legs churned frantically on the soapy floor.

Willie shouted, "Mop-man going down."

The noise in the T and A rose to frenzy level. The Tweedy Birds sprang to their feet. The warden tossed down his *PEOPLE* and yelled, "Get the bastard." Dr. Vu looked on in astonishment, addled by the sudden excitement.

Larry fell. Mop-man down. A sporting event bigger than sacking a quarterback or bulldogging a steer. The mop bucket bounced ahead of Larry as he hydroplaned down the corridor and slid headfirst into iron bars of cell three. Hot Dog's lethal hands shot through the bars and clamped onto Larry's head. Silence fell like a guillotine.

Tweedy Birds held their breath. TV cameras rotated. Maniacs listened for any clue.

Then a strange, inexplicable thing happened. Grappled in the iron grip of a killing machine, Larry began singing, his vibrant voice reverberating richly from the walls of T and A. He sang an old funeral dirge, a cappella.

And so to earth now entrust

What came from dust and turns to dust

And from the dust shall rise that day

In glorious triumph over decay.

…who dieth thus is living still.

An even stranger thing happened. Hot Dog in a gush of tears began stroking Larry's soft brown hair as if his grief-stricken soul were purging itself.

"I'll be a sunna bitch," the warden mumbled.

Larry continued singing while slowly inching away from the mawkish killer. When he changed tunes, *Danny Boy—the pipes, the pipes are calling from glen to glen, and down the mountainside,* Hot Dog bawled like a jilted lover. Tweedy birds cheered when Larry stood up in the corridor. He had escaped a most certain death.

Tool reached out through the bars of his cell and grabbed the mop bucket. With lightening speed, he removed the wire handle, jammed it into the lock on his cell door, twisted and jiggled until the lock clicked and the door swung open. For the first time in State Prison's history a live maniac stood in the corridor of the T and A without handcuffs and chains. The Tweedy Birds eyed the emergency staircase. For the second time this morning, Larry stared into the face of death. He kept singing.

Tool scanned the unfamiliar landscape of the corridor like an intergalactic traveler put ashore on a strange planet. His eyes were dark and hollowed, and his grisly face fringed by a bristly beard and an explosion of bird nest hair. His pale skin glowed in the dim light of the corridor. *Revenge of the Living* Dead--now playing. Stiffly, he moved towards Larry, his clomping feet slithering here and again on the soapy floor, the mop handle dangling from his hand.

Larry sang an old favorite, *You Are My Sunshine,* and he sang it with all the energy and voice he could muster. Tool stopped, cocked his head, and swayed with the rhythm. Larry danced with the mop, the East Coast Swing. Tool grinned and danced along--a clopping Clydesdale, breathing heavily--this the most exercise for Tool in over twenty years. Dropping the bucket handle, Tool took the mop from Larry's hands and held it to his chest. He followed Larry in a cha-cha up and down the slippery corridor, grunting and wheezing like a steam locomotive. Larry glanced warily over his shoulder at the emancipated maniac.

The other maniacs watched in stunned silence as the twosome danced past their cells. Tool seemed to be enjoying the dancing, hugging the mop, huffing and puffing, and listening to Larry's magical voice. Larry picked up the pace and the old psychopath pushed himself to the limit to keep up. Up and down the corridor they went, Tool gasping for air and turning purple about the lips. Waltzing now, Larry led Tool into his cell where the exhausted maniac collapsed onto his rubbery mattress. Larry quickly waltzed out with the mop and slammed the door. The Tweedy Birds applauded.

"Lucky bastard," the warden muttered.

To a chorus of Hotdog's wailing and Tool's raspy breathing, Larry tap-danced to the end of corridor with his mop. Right-brain Larry beamed triumphantly. Twice this morning he faced death and survived.

Doctor Vu, acutely aware he had witnessed something extraordinary, envisioned a revolutionary new therapy for maniacs. Music and dance to soothe the beasts. Yes, he would call it *entertaino therapy*. Someday, he'd not only be famous for his theory of brain-disordered criminality, but also for his Copernican treatment of maniacs. He could see a Nobel Prize looming. From inside the shark cage, he grinned at Larry.

Without warning, Olgesby hurled a handful of his morning excreta through the bars, smacking Larry in the face.

Chapter 16
BOOK REPORT

During bad times when things went awry, Kent's mother would say, "When it rains, it pours." How right she was. This deluge spit curses. Kent had been poisoned, had only a year to live, give or take a few months, Cleo had wrecked his Mercedes, and he was driving around in a nerd car looking for some nebulous, mysterious thing called a *homopragmatic truth*. No rainbow in sight.

A hundred miles from Harkerville, near the State Prison, Cleo directed Kent to a body shop that looked like a salvage yard. He didn't recognize his Benz until he took a second more sobering look: front end crumpled, windshield shattered, one door missing.

Kent looked confused. "I thought you said it was a fender-bender."

"Don't worry. They'll fix it like new."

The body-man, a geezer in greasy coveralls, told Kent, "Once I get the parts in, match up the paint, uh…should have it done in two weeks. Uh…need new motor mounts too. You can keep the Ford till the work's done."

The geezer ripped off the yellow and pink copies of the repair estimate and handed them to Kent. It made no sense to Kent to hang around two weeks in a strange place waiting for his Mercedes to be resurrected. He hmm'ed a bit, stuck the copies of the estimate into his pocket and drove off in the blue heap with Cleo. Kent suggested that they take a little tour of the Midwest, to think about things, to get their bearings, to figure out where and how to find a *homopragmatic truth*.

Cleo warbled, "Okay, I've got some vacation time coming."

They wandered aimlessly through the heart of America, each little town the *deja vu* reflection of the previous one: golden arches, red-roofed pizzerias, Wal-Marts, Dollar Stores, and Holiday Inns. The medium-sized towns looked much the same as the small towns, just more traffic and bigger shopping centers, Dillards at one end and Sears at the other. There's no escaping the generic sameness of the Midwest: same stores, same billboards, same movies, same similar people.

Sprawl had infected the larger cities, but urban heart surgery bypassed the bad parts with eight-lane, traffic-packed beltways that skirted above and around the socially and economically deprived inner city, law-of-the-jungle ghettos. In five days, they covered it all: Old West towns, zoos, I-Max, space museums, presidential libraries, and great balls of twine. In Kansas City, the blue Ford inched from traffic light to traffic light in the morning rush.

Cleo bluntly told Kent, "You know, I don't think you want to face up to the fact you've been poisoned? We've been driving around for days now and you haven't said a word about that truth thing you're supposed to find. I don't think you're really looking for it?"

"Honestly, I don't know where to begin."

The Ford shot up an entrance ramp and clattered down a congested freeway at fifty miles an hour. Cleo burped her Burger King French toast breakfast and stared absently out the window. Five miles farther down the freeway, Cleo turned to Kent and made a suggestion. "You know, we should find someone really smart and ask them to help us."

Kent shrugged. "If Tommy Tennyson doesn't know a *homopragmatic truth*, who does? He's the smartest person to ever come out of Harkerville."

Cleo rifled through her cosmetic bag for lipstick. "I mean someone really, really smart."

"Like who?"

"Selena Rosalina."

"What makes her so smart?"

Cleo stared in the rearview mirror and applied lipstick. "Because she overcame adversity and made it all the way to the top. I watch her TV show all the time." Cleo smacked her lips. "I've never seen anyone come on her show that she couldn't help."

"Really."

"Yeah, I read her best selling biography."

As they circumnavigated the city, Cleo told Kent *The Selena Rosalina Story*:

Selena, the illegitimate daughter of an illegal alien from Mexico, had come to California to pick fruit. She had her first baby when she was thirteen. At eighteen, when most kids were off to college, Selena the unwed mother of three children worked three jobs to support her kids, her mother, and her little brother.

"Most people would have just given up," Cleo declared, "but not Selena."

When Selena lost one of her three jobs, she turned the loss into opportunity by going to night school. She not only graduated with honors, she became certified in cardiopulmonary resuscitation. When Carl Harris, a TV executive, collapsed with a heart attack on a Los Angeles street, Selena and her three children happened along. Selena gave Harris mouth to mouth, while her five year-old jumped up and down on the lifeless man's chest. Doctor's claimed Selena saved Harris' life. The revived TV executive gave Selena a job in television. She worked her way up from gofer to afternoon talk show host. She even tried the movies, but that didn't work out.

"You're spontaneous, Selena. Your personality really comes across when you interact with people. Stick to television," Harris counseled.

Taking Harris' advice, Selena moved to New York City to become one of the most watched celebrities in the world when her afternoon TV show soared to the top of the ratings. Her real name was Carmen Ortiz. She chose the pseudonym Selena Rosalina, because she thought it sounded better and it rhymed.

Cleo wrapped up her book report: "It took a lot of smarts to do what Selena did."

Kent asked, "Do you think she knows a *homopragmatic truth*?"

"If she doesn't, I bet she'll tell us where to find one."

Kent sensed the rain in his life was letting up. He squeezed Cleo's hand and stomped the accelerator, hurling the old Ford east on the interstate, engine howling. They were headed to New York to find Selena Rosalina, the woman who just might save Kent's life.

Chapter 17
JUSTIN FREELY

On the Interstate, Kent and Cleo noticed a ragged bum sitting on the shoulder of the highway, his thumb in the air. Kent recalled his dad's warning to never pick up hitchhikers. They could be terrorists or serial killers.

Cleo looked at Kent, her brow furrowed with concern. "I feel sorry for that old man. He's probably someone's grandfather."

"Could be a terrorist or serial killer."

"I bet his grandchildren are wondering where he is. Have a heart; give him a ride."

"It's not my fault the old codger is down on his luck."

Cleo pleaded, "Please?"

Kent exited onto a service road and drove five miles to get back on the Interstate going the other direction. He ended up driving twenty miles to backtrack two miles. The bum was still sitting there, thumb in the air when Kent pulled over and honked.

"Hey buddy, need a lift?"

The codger moved as if his joints were super-glued. Kent could have sung the complete *Bye, Bye American Pie* by the time old man got to his feet. He had a big duffel bag with him.

Cleo nudged Kent. "Go help him."

The bum's large blue eyes peered out at Kent from a weathered face half-hidden by a scraggly beard. Kent picked up the duffel.

With a gap-toothed smile, the old man cautioned, "Be careful with that. I've something valuable in there."

The duffel smelled like a doghouse in winter. The old man wore a moth-eaten brown coat threadbare at the elbows, faded overalls, and porous shoes. Kent lugged the duffel to the car, wondering if he was the only poisoned millionaire in the world toting baggage for a bum.

"What have you got in there, a washer and dryer?"

The old man settled into the back seat with his arm around the duffel as if bonded to it. Kent climbed in the passenger seat. Cleo drove. Kent leaned across the seat and made eye contact with the old man.

"What's your name?"

"Justin," the hitchhiker answered in a cracking voice.

"Where are you headed?"

Justin's wizened face crinkled up like wrapping paper when his lips moved. "Nowhere in particular."

"Got any grand kids?"

"I'm only thirty-three."

Kent gasped in astonishment. "You're thirty-three years-old?"

"I know I look older. It's the mental anguish."

"I'm going through some mental anguish myself," Kent admitted.

"That right?"

"Yeah, I've been poisoned."

"I see."

"I'm gonna die in a year, give or take a few months, that is if I don't get the antidote."

"Then you better get it. Is it expensive?"

"Money doesn't matter. I'm a millionaire."

Justin nodded.

"I've got to find a truth called a *homopragmatic truth* before I can get the antidote."

"I see."

"Hey," Cleo shouted, pointing out the window, "look at that jerk."

A sleek black Porsche had pulled along side. The driver, a thin man wearing a ball cap, laid on the horn with his left hand and gestured wildly with his right hand.

"Just ignore him," Kent said, "probably a pervert with road rage."

Finally, the Porsche pulled ahead.

Kent asked Justin, "What kind of work have you done?"

"Your question implies that I'm not currently working and that is the case. I used to be an agent and financial advisor to athletes."

Kent nodded.

"Elliott Dumbrowsky was one of my clients."

"Who's he?" Cleo asked, glancing over her shoulder at the hitchhiker.

"Just one of the greatest collegiate linebackers of all times. Killed in car-truck collision on his way to sign a multimillion-dollar contract with the Colts. That accident cost me big time."

Kent's disarming nods and engaging smile kept Justin jawing.

"Another of my clients Chico Morales a potential homerun king and seven-figure superstar, smashed the shoulder of his throwing arm when he fell off a ladder painting his mother's house. He ended up an overweight prison guard.

"But my greatest discovery was Kumarmar Gamuka, a five-foot, one hundred pound Indian kicker. He was the greatest punter and field goal kicker of all time. Great distance. Great accuracy. And the sweetest little fellow you ever hope to meet."

Kent asked, "What college did Gamuka play for?"

"He never played football. It's a long story."

"I'd like to hear it."

Justin shifted in the seat. "Normally, I don't tell people about Gamuka, but you've a trusting face. Promise to keep this to yourselves?"

Kent and Cleo promised. At seventy miles an hour, the nerd Ford rattled like a corn picker with a loose drive chain.

"I discovered Gamuka when I was trying to sign up a tight end at the University of Wisconsin. Gamuka was kicking a toy rubber football to his five-year-old son outside a housing complex. I watched him kick the ball over a three-story building and across a nearby lagoon. I'd never seen anything like it. Although he had a terrific kicking leg, Gamuka never intended to be a football player." Justin's blue eyes sparkled and his face lit up as he spoke about Gamuka. "He had come to Wisconsin from Punjab University in India to study cosmology. His doctorate thesis was an amalgamation of physics and religion; he believed heaven existed in a universe entirely separate from the universe we live in, but accessible to it."

"Wow," Cleo gasped, "that's deep stuff."

Kent asked, "How did he know heaven was in a different universe?"

"It's obvious. We live in a universe with black holes, exploding stars, pollution, crime, cancer, and war. By definition, heaven's someplace else. It's more than a theory. Gamuka's been to other universes."

Kent and Cleo exchanged glances. *Coo-coo, dingy?*

Kent asked, "How did he get there?"

"Through a wormhole. That's the only real way to travel around the universe or between universes. Otherwise the distances are too great."

Kent remembered old Hoover saying it would take NASA's fastest spaceship four times longer than the entire period of written history to travel to the nearest planet outside the solar system. He could see what Justin meant. The universe was just too big for spaceship travel.

Cleo asked, "What's a wormhole?

"A wormhole is a connection, a short cut between distant parts of the universe and between different universes."

"I don't get it," Kent said with an expression of puzzlement.

Cleo yelled, "Hey look, here comes another jerk."

This time a jowly character with curly black hair in a Toyota Avalon rode the outer lane, honking, stretching body and limb to the limits of his seat belt, and making the same obscene gestures.

Cleo glared at the jowly driver. "What is this highway, Weirdsville?" She stomped on the accelerator. The old Ford inched ahead, shimmying like an unbalanced washing machine.

Justin told Kent, who maintained eye contact despite the distraction, what Gamuka had told him about wormholes. That space was curved, and the universe exists in a time-space continuum thanks to Doctor Einstein.

"Let me explain it this way," Justin said. "Got some paper?"

Kent dug around in his pocket for the pink and yellow copies of the Mercedes' repair estimate and gave them to Justin.

"Got a pencil?"

"In my purse," Cleo said. Kent retrieved a ballpoint from Cleo's purse and handed it across the seat to Justin, who then marked a little "x" with the ballpoint on the center of each paper, and laid the yellow paper atop the pink one.

"If a tiny ant wanted to go from the "x" on the yellow paper to the "x" on the pink one, he'd have to crawl down the yellow paper and then up the pink paper. Right?"

"Right," Kent answered.

"And if these papers were vast universes, the ant wouldn't have enough time to do it. Right?"

"Okay."

Justin jabbed the ballpoint through the yellow and pink papers at the x's. "But if there is a hole between the papers, the ant could go right through the hole in the yellow paper and come out the other side on the pink paper. Get it?"

Justin handed Kent the ballpoint with the papers skewered on the shaft.

"Yeah," Kent replied, twirling the impaled papers, "a wormhole." Kent liked the way Justin explained things--clear and visual.

Cleo asked, "How did Gamuka find a wormhole? "

"Good question. Wormholes are too small to be seen; they're part of the multidimensional world of subatomic particles. Only the mind can enter a wormhole. And only by using a special form of meditation Gamuka personally invented. One day, I found Gamuka standing in a freezing drizzle on the porch of his apartment, oblivious to the world, ice crystals forming on his eyebrows. His breathing had virtually stopped. And his heartbeat was barely perceptible. He had entered a wormhole and had lost all track of time. I figured he had been standing there for hours. I carried him inside before he froze. Several hours later, he returned from the wormhole exhausted but radiant, his eyes blazing with life and warmth. He told me he had seen God."

"What a trip," Kent gasped. "How's one do that kind of meditation?"

"It's very complicated. First, you must empty out the mind. Kill the senses. Become just self. You start by shutting out all sound, all feeling, even the urge to urinate. Then you must visualize Einstein's equations for General Relativity. You don't have to understand them, just visualize them. They all have that little square root sign. Then, if you try hard enough, you'll visualize the wormhole. Once you see it, the mind can enter it. I've never been able to do it myself, but Gamuka has made several trips."

Cleo asked, "What's all this got to do with kicking a football?"

"I'll try to tie it together. At first, Gamuka refused to sign a contract with me. He hated football, and you couldn't blame him. He weighed only a hundred pounds and had a very gentle nature. All he wanted was to do wormhole meditation and start a school in India to teach others. But he had no money. I convinced him that after a few years in the NFL, he'd have enough money to build a school and do wormhole meditation the rest of his life. So, he signed on with me.

"I couldn't wait to get him to a training camp. I even thought up a nickname for him, 'Big Foot', although he wore a boy's size seven shoe. I could hear the fans chanting, 'Big Foot! Big Foot!' I knew that someday the name 'Big Foot' would be as famous as 'Yankee Clipper' or 'Brown Bomber.' Because of his size and inexperience, eight teams turned him down for a try-out. Finally, the Vikings gave us a shot. Gamuka was terrific. Eighty-five percent accuracy for field goals over sixty yards. Ninety-nine point nine percent under sixty. Extra points were automatic. Punts were coffin corner with hang-time enough for a cup of cappuccino. No one in football had seen anything like him.

"That night after his try-out, I went to my motel room knowing a major contract was forthcoming. Gamuka and I would soon be millionaires." Justin's voice suddenly cracked with disappointment, "It never happened."

"Hey look!" Cleo cried, "The guy in the Toyota's back."

The Toyota driver almost crowded them off the road, waving his arms and shouting like a lunatic. Cleo swung the Ford sharply onto an exit ramp and the Toyota sped on by.

"Good move, Cleo."

The Ford rolled down the ramp onto a two-lane where Cleo wheeled into the parking lot of truck plaza and restaurant.

"I'm hungry," Cleo announced, "how about you guys?"

A fleet of eighteen-wheelers clogged the parking lot like a panzer division warming up for an invasion, clanking engines, black diesel exhaust, livestock stomping and moaning. Cleo drove between two idling monsters and parked.

"Looks like a truck driver's convention," she observed. "They say the food is always good at a truck stop."

"I hate trucks," Justin croaked, rancor in his voice, a glowering in his eyes. "A truck killed Dumbrowsky, my prize linebacker. My brother slid into the back of a flatbed on an icy road. Took off the top of his Volkswagen and his head. And my cousin Nick's in a nursing home with brain damage from a collision with a truck."

Cleo turned to Justin, a sympathetic expression on her face. "I'm so sorry to hear that."

"You know, I used to collect news clippings about athletes," Justin continued. From inside his ragged coat, he pulled out a chafed leather pouch gorged with newspaper cuttings. He shoved the pouch at Kent. "Now I keep tabs on truck accidents. Read those headlines, will you."

Kent glanced at some of the clippings:

FAMILY OF SIX KILLED IN HEAD-ON WITH TRUCK. TRUCK DRIVER TREATED FOR ABRASIONS AND RELEASED.

EIGHTEEN KILLED IN TWENTY-CAR PILEUP
WHEN TRACTOR-TRAILER JACKKNIFES ON ICY
HIGHWAY. DRIVER OF TRUCK TREATED FOR
MINOR INJURIES.

SCHOOL BUS COLLIDES WITH TRUCK. TEN
CHILDREN KILLED. THREE IN CRITICAL
CONDITION. SIX MORE SERIOUS. TRUCK
DRIVER ESCAPES INJURY.

TRAIN DERAILS IN CRASH WITH TRUCK AT
CROSSING. SEVEN DEAD. THREE MISSING.
TRUCKER TREATED AND RELEASED.

There were more.

Kent handed the pouch back to Justin. "You know, if a guy's going to be doing a lot of highway traveling, maybe he should buy a semi."

Justin looked at Kent. "Someday I'm going to write a book about it."

When the three of them got out of the Ford, Justin turned and said, "You guys go on. I'll wait here."

Kent asked, "What's the trouble?"

"I can't leave my duffel here."

"We'll lock it in the trunk, okay. It'll be safe there."

In the shadows of clangorous eighteen-wheelers, Justin cast furtive glances in every direction as Kent placed the ponderous duffel bag into the trunk and slammed the lid closed. He smiled at Justin. "There, locked up nice and safe. Let's go eat."

Chapter 18
RUMMELS

Inside the restaurant, Kent and company settled into a Naugahyde booth in the no-smoking section where stagnant clouds of exhaled smoke migrated over from the smoking section. Across the way, sleepy-eyed truckers dined on greasy food, sipped coffee, and talked on cell phones.

Kent leaned back and smiled at Justin. "Please go on with your story about Gamuka."

Before Justin could open his mouth, a red-haired waitress in a spotted uniform and tennis shoes waltzed over with menus. Justin studied his menu, his eyes slowly rising to catch Kent's gaze, his wiry white brows arching inquiringly.

"It's okay," Kent assured him. "I'm buying."

Justin ordered the fried chicken dinner with extra gravy on the mashed potatoes and cherry pie a la mode. Coffee with cream. Cleo got the same. Kent ordered a grilled cheese sandwich. Although anxious to hear the rest of Justin's story, Kent made no attempt to rekindle the conversation with the hitchhiker. Justin seemed preoccupied staring at the kitchen's service window, fork in hand, little beads of saliva foaming in the corners of his whiskered mouth as if the poor fellow hadn't eaten in days.

When the food came, Justin ripped away at the chicken with his teeth, swallowing strips of it without chewing. With two scoops and three gulps, he devoured the potatoes, the gravy a lubricant for his gullet. Coffee washed down the pie and ice cream. Sated, Justin settled back in his seat and watched the waitress refill his coffee cup. Driblets of gravy clung to his beard. Smiling politely, he told Kent and Cleo how lucky he was to have met such nice people as them, their trusting faces and all.

Kent put down his sandwich, clasped his hands together and looked at Justin. "What about Gamuka?"

Justin leaned across the table. "You must never repeat what I'm about to tell you."

Kent and Cleo nodded.

○──⚭──○

Justin began where he had left off, the night following Gamuka's Viking tryout:

Asleep in his motel room, Justin dreamed about a fat contract with the Vikings when someone banged on the door.

"Who is it," he called out.

A gruff and authoritative voice answered, "Special Agent Rummels."

Justin slipped on a robe and tromped barefoot over to the door. An overweight man in a tan topcoat over a gray suit stood in the doorway, a government look about him, hair unkempt, eyes limp, suit rumpled, a pudgy Walter Matthau.

Special Agent Rummels stuck his foot inside the door. "I'm from CRAWL," he announced.

Justin fidgeted with his robe. "CRAWL what?"

"It's an acronym for the *'Committee for Reaffirming the American Way of Life.'* We specialize in preventing economic destabilizations and cultural shock. Our methods are covert and no official records are kept. However, we are funded. Only a few months ago we bought a South Pacific Island chain from a dictator for a hundred and twenty-five million dollars and a fully furnished chalet in Switzerland. A small price for democracy. May I come inside?"

"I guess," Justin answered.

Rummels took off his coat, tossed it into a chair, and gazed up at the ceiling and down at the floor. He scooted the chair over to the bed, sat down, loosened his shoestrings, and plopped his feet upon the bed. "Ahh, that's better. Standing around just kills me. I've a lumbar disk and bad leg veins. I wear panty support hose, but my doctor has me elevate my legs at every opportunity."

"What does your committee want with me," Justin asked, standing barefoot beside the seated stranger.

"We work preemptively, Mr. Freely. We successfully handle about ninety-eight percent of all potential calamities in our area. However, once a catastrophe occurs, it's out of our hands. I'll be the first to admit we've had a few slip by us."

"Will you get to the point?"

Rummels shifted in the chair and craned his neck to make eye contact. "I'll be quite blunt. We consider your client Kumarmar Gamuka a potential but preventable economic and cultural calamity."

Justin cast an angry look at his visitor. "What are you talking about, that little fellow's the nicest guy you could ever meet? The only thing he does is meditate."

Rummels' lips curled. "And kick footballs."

"So what?"

"That's the problem, Mr. Freely. Eighty yard field goals. He'd ruin the game of football."

"On the contrary, he'd be a main attraction."

Rummels shifted again in the chair and rolled his pouchy eyes. "No one goes to a football game to see someone kick a field goal. People want action. Spectacular running. One arm catches. Body banging. Our calculations show Mr. Gamuka would kick the ball out of the end zone every kickoff. His coffin corner punts wouldn't be returnable. Just think. No punt returns. No exciting runbacks. His team would never lose. The Super Bowl would become the Super Bore. Football, as we know it, would be doomed."

"I can't believe this," Justin thundered, glowering at his unwelcomed guest.

"What you don't understand is that football is more than a game; it's a form of patriotism. Keeps the jingoism flowing between wars and keeps American men in a mental state of readiness."

Justin shook his head. "Football's just a damn game."

Rummels leaped up with his hand on his paunch and desperation in his eyes. He glanced anxiously around the room, rushed into the bathroom, and closed the door. Justin paced for ten minutes before Rummels, sitting on the stool, panty hose rolled at the ankles, pushed the bathroom door open.

"You wouldn't happen to have today's newspaper, would you? I need something to read."

Justin handed him the paper and closed the door. Fifteen minutes later, Rummels came out of the bathroom, buckling his belt, the newspaper under his arm. He dropped heavily into the chair, and threw his feet back upon the bed. His face was pale and his brows moist.

"Phew."

"You all right?"

"Got a bowel problem, hits me when I least expect it. Now let's see, where were we?"

"I said football was just a game."

Rummels tossed his head back and looked up at Justin. "Oh, how wrong you are. You don't understand just how delicate the fabric of our economy is. Without football, SUV and truck sales would plummet due to the lack of a male TV audience. Sales of beer, athletic footwear, fuel additives, fishing tackle, motorcycles…well, everything masculine, would dry up. Little things like ball caps, T-shirts, peanuts, and red-dye used to color hot dogs are immensely important to our economy. Not to mention the cultural upheaval that would result from the loss of a major sport."

Justin slapped his hand to his forehead in disgust.

Rummels pivoted and swung his feet onto the floor. "Mr. Freely, we have no choice but to stop Mr. Gamuka from ever playing football. How much would it take for him to agree to never play football and to leave the country?"

Justin perked up at the thought of a buyout. He did a quick calculation, factoring in his commission. "Say, twenty million."

"Come on, he's good but he's not Peyton Manning."

"Fifteen?"

Rummels tied his shoes and with a loud grunt stood up. From his pocket, he withdrew a handheld electronic device and punched in some numbers. At length, he mumbled, "That's still way too much money." Then in full resonant voice, "We may have to go with an annihilation. I wouldn't drive around in a car with Mr. Gamuka if I were you. A bomb or a drive-by are possibilities."

"How about ten million?"

Tucking his chin and making a roll of the fat on his throat, Rummels punched in more numbers. He studied the handheld, shaking his head. "I'm sorry. With that South Pacific Island chain buyout, we're a little strapped right now. Can you think of anything Mr. Gamuka would like to have? A car? Small airplane? World War II tank?"

His face glazed with disappointment, Justin answered in a subdued voice, "He wants to open a school for wormhole meditation in India."

"Sounds doable, I'll look into it. In the meantime, like I say, I wouldn't ride around with Mr. Gamuka. Oh, by the way, if you mention this conversation to anyone, you'll be placed on our annihilation list. You wouldn't want that, I assure you."

Rummels slipped on his topcoat and without saying another word walked out.

Chapter 19
THE ACCIDENT

The waitress replenished Justin's coffee cup. Justin stirred in two packets of sweetener, looked up, and grinned at Kent. "We've something in common. You've been poisoned and I'm on CRAWL's annihilation list."

"Why are you on CRAWL's annihilation list," Cleo asked as she forked up the last of her cherry pie.

"I struck a deal with Rummels. Gamuka would give up his football career for two years funding of a wormhole school in India. I didn't like it, but it was the best deal I could get. No commission for me. Not even a consulting fee. We were to meet with Rummels and sign papers the following Wednesday. 'Be on time," Rummels warned. He explained that a 'no show' would automatically trigger an irreversible annihilation order on Gamuka and me. No excuses accepted.

"When I explained the situation to Gamuka, he immediately sent his wife and child back to India. He planned to fly back after the deal was consummated on Wednesday. The next day I found Gamuka lying on a sofa in his apartment in a deep trance. I couldn't wake him up. I figured he was trapped in a wormhole but I wasn't sure, so I loaded him into my car and took him to a local hospital. The doctors were stumped.

"Seven days and nights I stayed at Gamuka's side. The doctors claimed he was in a coma. His weight dropped to a mere sixty-five pounds. While sitting in the ICU waiting room, it donned on me that we had missed our meeting with CRAWL, and that an annihilation order was now in effect. There was nothing I could about it, except stay out of sight.

"To make matters worse, the doctors diagnosed Gamuka as a 'clinical vegetable'. They wanted to take out all his organs and transplant them into other patients. That's when I stuffed him into a duffel bag and walked out with him. And just in time I might add. On the way out, I spotted Rummels walking through the hospital lobby toward the elevator."

Kent asked, "Gamuka's not in that duffel bag in the car trunk, is he?"

Justin lowered his gaze. "His body is. His mind is stuck in a wormhole somewhere."

Cleo put her hand over her mouth. "Oh, dear God."

Justin patted Cleo on the arm. "Please, don't worry. I'll take Gamuka and head south. We won't get you involved." He motioned to the waitress. "Could I have a coke to go, please?"

Justin stuffed his pockets with little packets of garlic breadsticks and crackers while Kent walked over to the cash register to pay for the meal. Outside in the parking lot, Justin glanced nervously around as the three of them made their way over to the Ford. Kent unlocked the car trunk and raised the lid.

"Could we see Gamuka," Cleo asked.

"Sure."

Kent and Cleo watched in lip-biting silence as Justin unzipped the duffel. A pungent ammonia odor floated up. Inside the bag, curled like a fetus, lay the pint-sized Gamuka, hollow-cheeked and sunken-eyed, a miniature Egyptian mummy swathed in stripped pajama tops and a diaper, his long black hair curled around him like an afghan, his skin flaky, his toenails whorled into little ram horns. The peaceful expression on his face was that of a contented baby, freshly rocked to sleep. Kent and Cleo felt like witnesses at an exhumation.

Woozy, Kent leaned against the car. Cleo placed her hand on Gamuka's chest. "Is he alive?"

Justin explained, "His body is in a vegetative state similar to hibernation. He has a pulse about every ten seconds. And about every six hours, he'll take a breath."

"Does he eat?"

"One small feeding a week. A diaper change once a month. He's been in the wormhole…let's see…a little over a year now."

Cleo felt a thump against her hand. "There's a heart beat. He really is alive!"

"Shhhh," Justin whispered. "CRAWL agents are everywhere."

Justin forced Gamuka's mouth open with his fingers, stuffed in some cracker crumbs, dripped in a little coke, and moved Gamuka's jaw up and down in a chewing motion. Gamuka swallowed. "That'll last him quite a while."

A Toyota Avalon rolled into the parking lot. The jowly man with curly black hair got out and walked towards them.

"Look, our friend in the Toyota is back."

"Must be a CRAWL agent," Justin gasped as he zipped up the duffel. "I've got to get Gamuka out of here."

Kent nervously cleared his throat. "Take your duffel and get in the backseat. We're not abandoning you to the mercy of a CRAWL agent."

The old Ford burned rubber out of the parking lot. Back on the interstate, Kent had the nerd car doing seventy-five. His eyes glued to the rearview mirror, Kent drove steadily for hours. The sun glowed red on the horizon. There was no sign of the Toyota. Kent turned on the headlights. Cleo slept in the front seat, Justin in the back snuggled to his duffel.

The car made a knocking sound and the steering wheel jerked violently in Kent's hands. He fought to control the vehicle. All at once the front end of the car dropped down screeching against the pavement. Sparks and chunks of asphalt sprayed the windshield. Kent watched helplessly as the front wheels sped down the highway ahead of the car.

"We're going to crash!"

The Ford careened left, plunged nose down into the median trench, teetered, and rolled over. The next thing Kent knew, he was lying on an ambulance cart at the side of the road in a neck brace. In the strobe of red and blue lights, he saw the jowly, curly-headed Toyota driver talking to a highway patrol officer. "I tried to warn them the front wheels were loose. But the darn fools just kept ignoring me."

Chapter 20
ENTERTAINO THERAPY

The prison clinic smelled of Pine Sol, Clorox, and rubbing alcohol, a noxious but necessary amalgam. Pine Sol for cleaning the floors and walls, Clorox for AIDS, rubbing alcohol for all the other germs. Larry Lakes assumed he had been ordered to the clinic for a vaccination or a routine exam. He sat thirty-minutes on a wooden bench in a waiting room filled with coughing, glowering inmates afflicted with fevers, bad livers, and prison blues. Finally, an orderly called out his name and led him down a corridor to Dr. Vu's office.

"Inside," the orderly barked.

The office wasn't much larger than an inmate's cell. Doctor Vu looked up from a cluttered desk, grinned and motioned Larry to sit. Vu picked up a telephone, punched some numbers, and following a short phone conversation in Vietnamese, handed the phone across his desk to Larry.

The soft purr of a voice coming over the phone was like having Julia Roberts blow into his ear. "Hello, Larry. I am Veronica, Doctor Vu's niece in Corpus Christi. He wants me to ask you if you would be kind enough to work with him on a special project?"

"W-w-what kind of project?"

"Please hand the phone to Doctor Vu."

Doctor Vu conversed with his niece and handed the phone back to Larry whose left foot vibrated like a plucked guitar string.

"Hello, Larry. It is I again. My uncle would like you to assist him in the T and A unit with a new kind of therapy for the criminally insane, which he has named *entertaino therapy*. He would like you to perform some musical numbers and skits. Would you be willing to help? He says that it would look good on your record, and he would arrange for you to have a private cell."

Without hesitation, right-brain Larry shouted, "Hell yes, I'll do it."

"Please hand the phone back to Doctor Vu, thank you."

The telephonic translation went on for sometime, Larry and Doctor Vu passing the phone back and forth. Larry said, "yes" to everything, to singing, dancing, and performing daily in the T and A. He'd take his chances with the maniacs; anything was better then being locked up with Eugene and his horny clientele of yard dogs.

"You will begin your new job tomorrow. Please hand the phone back to Doctor Vu."

Larry clicked his heels on his way out of the clinic. *Entertaino therapy, hot dog. Break a leg, baby.*

When the guards came to escort Larry to a private cell, Eugene grabbed him by the collar. "Listen punk, nobody walks out on me. I'll have your ass back here before you know it. You just wait."

Bedroll on his back, Larry followed the guards down the corridor. He wasn't dreaming of revenge and escape; he was making plans.

Fuck you, Eugene.

The next morning, swinging his mop, Larry two-stepped down the corridor of the T and A singing at the top of his lungs. At first, the maniacs looked at him as if he were crazy. After a few days belting out solid rock and country favorites, Larry had 'em hooked. Whenever Larry strolled into the T and A, the maniacs rushed to their cell doors, not to grab at the mop-man but to applaud him. Overnight, thanks to Larry's magical musical voice, the mop-man had become the maniacs' private satellite entertainment channel, the only cheer in the wretched lives of the sixteen troglodytes, a supernova in a drab universe of gray walls.

Each maniac had preferences: Hot Dog Jenkins liked sad songs, ballads, and poems; Tool preferred song and dance routines especially when the mop was involved; Willie loved cartwheels and handstands. Larry did them all. One day crooning the lyrics to "The Red River Valley," Larry put down the mop, reached through the bars, and patted the sobbing Hot Dog Jenkins on the shoulder. Doctor Vu was ecstatic. *Enteraino therapy* worked. Larry was living proof.

Larry added some comic routines, imitations, and clown acts. It wasn't life at the zenith, but right-brain Larry was doing what he liked doing best—entertaining. And he wasn't being sodomized.

Only Olgesby remained unimpressed by Larry's performances. Larry tried everything to amuse the turd-tossing butcher, pantomimes, belly dancing, and old Flip Wilson skits. Nothing worked until Larry tried ventriloquism using hand shadows. The chattering animated shadows on the walls of his cell captivated Olgesby, and he carried on lengthy conversations with them. Larry turned the talks into a fifteen-minute daily drama, which the tweedy birds broadcast over the PA system. A week later Olgesbee stopped throwing his shit.

The maniacs began saying two word pleasantries like "thank you" when they got their food, "Good night" at lights out, and "Good morning" when they came on again. One day, Hot Dog spoke a coherent, seven word sentence.

"I used to live in the Ozarks."

Amazingly, Tool responded with a six-word assertion, "My folks came from the Ozarks."

Larry became the first prisoner ever allowed inside the shark cage, where every afternoon he and Doctor Vu sipped coffee and discussed *entertaino therapy*. The enthusiastic Vu, his hands flying like semaphores in a storm, chatted with Larry for hours at a time. With great pride, he showed Larry his notes on *entertaino therapy* and the graphs and Venn diagrams he had drawn. Although Larry had no idea what Vu was saying, he nodded and made little guttural noises of affirmation and accord. One day, a Tweedy Bird asked Larry where he had learned to speak Vietnamese. That gave Larry an idea.

Doctor Vu had recorded the short conversation between Hot Dog Jenkins and Tool on tape, and when his niece translated it for him, he knew time was right for the next bold experiment in *entertaino therapy*. He had only to convince the warden.

Chapter 21
AEROBOCIZING

Victims' family and the press jammed the warden's office, clamoring for front row seats for the first execution in the state since lawmakers reinstated the death penalty. The condemned killer, Betty Stites, a twenty-two year old mother of three, had shot and killed some salespeople at a Sears store. She went to the store to return a pair of tight-fitting blue jeans that had split open in the back, and although she was 20 pounds heavier than when she purchased the jeans, she demanded her money back. When the salesperson refused to give Betty a refund, she stomped out of the store and came back an hour later with an assault rifle her husband had bought for rabbit hunting. She fired the weapon indiscriminately, the bullets bringing down three sales clerks, two in lingerie and one in furniture.

Betty's execution would be a series of firsts. First-degree murder. First execution in the state this century. First execution under the new law. First lethal injection in the state.

Doctor Vu snaked his way through the crowded office to the warden's desk where he stated his request bluntly in Vietnamese to the harried warden. "I like for the maniacs in T and A to go out into the corridors everyday for exercise and dancing routines. Your permission, of course."

The warden asked his secretary, "You any idea what he just said?"

"No, sir. Would you like me to get his niece on the phone?"

"I don't have time for that today."

A reporter from the Capitol Gazette must have noticed Doctor Vu's white clinic jacket and the stethoscope hanging around his neck, for he asked the warden, "Is this the doctor who will administer the lethal injection?"

"Yes," the warden replied, "I believe that is in his job description."

Doctor Vu mistakenly took the warden's "yes" to mean he had been given permission for the maniacs to exercise and dance in the corridors of the T and A. Vu shook the warden's hand with vigor. He also thought the reporters pressing close and shooting questions at him were interested in *entertaino therapy*. What wild enthusiasm.

"Doctor, do you have any qualms about administering a lethal injection to a twenty-two year-old mother with three young children?"

"Have you ever done a lethal injection before?"

"Does administering death violate your Hippocratic Oath?"

"What drugs will you use to kill Mrs. Stites?"

A victim's grandmother, an arthritic lady with blue hair, patted Doctor Vu on the back with her gnarled hand. "You will give the injection slowly so she can think about it, won't you, doctor? She will suffer, won't she?"

Doctor Vu raised his hand to quiet the mob.

"I'll answer all questions after my study is complete. We are just entering a bold new phase of *entertaino therapy*. It would be premature and reckless to comment further at this time."

A reporter asked the warden, "What did the doctor say?"

The warden shrugged.

Doctor Vu walked out of the warden's office more confident than ever of a Nobel Prize. Lord, he loved America.

The next day, emboldened by the warden's endorsement of *entertaino therapy*, Dr. Vu wasted no time implementing phase II with corridor Q. From inside the shark cage, Vu pushed the power button of his Yamaha compact disk player. BOOT SCOOTIN' BOOGIE echoed through the corridors.

Decked out in red shorts, gray sweat shirt, and a yellow headband, Larry stood on the broad expanse of concrete in front of the shark cage, perspiring, heart fluttering, left foot jerking. He would be out there alone with four deadly maniacs. He had to do it. It was part of a vague plan taking shape inside his head—a plan that would set him free.

He took a deep breath and shouted, "Turn 'em out."

The Tweedy Bird at the control panel threw switches and pulled levers. The four cell doors in corridor Q squeaked open.

Nothing happened.

"Exercise time," Larry shouted as he skipped up and down the corridor, the music blaring. "Everybody out. Come on boys, let's get with it."

Like wary prairie dogs, maniacs poked their grizzled heads out into the corridor then quickly withdrew them. The head bobbing went on for sometime before Willie shuffled out of his cell into the corridor, his spine cracking like popcorn as he straightened. Soon the others came, gimpy Neanderthals thawed from a block of ice. They looked like brothers with their bird nest hair and *Revenge of the Living Dead* anemic faces, except for Willie, who was black, bald, and six-foot-ten. They gawked at the shark cage, at each other, and at Larry. Then, as if guided by some universal impulse, they rushed back into their cells.

Larry had no fear of death, only of failing and being sent back to Eugene. He did flips down the corridor with the mop. He stood at the open door of Tool's cell, took a deep breath, and stepped inside. The music stopped. Doctor Vu covered his eyes.

Larry screamed, "Start the damn music."

With the music came Larry out of the cell followed by Tool hugging the mop, the two of them dancing down the corridor. Slowly came the others, one at a time, stiff-legged, awed, and Oglesby crapping his pants from all the excitement. A Tweedy Bird sneezed and the maniacs flew back into their nooks. All except Tool, who continued to waltz the mop like an Arthur Murray graduate.

It went on like that all day, maniacs shuffling out into the corridor then scurrying back to their cells like startled rodents. Only Tool stayed in the corridor, swaying cheek-to-handle with the mop, whirling it around, and on several occasions trying to hump it. When the session ended, Tool was reluctant to give up the mop, but he was so exhausted, Larry had no trouble taking it away from him.

Larry had survived his first day of *entertaino therapy*. He looked through the wire crosshatches of the shark cage at a grinning Dr. Vu. Music and dancing had truly calmed the beasts.

The next day, the maniacs were eager to participate, and corridor R was also opened up. By the end of the week, all sixteen maniacs were dancing around the shark cage under Larry's tutelage. That is, all but Hot Dog, whose knees had swollen up from all the dancing and were killing him. Over the next three weeks, Larry guided the maniacs through highly structured aerobic exercise and dance routines plus some chorus line numbers. Dr. Vu supplied the music, everything from Hill Billy Rock to Barbara Streisand. *Entertaino therapy* became infectious, and the Tweedy Birds began dancing and exercising within the crowded confines of the shark cage. Everyday the T and A rocked like a hop fest. The maniacs' dreary black hole existence rocketed into a universe of sound and motion.

To implement Phase III of *entertaino therapy*, Dr. Vu and Larry cropped the maniacs' hair and gave each one their own personal battery-powered electric shaver. Vu requisitioned for each maniac a blue satin warm up, red spandex shorts, white cross trainer shoes with blue trim, and a white

T-shirt with "T and A" in gold lettering. The maniacs looked more "white hat" than the guards. Then to the beat of "ACHY BREAKY HEART," Dr. Vu swung open the shark cage so that the space-cramped Tweedy Birds and maniacs could exercise and dance together. Hot Dog sat inside the shark cage in his new warm ups, watching the monitors and answering the phone, his knees the size of giant cantaloupes.

The good will between prisoner and guard was impressive. Not only had Vu invented a treatment for criminal maniacs, but just possibly a cure. Vu placed his hands on Hot Dog's shoulders, stared out through the wire cage at the aerobicizing Tweedy Birds and maniacs, and smiled a prodigious smile. At that moment, Larry was the only person in the T and A with a criminal thought in his head.

Chapter 22
THE PLAN

Doctor Vu and Larry often took strolls together along the brick paths that meandered through the prison grounds. As they sauntered along, Doctor Vu talked excitedly about *entertaino therapy*, and Larry pretended to understand everything Vu said. When they passed by a guard, especially one of the guards at the gate, Larry emulated Doctor Vu's Far East twang with nonsensical syllables like *uh-lee-mau, hoy-no, chu-cong*. The guards were impressed with Larry's apparent command of a foreign language.

One day, walking along near the prison gate, Vu turned to Larry. "I don't know what you're saying, Larry. But it doesn't sound like English."

The guard at the gate, a dazed expression on his face, asked, "What did the doctor say?"

Larry answered, "He wants to know what time it is."

The guard glanced at his watch. "It's three thirty-five."

Larry turned to Vu. "Uh-lee-mau. Hoy-no."

Vu shrugged. "I don't know what you said. It didn't sound like English."

The guard asked, "What did the doctor say?"

"He said thank you and you're doing a good job."

"Tell the doctor, he's doing a good job, too."

"Chu cong, wu lee."

Vu said irritably in Vietnamese, "I have no idea what you just said."

A few days later, Larry finalized his escape plan. He would create a disturbance in the T and A which would set off an alarm. That would occupy every guard in the prison, leaving only the guards at the gate between him and freedom. He planned to use Doctor Vu to get through the front gate. If all went well, he would drive off in the doctor's new Honda, leaving Vu in the parking lot to confuse anyone who came along asking questions.

Larry walked in the evening shadows of Building B on his way to his private cell in Building D. He took the long way around to avoid any chance meeting with old friends. Now that his escape plan was complete, he had only to implement it. He would succeed. He had to succeed.

He rounded the corner of Building D and his heart nearly stopped. Slouched against the gray stone building, Eugene puffed on a cigarette. Larry knew better than to run. He nervously crumpled up the prison pass in his pocket. Being an official clinic orderly, thanks to Doctor Vu, Larry could go anywhere on the prison grounds with his pass. But how did Eugene get outside the cellblock? Stupid question. Larry glanced up at the guard watching from the second floor window. Eugene had bought the guard off.

Eugene flicked his cigarette into the air, and Larry hung his head and shambled over to his old master. Eugene slapped him hard across the face. "Look at me, you chicken shit, bitch. No one runs out on me."

Eugene's iron fist smashed into Larry's face and blood flew from Larry's nose. Larry fell against the building and slid to the ground. Eugene kicked him in the ribs and kept kicking. Larry rolled up in a ball.

"I made a deal with the bulls, punk. They'll let you move back in with me, but you have to request it."

Another kick, and the breath went out of Larry. He felt the sharp pain of a cracked rib as he gasped for air.

"And if you don't fuckin' request it, I'm puttin' a contract on you."

Eugene's heavy foot slammed into Larry's head. Brain jarring. Flashes of light in both eyes.

"You better fuckin' be there when I get back from the yard tomorrow."

Two parting kicks, one to the kidney and one to the drawn-up legs. Eugene glanced up at the guard in the window, nodded, and walked away. Larry lay motionless; it hurt to breathe. A contract was a death sentence. The assassin was paid in cigarettes--three fucking cartons of Camels. With his connections, Eugene would have no trouble making a contract. Larry crawled to his feet and wiped blood from his face with the back of his hand. If he didn't do what Eugene said, he'd be dead before Betty Stites got her sleep injection. He had seen a contract fulfilled before--the knife blade broke off in the man's back and he staggered around the yard bleeding, begging for help. He died there in the prison yard, in that huge circle of men, and for cigarettes, and no one cared. Larry made up his mind. Tomorrow, he would implement his escape plan.

Adios, Eugene.

Chapter 23
THE ESCAPE

The maniacs and Tweedy Birds exercised like Richard Simmons Cadets: arms flailing, knees pumping, sweat flying and the music blaring. Inside the shark cage, Hot Dog watched it all on TV monitors while Doctor Vu scribbled notes on a yellow pad.

Some time ago, Larry had noticed Olgesby eyeing Tool's mop. Occasionally, when Tool wasn't looking, Olgesby affectionately caressed the woolly strands of the mop. The next time Tool put the mop down, Larry planned to hand it over to Olgesby. He was sure that would start the maniacs fighting, maniac against maniac, then the violence would spread, maniac against Tweedy Bird. Once the melee got going and a general alarm sounded, Larry would sneak into the shark cage, lock it behind him, and force Dr. Vu up the spiral staircase onto the roof. With Vu as a patsy, Larry would talk his way out the front gate by pretending to interpret for the doctor.

Today was the day.

"Come on. Let's get with it. Jumping jacks. One, two, three."

Tool usually laid the mop down so he could clap his hands above his head while doing jumping jacks. Larry waited beside the shark cage to snatch up the mop and hand it to Olgesby.

Without warning, the steel door of the T and A flew open. A dozen armed Bears poured in followed by the warden in a blue suit and red necktie. A surprise inspection. Larry's face sagged in a fish-mouth of gloom. "Damn, of all the luck."

On his surprise inspections, the warden had seen some strange things, but nothing like this. He shouted shrilly, "Cut that damn music."

Hot Dog shut down the CD player. The Tweedy Birds in their sweats cowered toward the shark cage, separating from the maniacs. The warden gawked at the fifteen clean-shaven, cropped, ruddy-faced maniacs in their spandex shorts and T-shirts. They all looked like recent Navy Seal graduates.

"Who are these people?"

The guards stammered and stuttered in a vain attempt to explain things. Dr. Vu stomped out of the shark cage like an angry baseball manager and demanded an explanation for this rude interruption of his therapy session. A Bear raised his weapon and Doctor Vu gingerly stepped back inside the cage.

The warden shouted, "Get those prisoners back into their cells. Now."

Larry's escape plan was ruined. *I'll never get another chance.* He hoped the warden would place him in solitary for a long time, away from Eugene and his grimy friends. Larry's fingers laced the wire of the shark cage and his head dropped in defeat.

The Bears and Tweedy Birds surrounded the maniacs. The plan was to cuff them one at a time. A bear noticed Tool hugging the mop and jabbed his rifle at Tool's chest.

"Drop the mop, dingbat."

Tool protectively moved the mop behind his back, and the bear reached around him and grabbed it. A disastrous mistake. With light speed, Tool disarmed the bear, shoved the muzzle of the assault rifle into bear's nose, and squeezed the trigger. TAT! TAT! TAT! The bear's head exploded in a spatter of blood, bone, and brains, the headless body convulsing and lurching in a dance of death.

Tool opened fire on the other Bears, dropping two of them. The remaining Bears fired back. Willie yanked a smoke and tear-gas grenade from the munitions belt of a dead bear, pulled the pin, and rolled the grenade across the floor. A sickening, billowing, yellow smoke engulfed the T and A. Wounded men screamed, guns blazed, bullets ricocheted from walls creating transient red streaks in the blinding yellow fog.

Larry rubbed his eyes and saw hope in the midst of chaos. He slunk into the shark cage and locked the door behind him. In the enveloping yellow vapor he managed to find Vu standing beside his Yamaha disk player. He grabbed Vu by the wrist and literally dragged him up the spiral staircase. At the top of the staircase, Larry flung open the trapdoor and shoved Vu out onto the roof into sunlight and fresh air.

Larry turned to close the trapdoor to find Hot Dog standing in the doorway in his spandex shorts and T-shirt, his chest rising and falling in great heaves, his red eyes bulging, his hands clenched, his mouth frothing. A powder keg ready to explode. Above the din of mortal combat issuing from the T&A, Larry chanted to Hot Dog in a woeful and solemn voice an old poem his grandfather often recited to him:

> *Tell me not, in mournful numbers,*
>
> *Life is but an empty dream!*
>
> *For the soul is dead that slumbers,*
>
> *And things are not what they seem.*

Hot Dog simmered a bit, but the glare in his eyes would have chilled a werewolf.

Dr. Vu raced around the roof looking for a way down and saw a large red button attached to a metal box and pushed it. A rope ladder shot out the metal box and over the side of the building. By pushing the red button, he unwittingly released a paralyzing nerve gas into the interior of the T and A, saving several lives.

Larry climbed down the rope ladder to the ground below followed by Hot Dog, snorting and frothing, his eyes blazing with madness, and then came Vu babbling in his native tongue. The prison grounds were calm, no alarms going off; the rest of the prison was apparently unaware of the bloodbath in the T and A. Larry walked nonchalantly down the brick path between the main prison buildings, trailed by a discombobulated doctor and a seething maniac with swollen knees and dressed like an Olympian.

> *Life is real! Life is earnest!*
>
> *And the grave is not its goal;*
>
> *Dust thou art, to dust returnest,*
>
> *Was not spoken of the soul.*

Two guards walked out of building C headed for lunch. Dr. Vu ran up to them, shouting in Vietnamese, arms and hands flying, "There's a riot in the T and A. Men are being killed. You've got to do something."

With a huge smile Larry interpreted for the guards. "Dr. Vu's just won the Publisher's Sweepstakes. He's a millionaire!"

The guards shook Vu's hand, patted him on the back, and then headed off to the employee's cafeteria. Dr. Vu screamed at them, "You Americans are all crazy. Every damn one of you."

Larry led Vu and Hot Dog to Building B, Vu's tongue wagging, Hot Dog's brain firing horrible messages down taut nerves to his deadly hands. Larry crooned in the killer's ear.

> *Art is long, and Time is fleeting,*
>
> *And our hearts, though stout and brave,*
>
> *Still, like muffled drums, are beating*
>
> *Funeral marches to the grave.*

Larry marched up to the guard at the entrance of Building B. "Doctor Vu wants to examine the mattresses for lice."

The guard glanced at Hot Dog. "Whose the ballhead?"

"Dr. Vu's training him to be a lice inspector."

Vu erupted in a tirade, shouting to the guard about the massacre in the T and A. "What's he so excited about," the guard asked.

Larry shook his head. "Warden's on his ass about the lice problem. Haven't you heard? It's an epidemic."

"You picked a good time to inspect. Everyone's at lunch."

The guard threw an electronic switch opening all the cell doors. Vu and Hot Dog followed Larry from cell to cell where Larry pretended to inspect for lice. Vu shrugged. "There's a riot in T and A, and you're looking under mattresses. Oh, to hell with it."

Larry stopped and stared into his old cell, where Eugene had turned him into punk, where he had suffered indignities no human being should suffer. Larry led Hot Dog over to Eugene's bunk, motioned him to lie down and covered him with a blanket.

"This is your new cell, Hot Dog, your very own private place."

> *In the world's broad field of battle,*
>
> *In the bivouac of Life,*
>
> *Be not like dumb, driven cattle!*
>
> *Be a hero in the strife!*

When they left the cell block, Larry told the guard that Dr. Vu was leaving Hot Dog behind to do a head inspections on all prisoners when they returned from lunch.

Larry then led Vu to the prison's front gate where he explained to the guard there that he and Dr. Vu needed to go to the parking lot to get some emergency medical equipment from the doctor's car.

"Not without an outside pass, you don't."

Doctor Vu made another effort to communicate. "There's a riot in the T and A. And I think Larry here is trying to escape."

The guard asked, "What's he in such a huff about?"

"He said if you don't let us pass, he's reporting you to the warden and to his state senator."

"Really," the guard said with a sardonic tone.

"Yeah. He's really pissed. Just listen to him."

"What's he saying now?"

Larry rubbed a bead of sweat from his forehead. "He's saying this is an emergency and if someone dies because you didn't open the gate, it'll be your fault.

And he will testify against you. He's really mad."

"I can see that. Tell him not to get ruffled. But you get your ass right back here. Understand?"

"Uh-lee-mau. Hoy-no."

Out in the parking lot, Larry took Vu's car keys away from him. When Larry slid into the driver's seat of Vu's Honda, Vu jumped into the passenger seat.

"This is my new Honda and I'm not getting out."

Larry drove off with a hostage. He glanced into the rearview at the disappearing walls of State Prison and smiled.

> *Let us, then be up and doing,*
>
> *With a heart for any fate;*
>
> *Still achieving, still pursuing,*
>
> *Learn to labor and to wait.*

When Eugene returned from lunch and discovered Hot Dog in his bunk, his last words were, "Hey, shit head, what the fuck you doin' in my bunk?" The next day Eugene's mangled remains were shipped in a plastic bag to a mortuary back home.

Chapter 24
BOLTON MENTAL

Dr. Frank Chisholm, chief psychiatrist at Bolton Mental Hospital, a tall man with a square jaw, receding hairline, and a tense face, relaxed in a large cushioned chair with a glass of ruby port at the Bolton Country Club. Downstairs, his wife played after-dinner-bridge in the game room. Frank had come to hate being a psychiatrist. He was what one might call, well, jaded, too much responsibility too long, and no end in sight. Being chief psychiatrist of Bolton Mental Hospital was like being the captain of a leaking oil tanker. The once famous institution for the mentally ill founded by Frank's grandfather was sinking in red ink. Frank had just taken out a third mortgage on his home to meet payroll and keep the ship afloat.

Swirling his port and whiffing the bouquet, Frank listened to the idle conversations of his friends, mainly doctors and lawyers, hoping they would not stray onto subjects such as economics. His retirement funds eaten up in bad debt, Frank had no interest in talk about money and stocks. While his retired colleagues basked in the tropics or toured European capitals, Frank, now sixty-four, was still analyzing neurotics, drugging schizophrenics, and passing electric current through the brains of the melancholy.

Finally, the conversation shifted to golf as all conversations at Country Clubs eventually do. Frank put down his glass, stood, and with a twist of his rangy torso demonstrated to his friends the swing that got him a birdie on the third hole today. Before he could finish his show-and-tell, his cell phone played the Vienna Waltz.

"Dr. Chisholm here."

The voice on the phone buzzed in Frank's ear with the shrillness of high-speed dental drill. "This is Ball, sir, the night intern. We got something a bit unusual here in admitting, shipped over from the ER at General."

Frank stepped over to the plate glass window overlooking the fairway. "Well, what is it, Ball?"

"I think it's a Folie a Deux, sir, but there's three in this case. One has a severe fetish disorder."

"What kind of fetish?"

"A smelly duffel bag. He won't let anyone near it."

"Listen, Ball, be careful. Don't take the duffel away, it might set him off."

"Sir, I don't feel comfortable with this. I've never really seen a Folie a Deux before. Would you come take a look?"

"I'm at the country club. My wife is playing bridge." Frank detested seeing patients after hours. That's what social workers, psychologists, and interns were for.

"Okay, sir, but I'll have to record your refusal on the chart."

"All right, Ball. Put them in the Observation Room and I'll come take a peek."

Damn interns. Frank rued the loss of resident doctors, psychiatrists in training, the funds for which had also disappeared in red ink. Bolton Mental was stuck with a handful of interns just out of medical school who used little black recipe books to diagnose and treat, and who wrote long rambling notes on patients' charts that often made the attending look like a fool in the courtroom.

Intern Ball, a short young man with an Adolf Hitler mustache, met Frank in the admissions department. They walked together down a deserted hallway toward the observation room, their footsteps echoing from the tiled walls.

"They all three think the one's been poisoned," Intern Ball reported, his face squished up in a look of puzzlement.

"What kind of poison?"

"They don't seem to know, sir."

Frank shook his head. "Figures."

"They overturned their car on the interstate. No significant injuries. The ER doc thought they were all crazy and sent 'em here. Guess where they were headed?"

"To see the Queen?"

Ball snickered. "Almost. They were on their way to find Selena Rosalina. She's supposed to help them find the antidote for the poison."

Frank shook his head again. "Celebrity baiting."

"What's that, sir?"

"They throw out names of celebrities to lure people into their delusions and to make themselves feel important. It's compensatory for low self-esteem."

At one time in Bolton Mental's glorious past the Observation Room had a one-way-see-through-mirror where psychiatrists could observe patients without themselves being observed. A few years ago, an agitated patient smashed the mirror with a chair. Due to budgetary restraints, the area was dry-walled, painted, and the mirror replaced by a peephole in a wall clock.

Frank screwed his eye up to the peephole and observed Kent, Cleo, and Justin sitting on fold up chairs in the Observation Room. Kent held Cleo's hand, and Justin sat with his duffel between his knees. They chattered like sparrows at a bird feeder.

"The hobo with the bag looks paranoid. Could be dangerous. The other two look fairly normal," Frank commented.

"Do you think it's a Folie a Deux, sir?"

"Let's see, that's two people sharing the same delusions, isn't it?"

"Yes sir, it's right here in the DSM handbook."

"I suppose you could call it a Folie a Deux. Turn up the volume, I can't hear what they're saying?"

"The speaker system's broke, sir. Can you read lips?"

"No. Can you?"

"A little."

Frank stepped back and Ball stood on a chair and put his eye to the peephole.

"They've stopped talking, sir. Wait. Now they're talking. Wondering why they're here. The old hobo with the bag is talking about...uh, I think he's saying the word CRAWL, as if it were a noun instead of verb. That CRAWL is behind the whole thing, and that they're all going to be murdered. What do you suppose CRAWL is, sir?"

"Who knows? Anything else?"

"The woman is telling the guy holding her hand that she's hungry. She's asked him if he thinks they are going to get anything to eat."

"Okay. I've heard enough. Put them on separate wards. Admit the hobo to the Contamination Room and get him cleaned up. He looks like a 'FIG'."

"What's a FIG, sir?"

"Didn't you read the novel 'The Intern by Doctor X' when you were in medical school?"

Ball shook his head.

Frank shrugged. "I'm getting old. A FIG is a 'Fucking, Indigent Geriatric'."

"That's degrading, sir."

"I didn't write the damn novel. I just read it…a long time ago."

※

Frank Chisholm drove home slowly from the country club. His oil-burning Mercury Cougar showed ninety-seven thousand miles on an odometer that had quit years ago. Frank didn't care much for cars. They were just a means of transportation. At least, that's what he told people, especially when he thought they were wondering why he was the only specialist at the country club without a European sports car.

As Frank pulled into the driveway of his heavily mortgaged, forty-year old ranch-style bungalow, he thought about the old hobo with the duffel and the odd couple with the same magic lantern show playing inside their heads. Folie a Deux. *Maybe I'll write this one up. Two people sharing the same delusions. A hobo with a fetish.* He knew he would never write it up, but it made him feel good to think he might. To think he wasn't over the hill yet.

Tomorrow he'd put Morgan, the psychologist, on this case. Collect the facts. Run the tests. Develop a strategy. Declare war on those mad delusions. And to what end? After thirty-five years of practicing psychiatry, Frank was convinced the whole world was crazy, not just patients, but doctors, automobile manufacturers, the whole damn ball of earth. He killed the Cougar's engine and headed for the front porch.

He turned the key in the front door and remembered his wife was playing bridge at the country club, a Freudian slip of the memory. His wife was seldom in his conscious thoughts anymore, although skank images of her roamed the unfathomable, dark recesses of his unconscious. And she had forgotten about him for the most part, at least those parts he thought of as him. The parts that craved the loving touch of a woman, the attentiveness of an admiring listener, that sought the companionship two souls were meant to share as they walked hand and hand down the rough, winding road of life.

The Cougar growled as it turned over. He drove even more slowly back to the country club, dreading the return ride home. For years, Frank and his wife had lived together like parasites eating away at each other's marrow. They no longer fought. It was worse; they ignored each other--no sex, no children, no love, just a stagnant cohabitation.

He masturbated regularly three or four times a week in the shower with the water running and a little fantasy show playing in his head. His fantasy always involved Tracy Fedler, the shapely business manager at Bolton

Mental. Although Frank would give up his right testicle for a night in the sack with Tracy, he knew he could never have her except in his mind, especially in the shower, the two of them, the water running, and the bathroom steaming, and him jerking off like a teenager. Sometimes, he took two showers in one evening. Hell, he'd give up one of his limbs for a night in the sack with Tracy. Well, maybe not a limb, his golf game was pretty important to him.

While Frank practiced psychiatry, played golf, and masturbated in the shower, his wife played bridge and collected Hummel plates and Beanie Babies. They slept in separate bedrooms, occasionally passing each other in the hallway on the way to the bathroom—ships in the night.

What had brought about this separation within a marriage? The Chisholms didn't know. She had married him because he was a doctor and because the bronze statue of his great grandfather had always stood in the middle of Town Square, old Colonel Chisholm rearing up on his horse like Peter the Great. The colonel, an anti-slavery freebooter, had been either a traitor or a hero of the Civil War, depending on your point of view. By smuggling troops in and out of Bolton, the colonel saved the lives of 800 bogged-down Union soldiers. As a result, the Union Army emerged victorious in the battle for Bolton and the town had been either saved or lost, again depending on your point of view. The polemics of that famous battle still rages in Bolton to this day.

Frank married his wife because he had known her since childhood and played high school football with her brother. After a few calm years of marriage, they started fighting. Why? The Chisholms couldn't remember. They stayed apart emotionally, but kept the marriage. Why? Because divorce was unthinkable. After all, he was head psychiatrist and chief executive of Bolton Mental, and she was a doctor's wife. He was a deacon of the church, and she belonged to four bridge clubs. To outsiders, the Chisholms appeared to be a wholesome, well-adjusted couple, living proof that endearing relationships and long marriages are worthwhile.

Talk about Folie a Deux.

Chapter 25
INPATIENT

Still groggy from the sleeping pill the nurse poked down his throat last night, Kent with great deliberation spooned up his Cream of Wheat breakfast, a good portion of it onto his white hospital gown. His eyes out of focus, his head spinning, he glanced around the whirling dining area, which had the no-frills-starkness of a Salvation Army soup kitchen, wooden tables, bowls, a spoon big as ladle, and strangers in white hospital gowns struggling with their Cream of Wheat. Kent put his spoon down, clasped his hands to his head and squeezed, trying to make sense of the events of the past evening.

He recalled the accident on the interstate and the three of them, four if you count Gamuka inside the duffel, being taken to an emergency room in ambulances. When the doctor in the ER asked Kent if he had any medication allergies, Cleo insisted Kent tell the doctor about being poisoned.

Yes, that's when it all started. It's getting clearer now.

The doctor stared at them suspiciously when they mentioned the poison. When they got around to the part about going to New York to ask Selena Rosalina to help them find a *homopragmatic truth,* that's when the doctor asked the security guard to search them. He was probably thinking then they were all crazy, especially after Justin bit the security guard's hand when he tired to take his duffel away.

That's it! That doctor in the ER was responsible for us ending up here in a mental hospital. Dam, if I had only kept my mouth shut.

Kent rubbed his eyes with his palms. Here he was sitting in the soup kitchen of a nut house, licking Cream of Wheat from his lips, trying to beam himself up, while a deadly poison was eating away at his insides. *Where are Cleo and Justin? We're losing valuable time sitting around here. We need to get to New York to find Selena Rosalina.*

He looked up at the nurse who walked into the dining area, a scowl chiseled on her face. Her hair was done up in a bouffant, rigid as a woodcarving. The patient's called her Attila the Hun. Kent straightened when she called his name. The other patients fled the dining area for the Day Room. She tossed a ballpoint pen onto the table along with some papers.

"Read, then sign 'em," she snapped, her arms folded across her flat chest. She tapped her foot and waited while Kent studied the papers. Minutes passed. To Kent, the papers looked like the extended warranty on his Mercedes, small print, long sentences, tangled phrases. After several minutes of intense perusal, he looked up at the nurse. "What's it say?"

"It says you're agreeing to six weeks of inpatient psychiatric treatment here at Bolton Mental."

"There's no way I'm signing this."

"If you don't sign, the doctors will take you to court and have you committed for six months. Suit yourself."

Kent glanced around the room. "Where are Cleo and Justin?"

"They're not on this ward."

"Then where are they?"

The nurse uncrossed her arms and put her hands on her hips. "You're a Folie a Deux. Visiting old friends and acquaintances right now would be bad for you. You'll make new friends on the ward."

"What's a Folie a Deux?"

"You'll find out soon enough. Now, sign the papers."

Kent signed the papers. He had no choice, a poisoned man sitting on a time bomb, and he wasn't going to come up with a *homopragmatic truth* hanging around a nut house. Six weeks was bad enough. Six months could be fatal.

Kent finished his Cream of Wheat and strolled out into the Day Room. Quiet as a funeral parlor in there. Morning sunlight slashed through thick glass windows, dust motes dancing in the shafts. A dozen white-gowned crazies in contorted postures dozed in front of the television, where on channel three, some guy in an expensive suit bantered with his girl sidekick, something about parking tickets and women drivers. Behind the row of slumbering patients, six chipped and battered game tables strewn with cards and magazines stood abandoned, chairs askew. A disorderly scattering of dominoes and checkers dotted a concrete floor painted gray. Near the door, a drinking fountain sent up a continuous gurgling arc of water. In the medication room, behind a wire screen, Attila the Hun rattled pills and puffed on a cigarette, while listening to classical music on the radio. Kent walked over, sat down in front of the TV, and yawned.

Chapter 26
CRAWL

CRAWL agent Rummels got a major break in the Gamuka case when the CIA shared with CRAWL information gleaned by its Satellite Surveillance System, SSS. These 34 orbiting telescopes ostensibly scanned the heavens in search of white dwarfs and black holes, but when aimed at earth they could count the exact number of eggs in a robin's nest in a New Jersey park. During routine surveillance of the nation's highways, SSS picked up images of a ragged hitchhiker traveling with large duffel on the interstate. Rummels figured this to be Justin Freely and suspected Gamuka was inside the duffel. He traced the hitchhiker to a vehicular accident outside of Bolton and then to Bolton Mental Hospital.

A data search at the CRAWL computer center revealed Bolton Mental to be a financially unstable institution but a secure lockup for crazies. Rummels left immediately for Bolton to carry out the annihilations of Justin Freely and Kumarmar Gamuka. He planned to use a lethal overdose of tranquilizers. Kumarmar Gumka was number one on CRAWL's most wanted list. No one welshes on a deal with CRAWL and survives.

Following his wake-up call at the Bolton Holiday Inn, Rummels rolled out of bed, watched the news on a morning show, and showered. Toweled but sweaty, he leaned against the bathroom door and fought with his panty support hose. The phone rang. Panty hose stretched between his thighs, he hobbled over to the phone like a Brahma bull waddling out of a mud hole, dewlap flapping.

"Rummels here."

Over the phone came the voice of Rummels' CRAWL supervisor in Washington. "You're to abandon your present assignment and proceed immediately to the Far East."

"What's the new assignment?"

"M.K."

M.K. stood for Moko Kaku. Rummels' supervisor went on to explain that M.K., the ex-chieftain-dictator who had given up his South Pacific archipelago for one hundred and twenty-five million dollars and a commodious Swiss Alps chalet, had reneged on the deal.

Moko Kaku's twenty-three wives divorced the Polynesian dictator only three weeks after they all landed in Switzerland. Attorney's fees and alimony payments quickly ate up Moko's money. In addition, his wives filed charges of bigotry and spousal abuse against the former chieftain. Worse, the Swiss government ordered Moko to cease spear-hunting dairy cows grazing on mountainsides and demanded he return all the cowbell trophies he had collected. Losing his wives was one thing, but giving up his hunting trophies was the real kicker, a colossal put-down for the greatest hunter and pig sticker in entire history of the Kaku Islands. In the dead of night, Moko took a flight out of the Geneva bound for the Far East.

Moko was beloved by his subjects, who believed him to be a direct descendant of the Kaku mountain god. CRAWL feared Moko's return to the Kaku Islands would lead to open rebellion and endanger plans for offshore drilling by American and British petroleum companies.

Ordered to intercept and annihilate Moko Kaku before he reached his homeland, Rummels didn't like the idea of giving up two birds in the cage of a mental hospital for one in flight. But orders were orders. Justin Freely and Kumarmar Gamuka would have to wait.

McDonald, a young CRAWL agent without an annihilation license, was put in charge of the Gamuka case until Rummels returned. A skinny, freckled-faced kid with red hair, pimples, pocks, and cowlicks, McDonald could only observe and report. The neophyte agent decided the best way to keep an eye on Justin Freely and Kumarmar Gamuka was to get himself admitted to Bolton Mental. That meant faking a mental illness. He chose depression because he once lived with an aunt who was depressed. Depression was easy, just sit in a dark corner with your head down and don't say much.

Chapter 27
TRACY

Bolton Mental's administration building, a converted three-story stately antebellum, lay in near ruin, the paint on the Corinthian columns curled up like tiny volutes, the grounds gone to seed, the shrubbery overgrown, and the sweeping asphalt drive riddled with potholes. Colorful star-shaped mosaics in the rotunda greeted visitors, the Gestalt effect of the designs best appreciated by looking straight down at the astral shapes from the third floor balcony. A receptionist sat at a desk just to the right of the rotunda, and down halls in both directions were offices.

Tracy Fedler, the hospital's business manager and the subject of Frank Chisholm's shower fantasies, a forty-year-old divorcee, strolled across the rotunda toting a laptop and a cup of coffee, her high heels clicking like rhythm sticks. Tracy's diligent bookkeeping and her hard nose approach to the business side of running a mental hospital had kept the place going during difficult times. Her clothes were modish, skirt a little short, sweater a little tight. Unlike the deteriorating administration building, she was well-preserved, shapely legs, a bedroom smile, and a slenderly curvaceous body.

Tracy walked into a conference room and sat down at a gleaming mahogany table across from Frank Chisholm who had his own steaming cup of coffee and, due Tracy's sudden presence, a seething libido. He couldn't take his eyes off her. Also present were the head nurse, a secretary, and Morgan, a plump, smooth-faced psychologist in a tweed suit and a red and yellow polka dot bow tie. Morgan had glazed eyes, no doubt the result of countless hours at the analytic couch. Frank thought of Morgan as a 21st Century Freud with a bag of 19th Century theories and the diagnostic acumen of a freshman medical student.

The first order of business was new admissions, and the secretary called out the name, "Justin Freely."

The head nurse's face flushed angrily. "That's the old duffer with a smelly duffel. He eloped last night."

"Eloped," Morgan shouted, his eyes wide and stark. "No one escapes from here. We're the most secure mental hospital in the state."

"Well, he's disappeared. We can't find him."

Morgan muttered, "Gee, I hope it doesn't get out that we lost a patient."

Tracy Fedler shrugged. "It's just as well he's gone, he had no insurance."

Frank stared at Tracy's dainty wrists, their only blemish a liver spot or two, her hands were delicate instruments of touch, her red acrylic nails works of art, her perfume an aphrodisiac. His eyes followed her slender arms up to those fragile shoulders and then fixed longingly on the jutting mounds of her blouse. Soon, he was fantasizing, his lips moving down the nape of her neck, his hands gently unsnapping the blouse.

The secretary's voice broke rudely into Frank's fantasy. "Mr. McDonald's the next patient. He's depressed."

Morgan straightened his tie and glanced at Frank. "When I saw him he wasn't communicative. I recommend electric shock therapy."

"Good," Tracy agreed, "he's got government insurance with full coverage."

Morgan beamed. "In that case, we'll work in some group therapy too. May help his catalepsy."

Morgan used words like 'catalepsy' as if he knew what they meant. Frank shrugged, what the hell, let the underlings play doctor. They loved it. Frank hated it. Frank tried to think about golf, but with Tracy sitting there across the table, golf was out the question. He finally decided what internal organs he'd give up in exchange for a week in the sack with Tracy, one kidney and the right lobe of his liver.

The secretary announced the next patient. "Kent Mullins."

Tracy smiled. "We're on a roll, this one's got insurance too."

Frank cleared his throat. "That's the Folie a Deux from the car accident who thinks he's been poisoned." *Sic 'em, Morgan. Put the flake on the couch and do a Lewis and Clark into those unexplored tangles of gray matter.* "This patient will need extensive testing and psychotherapy."

"Yes sir," Morgan agreed. "I'm right on it."

Frank asked, "What happened to that girl with him? Cleo something or another."

"We discharged her," Morgan reported. "I didn't think having them both here at the same time was a good idea. He's the independent element in that relationship, so we kept him." Morgan launched into a short lecture, material he probably looked up just prior to the meeting. "Folie a Deuxs have a certain synergism, they share a psychic energy that feeds off their mutual delusions. Usually one is more dependent and the other more independent. In this case...."

In the virtual reality of his imagination, Frank removed Tracy's blouse and bra, and his fingers gingerly explored her firm, up-tilted breasts. So very busy was he that he tuned out the others. Soon Tracy was completely undressed. How natural she looked sitting there naked.

"Dr. Chisholm." The secretary's voice disrupted Frank's reverie. "We have just one more patient."

Restored to consciousness, Frank straightened and glanced around the table. Tracy's lips curled into a smile and she winked at him. At least he thought she did. Something made his heart pound. *My god, she may have winked at me!* His hands trembled and hot coffee stung his fingers.

The nurse emitted a troubled sigh. "Believe it or not we have another Jesus. Admitted last evening."

"Christ, not another one," Morgan cried. "That makes three this year."

"The police picked him up at a slaughter house," the nurse said. "Get this, he was giving last rites to cattle. Seems he's come back to earth this time to save the animals."

A ripple of laughter spread over the room.

At one time, Frank enjoyed stripping away the holier-than-thou facades of Jesus impersonators, exposing the guilt-ridden inadequate slobs for what they really were--guilt-ridden inadequate slobs. Nowadays, he left even the debunking of impostors up to the underlings. He had seen and heard it all before, had his fill. Suddenly, he and Tracy were nude in the shower, locked in each other's arms, warm water cascading over their bodies, her hair clinging to her skin. He panted audibly.

Another intrusion. "Dr. Chisholm, would you like some fresh coffee?"

"Thank you, yes. A little soap and sugar, please."

Chapter 28
VERONICA

Larry Lake's escape from prison didn't make headlines, just a blurb on the back page of a newspaper Larry picked up at a gas station. The front-page screamers were stock market oscillations and nerds gunning down jocks in the classroom. Larry could hardly wait to see the look on Cleo's face when he walked back into her life, but the reunion would have to wait. His first priority was to keep out of sight, away from the police and the highway patrol. That's why he took to back roads, where Vu's Honda kicked up gravel and bounced in and out of ruts and chuckholes at high speed. Strapped into the passenger seat, jostled, disheveled, his car taking a beating, Vu scolded Larry and shook his fist at him.

"Shut up," Larry snapped. "Don't you know I can't understand a fuckin' word you're saying? I was faking all those conversations we had back at prison. Oh, what the hell, you can't understand me, either."

When the left front wheel hit a chuckhole the size of a meteorite crater, Vu's head slammed against the car roof and the owner's manual and a cell phone flew out the glove compartment. Larry fought to keep the car on the road.

"Why didn't you tell me you had a fuckin' phone?" Larry grabbed the cell and handed it to Vu. "Call up your niece."

Vu rubbed his head.

"Your fucking niece. Call her up!" Vu punched 911 and Larry jerked the phone away. "Your niece, asshole." Larry did an imitation of the niece's sexy voice. *Hello there. This is Dr. Vu's niece. How is everything?* He shoved the phone back to Vu.

The imitation was apparently accurate, and Vu punched in his niece's number. Larry grabbed the phone and waited for that sexy voice to massage his eardrum.

"Hello there."

"This is Larry Lakes."

"How are you, Larry?"

"Fine."

"Would you please put my uncle on the line? Thank you."

"No. I want to talk to you."

"Go ahead. I am listening."

"I've escaped from prison and your uncle's my hostage. You do exactly what I say, he won't get hurt." The road vibrations gave Larry's voice a staccato quality.

"Okay. What may I do for you?"

Larry was speechless. What can she do? He couldn't think of anything.

"Larry, are you still there?"

"Yeah, I'm here."

"I see on my caller ID that you are calling on my uncle's cell phone."

"So what?"

"That means you are probably in his new Honda, correct?"

Vu let go with a barrage of undecipherable utterances, expletives most likely, and grabbed for the phone.

Larry shifted the phone to his left hand and mouthed, "Shut up!"

Vu's niece replied, "I thought you wanted to talk with me?"

"I meant for our uncle to shut up. Say, what is your name anyway?"

"Veronica."

"Listen, Veronica, I've got to find someone and I don't know how to go about it. My ex, Cleo, and a guy named Kent Mullins."

"Why not call them up?"

"I don't want them to know I'm trying to find them."

"I see. You want to surprise them. Being an escaped convict, you are probably plotting some kind of revenge or seeking to renew a love relationship. Correct?"

"How did you know that?"

"It's only logical. I am very good at logic. I am a systems analyst."

"A what?"

"Considering your present situation, I do not think we should get into that at this time. Let us just say I work with computers. I take it you have not left the state yet and you are probably driving on back roads to stay out of sight."

"What are you, some kind of fuckin' fortune teller?"

"Larry, I do not appreciate vulgarities."

"Sorry. I didn't talk like that until I went to prison."

"Listen, I think it would be safer if you took a busy thoroughfare and got out of the state as quickly as possible. A red Honda on country roads looks a little queer."

"Queer!"

"Excuse the ambiguity, I should have realized you may have been sensitized to that word, being a prisoner and all. I meant queer in the sense of being conspicuously unusual. If you were driving a pickup or a tractor, that would look more normal, considering your present surroundings. Anyway, you should change vehicles. The police will be looking for a red Honda."

"Hey, you're right. Absolutely right."

"I suggest you go to a metropolitan area, scan large parking lots for cars with keys in the ignition." Vu reached for the phone again and Larry slapped his hand. "Try places like supermarkets, ball parks. The probability is one in fifty. That means statistically two out of every one hundred parked cars will have the keys in the ignition. And Larry, choose an older car, they are less likely to have anti-theft devices."

Vu shouted angrily at Larry, vile profanities no doubt.

"Veronica, would you explain to your uncle that I'm a desperate man and that he should behave. I hate to say this, but he's really bull-headed."

"I know. Everyone on my mother's side is that way. Would you hand the phone to my uncle, please? Thank you."

Vu took the phone, hunched down in the seat, and listened quietly while peering at Larry out of the corner of his eye. He nodded several times and with some reluctance, handed the phone back to Larry. Quiet for the first time since becoming a hostage, Vu sat with his hands folded and stared straight ahead.

Larry asked, "What did you say to him?"

"I told him that if he did not behave you were going to kill him."

"Ah c'mon, I wouldn't actually do that, really. I kinda like the old fart."

"Call me back after you switch cars and we will talk about how to find those people you are looking for. Bye."

"Bye, Veronica."

Chapter 29
ON THE RUN

At a flea market on the grounds of a defunct drive-in theater, Larry spotted among the parked cars a black Cadillac with keys in the ignition. While the flea market crowd bought and sold each other's junk, Larry parked Vu's Honda in some weeds behind the wind-tattered big screen. Larry got out of the Honda and when Vu climbed out, Larry shoved him back into car, but kept the keys. "You stay here. I don't need a hostage any longer."

Larry got into the caddy and drove off. Easy as fishin' with a net. He hadn't driven five miles when the cell phone buzzed.

"Hello."

"This is Veronica. Have you and my uncle switched cars yet?"

"Yeah."

"What kind did you get?"

"A black caddy."

"Did it bother my uncle to give up his Honda, I know he was very attached to it."

"He didn't say a thing."

"Are you two wearing the same clothes you wore when you escaped prison?"

Larry glanced down at his red prison trousers. "Not a good idea, huh?"

"Not at all."

"I wonder why I didn't think of that."

"You've been under a lot of stress. Allow me to do the thinking for you for while. I'll call you back shortly with instructions for getting new clothes."

"It's so nice of you to help. How can I ever repay you."

"Just be nice to my uncle. I think he really likes you."

Larry whipped a U-turn and drove back to the flea market where Vu sat stoically in his Honda staring out the windshield. Larry rolled down the window of the caddy and motioned to Vu. "C'mon, get in. I guess we're stuck with each other."

Vu didn't protest leaving his new Honda behind, but Larry could tell from his sagging face and the frown lines on his forehead that it bothered him.

Veronica called back and directed Larry to a Goodwill store in the next state where Larry and Vu bought new old clothes with the last of Vu's money. Vu got overalls, a flannel shirt, and a ball cap. Larry walked out of the store in faded jeans and a western shirt with pearl snaps for buttons. At Veronica's suggestion, Larry threw his prison garb off a nearby bridge into a river, hoping they'd wash up miles downstream throwing the authorities off his trail.

Also on Veronica's advice, Larry obtained a ten thousand dollar cash loan using Vu's American Express card. Veronica had to talk persuasively to get her uncle to go along with the transaction. Next Larry bought a used Buick and ditched the Cadillac. He dyed his hair black and shaved, leaving a mustache that made him look like the short guitar player the on the old Dunn and Brooks duo. In the meantime, Vu's contact lens dried out and he couldn't see past his elbows.

Taking refuge at a Motel 6, Larry stretched out on the bed while Vu scrunched up to the TV to watch what he could of the news. Nearly blind without his contacts and not understanding what anyone was saying, Vu wasn't enjoying being a hostage. Life had become a series of food and restroom stops. Often Vu was forced to eat when he really wanted to go to the bathroom, and vice versa.

The cell buzzed and Larry picked it up from the bedside table. Veronica's sweet voice purred in his ear, "Hello there. How are you and my uncle doing?"

"Did I tell you his contacts dried out?"

"Perhaps it is better that way."

"I like it better. He's easier to get along with."

"I've gathered some of information on those people you told me about. It seems Kent Mullins and Cleo, your ex, have not been seen in Harkerville for sometime. There are rumors they may have run off together."

"How do you know that? You live, what, down in Texas somewhere?"

"In this age of social media, we all live in one big community. My computer checked out everyone in Harkerville who is on Facebook. Then it made random calls to Harkerville residents. The program I use carries on 100 simultaneous conversations using pre-recorded questions. The program keys in on words such as Cleo, Kent, geographical areas, and certain action verbs, and then cross-references all significant responses with a target word list. As a result, the information grows exponentially.'

"Wow, you really did that? I used to be good with computers, back in high school."

"Yes, and then you flunked out."

"How did you know that?"

"I have all accessible knowledge about Harkerville on two flash drives. Ask me anything about Harkerville."

"I can't think of anything."

"Do you know Sally Coles?"

"Sure," Larry said, "what about her?"

"She has laryngitis and Dr. Jenkins advised her not to sing at Dixie Pratt's wedding."

"I used to sing at weddings. I like singing."

"I know that."

"Who's Dixie marrying?"

"Sandy Brock."

"That old buzzard. She's probably marrying him for his money."

"That is exactly what I thought. Anyone else you would like to know about?"

"Yeah. Ed Jones, the banker."

"Let's see. Oh yes, Mr. Jones sold his shares in Green Pasture Fertilizer and Pesticide and moved to Switzerland with his family."

Larry's voice dropped an octave. "The bastard. The sonnabitchin-motherfuckin' bastard."

"I told you, Larry, I do not appreciate vulgarities."

"Sorry. Jones is one of those who set me up. I took the rap, and he's living like a king in Sweden."

"Switzerland, in the mountains near St. Moritz. You may be interested to know that Terry Crow retired from the police department after forty-two years of service. Anyone else you care to know about?"

"Just Cleo and her lover boy, Kent Mullins."

"I ran a computer check of all major credit card companies and it appears Kent is using his *Vita Platinum Card* exclusively."

"You're good, you know that."

"I told you I am a systems analyst. In today's world, that makes me the equivalent of a J. Edgar Hoover without the cross-dressing. That's a little joke, Larry. Never mind. I did follow Kent's credit trail through motels, restaurants and strip malls. The trail ended at a service station outside of Bolton."

"I know where Bolton is."

Vu, whose face had been plastered to the TV, leaped up, pointing at the television, yammering away in his native tongue. There on the screen was his picture along side Larry's mug shot. Vu's picture must have been an old one, possibly taken when he was in medical school, since he looked much younger. Vu danced around the room shouting.

Larry asked, "What's he so excited about?" He held up the phone so Veronica listen to the shouting.

Veronica said, "He thinks he is on television because he discovered *entertaino* therapy for the criminally insane. He thinks he is famous."

"He's got it all wrong. That's not what they are saying. They think he helped me escape. He's not a hostage anymore, he's a fugitive just like me."

"Please break it to him easy. This is going to be very upsetting."

Larry paused. "You tell him."

He handed the phone to the trumpeting Vu and watched the glitter drain from his cheery eyes. Vu had gone from prison doctor to hostage to accomplice. His head sunk to his chest and he dropped the cell onto the bed. Not only had he had lost his new Honda and his contact lens, he was now a common criminal. The two men exchanged glances, reading the other's minds. *We may not speak the same language, but we're in the same boat.*

Larry rolled across the bed and picked up the phone. "Listen, I'm heading to Bolton in the morning."

Veronica said coldly, "I would not go there. The police may be watching Cleo, thinking you will contact her. They often do that with first-degree relatives and ex-spouses of escaped prisoners."

"I bet your right."

"Go somewhere like the East Coast. Get out of the heat for a while and give yourself time to think things through."

"Veronica, I can't tell you how much I appreciate what you're doing, especially with me taking your uncle hostage."

"Glad I can help. Tomorrow I am flying to Bangkok on business. I will be there for sometime. I will call you when I get back."

Larry glanced around the small room. Vu was gone.

Larry threw the door open and looked up and down the hallway. No sign of Vu. He raced downstairs to the front desk and asked Pakistani night-clerk, "You see a dude in overhauls and a ball cap come by?" The night clerk shook his head.

Larry rushed out into the parking lot, shouting, "Vu. Vu." No response. Shrouded in a suffocating loneliness, Larry slumped back to the motel room and fell across the bed, a glaze of despair on his face.

He heard the toilet flush. The bathroom door flung open, and Vu stepped out snapping the shoulder strap of his overalls. Larry could have kissed him.

Chapter 30
EXAMINATION

A twelve-foot chain-link fence topped with barbed wire surrounded the campus of the Bolton Mental as if it were an extermination camp. A massive iron gate cast an abject shadow over the grounds, a vestige of the institution's former greatness, when crazy was a crime and not a disease. Building B housed the newly admitted patients, those who had yet to be tested, analyzed, and categorized.

Like Dante roaming Purgatory, Kent wandered about on the ward asking questions. "Hi, I'm Kent Mullins. What's your name? How long have you been here? Do you like it here?"

Nearly everyone opened up to Kent, his friendly smile and youthful innocence a wooer to conversation. Many of the patients were *transmitters*, eager to share every insignificant detail of their lives. Others were manic, to whom nothing seemed impossible and for whom an invitation to the Emperor's Ball was always imminent. With gusto they unloaded their great schemes and revolutionary theories on Kent. The paranoids whispered dark secrets to him.

After an exhaustive day of listening, Kent plopped down in a chair to watch the Evening News. All around him patients snoozed as if the television emitted hypnotic gamma rays. On Kent's right dozed Alonzo, who wore a scarlet head rag, an old hippy with a roadmap face and a brain singed by dope back when the Beatles were belting out "Hey Jude." On Kent's left, sat Jesus-3, a wide-awake, ordinary-looking man with hazel eyes.

Jesus-3 turned to Kent and asked, "Did you know more than three hundred and thirty million animals are slaughtered everyday by human beings? That's a gigantic holocaust. And not a word about it on CNN."

"Really?"

"Yes, really. News reporting is very biased. They only tell about people, mostly. And it's usually bad stuff."

Kent tried to change the subject. "Look, the stock market's down."

"Frogs are disappearing all over the world."

"I didn't know that."

"How could you," Jesus-3 blurted, "The news is biased."

Alonzo woke up, yawned, leaned forward and looked at Jesus-3. "Got a question for you, man. Like, why are we here? Not here, here. I mean here, anywhere?"

Jesus-3 grumbled, "You won't find out by watching the fucking news, that's for sure."

Kent grinned, got up and politely walked away. He was learning to step around the loose marbles, to avoid fruitcake conversations.

McDonald sat in a corner, glum as judge, staring at his shoes. The redheaded, undercover CRAWL agent, Rummels' stand-in disguised as a depressive, got two electric shock treatments every day. Kent noticed how McDonald would stiffen up when they came to strap him onto a gurney. When you're depressed, you get shock treatments whether you like them or not. Doctor's orders. After only a dozen or so treatments, McDonald began to tremble all over, even when he dozed off in his chair. Salvia constantly drooled from his downturned mouth, soaking the front of his gown. Nice looking kid going to pot; depression must be a terrible thing.

Kent walked over and smiled at McDonald. "Looks like rain."

"Uh-huh."

"Stock market's down."

"Uh-uh."

"You got any pets at home?"

McDonald shook his head.

Kent grinned and said, "I had a Beagle once."

"Humph."

"How many more shock treatments do you get?"

McDonald sprayed salvia. "I don't want talk about it."

"Okay."

"Phew."

Despite having a private room and a soft mattress, Kent had trouble sleeping at Bolton Mental. If nightmares about Tommy Tennyson and his poison didn't keep Kent awake, worrying about Cleo did. He'd not heard from her since coming to this nuthouse almost two weeks ago. There was a rumor that Justin had escaped, taking his duffel with him. How'd he do it? Bolton Mental was a Bastille with padlocked doors, fences, barbwire, Nazi nurses, orderlies, interns, and armies of social workers swarming over the ward. Kent reassured himself. *Just sit tight, put in your time and eventually you'll get to New York and Selena Rosalina.*

One day, Attila informed Kent that Cleo had been discharged from the hospital.

"Where'd she go?"

"Wherever. It's a free country."

Kent figured Cleo went back to Harkerville. After all, she had a job there. Unbeknownst to Kent, Cleo took a room at a cheap motel in Bolton called The Snore. Everyday she came to the hospital to plead for Kent's release, explaining to the hospital's receptionist that Kent desperately needed to find the antidote that would save his life. After several days of listening patiently to Cleo's pleas, the normally polite and low-keyed receptionist looked through the glass window with a hole in it and said, "I believe your involvement with Mr. Mullins is making both your mental conditions worse."

"Mental, your ass," Cleo snapped. She stopped coming to the hospital; instead, she left phone messages for Kent. Messages he never received.

Early one morning, interns in white jackets, stethoscopes bouncing on their chests, swooped down on Kent like a Mongol raiding party. They beat on his tendons with rubber hammers, stuck little plastic cones into his ears, flashed bright lights in his eyes, jammed needles into his veins, shoved a finger up his ass, and stuck gummy electrodes onto his scalp. They studied the hollow of his breastbone with keen interest, calling it by some Latin name.

Then came the psychologists with their word associations, inkblots, problem solving puzzles, and dozens of multiple-choice tests that Kent couldn't read. Finally, a social worker, a plump blonde with brown roots and a gallon jug of diet cola, interrogated Kent. She refused to believe he had been poisoned, or that he was millionaire, or even that he'd graduated high school. She didn't believe anything he said. She just sat there asking questions, looking at him skeptically, sucking on a straw, and shaking her head.

The upshot of all this testing was a fifteen-page report that concluded Kent was an intellectually challenged, anxiety-ridden, neurotic who harbored marked delusional ideation and needed intensive psychotherapy.

Then came Morgan.

Chapter 31
THERAPY

Bookcases lined three walls of Morgan's darkened, oak paneled office. A pastel Aubusson rug covered a good portion of the polished hardwood floor. Two brass elephants the size of Saint Bernards flanked an uncluttered desk.

"Why don't you lie down on the couch over there," Morgan suggested to Kent as he closed the door.

Kent stared at Morgan with a look of displeasure. "I'm not tired."

"You don't have to be tired to lie down."

"I'd rather sit up."

"You can relax much better lying down."

"I'm relaxed."

Morgan asked, calmly but firmly, "Why are you resisting my efforts to help you?"

"Because no one around here believes I've been poisoned."

Morgan nibbled on the stem of an unlit meerschaum pipe. "I believe that you believe you've been poisoned."

"I really need to get out of here as soon as possible."

"Perhaps, if you cooperated, it would speed things up."

Kent was unsure if he should press the issue of being poisoned. The more he talked about it, the crazier people thought he was, and he didn't want to prolong his stay at Bolton Mental. But he figured Morgan, being a psychologist, would keep an open mind. And Kent desperately needed to talk with somebody.

Kent asked, "Why don't you just call Tommy Tennyson and ask him about the poison?"

Morgan took the pipe from his lips. "Be reasonable. If this Tommy Tennyson fellow really poisoned you, he would surely deny it. If he didn't poison you, he would naturally deny it. So, it really makes no sense asking him."

"I suppose you're right."

"Of course, I'm right. Why don't you lie down on the couch?"

Kent sank into the soft leather, folding his hands on his chest.

"This may be painful at times," Morgan explained, pulling up a cushioned chair. "Especially when we bring into the open things you've hidden away in your subconscious. It's like opening an old forgotten chest in the attic and rediscovering things long forgotten. The trauma of the past can be roadblocks to our future. However, once the traumas are out of the box, the roadblocks disappear. Do you understand what I'm saying?"

"I think so."

"Good. Now close your eyes and relax. The results of our questionnaires indicate you were much closer to your mother than to your father. Is that right?"

"I suppose so."

"Did your father ever play ball with you?"

"I don't remember. I wasn't very good at sports."

"Did your father ever take you to the movies?"

"Once. E.T."

"Only once?"

"My mom usually took me places."

"Not your father?"

"He was busy."

"I see," Morgan said softly, leaning forward in his chair. "Now I want you to think back to when you were very small. Relax, take your time."

"How small?"

"Back before you started school. Around age three or four."

"I can't remember anything much before the age of five."

Morgan shifted in his cushioned chair. "Why can't you remember?"

"I don't know."

Morgan's voice deepened. "That's because something bad happened back then. Something so bad you've blocked out all memories from that period of your life. Now think back to the time your father first touched you on your private parts."

Kent shot up from the couch. "My dad never did anything like that."

Morgan's hand pressed against Kent's shoulder and gently eased him back onto the couch. "But you don't know that for sure, do you? You just said you couldn't remember anything before age five."

As Kent sank into the soft leather couch, Morgan got up and quietly lowered the window shade. The office turned dark as an attic. "Now close your eyes and try to remember your early childhood. It's very important."

Kent's eyelids felt like lead curtains.

Did my dad really do that? He wouldn't have, would he? At least I don't remember it. Maybe that's because it's too painful. My God, I was a sexually abused child. Is that why I wasn't able to read like other kids?

After only four sessions on the couch, Kent learned that his father, a man he had respected and loved, was actually a lowly pedophile. His father had been the apex of a love triangle of the most sordid kind. Kent's father had lusted after Kent. And Kent's mother lusted after his father. Kent, surprisingly, lusted after his mother. Morgan cushioned the blow of the last revelation by explaining to Kent that it was very common for little boys to lust after their mothers.

"Gee, I don't remember any of it, " Kent confessed.

"That's why you're undergoing therapy. I warned you that unearthing repressed material can be painful, but it has to come out."

Over the next several sessions, Morgan reconstructed Kent's childhood as an archeologist fits together the shards of ancient amphora, filling in the missing pieces with new clay. At first, Kent yo-yoed between two realities; the one he thought he had lived through and Morgan's terrifying re-creation of his past. He moved in and out of the two worlds like a man with a double life. Kent, who was always asking questions, searching for truth, hadn't anticipated that truth could be so unsavory. In time, he came to see things clearly, illuminated by the beam of Morgan's searchlight shining into dark corners of his subconscious. Kent began to hate his father.

"Hate can be a healthy emotion," Morgan explained.

After a few more turns on the couch, Kent learned Tommy Tennyson hadn't really poisoned him. Morgan exposed that delusion to be nothing more than a defense mechanism Kent employed to punish himself for the awful things his father did. Morgan explained that victims of sexual abuse often punish themselves. Kent soon realized his relationship with Cleo was an unhealthy one. She had nurtured his delusions and distorted his perception of reality. When Morgan handed Kent the stack of never-received phone messages from Cleo, Kent refused to look at them. A sure sign he was getting better. With Morgan's help, Kent figured out that Gamuka, a tiny man with the heart rate of a tortoise, hibernating inside a duffel bag, was a hallucination. Kent finally realized just how sick he had been.

Freed from his delusions, Kent was getting answers to questions he would have never thought to ask. No longer a man dying from an untraceable poison, no longer besieged by false beliefs and unfounded fears, no longer trapped in an unhealthy relationship with a woman who distorted reality for him, Kent was getting well.

Morgan smiled at his prize patient. "Congratulations, you've made great strides. I believe you're ready for group therapy."

Chapter 32
SINGAPORE

Rummels traveled half way around the world before catching up with Moko Kaku, the ex-dictator of the Kaku archipelago, at the Singapore airport. A newspaper under his arm, Rummels strolled up to Gate 6 in a Hawaiian print shirt, khaki Bermuda's, and sandals. He emptied his pockets and placed his change, keys, and a cigarette lighter disguised as a ballpoint pen into a small plastic bowl and walked through a doorframe metal detector. Once inside the waiting area, he re-pocketed his items and settled into a seat near a huge plate glass window overlooking the runway. In front of him sat Moko, waiting for his flight and watching with fascination the giant silver birds taking off and landing. Rummels studied Moko's reflection in the window. A small man with a thick torso, a sun-weathered face, strong jaw, and the eyes of a falcon, Moko looked something like a Comanche war chief in a Western movie. The unbuttoned gaps in his tan trench coat revealed a sealskin vest and loincloth, Moko's usual attire.

Rummels glanced up at the NO SMOKING sign in the waiting area and fingered the pack of Camels in his shirt pocket. Smoking in the Singapore airport could land a man in jail. Fortunately, passenger traffic was light this time of the morning. Confident that no one would suspect a stodgy vacationer with ropy leg veins of being an assassin, Rummels prepared to strike. He unfolded the newspaper, held it up, and in its shadow removed a pink capsule from his pocket and swallowed it. The capsule contained a protective antidote for the lethal smoke toxin he would use to annihilate Moko.

Once the antidote took effect, he'd light up a poisoned cigarette with his ballpoint, tap Moko on the shoulder and blow killer-smoke into the dictator's face. He'd stomp out his cigarette before any one noticed. Moko would be dead within seconds. Slowly, Rummels lowered his newspaper and stared at the back of Moko's head. He wondered if the little dictator was thinking about his beautiful homeland.

Rummels had visited the Kaku islands during the initial negotiations between Moko and CRAWL. He recalled the crystal clearness of the water and the extraordinary whiteness of the beaches. The main island was a natural harbor with lagoons and waterfalls, and from the beach one could see the distant cloud-ringed, green peaks of the Kaku Mountains. The melodious song of the red-collared lorikeet in chorus with the distant roar of the sea still rang unforgettable in Rummels' memory. He longed for the bittersweet taste of Kona coffee. His mouth watered as he called to mind the unbelievable abundance of food on the islands: octopus, snapper, turtle cooked in coconut oil, shark fin soup. Not to mention the kiwi, breadfruit, mangos and the exquisite taste of the rare Kaku nut.

Last evening, Rummels had enjoyed a Cantonese dinner here in Singapore, although he had overindulged. The sauce had left him with a touch of dyspepsia, and he had not had his usual morning movement--cause for concern when plagued by a spastic colon.

Rummels face flushed with heat and his fingers tingled, a sure sign the smoke antidote was circulating through his body. He glanced around. All clear, he took the pack of Camels from his shirt pocket and carefully tapped out the cigarette with a small red dot at one end. He placed the cigarette between his lips. He had only to light the cigarette, tap Moko on the shoulder, and blow.

As Rummels groped among the loose change and keys in his pocket for his ballpoint lighter an intense pain seized him. A horrible wrenching of the gut, wild steeds were tethered to his colon and running in opposite directions. He doubled over. Sweat poured from his face. Then came the urgency of an impending evacuation. With the deadly unlit Camel dangling from his lips, the newspaper in one hand, his ballpoint lighter in the other, he raced out of the waiting area and down the corridor to the Men's Room. He scolded himself for having put hot pepper and salsa on his scrambled eggs this morning.

The Men's Room was empty except for a Chinese janitor cleaning the lavatory. Rummels flew into the nearest stall, dropped his Bermuda's and plunged onto the toilet seat. Endorphins bathed his brain as his tortured intestines fluttered in the ecstasy of relief. A smile creased his face. Then came a second volley of cramps. Oh, the pain. Stoically, he sat, knowing intense rapture would follow. He opened his newspaper, every article intriguing. There's nothing like a newspaper at a time like this.

Slowly, the exhilaration of relief subsided and the newspaper became less interesting. In an attempt to prolong his pleasure, he absently lit the cigarette between his lips and inhaled deeply. Ringlets of smoke floated out of the stall. He lingered, squeezing out every increment of pleasure. The endorphins ebbed, and when Rummels stepped out of the stall, reality smacked him in the face. Beside the lavatory, dead on the floor lay the janitor, a victim of the lethal smoke. Rummels quickly tossed the butt of the red-dotted cigarette into the stool and flushed the evidence. One had to be careful here in Singapore where death sentences and canings were meted out like traffic tickets.

He carefully stepped over the body and raced out the restroom back to Gate 6. Moko was gone. Out on the runway, Silk Air's Flight 606 bound for New Zealand taxied for takeoff. Rummels stood at the plate glass window and helplessly watched the 727 lift skyward and disappear into a layer of cumulus clouds. There were no CRAWL agents in New Zealand to intercept Moko. The little dictator would waste no time in taking an aquaplane from New Zealand to one of the lesser islands, then boat to the main island of Kaku under the cover of night, Moko sailing over the reef like Washington crossing the Delaware, a hero to his people.

The next day while Rummels dined in Kuala Lumpur on shrimp and vermicelli, Moko and his faithful followers seized the Kaku archipelago's administrative headquarters in a bloodless coup. They took twenty-five American administrators hostage, along with five Marine guards.

Moko was back in charge.

Chapter 33
BLACKJACK

Larry grew weary of driving up and down the East coast, hiding out in cheap motels, eating drive-through cheeseburgers and baby-sitting Vu. He longed to talk with someone. Veronica was in Bangkok on business and unavailable. Boy, how he missed talking with her. Vu seemed weary of it all too, but he had picked up some eyeglasses at a yard sale in Baltimore and was at least enjoying the scenery.

While driving through Virginia, Larry decided to teach Vu English. He began with the word "*No*," which was self-explanatory when spoken loudly and coupled with a facial expression of displeasure. "*Yes*" came with a grin and a nod. "*Maybe*" with a shrug. Larry pointed at various objects sailing past the car window and made the appropriate sounds to go along with the objects. Vu picked up the sounds quickly, imitating Larry accurately.

After teaching Vu the nouns parading by the car window, Larry taught him things like red and blue, hard and soft, hot and cold, sweet and sour. Then came relationships. Up and down, right and left, over yonder, get-the-fuck-over-to-your-side-of-the-bed. Before long, they had covered a good part of the lexicon. These two men from opposite ends of the earth, so different—Vu, scientific, logical, a physician; right-brain Larry, a song and dance man, a used car dealer, a fugitive—they were now, after all this time and all these miles, connecting the same way an infant connects with adults, through the learning of language.

Subject and verb agreement came naturally to Vu, as did pronoun and antecedent, verb tense, and those troublesome modal auxiliaries. One morning to Larry's surprise, Vu spoke complete English sentences using both concrete and abstract nouns. "This car smell like a pig sty. I don't mean to be impertinent, but shouldn't we run this bucket of bolts through a car wash?"

"I can't believe how quickly you've picked up English. You must be a fucking genius."

Vu smiled. "Thank you. I try many times to learn English using grammar book. But I learn best seeing and hearing. You a good teacher."

Larry corrected, "You *are* a good teacher."

"Right, you *are* a good teacher."

Having someone to talk with made life on the run more bearable, but Larry was still sick of living out of a car and eating cheeseburgers.

Larry looked at Vu. "You know what?"

"What?"

"Let's go to Atlantic City. I hear it's the Big Rock Candy Mountain. A guy can strike it rich there. Miracles happen, you know."

Vu nodded. "Let's go for it."

Larry pulled over to the side of the road, cut the engine, and counted the remaining cash from Vu's American Express loan. A little over two thousand dollars. Larry decided to try the slots. *What the hell?*

༄༅

Atlantic City was a pleasant shock to Vu's nervous system. He had never seen so many dazzling lights, so much merriment, and so much disorder, the fabled gold-paved streets of America. The excitement of being there ran through him like the zesty warmth of strong liquor. He recalled when as a young man he visited Saigon for the first time, and tasted *arrack* the distilled spirits of rice for the first time, and drank French wine for the first time, and had a woman for the first time. Like the *firstly-ness* of Saigon, he fell in love with the excitement of Atlantic City.

Larry went right to the slots. Win a few and lose a lot. By the middle of the night, the money like the color in his face drained away. While Larry fed the machines, Vu, in his Goodwill togs, heart racing, eyes goggling, took it all in, the clinking of coins, the ringing of bells, the keno, the roulette, the crapshooters, the 'let it ride', the poker games, the pretty girls, and the blackjack. Blackjack! Just like in Saigon. Vu walked over to the slots and with raised brow watched Larry lose to their last one hundred dollars.

Larry looked up. "You think you could do better."

Vu smiled. "Yes, I do better."

"Bullshit."

Larry cranked the machine's electronic arm and twenty coins clanged into a metal tray. He scooped them up, counted them, and handed ten coins to Vu. "Better get some grub."

Vu went directly to the five-dollar blackjack table where he watched for a while, then stepped up. The dealer stared with disdain at the scruffy Asian in overalls and ball cap. Vu bought two five-dollar chips and placed one. A mathematical prodigy who studied probability before going to medical school, Vu learned long ago in Saigon that blackjack need not be a game of chance. He'd need a little luck with the first couple of hands if he were to keep playing. He quickly memorized as many cards as possible out of the six decks; that alone made the odds fifty-fifty, taking away the House's slight advantage. He lost the first hand.

His hand trembled as he laid down his last chip. If he lost, there would be no supper tonight and no breakfast tomorrow. His brain worked like programmed software in a high-speed computer, memorizing cards and calculating probabilities using the Mises-Reichenback Frequency theory. To the dealer, he looked like a stiff in a ball cap who just placed his last five-dollar chip on the table. Vu knew the probability of the next card being a five or below was in his favor. "Strike me," he told the dealer. Vu jumped straight up when the dealer turned over a five of spades. Twenty-one. Vu kept playing, knowing that if he played enough games, he would come out ahead. And if he played a lot of games, he would come out a lot ahead.

The night wore on and Vu's winnings mounted, the odds always slightly in his favor thanks to probability computation and brute memorization. Three dealers later, he was still winning. At seven in the morning, Larry slumped through the casino busted. He had wanted to save out a little for gasoline, but the slots had got it all. He saw Vu at the blackjack table and ambled over. He stared in wonderment at Vu's hefty stacks of chips. Vu won the next three hands.

Later at the IHOP while Vu devoured a stack of pancakes, Larry counted his winnings. "Over eighty thousand dollars, here!" He slapped Vu on the back. "You lucky bastard."

Vu wiped maple syrup from his chin. "Not luck. I know blackjack. In Saigon it called *vengt et un.*"

"I can't believe you beat the house. Do you think you could do it again?"

Vu grinned. "Sure. I know blackjack."

On the way out of the restaurant, Larry snapped his fingers and did a little jitterbug with a half-turnout. "I've got me a flapjack eatin' blackjack player, and we're gonna tear this town apart."

Chapter 34
WAKING UP

Thanks to psychotherapy the desperation in Kent's life had vanished, or at least he thought it had. There was no need to make a mad dash to New York in search of a *homopragmatic truth*. And soon he'd be getting out of this nuthouse. No longer a fatally poisoned man, he should be relaxed, but he wasn't. He turned one way than the other on his narrow bed. *Why can't I sleep?*

He closed his eyes tightly and tugged the wool blanket over his head and pretended to be at the North Pole inside an igloo with a snowstorm raging outside. He always slept soundly during storms. This trick of the imagination wasn't working. Wide-awake, he once more went over what he had learned in psychotherapy. He had never been poisoned. He wasn't going to die. His father had been a pervert. Cleo distorted reality for him. Gamuka didn't exist and neither did the CRAWL agent Rummels whose assignment supposedly was to annihilate Gamuka and Justin. All fictions of the mind.

Yes, I'm cured. So why do I feel worse now than before? Why can't I sleep?

In his state of sleeplessness, Kent thought about a *homopragmatic truth*. A truth that brings about its own existence. Knowing a *homopragmatic truth* and the effects of knowing it are one and the same. He was amazed that he, all by himself, had thought up such a thing. *How did I do it?* "A *homopragmatic truth* is a piece of knowledge so enlightening, so brimming with veracity, so eye-opening, so all encompassing that once you posses it, your life is forever changed, and nothing will be the same again." *Where did I come up with those words? And veracity especially.*

He remembered Cleo looking *veracity* up in a dictionary. Veracity and truth meant pretty much the same thing. *How had the word veracity slipped into my vocabulary?* He couldn't have heard it from Tommy Tennyson. According to Morgan, all that stuff about Tommy Tennyson was a bucket of psychic bullshit. Kent's head ached. Thinking can get so complicated. He wished all thoughts would go away, that he would fall asleep.

He rolled up in his blanket like a papoose and pretended he was twelve-years old inside a sleeping bag at Boy Scout camp. Wind howled through the tent as a storm brewed outside. He imagined flashes of lightening. Thunder. It was working. Blessed drowsiness. The Twilight Zone. He dozed off.

Something tugged on Kent's shoulder. His eyes flew open, and he shot upright in bed. A shadowy figure beside the bed whispered, "Shhh, don't yell. It's me. Justin."

Kent's flipped on the bedside lamp. It was Justin. He looked run-down ragged, his hair unkempt, and his beard stragglier and grimier than before. His clothes reeked with the musty odor of a damp basement. "I thought you had eloped."

Justin grinned. "I've been hiding out."

"How did you get onto the ward?"

"Picked the lock. Piece of cake."

"But the night nurse?"

"She's asleep."

Kent wondered if Justin was a delusion. He seemed pretty real standing next to the bed and smelling musty.

"The night we were admitted, they put me in the Contamination Room," Justin explained. "They said I was a coprophiliac."

"A what?"

"They thought I was carrying around shit in my duffel. That's what the nurse told me when she tried to take it away. I had to fight her off."

Justin sat on the edge of the bed and began a tale loonier than any Kent had heard since coming to Bolton. "When the nurse went for help, I frantically searched Contamination Room for somewhere to hide Gamuka."

Kent wanted to shout, there is no Gamuka. He's just a hallucination. Instead, he choked back the words, took a deep breath, and bit his tongue.

Justin went on with his story. "I wasn't the only one in the Contamination Room. There was this Jesus fellow they brought in from a slaughterhouse, covered in cow manure head to toe. Gee, talk about stink. Anyway, the Contamination Room is really old, limestone and rotting timber. It's where they put street people until they're cleaned up and free of germs."

Kent nodded and emitted a series of "uh-huhs."

Justin took a breath and said, "In there is a boarded-up old fireplace. Hasn't been used in years. Anyway, I was running around with my duffel, looking to hide it, when this Jesus fellow tells me the boards covering the fireplace are loose. 'You might try hiding behind them,' he said. So, I slip behind those boards with my duffel."

Kent looked skeptically at Justin. *Folie a Deux all over again. I wish Mr. Morgan could hear this.*

Justin's eyes grew wide. "Standing there in the dark, I realized Gamuka and me were trapped behind those boards, nowhere to go. The nurse would be coming back with help and they'd find us. Then that CRAWL agent Rummels would eventually get wind of it, and Gamuka and I would soon be annihilated."

"So, what did you do?"

"I got all worked up. Mad as hell. It wasn't fair. We're having to die just because Gamuka can kick a football farther than any other human being on the planet."

Kent shrugged. "And…"

"I went nuts. Began kicking the hell out of that old fireplace. Out of my head, crazy. Flailing away with my feet like a lunatic, soot and dust flying, my shoes coming apart. Then, all at once, the back wall of the fireplace opens up like a door on a hinge. A gush of stale air almost knocks me over. I looked inside. Black as midnight in there. I pick up the duffel, step inside and shove the firewall closed. Couldn't see a thing. Like stepping into a tomb."

Kent suspected more than ever Justin was a delusion or a nightmare. If a nightmare, at least Kent was sleeping.

Justin continued, "I groped around until my eyes adjusted to the darkness. It's Carlsbad Caverns down there. Passageways going in all directions. I hid there for two days until I got so hungry I had to come out. There's plenty to eat in the hospital kitchen. But you gotta watch out for the nightshift, they're in and out of the kitchen all night long snacking. I stole a flashlight from one of the wards. You wouldn't believe what's down there in those dark underground passageways."

Kent closed his eyes and rubbed his forehead to ward off a headache. *How long was this nightmare going to last?*

"Bones and skeletons, crumbly old uniforms with brass buttons, and even some old rifles. I hid my duffel on a stone ledge out of reach of the rats running around down there."

Kent sighed. *I bet Becky Thatcher and Injun Joe are down there too?*

Justin hesitated momentarily, looking around the room and then at Kent. "Thought I heard something."

Kent pointed with a quick roll of his head. "The guy across the hall talks in his sleep."

Justin scratched at his bristly beard and went on with his story. "Anyway, as I was saying, I stay underground all day, come out each night to raid the kitchen. I only eat once a day. One of those underground passageways opens into the shaft of an old well. I climb up the shaft every night and go for a walk around the grounds. The fresh night air is rejuvenating after being stuck down there all day. Which reminds me, Cleo wants to meet you at the hospital gate."

"Cleo!"

"Yeah, Cleo. Your girlfriend. Comes to the gate every night asking about you."

"I don't want to see her. She distorts reality for me."

Justin stared dubiously at his friend. "You know, the other night hiding in the kitchen, I overheard the night nurses saying this Morgan guy was playing with your mind."

"Nonsense. He's helping me. Did I tell you, I wasn't poisoned? It was all a delusion."

"Whatever. But you owe it to Cleo to talk to her."

Kent stared at the scraggly vagrant who had popped in out of nowhere, telling incredible tales and handing out advice. "Justin, you're just a Folie a Deux ghost. When I wake up, you'll disappear."

"Yeah?"

"You're a delusion, you're not real."

Justin grabbed Kent's wrist with both hands and twisted.

"Ouch," Kent yelled. "What do you think you're doing?"

Justin smiled. "If I'm not real, why did you yell?"

Kent massaged his wrist. "Okay, you're real. But Gamuka isn't."

"Oh yeah, he's as real as you are."

"No he's not."

"Come on and I'll show you?"

All his life Kent had asked questions, searching for truth, never being afraid of the truth, and he wasn't afraid now. *What's it hurt to look at someone who doesn't exist?* "I'll do it just to prove you're wrong."

"Okay," Justin said, "follow me."

Chapter 35
FOLLOW ME

Kent and Justin tiptoed silently by a wire mesh door where the night nurse snoozed with her feet on a desk and her head lolled on her shoulder. Quietly, they descended a back stairway to an unlit corridor that ended at a locked door. Justin picked the lock with a piece of wire. Slick as slime. He knew what he was doing. Another corridor, another door, another lock.

They slunk past the hospital pharmacy with its smell of tinctures and antiseptics. Down another flight of stairs. They heard footsteps and quickly ducked under the stairway. A pudgy orderly lugging a laundry bag and whistling "Yellow Rose of Texas" moseyed by, keys jingling on his belt. They waited until he was out of sight and moved on. Their long trek ended when Justin unlocked and shoved open the door to the Contamination Room. The spacious room looked like the great hall of an old, deserted castle.

Justin walked over to the fireplace, stopped in front of the hearth, turned and looked at Kent. "Promise me you won't tell anyone about this. And if anything happens to me, promise me that you'll take care of Gamuka and keep an eye out for Rummels the CRAWL agent."

Kent reluctantly held up three fingers. "Scout's honor."

Justin shoved apart the boards covering the fireplace, bent down, stepped into the hearth, and placing his hands on the firewall, pushed. The wall moved with the creepy, creaky sound of a crypt being violated.

Kent stared into the black hole behind the firewall and his stomach knotted up. *Oh God, no. This can't be real. Not when I'm just getting well. Was Gamuka really in there somewhere, inside Justin's duffel?* Kent's throat tightened. He felt there wasn't enough space in his chest for the erratic pounding of his heart. In a panic he raced back across the room and flung open the door.

In the doorway stood Jesus-3, a placid expression of benediction on his face.

Kent stiffened. He glanced back across the room at the fireplace and then turned back to Jesus-3. "What are you doing here?"

Jesus-3 smiled. "That question has a very long answer. Did you know they slaughter innocent little lambs to make food for cats and dogs? You can't blame the cats and dogs; they have to eat what they are given. And people are forced to buy what's on the grocery shelf. Why are you sweating, Kent? You look frightened. What's bothering you, my son?"

Kent stood there, his head spinning with doubt and confusion, his every fiber trembling. Jesus-3 folded his hands, the soppy benign smile on his face broadening. "Whatever it is, face it with courage and seek the truth. And the truth shall make you free."

Kent slammed the door and fell against it, his chest rising and falling as if he had just run a marathon.

Justin poked his head out of the fireplace. "What are you waiting for?"

Kent reasoned that if he didn't go through with this, he could never be sure he was cured. He walked over, took a deep breath, and stepped through the fireplace into Justin's subterranean world.

Guided by Justin's flashlight, the two men groped along the crumbling passages. Kent shuddered at the sound of something crunching under his feet.

"What is that?"

"Bones left over from the Civil War."

As they crept along the darkened passage, Justin explained that he had eavesdropped on the nightshift's conversations in the hospital kitchen while he hid in the pantry eating his daily meal. It amazed him that people still theorized and argued about a Civil War battle that occurred 150 years ago and about the mystery of how Colonel Chisholm smuggled Union troops in and out of Bolton. Justin, a stranger in Bolton, had figured it out. He discovered the bony remains of soldiers and other remnants from the Civil War in these dark, crumbling passages under the hospital--the old colonel's underground railroad. The best kept secret of the Civil War.

Kent's heart flip-flopped when Justin's flashlight illuminated the hollowed-out eye sockets of a skull half-buried in the floor.

"Watch your step," Justin warned.

The flashlight beam ran up the wall to a stone ledge where Justin's gray duffel lay in heap like the carcass of an animal. Kent stood paralyzed and speechless.

Justin chuckled. "I told you." He handed Kent the flashlight. "Hold this while I feed Gamuka."

With the gentleness of a midwife, Justin delivered Gamuka's head from the duffel, the shrunken face, eyes peacefully closed, a miniature mummy resting in its crypt. The flashlight jiggled in Kent's hand as he tottered between belief and disbelief. The pungent odor of unwashed flesh confirmed for him that the diminutive field-goal-kicker-philosopher existed. *I've been a fool.* All Morgan's theories and reconstructions had been nothing but mind games built on a scaffolding of lies, now collapsing like an imploded building. Kent's grip tightened around the flashlight. If he had gone on believing Morgan, he would have surely died from Tommy Tennyson's poison. He may yet. But now he had a fighting chance. A chance to find a *homopragmatic truth* and to gain the antidote. A chance to live.

Justin fed Gamuka his usual diet of breadcrumbs and crackers. This time he didn't have to work the jaws. Gamuka swallowed the food like a hungry nestling, his eyes opening and closing, lips smacking.

Justin turned to Kent and grinned. "He's opened his eyes a lot lately. Even stared at me. I think he's working his way out of the wormhole."

"I want to go to the gate. I want to see Cleo."

"Hey, you've finally come to your senses."

Chapter 36
KUALA LUMPUR

Rummels, the CRAWL agent with an annihilation license, walked out of his hotel room in Kuala Lumpur, suitcase in hand and plane ticket in pocket, headed back to the States to annihilate Justin and Gamuka ASAP. Before he could close the door, the phone in the room rang. He set down his suitcase, stepped back inside and picked up the phone.

"Rummels here."

His CRAWL superior in Washington said, "The CIA has just issued an Order of Abnegation concerning the Kaku situation." Rummels knew the word "Abnegation" in the operative jargon of governmental intelligence meant we want something done, but we don't want to get our hands dirty.

Rummels asked, "What is it you want done?"

"You'll know soon enough. Sit tight where you are and await further orders."

"But I have a plane to catch."

"Forget the plane."

"It's pretty hot here," Rummels whined, "there's no air conditioning." His complaint failed to register and the phone went dead.

Rummels stripped to his underwear and waited for the call while sitting under the rotating blades of a ceiling fan and soaking his feet in ice water. The second call came within the hour. His superior informed him about the hostage situation in Kaku and that the press had not yet got wind of it. "The rescue of hostages and the arrest of Moko Kaku has been ordered. Operation Kaku is your baby."

"Wait a minute," Rummels sputtered. "I've only done negotiations and annihilations. Never a hostage rescue."

"You're doing this one. It's just a few people on a little fucking island. No big deal. And remember to keep the CIA's name out of it in case something goes wrong. They've gotten a lot of negative press lately, and if they were associated with a bungled invasion of an island kingdom with a population less than Branson, Missouri minus tourists, it wouldn't look good."

Rummels asked, "What could go wrong?"

"Nothing, if it's done right? You fucked up the Moko annihilation. If you fuck this up--I don't have to tell you what that means."

Sweat dripped from Rummels' brow. If he botched the assignment, if Kaku became another "Bay of Pigs", CRAWL would doubt issue an annihilation order with his name on it.

"Your assignment is to be carried out quickly and covertly before anything leaks to the press. You have full requisition and conscription powers as defined in the CRAWL handbook. Prepare your plan immediately, get it approved, and implement. This is Top Priority."

Rummels puffed on his asthma inhaler, dried his feet off, powdered his ankles, and looked wearily at his panty hose hanging limply on the back of a chair. He decided he would use the Powell formula for Operation Kaku. Have a clear objective and then obtain that objective with overwhelming force. But stay out of jungles and mountainous terrain, if possible. In other words, pick on someone smaller and weaker than you are, corner them where they can't hide, then kick the shit out of 'em. Notre Dame playing Junior High football.

He took two more puffs on his inhaler and thumbed through his CRAWL handbook to the section on clandestine operations. Just as he suspected, a Catch-22 under rule 20914-635, "the U.S. military does not have to comply with requisition and conscription orders from non-military governmental agencies." In short, Rummels would have a hard time requisitioning men and first-rate equipment from the military. He swallowed a colon pill and got on the phone.

He located and requisitioned twenty-two SH-49F Seahawk helicopters mothballing in Japan, waiting to be shipped State's side for demolition. The Seahawks had sixty-foot rotator blades, rather than the standard fifty-three foot eight inch blades. The next day, the Philippine government released to Rummels the USS Nixon, a nuclear aircraft carrier the US Navy had abandoned when shore installations around Manila Bay closed. An A4W pressurized nuclear reactor powered the Nixon. On board were enough plutonium rods to fuel six trips around the world. The Philippine government was anxious to get rid of the Nixon since no one was paying the dock fees any longer.

Air National Guardsmen from three states volunteered for the action in lieu of their regular two-week summer camp. Rummels arranged helicopter simulator training for them in Japan. Coast Guard volunteers at the Department of Transportation, six with carrier experience, were flown immediately to Manila.

He placed an ad on Facebook: "Commando volunteers wanted for a covert sea and air invasion of a dictator-led principality." Fifty state militias volunteered. He selected two by the draw.

Everything was set, men and ship to rendezvous in Tokyo Bay at 2400 hours. He had seventy-two hours to whip the invasion force into a state of readiness. Time was running and the press was sure to get wind of the hostage situation soon. All he needed was final approval.

He cut through the governmental red tape by explaining his assault and invasion plans over the phone to a Kelly Girl temp at the DoD. The Kelly Girl, filling in for a secretary on sick leave, agreed to pass the information along to the Deputy Assistant Secretary's secretary when she returned to work. The Kelly Girl told him, "Your plan sounds pretty good to me. You should have no trouble getting it approved."

That was good enough for Rummels. Operation Kaku was a GO!

Chapter 37
GOOD-BYE VU

A casino's definition of a cheater is anyone who consistently wins. All cheaters have a system and all systems have flaws. If you watch a cheater close enough and long enough, you'll discover the flaw. The Atlantic City casinos kept a close eye on the portly Asian who consistently won at blackjack. However, electronic surveillance revealed nothing. The pit boss standing behind the dealer noticed no funny business. The gambler played his hand like all the other high rollers. The gambler's sidekick wasn't helping him either, no spilled drinks, no distractions, and no hand signals. All the sidekick did was play the slots, and they were eating him alive. The casinos put a detective on the case, an ex-FBI agent specializing in casino cheats.

The detective followed Vu and Larry in and out of the casinos, up and down the Boardwalk, to the shows, down ringside at the fights, from a cheap motel to a five-room suite at Merv's. The two suspects seemed to be ordinary guys having a good time. They were heavy tippers. They liked massages, good food, and expensive cigars. They bought a Lincoln Navigator. They slept late, wore expensive duds, and gambled all night. That's what Atlantic City was all about. To the detective, these two appeared legitimate, the one having an unusually hot run at blackjack.

Vu in a spangled Liberace jacket stood in front of the suites girandole mirror fluffing the pompadour of his Elvis wig. Larry slumped into a chair, still in his underwear. Vu glanced at Larry's reflection. "You're not dressed?"

"I'm staying in tonight."

"Are you crazy? Good food. Pretty girls. *Vengt et un.* Come on, Larry. We'll tear the town apart."

"You go on."

Larry's prison scars showed, the prematurely gray hair, the crow's feet of worry, that scowling *I don't give a shit* look. Despite the scars, Larry was incapable of hiding emotion. Vu read him like e-mail. "All right, Larry, out with it. What's wrong? You want a prostitute for the night."

"Nothin's wrong, I'm just staying in."

Vu sat down on an ottoman. "You're worried they'll catch you and send you back to prison."

"I'll never go back alive."

"Are you lonely for the girl back home?"

Larry walked over to a closet, took out a suitcase, and tossed it onto the bed. "I'm leaving for Bolton in the morning."

Vu stood up. "Take the Navigator and all the money you need. I'm staying here."

Larry gazed into the brown sagacious eyes of the immigrant physician-gambler who unwittingly helped him escape from prison. Whose niece, thanks to brains and skill, had landed them safely on the East Coast. Now Vu was giving him yet another car and more money. He owed Vu everything.

"We're splitting up," Larry said in a fragile, tremulous voice. "If you rat on me, Vu, I'll…." In a gush of emotion, Larry rushed over to the only friend he had and wrapped his arms around him. They embraced nearly a minute, Larry in his underwear, Vu in his spangled Liberace jacket and Elvis wig.

"I'll miss you, Vu."

"Somewhere, sometime we'll meet up again."

Chapter 38
ON THE ROAD

Larry pulled down the visor to block out the late afternoon sun and downed his last can of Bud Light, while hurling ninety miles an hour across Indiana in the Navigator. He thought about Cleo and how beautiful she was. But for some reason he couldn't visualize what she looked like. He had the same problem in prison. He could see her smile, her gleaming white teeth, that wide sensuous mouth. He could hear her high-pitch giggle. He remembered the incredible softness of her skin. Yet he couldn't put it all together into a composite. No matter how hard he tried, he couldn't envision that beautiful face. It was as if her features were out of focus. He pounded the steering wheel. *This is stupid. I was married to her for twelve glorious months.*

He thought about Veronica. A woman he had never seen. What a voice. So sexy. Velvety. He wondered what Veronica looked like? If anything like her voice—wow. He was thinking about two faceless women. Skin and Voice.

He tossed the empty beer can out the window, and his cellular phone came alive with Scrugg's Bluegrass. *Veronica's back from Bangkok.* He couldn't locate the phone. He rummaged through the junk in the back seat with his right hand, while steering with his left. The phone kept playing. The Navigator crossed lanes. A trucker laid on his horn. Larry jammed his foot into the accelerator. The speedometer jumped to one hundred and ten. Larry felt something compact and plastic under a suitcase. *The phone.* "Hello, Veronica. Is that you?"

Her voice was instant Viagra. "I missed you, Larry. Did you miss me?"

"Yeah. A lot as matter of fact."

"Where are you?"

"I'm on a four lane outside Evansville, Indiana."

"You are on your way to Bolton, are you not?"

"I was thinking about it."

"Are you still in love with her?"

"I don't know. I can't figure it out."

"How fast are you going?"

"About ninety. A little more."

"It is rather foolish for a man wanted by the law to speed on a major highway. Do you want to get caught?"

"No."

"I did a lot of thinking in Bangkok."

"Really?"

"I think we should…. Larry, what is the noise in the background? I think I hear a siren. Better take a look."

The shrill sound of a siren screeched in Larry's ears. He glanced in the rearview mirror and saw flashing red and blue lights. The highway patrol! *Motherfucker.* He could smell State Prison.

Veronica asked coolly, "Is it the highway patrol?"

"I'm going to outrun them. They won't take me alive."

"Just remain calm. Slow down. I will help you."

"Slow down? Are you out of your fuckin' mind?"

"You know I do not like vulgarities. Now I want you to slow down and pull over to the shoulder."

"Hell no!"

"Trust me. I can get you out of this."

Larry squeezed the steering wheel. "It goes against my better judgment, but…I'm pulling over."

Veronica's voice was unchanged. "Look in your mirror and tell me what you see. Any information may be helpful. I am using a very powerful computer."

"All I see is a patrol car and flashing lights. My ass is mud."

"This is very important. Do you see any numbers on the car or any kind of identification?"

"What?"

"Remain calm. I am going to help you. My search data gives only three highway patrolmen in that area."

"He's getting out of his patrol car."

"This is important, do you see any identifying numbers on the car?"

"It just says, Indiana Highway Patrol."

"Numbers, Larry."

"Okay. Five, three, one, eight. Oh, shit!"

"What is wrong?"

"I just wet my pants."

"Okay, I have it. The officer's name is Ray Johnson. His father is Herman Johnson who works at a dairy processing plant in Evansville. Tell him you know Herman. That you and Herman are good friends."

Holding the cellular to his ear, Larry lowered the window. A Darth Vader face stared at him grimly through wrap-around mirrored sunglasses.

"Sir, I clocked you at ninety-eight miles an hour. I'll need to see your license and registration, please."

Larry tried to speak but the words wouldn't come out. Frozen with terror, he sat motionless in his wet pants, the cell phone plastered to his ear. He suddenly remembered how he would breathe deeply to calm himself before giving talks on growth to farmers or singing solo at weddings. He inhaled until he thought his chest would rupture, and then blew out all the air. He could feel sweat running down the back of his neck. Surprisingly, a feeling of calm swept over him. He heard himself say with vigor, "Why, I'll be. Aren't you Herman's boy?"

The officer's stone face cracked. "You knew my dad?"

"Yeah, you look just like him. Use to work with Herman at the dairy. Your dad and me were best friends. My name is Smith. They called me Smitty at the dairy."

"You don't look that old, Smitty."

"I-I-I was a lot younger than Herman. How is old Herman, anyway?"

"He's dead."

"That so? Was it his heart?"

"Killed by an electrical short in the refrigeration room while scooping cottage cheese. Fried him like bacon. Mom and I are suing the dairy."

"I would think you would. They never did take very good care of that refrigeration room."

"That's the way mom and I feel about it. Say, are you talking with someone on that phone?"

Larry froze again. *Yeah, I'm talking to the niece of the man who helped me escape from prison. You want to put the handcuffs on now or wait until I get out of the car?* Veronica's voice whispered in his ear. "Tell him I am your wife and that I am in labor, having a baby in a St. Louis hospital. That you're rushing there to be with me."

Larry stammered, "I-i-it's the wife on the phone." To Veronica, "I'm right here, dear." He smiled at the bear. "She's having a baby in St. Louis. She's in labor. Breathe deeply, dear. Remember what the doctor said, it's all in the breathing." Larry took another deep breath. "You'll never guess who I'm talking to. Herman Johnson's boy. You remember Herman from the dairy?"

Veronica whispered, "Ask him about the twins."

"She wants to know how the twins are."

"They're fine. Tell her, thanks for asking." The bewildered patrolman removed his hat and sunglasses and morphed into an ordinary-looking guy. He leaned on the car door and scratched his head as he stared at Larry. "How did she know about the twins?"

"Honey, he wants to know how you knew about the twins." Larry emitted a nervous chuckle. "She talks with your wife Susan at least once a month. They went to school together at Stephens College."

The bear squinted at Larry. "It's a darn small world. Your wife in labor explains your speeding. But what about this?" He held up a crumpled beer can.

"Oh, that. I'm always picking up beer cans. It's a compulsion. I believe it's every citizen's duty to keep our highways clean. That one there just happened to get away from me."

Sunglasses back on, hat on, the bear smiled at Larry. "I wished everybody was as concerned about our highways as you are. Now you drive careful, Smitty. I wouldn't want that new baby to start life without a father."

"If it's a boy, we're naming him Herman." Larry waved as the patrol car pulled away.

"You were pretty cool," Veronica said.

"I wet my pants."

"That is quite understandable."

Larry headed down the highway, his finger on the cruise control. "Veronica, how in the world did you come up with all that information?"

"I told you, I am the high tech equivalent of a J. Edgar Hoover."

"I don't know what I'd do without you."

"I am glad you feel that way. How is my uncle?"

"Having a ball making a fortune in Atlantic City."

"He must be playing blackjack. Listen, I would like to meet you in St. Louis."

Larry swallowed hard. "What for?"

"You do not want to meet with me?"

"Oh sure, I want to. I just meant that it's a lot trouble for you."

"No trouble. I want to visit with you in person. I will call you back and let you know when to meet my plane."

Chapter 39
DOWN AT THE GATE

In the dead of night, as the hospital slept, Justin picked the lock to Ward 2. He awakened Kent and together they walked off the ward right past the slumbering night nurse. Stealthily, they hurried down a series of corridors finally arriving at the Contamination Room. They slipped through the firewall of the abandoned fireplace and into the labyrinth of underground passageways. Justin led Kent some 300 feet along one of the passageways before stopping. "Gets a little slippery here, watch your step."

In utter darkness, Kent followed Justin up a flight of moss-covered spiraling stone steps of an abandoned well. When they reached the top Justin shoved aside some loose boards and the two men stepped out onto the hospital grounds. Slowly now, like commandoes on a night raid, they slunk along a high chain link fence that glistened silvery in the moonlight. At the crest of small hill Justin stopped. "There she is, down by the gate."

Kent's mood soared when he saw Cleo standing under a street lamp on the other side the hospital's cast iron gate. He raced up to the gate and yanked on the heavy chain securing it. Cleo greeted him with a nasty stare.

"I've been worried to death about you," she grumbled as she stepped up to the gate. "Why didn't you return my calls? I'm cleaning rooms in a flea-trap motel for my keep and don't you even care. I should've gone on back to Harkerville." She rocked nervously back and forth on the balls of her feet. "Not knowing is the worse thing. It tears a person apart emotionally."

Kent clung to the iron bars of the gate like a caged animal. He kept quiet, letting her get it all out, her voice cracking with emotion, her teary blue eyes shimmering in the light of the streetlamp. He wanted to hold her in his arms, but the Iron Gate and her anger held him back. He glanced at Justin cowering against the fence in the shadow of the gate. Justin shrugged as if to say I can't help you. Kent bit his tongue and waited patiently for Cleo's anger to cool.

Cleo stepped closer and said in a softer less rancorous voice, "I missed you so much." He slipped his hand through the iron bars and touched her hand. Soon they were talking as if nothing were ever wrong between them. Kent took off his left shoe and removed his Vita Master Card from inside his sock. He shoved the card between the bars to Cleo.

"Buy a car and get new clothes for everyone including Justin and Gamuka. In two weeks when I get discharged from this nuthouse, we're heading to New York. I'm sorry about your phone calls. That psychologist Morgan screwed everything up."

"I can vouch for that," Justin threw in. "He had Kent thinking Gamuka was a hallucination, can you believe that?"

Kent and Cleo pressed their faces up to the gate and their noses touched. They lowered themselves to the ground, held hands through the gate and talked about going to New York to find Selena Rosalina.

"CRAWL will have a hard time finding us in New York," Justin interjected. "It's a huge place crammed with people."

Cleo sighed. "Two weeks, I can hardly wait."

Chapter 40
GROUP THERAPY

At Morgan's group therapy session Kent sat quietly, holding back his anger, reminding himself that he and Cleo would soon be on their way to New York in search of a *homopragmatic truth*. *Stay cool.* He blinked to conceal the glare in his eyes as he stared across the circle of people at the man who had nearly destroyed him, his past and his future. If anybody in this group needed therapy, it was the sludgeball psychologist with the bow tie. Kent glanced up at the wall clock. Fifteen minutes of group therapy to go. He shifted in his chair to relieve the tightening in his muscles.

Morgan, the only one in the group talking, lectured on his favorite topic, boys lusting after their mothers, Freud's "Oedipus Complex." Two nurses and a social worker, Morgan's cheering section, took notes. Alonzo and two others nodded off, heads dangling like ripened fruit. McDonald sat staring at his feet, saliva tickling from his mouth, his head moving in little rhythmic jerks. The kid looked like an old man. Word on the ward had it that McDonald, due to a clerical mix up, had received four times the usual number of electroshock treatments. An overdose of several hundred volts. The interns called his drooling, trembling and head jerking "FBS," Fried Brain Syndrome. That's what happens to a brain on electricity.

Jesus-3, whose only distinguishing characteristic were the bright yellow specks in his hazel eyes, sat stroking the air with the palm of his hand. The stroking motion perturbed Morgan, who stopped his monologue and asked, "What are you doing?"

Jesus-3 smiled. "Petting my cat."

"I don't see a cat."

"That's because you're blind to the suffering of animals."

Morgan said with a bit of asperity in his voice, "There is no cat."

"Yes there is. His name is Omni."

A nurse chuckled. "Funny name."

Jesus-3 shook his head sadly. "Omni is an unusual cat. He's symbolic of all the animals you human beings have murdered."

Morgan shot Jesus-3 a waspish look. "You think it is wrong for humans to kill animals?"

Kent was glad Morgan focused on Jesus-3. He wanted no confrontations. He might lose it, attack the charlatan shrink and end up staying longer in this nuthouse.

Jesus-3 answered Morgan with a question, "Have you ever looked down at the earth from twenty-thousand feet up in an airplane?"

"What are you getting at?"

"The houses on the ground look like dots on a piece of paper, and people are as invisible as viruses. I'm telling you, twenty-thousand feet is nothing to the Father."

Morgan crossed and uncrossed his legs and nibbled the stem his meerschaum. "Are you trying to make a point?"

"In a nutshell, Mr. Morgan: if God, Who is great and wondrous, loved and succored human beings; then why does humankind, who is nothing in comparison, not love the animals who are only a little less than they?"

Morgan shot a smug smile to his cheering section. "I love animals. I have a poodle at home."

Jesus-3 sighed. "And yet you eat steak."

"I'll eat whatever I please."

"And what do you feed your poodle?"

"Dog food, of course."

McDonald looked up from his feigned melancholy, a bit of spirit in his passionless face.

Jesus-3 asked, "And what is dog food made of, Mr. Morgan?"

"Who cares?" Morgan turned to his cheering section. "Freud discovered in his own life an infatuation for his mother and jealousy towards his father. He saw a certain survival quality in this. A little boy falling in love with his mother is developing feelings that could one day lead to the procreation of the species. And…"

"Ground up horses," McDonald blared.

"What are you shouting about," Morgan asked.

Thick strands of slobber swung from MacDonald's lips. "I grew up down the street from a dog food factory. There was this big corral with palominos, Shetlands, donkeys, and mares with colts. One day I watched them drive the ponies up this wooden chute into a dirty brick building. They murdered all the horses. Shot them in the head. Hanged them upside down on hooks. Slit their throats … "

Morgan stared harshly at the redheaded depressive. "That's quite enough."

Jesus-3 patted McDonald on the shoulder. "It will be all right, son."

Morgan glared at Jesus-3. "In the Bible, the Israelites sacrificed animals in the temple all the time. God demanded it of them. What do you say to that?"

Jesus-3 tensed. "You Americans. You think you invented protectionism. The Israelites were wandering, horseless cowboys, exploiting and murdering animals. It was a way of life. The priests were just promoting and protecting the tribal business practices, while at the same time putting a little meat on the table for themselves."

Morgan's lips curled. "That's blasphemy! How can you dare call yourself Jesus? If you ask me, you're the devil."

Jesus-3 grinned. "Look who's having delusions now."

Morgan's face turned blood red. Words choked in his throat. A nurse brought him water in a paper cup. He loosened his tie, took a deep breath, looked at Jesus-3 and declared, "You're a delusional pervert. A cataleptic, paranoid confabulator. "

Jesus-3 retorted, "And you're a pedantic dunce who doesn't know a fucking thing."

Quips and gibes flew. The circle, wide-awake now, listened intently as therapist and patient battled like two scorpions on hot sand. The tongue-lashings stopped when Jesus-3 called Morgan a "moron." The enraged psychologist flew out his chair, hands clenched. The social worker and the two nurses grabbed him by the arms to restrain him.

Chapter 41
ST. LOUIS

All three remedies for chronic megapolisitis had been tried on St. Louis: sprawl, bypasses, and high-rise ghettos. Larry flew over ribbons of freeway in the Navigator like a pilot in a Lear jet. He studied the road signs diligently. He turned off the freeway looking for gasoline and ended up in the heart of a law-of-the-jungle ghetto, where hordes of people openly barbecued food and congregated in the streets as if it were a national holiday. Puzzled faces stared at him as he tooled along, glancing at his fuel gauge. Everything that looked like a service station was boarded up. He sat high in the Navigator like a Mughal emperor on an elephant's back, ignoring the teenagers throwing rocks and empty beer cans at his windshield. He looked straight ahead and plowed through the ghetto, leaving crumpled trashcans and upturned barbecue grills in his wake.

Freeway signs led him to the airport. He parked in short term and took a long-term wait at gate nine. Veronica's plane wasn't due for another hour. He walked around. *Why was she coming all the way to St. Louis to meet me, an escaped convict, a man she knew only over the telephone?* It didn't make sense. But he owed her. Without her help, he would have never made it this far. Shit, she had saved his life. Maybe this was like falling in love over the Internet.

At a food kiosk he bought a chilidog and a cola. Later, he browsed the books in the gift shop and wondered why someone hadn't written a "Chicken Soup for Death Row Inmates." Back at gate nine, he paced.

What would Veronica look like? Despite her sexy voice, he imagined her to be a nerd with a computer brain, a dumpy couch potato body, her hair in a bun, thick glasses, black high-tops, and a digital watch with a GPS. It didn't really matter what she looked like. Whatever she asked, he would deliver. Even if she were an un-humped skag looking for a weekend shack-up.

The 727 landed, reversed engines, and taxied to the gate. No one in the jet way queue looked like what he thought Veronica should look like. *Maybe it's a setup.* He was at an appointed place at an appointed time. But the cops would have a hard time recognizing him with his waxed mustache, his expensive black sheepskin blazer, five hundred dollar V-neck cashmere sweater, tweed pants, and square-toed Fatelli's. *Maybe I ought to get the hell out of here anyway.*

He heard that familiar sexy voice. "Larry, is that you?"

He closed his eyes, turned, and opened them. His impression was that of the most beautiful woman he had ever seen. That impression did not include her diamond earrings, gold choker, Gucci purse, and a laptop in a slim leather case. It did include a dark pantsuit, which her slender body filled out subtly in the right places, button lips and dark eyes that gleamed like moonstone. Her lustrous black hair was cut short with ruffs of curls. His eyes moved down her neck, a tapering anomaly so slender and long, so exquisite, he envied the choker gripping it.

"Veronica?"

"Larry," she chuckled. "You look exactly like I thought you would."

"Yeah. You too. Any luggage?"

"One small suitcase."

Rush hour on the freeway was a smelt run. Cars crammed six lanes, sluicing towards the spawning beds of the suburbs. Veronica glanced at the GPS on her wrist. "You better get over, we turn right at the next exit."

With abandon, Larry wheeled the Navigator across two lanes. In traffic, he was a road warrior. The Navigator could crinkle a compact or an import and Larry loved the respect.

Veronica said, "You are a good driver."

"That's all I've been doing since I escaped."

Following Veronica's instructions, Larry took a right off the freeway onto another freeway. Five miles of silence ensued before Veronica said, "You are probably wondering why I wanted to meet with you?"

Larry glanced at his passenger. "I swear you're some kind of mind reader."

"I am starting up a new computer company and I could use someone like you."

"You don't know anything about me, other than I'm an escaped convict."

"My uncle told me anyone who could turn a cell block of raving maniacs into human beings had to be a good person. He likes you, and he is a pretty good judge of character."

"I think he's pretty fuckin' nice too."

"Please watch the language."

"Sorry. The longer I'm out of prison the less I cuss."

"I understand."

"Thanks."

"Certainly."

Larry asked, "What were we talking about?"

"About my not knowing anything about you. But I do. Back in Harkerville, you were the toast of the town. You sang at weddings and funerals. You sold everyone a used car. You made Green Pasture Pesticide and Fertilizer a booming business. You were a celebrity."

Larry squeezed the steering wheel. "Someday those bastards at Green Pasture will pay for what they did."

Veronica smiled. "I want you to forget about revenge and start thinking about a new life. I need someone to handle our foreign markets. You would be living overseas with a fresh start. You would not have to worry about going back to prison."

"You really mean it?"

"Yes I do."

"But I don't know anything about your business."

"Turn here, please."

Larry wheeled the Navigator down an exit ramp onto a two lane. At a blinking light, they dipped into a glass and concrete canyon, hotels and corporate headquarters. Veronica pointed out the window. "Our hotel is right over there."

Carrying the suitcase, Larry followed Veronica from the hotel's front desk to the elevator. Up seven flights. He liked the way she moved, so self-assured, almost arrogant. He felt like the tail of comet as he pursued her down the hallway to room 736 She unlocked the door. "Come on in."

Larry flipped on the lights of the two-room suite with a king size bed. Veronica opened her laptop and set it on a desk near the bed.

"Close the door," she commanded in a clear, low voice. On the table by the window were a bucket of ice with champagne, two glasses, and a vase with a dozen red roses. "You'll like this place, it is nice and quiet, three restaurants, a pool, gym, and Wi-Fi. I ordered the champagne from the airplane. I wanted to celebrate your coming to work for me."

"I haven't agreed to it, yet."

Her hand swept across his chin. Her smile was polished ivory. "You will. We would be working together from time to time. And you will make more money than you ever dreamed."

He knew she was aware his eyes were feasting. She turned off the lights. A haze of laser-blue from the laptop's screen illuminated the room. She popped the cork on the champagne and poured two glasses.

She handed him a glass, kicked off her shoes and sat on the bed. She patted the mattress. "Come sit."

The only other times he had tingled all over like this were when he was with Cleo. He was glad he had forgotten what she looked like.

He couldn't think of anything to say as he sat down on the bed. After all those months trapped in that prison cell with Eugene, he was now sitting next to the most beautiful woman in the world and looking at her over the rim of a champagne glass. Veronica smiled between sips. Larry smiled. After three glasses of champagne, they giggled at nothing. Without warning, Veronica smashed her glass against the wall. Larry smashed his glass. They laughed so hard tears rolled down their cheeks.

Veronica lay back on the bed and whispered, "Kiss me."

Larry touched her lips, his tongue sliding in and out, exploring her mouth. She rolled away, stood, took a condom from her Gucci purse and tossed it onto the bed. Larry's left foot twitched.

She removed her top slowly, a button at a time. She held it up and watched it drift to the floor. Smiling, she slid her pants down over her legs in a deliberate, graceful motion. She stepped out of her thong panties, unsnapped her bra and slipped it off over her arms. In the subdued light of the laptop's screen, she stood before him naked--a boyish, unblemished goddess. Her gentle curves were impressionistic, suggestive of something more. Her belly was nearly as slender as her neck, the navel a mere eddy in the smooth unvarying flow of skin that was she. Small, firm breasts jutted from her chest like projectiles ready for launching, the nipples hard and beckoning.

With the same dexterity she did everything, she undressed Larry. Like a mannequin, he sat there motionless, except for the twitching of his foot. Off came his sweater, his pants, his shoes, everything. She applied the condom like an artist covering a work of art. She kissed him there. Her legs straddled him, her pelvis swiveled. Larry groaned. She rolled over. "Come on, Larry. Fuck me."

He plunged deep inside her, her hands digging into his back, his hands everywhere, their bodies amalgamating in a gyrating dance of the flesh. For the first time since escaping prison, Larry wasn't looking over his shoulder. He didn't care what happened next; he was living for this singular, rapturous moment. He plunged deeper, almost violently into the moaning, lurching, exquisite protoplasm beneath him.

Chapter 42
HIGH TECH

While Kent Mullins underwent group therapy at Bolton Mental, Larry Lakes cohabited with Veronica at that St. Louis hotel, where they made love and Veronica reviewed with him the entire computer revolution. Within six days, he was teleconferencing, uploading, downloading, networking, and multitasking. Sometime in those last few days, Larry's brain had shifted to the left, to the analytical, gadgety side.

Veronica said, "Boy, you catch on fast."

"In high school I was pretty good with computers. But I didn't enjoy it much." Despite sharing a hotel room with a beautiful, attentive woman, Larry felt blue, as if the color was being bleached out of his world.

Cuddled to Veronica, Larry lay awake one night and mentally compared her with his memories of Cleo. It was like comparing diamonds and rubies. They were different, but equally exciting and marvelous in bed. Both were assertive, intelligent women. Although he couldn't remember what Cleo looked like, he did remember she was very beautiful. Maybe as beautiful as Veronica. Her skin was softer than Veronica's. Her breasts larger. But size isn't everything. On a scale of one to ten, they were both ten in his opinion. Yes, equally beautiful. Equally exciting. But Cleo had abandoned him. She was no better than banker Jones or Eugene and his horny yard dogs. Veronica had lifted him out of the pit of despair and offered him the world. If he ever had to choose between them, it would be easy.

Or would it?

One morning in bed, Veronica told him, "You're a natural. When it comes to computers you're best I've ever seen, even better than me. You taken to high tech like Mozart to the piano."

"You mean I get the job."

She leaned over and blew in his ear. "Yes. You'll be charge of our foreign office. You'll be making big bucks."

"Where?"

"Bangkok."

"What kind of business is it?"

"Import, export. But you don't have to worry about the details. You'll only be involved with shipping, it's all done on the computer." Veronica rolled out of bed, slipped into a thin silk gown, and walked over to the printer connected to her laptop. "I have your plane tickets and your passport. You leave tomorrow."

"Aren't you coming?"

Veronica sat beside him on the bed and smiled. "I've got to go back to Texas on business. But we'll get together from time to time."

Larry stretched. "I've got to see someone first."

Veronica's smile changed quickly to a grimace. "Your ex, Cleo, is it not?"

Larry rose onto his elbow. "How did you know?"

"You talk in your sleep."

Larry yawned. "I'd like to see her one last time."

Veronica turned away. A second later, she whirled back around, composed and smiling again. "You cannot go to Bolton. It is much too dangerous. There will be plenty of time for that after the heat dies down."

Larry cleared his throat. "I'm a little nervous s going to Bangkok without you. I'll miss you."

Veronica planted a kiss on his cheek. "You'll do just fine."

Chapter 43
GATE SERMONS

For the fifth night in a row Kent and Cleo rendezvoused at the hospital gate. Justin stood a measured distance away so not to disturb the two lovers as they talked. Kent pressed his face to the cold iron bars and stared longingly at Cleo.

"How do you like my new clothes," Cleo asked, spinning around in front of the gate on low heel opera pumps. "I got the jacket, the sleeveless shell, and the skirt at a half-off sale, and the pumps at Pay Less. Saved a fortune. I'll need at least two more outfits before we take off for New York. Oh, I gave the motel notice. Had my hair done. How do you like it?" She spun again.

"Looks wonderful."

A man forgets how beautiful a woman is until she's all dressed up and there's twelve feet of fence and an iron gate separating them. Shopping had been a mood elevator for Cleo. She literally danced in front of the gate.

Cleo trilled, "Guess what? Got us a red Camaro. Used, but in perfect condition. Only fifty thousand miles on the odometer. I had a CD player installed. I hope I'm not maxing out your Vitae Platinum Card."

Kent's fingers curled around the iron bars. This was like a convict having a conjugal visit without the conjugal. "Don't worry about the money. I'm a millionaire, remember."

Justin noticed someone walking across the grounds in the darkness. "Look, someone's coming!"

Kent's eyes strained at the figure moving towards them. "It's Jesus-3. How did he get off the ward?"

"Who?" Cleo asked.

Kent said irritably, "Some nut who thinks he's Jesus."

Jesus-3's white hospital gown rippled in the breeze and glimmered in the moonlight as he walked right up to the gate. "Good evening, Kent. Why Justin, I haven't seen you since that night you were admitted and disappeared into the fireplace. Everyone thinks you eloped."

Justin paled. "Please, don't tell anyone you saw me here. It's a matter of life and death."

"My lips are sealed. Did you happen to see the deer playing in the meadow beyond the fence? Graceful creatures." Jesus-3 glanced at Cleo. "And who are you?"

"My name is Cleo."

"May I sit and visit?" Jesus-3 asked.

"Surely," Cleo answered.

Jesus-3 sat on the grass near the gate. Kent frowned. He knew that once Jesus-3 started talking there's no stopping him.

Jesus-3 looked at the others. "My friends, I must tell you the Father has many garden planets throughout the universe, but this is one of the worse. Man is murdering all living things. The sin here is quite grave." His tone became serious. "Somehow man must learn to live in peace with his brothers and sisters the animals."

Kent, Justin, and Cleo exchanged nervous glances. Jesus-3's presence here at the gate was an unexpected turn. Kent didn't want the night nurse to find out about his nightly visits to the gate. To sneak off the ward was a major infraction of the rules. He didn't want anything to interfere with his impending release from Bolton Mental.

Jesus-3 sitting comfortably on the grass spoke of his experiences at slaughterhouses comforting condemned animals. He'd blessed the animals, prayed for them, and even walked with some of them into the "kill rooms." He told horror stories of cattle butchered alive, their bellies ripped open, their hide being pulled off as they sailed down the assembly line in immeasurable pain, their eyes rolling in terror.

Kent had heard it all before on the ward. At first, Cleo was repulsed by the stories. But Jesus-3's soft voice mesmerized his listeners and put their minds at ease. He appeared to be a man free of guile and hypocrisy, genuinely concerned about humanity's treatment of animals. He next preached a short version of the Sermon on the Mount with such pathos that it made Cleo's eyes teary.

The next night was unseasonably warm, and a drift of gray clouds hid the moon. Cleo returned to the gate with a friend, a young illegal immigrant. "This is Carmen Salazar," Cleo told Kent and Justin. "She got me the job cleaning rooms at the Snore Motel. If it wasn't for her, I'd be sleeping in the streets."

To Kent's chagrin, Jesus-3 came walking down the hill to the gate, the yellow spatters in his hazel eyes twinkling like points of light in the darkness. "Here he comes again," Kent warned.

Cleo introduced Carmen to Jesus-3 who welcomed her in Spanish. They all sat down in the grass beside the gate, men inside, women outside.

Jesus-3 spoke softly and melodiously, "My Father sent me here the first time to teach you human beings to love one another, to turn the other cheek, to help the poor, and to love one's enemies as well as one's neighbors. In heaven it was believed that in the normal course of events, you human beings would extend these beatitudes and blessings to your sisters and brothers the animals. The Father thought of all the creatures on earth, surely you human beings would have shared your blessings. But you haven't, and that's why I've come back."

Kent whispered to Cleo, "This is like going to church every night."

Cleo sighed. "I think he's wonderful."

Jesus-3 repeated his rendition of the Sermon on the Mount and concluded, "This is the Father's message: love your neighbors, love your enemies, and love the animals."

On the third night, not only Cleo and Carmen came to the gate, but also the manager of the Snore Motel with his wife and six kids. Jesus-3 preached about love in a world full of evil, where life is difficult, and sickness and death seem to ultimately conquer. He preached a message of hope and promise, telling his audience that only through the love of human beings for one another and for all of God's creatures can God's kingdom on earth as in heaven be done. He recited the beatitudes with poignancy, and all who listened were impressed. The next night a Baptist minister and some of his congregation showed up at the gate to see this man who calls himself Jesus. After a brief sermon, Jesus-3 asked them to all come again and to bring their pets, especially the sick and injured.

They did.

Chapter 44
AND PEOPLE TOO

Each night at the gate with a wave of his hand, a smile, and a blessing, Jesus-3 healed not only German Shepherds with bad hips, Saint Bernards in heart failure, and old Cockers gone senile, but also cats, ferrets, goldfish, iguanas, parakeets, pet rodents, and farm animals. A short sermon followed each healing session. Night after night, they came, an endless menagerie of infirm pets and livestock led by their caring owners.

Kent said to Justin as they watched the activities at the gate, "He's turning this hospital into a petting zoo."

Justin sighed. "Well, if you ask me, it might be an improvement."

It seemed to Kent that all meaning and order in the universe had evaporated? The Tommy Tennysons and Mr. Morgans were in charge, poisoning people, lying to them, and now a Jesus impostor was preaching animal gospel to a large crowd in the middle of the night at the front gate of a mental hospital. And people were buying it. Even Cleo was out in front of the gate, herding animals, and helping with the healing sessions.

The weather turned cold and still people and animals clogged the narrow streets around the gate each night. Revival notices floated about town. *BRING YOUR PET. GATE SERMONS NIGHTLY.* A local television station televised the healing sessions and nightly sermons right after the ten o'clock news. Crowds became throngs. Church choirs belted out hymns as Jesus-3 healed hundreds of critters each night. Police were dispatched for traffic control. Justin stopped coming to the gate for fear of being noticed on television by CRAWL. Kent came to see Cleo, but because of the crowd, they could only wave and throw kisses to each other.

One night, Jesus-3 reached through the gate and touched a poodle with arthritis. An old man holding the poodle jumped up and down and shouted, "I've been healed, my arthritis pain is gone." He threw down his cane and raced away with his poodle on his shoulder. The whole episode was televised. Word spread. Multitudes came nightly to the gate to be healed, some with their pets, many without. Kent sat in the grass near the gate and watched the madness night after night, comforted by the knowledge that soon he and Cleo would be off to New York.

❦

Frank Chisholm hadn't an inkling of what was going on at the hospital gate. Busy sublimating his sexual desires for Tracy Fedler into his more acceptable passion golf; he chased the little white ball around the links from sunup to sunset. In a freezing drizzle, when more sane aficionados of the sport retreated to the clubhouse to watch Tiger Woods' putting videos, Frank was out there swinging his irons and woods like a man possessed. Playing golf was his way of taking a cold shower. Because when he took a hot shower, Tracy was there in the video of his mind, and he behind the shower curtain doing a hand job. He wanted Tracy in his bed, not his head. If he couldn't have her in his bed, he'd like her out of his head. And that's why he was sublimating. After all, he was the head psychiatrist and chief executive of Bolton Mental. He golfed even when the water hazards froze over.

After a long passionate late evening shower, Frank walked into the living room in his bathrobe and turned on the TV. His wife sat in a recliner sewing nametags onto little sweaters for her Beanie Babies. Frank squinted at the TV. There stood Jesus-3 at the hospital gate preaching to an enormous crowd.

"What the hell's going on?!"

Frank shut off the TV, picked up the phone, and called Morgan.

"Haven't you debunked that Jesus character yet? What do you mean, you're working on it? He's on television, preaching. Well, turn on your TV. Listen, I want this guy restricted to the ward and an orderly watching him every minute. I don't want any more public exposure. And have the intern zonk him with a sedative." Frank slammed down the phone. "Damn underlings. If you want something done right, you have to do it yourself."

His wife looked at him with a half smile, holding up a Beanie Baby nametag. "How do you like the name Okapi?"

Frank, not used to hearing his wife's voice, stomped off to his bedroom. He wished the army of Beanie Babies sprawled over his wife's bedroom would somehow suffocate her during the night. *Thirty-five years of marriage and how do you like the name Okapi?*

❦

Mr. Carl Harris, a successful Los Angeles TV producer, who after a near-death experience from a heart attack had given up his mistress, race car driving, and flying in airplanes, had a blowout on his SUV while driving across the country. Luckily, he wasn't injured. The owner of Bolton Conoco charged him an extra twenty-five bucks to put on new tires after hours. Waiting in the grimy service station, Carl sipped on a can of Pepsi and watched Jesus-3 deliver an entire gate sermon on local TV. Huge crowd. A terrific sermon. And this character claimed to be Jesus.

An hour later, lead-footing down the interstate on new rubber, Carl got an idea. He called his assistant in L.A. "Mike, I need a camera crew right away. A place called Bolton. This is big. Jesus may have come back."

Chapter 45
DOCUMENTARY

Frank burst into Tracy Fedler's office without knocking, breathing heavily, his eyes wide with excitement. "Guess what? I just got a call from Carl Harris, the TV producer. You know, the one who discovered Selena Rosalina. He wants to do a documentary on Bolton Mental."

Tracy swiveled from her computer, leaned back in her chair, and crossed her legs. Frank felt a stirring in his loins as he eyed the smooth contour of her knees.

"Why us, Dr. Chisholm?"

"Mr. Harris said a computer selected us. He wants to document the modern advances in psychiatry at randomly selected hospitals."

Tracy's mouth curved to a generous smile. "That's great."

"Yeah, but what if it doesn't come out right," Frank stammered, frowning. "What if they paint a negative image of us?"

Tracy swiveled back to her computer. "Look at this."

Frank leaned forward, his chin brushing her shoulder. He inhaled her perfume as he stared at the computer's screen. His heart pounded and tremors raced through his limbs. *My chin actually touched her.*

Tracy craned her neck to look at Frank. "The long column represents accounts payable; the short column, receivables. We have about two months before the cash box dries up. Bankruptcy."

Bolton Mental going belly-up. Frank had known it all along; he had just refused to think about it. The end of Bolton Mental meant the end of his career. He had no retirement. No savings. Nothing but his golf clubs and a collection of fuckin' Beanie Babies. He would end up a FIG. He forced a smile. "Maybe business will pick up if we get a some good PR from this documentary?"

Tracy shrugged. "Worth a try."

Being this close to Tracy set off a montage of shower flicks in Frank's head. He stumbled out of Tracy's office dazed, with an erection, covered in goose bumps, an idiotic grin on his face. He didn't look like a man on the brink of bankruptcy.

"Good luck with the documentary, Frank."

Frank! She called me Frank.

In the Emerald Room of the Bolton Holiday Inn, Carl Harris gave final instructions to his film crew. "I want two of you recording with hidden cameras everything this Jesus patient does and says. The rest of you wander around the hospital and pretend to be filming a documentary."

Chapter 46
BLOOD OF PATRIOTS

Moko Kaku broke the story of the Kaku Islands uprising to the world at a surprise press conference. The bellicose dictator brandishing a machete, his face engraved with deep lines of rancor, came across with the television presence of a gargoyle as he laid out his demands for release of the hostages: guaranteed sovereignty for his island kingdom, lots of money, and the return of Moko's confiscated cowbell trophies. Many viewers out in TV land thought Manuel Noriega had escaped from Federal Prison.

Sitting on hardback chairs in the day room, Kent, Jesus-3, Alonzo, and McDonald along with a dozen others watched a CNN special on the Kaku uprising and hostage situation. Jesus-3, repulsed by the images of hooded and bound hostages paraded about at spear point, surged onto his feet, his face blushed with indignation. He jabbed an incriminating finger at the TV. "You see," he shouted to the others in the day room, "you human beings are even unloving to your own kind. War, terrorism, hostage taking--all man made inventions. Why Father succored you human beings, I'll never know."

Alonzo, unraveling his head rag, hollered out, "Right on, man. There's a lot of bad shit out there."

McDonald, slobbering and trembling, nodded in agreement.

Across the nation American religious leaders, politicians, and other zealots clamored for action. A quick public opinion poll by CNN showed ninety-one percent of Americans favored a speedy military resolution to the Kaku hostage crisis.

※

Washington D.C.

White House

The President of the United States met with the Director of the FBI, the Head of the CIA, the Vice President, Joint Chiefs, and selected members of his cabinet.

"What the hell is Kaku and where is it?" The President demanded.

His advisors ensconced in comfortable leather chairs in the Oval Office stared blankly at the President.

The head of the CIA, a reserved man of quiet dignity, spoke up, "It's a very small South Pacific archipelago."

The President got up from his desk and paced. "We don't want a prolonged hostage situation on our hands. What do we do, gentleman?"

The Secretary of Agriculture, a regenerated politician with a helmet-like toupee and Howdy-Doody facelift, commented, "Whatever we do, we must be decisive. The American people demand it."

"How about a strike force," proposed the HUD secretary, a former baseball star with presidential aspirations of his own.

The Head of the CIA cleared his throat. "I'm afraid there's a strike force already on the way. Militia volunteers."

The President slapped his forehead. "Just what we need. A bunch of vigilante assholes with assault weapons. And the whole world watching. Who ordered it?"

"The CIA abnegates, sir."

The Secretary of Defense, a token minority with military medals, wagged an incriminating finger at the CIA chief. "It's one of your fucking ghost agencies."

"The CIA abnegates."

The President sat down and buried his head in his hands. "Call them back and get a real strike force in there. How about some Navy Seals?"

General Pitcher of the Joint Chiefs stood up. "They've cut off radio contact, Mr. President. I'm afraid the invasion is on whether we like it or not."

The President looked around the table. "I'm going to have somebody's head for this."

"The CIA abnegates, sir."

The FBI Director, a bald man with large ears, said reassuringly, "Don't worry, Mr. President. The Kakus have no army, no defenses, and no radar. They don't even have barbed wire fences. A Cub Scout troop could take the islands. It'll be a slam dunk."

The Secretary of Education, a senior advisor, spoke with a clear and resonant voice, "Sir, I think we should go along with this vigilante force as if it were our plan from the start. We have to appear to be in control."

The Secretary of State, the intellectual in the group, added, "With the right spin, this could be a coup for us. Could even bring some of the gun nuts and fringe elements into the party." He glanced at the others. "Here's the spin. American patriots volunteer to rescue hostages and free an island kingdom from the deadly grip of a ruthless dictator."

The president glowered. "If anything goes wrong…"

"The CIA abnegates, sir."

Later that evening the President of the United States usurped regular television programming to speak to the nation. Along with millions of others across the country, Kent and his compatriots at Bolton Mental looked on as the President compared Moko Kaku with Adolf Hitler, Benito Mussolini, Bin Laden, and Genghis Khan. "Moko Kaku is a ruthless dictator, an aggressor, a hostage-taker, and an enemy of democracy." With Gulf of Tonkin resoluteness, the President told the American people, "A Special Strike Force is on its way to Kaku this very moment to rescue hostages and free the people of Kaku from the iron grip of tyranny. This force is comprised of ordinary Americans risking their lives for freedom and justice."

When the President quoted something about *blood of patriots and tyrants*, Jesus-3 bolted from his chair, stuck his face up to the television and shouted at the President, "Forget it motherfucker. There will be no invasion. I'll destroy that Strike Force down to the last man. There's been enough bloodletting on this planet."

A member of Carl Harris' film crew recorded the entire Jesus-3 outburst with a miniature camera hidden in his shirt pocket.

McDonald looked at Jesus-3 and blurted, "You can't be Jesus. You just said, 'motherfucker'."

"I was pissed off," Jesus-3 retorted. "Mark my word. There will be no invasion."

Chapter 47
OPERATION KAKU

The prow of the USS Nixon cut through the blue-green fabric of the Pacific like tailor's shears. Rummels, standing on the bridge, the salty nip of the sea in his face, peered at the iridescent sunset reflecting off calm waters. His eyes moved to the twenty-two Seahawk helicopters tethered to the flight deck. Gleaming rotor blades folded over the chopper's fuselages like resting wings on giant dragonflies.

Rummels had put his team together in record time. Ordinary citizens molded into a strike force. He felt proud. This was his operation, his responsibility. Pride quickly vanished, swept away by a black fear. This was also his last chance. One more fuck-up and his head would be on the CRAWL chopping block.

The main island of Kaku lay fifty miles straight ahead. Darkness would soon veil the deep, and Rummels would shout out the orders setting Operation Kaku into motion. He visualized it. The man to his right, Major Moloney, a butcher by trade and weekend warrior for the thrill of it, would repeat Rummels' commands over the ship's intercom. Pilots would scramble onto the flight deck. Engines would roar and the blades of the twenty-two Seahawk helicopters would open up like giant umbrellas. Once the rotator heads engaged, the blades would become whirling circles of steel, whipping the deck air into a tempest.

Rummels would order onto the deck two platoons of Militia, fully equipped and combat ready, faces inked for night fighting. They would board the Seahawks for the short flight to Kaku City on the opposite side of the island. The hostages and their captors would be asleep when the Strike Force swept down. The operation should be bloodless. Rummels doubted a single shot would be fired.

As the sun sank to the crest of the sea, Rummels thought about the aftermath. The freed hostages sailing home with him on the Nixon. Moko Kaku in shackles. A ticker tape parade. Television appearances. A book deal. A political career.

It was time. At twenty-three hundred hours, Rummels shouted out the fateful orders. Major Moloney relayed the orders over the intercom. The choppers roared to life. The rotators engaged and the Seahawks' steel blades lifted, spinning like…suddenly THE GATES OF HELL BLEW OPEN! A horrific, discordant clanging rang out, a deafening noise louder than a million Maytag washers hitting the rinse cycle at the same time. Sparks big as thunderbolts flashed across the deck. The Seahawks' sixty-foot blades were six feet, four inches too long for the Nixon's deck pads. The helicopters' whirling blades clashed together like gargantuan swords, disintegrating and spraying the deck with hot shrapnel.

Crippled helicopters careened about like bumper cars. A piece of flying rotator slashed into the ship's radar and communication tower. A chunk of steel ripped through the engine control panel dumping fifteen Plutonium rods into the reactor chamber of the A4W. Other choppers burst into flames. Trapped pilots screamed in agony. Gas tanks exploded like torpedoes. Debris and body parts rained onto the deck. The USS Nixon lit up like a floating casino. Rummels' bowels twisted into knots as he watched the devastation in stunned disbelief.

"The helicopter blades are too fuckin' long," screamed Major Moloney.

Rummels doubled over in pain. It hadn't occurred to him different helicopters might have different size blades. *Why hadn't someone told me the Nixon's lift pads weren't designed for Seahawks?*

Colonel Henry, the officer in charge of the assault force, ordered his combat-ready commandos onto the deck, two platoons coming from opposite directions, foredeck and aft. The sight of exploding helicopters and the ship's deck in flames told them the Nixon was under siege. They immediately hit the deck and fired into the night air and at each other. The sound of automatic rifles and screams of men cut down by friendly fire added to the pandemonium.

Rummels shouted over the intercom, "Cease firing, men. You're shooting each other." Weapons' fire quickly drowned out his voice.

Two hours later, when ammunition ran low, the firing stopped. Colonel Henry stepped out from a bulkhead and shouted above the cries of the wounded, "We're not under siege, you idiots. Regroup."

Organized into teams, his men battled the deck fires, carried the wounded below, stacked the dead into neat piles, and shoved the burning helicopters over the side.

Rummels listened soberly to a junior officer's damage estimate. "Sixty-five dead, forty wounded, sir. Twelve Seahawks lost. Ten choppers remain intact. We're assessing the damage in the engine room now."

Operation Kaku hadn't even begun and over half the choppers and a quarter of the Strike Force were lost. Rummels knew there would be no best selling book. No political career. He sucked deeply on his asthma inhaler. If he didn't get Operation Kaku going and the hostages freed, a CRAWL annihilation order with his name on it would be forthcoming.

He instructed the junior officer, "Forget about assessing the damage below. Get this operation under way. Now!" He turned to Major Moloney. "We got ten helicopters and four hours of night cover. Get moving."

"Right away, sir."

Rummels and his junior officer watched the troops cram into the ten undamaged helicopters, which this time had plenty of room for the blades to open. At last, the helicopters lifted off into the night air. Operation Kaku was underway.

The junior officer turned to Rummels. "Pretty crowded up there, all those men in just ten helicopters."

"It's only a short jaunt."

"Sure is dark tonight, sir."

"Black as a bear's ass out there."

The junior officer smiled. "With night-vision goggles, the pilots shouldn't have any trouble, sir."

The color blanched from Rummels' face. He stared dumbfounded at the junior officer. "Night-vision goggles?"

"Yes sir. Night-vision goggles."

Rummels couldn't remember requisitioning any night-vision goggles. *Oh, shit!* Deadly mountainous terrain stood between the seashore and Kaku City. The Seahawks were flying blind. With the radio tower down there was no way to communicate with the choppers. The Strike Force was doomed. If any of the troops survived the crash-ups in the mountains, Moko's warriors would finish them off. A fatal fuck-up. Once word got back to Washington, Rummels would be good as dead. Sweat poured from his face as he climbed down from the bridge. He ordered a deck hand to prepare a motorized lifeboat for launching.

"I'm going to boat in and supervise the invasion."

The deck hand saluted. "Yes, sir."

"And fill the life boat with plenty of rations and lots of drinking water. All you can find."

"May I ask what for, sir?"

"You may not. Now get the boat ready."

"Yes, sir."

Fifteen minutes later, Rummels climbed into the lifeboat to make the run of his life, to get as far away from CRAWL as possible. As he stood in the boat waiting to be lowered into the sea, the junior officer walked up.

"Sir, there's been severe damage to the engine room. Fuel rods have spilled into the A4W reactor and pressure is building up."

"I can't be bothered with that now. I'm leaving to supervise the invasion. Lower the boat, men."

The junior officer leaned over the gunwale and shouted, "But sir, you'll never find your way to Kaku in the dark. Besides, you won't be able to see anything."

As his boat descended to the sea, Rummels shouted back to the junior officer, "Don't worry about me. Just carry on."

⚜

Three hours at ten knots into the ocean's darkness, Rummels cut the lifeboat's engine. He was far enough away from the Nixon to drift and sleep. In the morning, he'd plot a course to some insignificant island in the Molucca Sea. He hoped he would be reported to CRAWL as "missing in action."

Thirty miles away, the Plutonium rods in the Nixon's reactor chamber turned white-hot. Some of the rods melted through the carrier's steel hull, vaporizing tons of seawater. When the remaining rods reached critical mass the Nixon turned into a Plutonium bomb.

Rummels was awakened by intense light issuing from a bright spot on the horizon. He stared in disbelief as the spot grew into a giant, luminous mushroom that lit up the night sky. Then came a sonic wind, blowing his hair straight back, rattling the ribbings of the lifeboat, and loosening the fillings in his molars. His fingers dug into the gunwales. The sea swelled into a mighty wall of water and raced towards him like Armageddon.

Chapter 48
THE SECOND COMING

Carl Harris took the Candid Camera shots of Jesus-3 shouting at the television set, warning the President not to invade the Kaku Islands, deleted the word "motherfucker" and spliced in recent footage he'd received of smashed up Seahawk helicopters on Kaku mountainsides. He added video taken by Filipino fishermen of a mysterious light that lit up the Pacific in the middle of the night. He edited in shots of a huge tidal wave that apparently sunk the USS Nixon and battered miles of coastline from Australia to Taiwan.

He then repeated the Jesus-3's warning. "I'll destroy that Strike Force down to the last man." He threw in some Jesus-3 gate sermons he'd purchased from a local TV station in Bolton, and sold the documentary to CNN for three million. CNN titled it, "The Second Coming." It became the most watched documentary in television history. At the end of the documentary, Carl asked, "Did this man or being who claims he is Jesus really destroy the Kaku Strike Force? Are you prepared for the Second Coming?"

Within hours after the "Second Coming" aired, cars and buses clogged the highway into Bolton. Exhaust fumes thick as LA smog choked the air. Stop and go bumper-to-bumper traffic inched toward the new Shangri-La. Soon religious pilgrims filled the streets of Bolton, hoping to glimpse Jesus-3, to touch the hem of his gown, to fulfill twenty centuries of waiting and anticipation. The air reverberated with joyful noises. The clamor exceeded that of a Midwest University football game.

On the crowded sidewalks, habited nuns, collared clergy, and glabrous monks blended with a veritable cross-section of America: the homeless, veterans, MADD mothers, animal rights groups, gay activists, pro and anti abortion people, the press, fossil fuel lobbyists, beverage vendors, and thousands of others seeking manna and attestation. From park benches and street corners, non-celebrity Bible-flapping evangelists cried out the end of the world. Porta potties were placed strategically around town. School gymnasiums and church basements opened to handle the flood of humanity pouring into Bolton. City crews set up emergency shelters. Merchants gleamed; business had never been better.

There were skeptics. The "Guns for Jesus" militia protested with a drum-drubbing march down main street, rank and file, a hundred strong, a hybrid of Hell's Angels and the Nazi Youth Movement: shaved heads under steel helmets, vanilla bodies cloaked in combat fatigues, tattooed arms exposed to the shoulders. They brandished Confederate flags, crosses, assault weapons, and signs that read *Animals Suck, Jesus Hates Fags, Down with the Antichrist, Kill the Faker*.

A growing crowd pressed onto the hospital grounds, chanting, "Jesus! Jesus! Jesus!"

Dr. Frank Chisholm had quarantined Jesus-3 to the ward and assigned extra orderlies to keep an eye on the troublemaker. He then made Bolton Mental off limits to all visitors and the media. The crowd of religious pilgrims surged forward to the hospital's Gate. Local and State Police officers locked arms in front of the gate to keep them back.

"Jesus! Jesus! Jesus!"

Kent stared out the window of Ward 2 at the mayhem and chuckled. He was a sane man trapped inside a mental hospital, while outside the whole world had gone nuts.

Kent thought Justin was going nuts, too. Last night Justin again evaded orderlies and nurses to slip into Kent's room, nervous as an expectant father, wringing his hands, worrying about Gamuka, who just when he seemed to be coming out the wormhole, slipped back into a stupor worst then before.

"His heart beat completely disappears and his body turns ice-water cold. And there's another problem," Justin announced in an alarming tone, "that kid with a pimply face, McDonald, he's following me around the hospital at night like a slobbering bloodhound. It's getting harder and harder to lose him. I bet he's a CRAWL agent. It's just a matter of time before he discovers Gamuka's hiding place."

Kent looked incredulously at Justin. "I heard the interns say electric shock treatments had cooked McDonald's brain. He's wandering around at night because he's confused and lost. He couldn't hurt a flea."

"If you're wrong, Gamuka and me are dead meat."

Chapter 49
TRACY'S PLAN

Tracy knocked on Frank's office door, opened it, stuck her head inside, and smiled. "Mind if I come in?"

Frank leaped up from his desk in a total body reflex, his smile too huge and juicy to suggest mere politeness. "Please do come in. Would you like some coffee?" Frank feinted toward the coffee pot in the corner, never taking his eyes off Tracy.

She strode over and placed her hand on Frank's forearm. "No thanks. I need to talk to you about something very important."

Standing face to face with the ruling passion of his life, Frank felt an irregular patter to his heart, and his eyes glazed over like a man on a drug high. *She touched my arm.* Tracy looked terrific in her green blazer and sky blue skirt tapered to slightly above the knees. Her voice was a silken whisper. "I think we can turn a major problem into something advantageous. Frank, are you listening to me?"

"Sorry, oh yes, uh-huh, I was preoccupied."

"That's quite understandable with all that's going on. That's what I want to talk about. Jesus-3."

Frank frowned. "That maniac is driving us all nuts. If I keep him secluded, all this uproar will eventually settle down. I know how to handle his kind."

She looked steadily at Frank. "We're getting calls from all the major networks. They want to telecast the gate sermons. They want Jesus-3 on national TV."

Frank blinked in confusion. "I just don't get it. All he does is lecture about being kind to animals and gives that same old Sermon on the Mount speech."

"It's not what he says. The public thinks he's performed a miracle by calling on the forces of nature to destroy the Kaku Strike Force."

"You don't believe that, do you?"

Tracy shrugged. "It doesn't matter what I believe. The public's bought it."

Frank Chisholm did the impossible; he turned away from Tracy and stared out the window at the riotous crowd at the hospital gate. Folie a Deux on a mass scale. "No way am I going to let that impostor turn my hospital into a circus."

Tracy positioned herself between Frank and the window, her hand on his chest. His heart thumped heavily now. He gasped. *My God. She touched me again.*

Tracy spoke softly. "We've gotten generous offers from all the major networks." Her fingers moved under his tie. "They all want to do a special on Jesus-3. CNN is proposing a live debate between Jesus-3 and some guy from the American Theological Institute. It's a package deal, two gate sermons and one debate."

"Really."

"Yes. The networks are bidding against each other. The top offer so far is four million. I think we could get five for the full package."

She unbuttoned his shirt. Frank was a man dying of thirst, standing on the edge of an oasis. Tracy looked up at him and smiled. "Five million, Frank. The two of us could go anywhere in the world. I could deposit the money in a Swiss account for us. All you have to do is say the word."

Frank's shirt was wide open now, his tie over his shoulder. Tracy bent and kissed his left nipple. Frank wheezed as if the wind had been sucked out of him. He tried to speak but his tongue hung in his mouth stiff as frozen meat. He was paralyzed, except for a silly grin slowly widening into a huge smile. The smile of someone who had just won the lottery. And the gods were smiling back, handing to him the goddess of his fantasies and five million bucks. Adios FIGville. He would have Tracy and more money than he ever dreamed. They could go anywhere in the world. It would be weeks before his wife realized he was missing. She'd probably learn of it some Saturday afternoon at bridge club.

He swept Tracy into his arms and pressed his lips hard against hers. He could hear the shower running and could feel its wetness. But this was no fantasy. Tracy was right here in his arms. He was kissing her.

Tracy pushed against his chest to free herself as she gasped for air.

"Frank, you're hurting me."

"I can't wait. I must have you." He circled her waist with his right arm, his left hand working the hem of her skirt up her thighs.

"Frank, the window is wide open and the door is unlocked."

"I don't care."

With amazing strength, Tracy whirled and shoved him up against the window.

"Cool it, Frank! You could ruin everything. We've got to be careful."

"Of course, you're right," Frank stammered, "I lost my head."

Tracy straightened her skirt. "I'll call the network and make the deal. Once we get the check, we're out of Bolton. And Frank, I'll make it so good for you."

Frank was a little boy who had just been scolded then promised a new bicycle. At the door, Tracy turned, walked back over and pecked him on the cheek.

"We're doing the right thing, you know. We're doing it for us."

"Yes, Tracy. For us."

Later that afternoon, Frank rushed over to Jesus-3's room on Ward 2 with a box of Russell Stover Chocolates tucked under his arm. With a wave of his hand, he dismissed the orderlies assigned to guard the patient. He gazed down at Jesus-3 sitting on the edge of his bed. "I'm Dr. Chisholm, your psychiatrist." He handed Jesus-3 the box of chocolates. "You're not confined to your room any longer. I've sent the orderlies away."

"Thank you. Anything I can do for you?"

Frank smiled. "Well, yes, there is. I'd like you to resume your Gate Sermons."

Jesus-3 let out a grunt. "Don't think so. Father doesn't really care for television evangelism. Too many money changers in that temple."

"I could get you canteen and movie passes. For six passes all you'd have to do is two sermons plus one live television debate with a professor from the American Theological Institute."

Jesus-3 looked at the floor, averting his gaze. "I'm sorry, Dr. Chisholm. I've come to earth this time for the animals and they don't watch television."

"Would you like to have your own private big screen TV? You could keep it right here in your room."

Jesus-3 shook his head.

"A car? A slightly used Mercury Cougar." Jesus-3 made no response. Frank frowned. "Not interested in material things, huh?"

Alonzo standing in the doorway said, "Hey, man, I'll do some sermons for you."

Frank closed the door and sat down on the bed beside Jesus-3. He lowered his voice. "What if I released you from the hospital with a notarized certificate stating that you are sane. With that certificate, you could resume your animal ministry. Just two sermons and one debate. What do you say?"

Jesus-3 looked up at Frank and smiled pleasantly. "Okay, I'll do it. I'm just spinning my wheels here anyway. I should be about my Father's business."

Frank lit up like a cocaine snorter with a fresh fix. He hugged Jesus-3 and waltzed off the ward happy as an attorney whose client had just been awarded punitive damages.

Chapter 50
GATE SERMON I

Klieg lights cut through the evening's darkness and lit up the hospital's grounds around the gate and the street beyond like daylight. Camera crews waited expectantly, ready to televise the first of the two gate sermons Jesus-3 had agreed to. Outside the fence, a huge crowd milled impatiently. The side door of Building B opened. A security guard stuck his head out, looked around and motioned for Jesus-3, Kent, and McDonald to step out.

The three patients walked slowly toward the gate, Jesus-3's white hospital gown fluttering in the cool breeze. Kent and McDonald wore street clothes. When they neared the gate, the crowd went wild. A gigantic roar punctuated with hallelujahs filled the air. The spontaneous singing and loud cheering could have drowned out a *Grateful Dead* concert. The stroboscopic effect of camera flashes and fireworks heightened the acid rock ambiance.

Kent had accompanied Jesus-3 hoping to see Cleo, but in the bright lights he saw only a faceless multitude. McDonald asked to come along after he'd received a call on his cell phone from CRAWL headquarters. CRAWL superiors granted McDonald an emergency annihilation license over the phone and informed him that he was the most strategically located CRAWL agent in the world. They ordered him to protect Jesus-3 at all cost until they figured out whether he was friend or foe. They also ordered McDonald to proceed with the annihilations of Kumarmar Gamuka and Justin Freely.

McDonald stumbled towards the bright lights, drooling, shaking, his eyes crossing erratically. All at once, he tripped over his feet and fell face down. Jesus-3 bent down and helped him back to his feet. The crowd cheered as if a miracle had been performed. Kent noticed the metallic glint from an object under McDonald's shirt.

Jesus-3 stepped up to the gate, his white gown luminescent in the bright lights. Cheers and praises filled the exultant air. The lame, the sick, the old, reporters, and hundreds of others with camcorders and cell phone cameras rushed to the gate. To maintain a free zone in front of the gate Police and National Guardsmen fended off those to whom seeing-was-believing but touching was absolute proof. Fathers held up their children to be blessed. Grandmothers wept. The afflicted and suffering stretched out their arms to be touched and healed. Hallelujahs rang out.

Jesus-3 attempted to speak, but twanging guitars, blaring flutes, and church choruses belting out hymns drowned him out. Thousands of rejoicing, arm waving believers sang and danced hysterically in front of the gate. Jesus-3 held his hands aloft to quiet the crowd but it had no effect.

"Could you hold down the noise for a few minutes? I'd like to say something."

His words were unheard. The night's religious fervor had no limits; the crowd, a single organism now, swayed and moved like a giant ameba. The air filled with noise and song and jubilation.

BOOM! An earsplitting explosion shook the ground. A gust of fiery wind ripped opened the fence and hurled the Iron Gate into the air.

Someone shouted, "Bomb."

The music stopped; screams filled the night air. The frighten crowd trampled the old and the lame in a mad stampede for safety.

Three men with "Guns For Jesus" armbands charged through a gaping hole in the fence, firing handguns at Jesus-3 trapped helplessly under the dismantled gate. Bullets zinged off the gate's iron bars. Two of the assailants were cut down by police fire. The third assailant raced over and aimed his gun directly at Jesus-3's head. The feeble McDonald, surging with adrenaline, leaped through the air like a Jedi, a butcher knife in his hand. He tore the gun from the assailant's hand and plunged his knife deep into man's chest. The assailant fell dead.

A dozen policemen lifted the heavy gate off Jesus-3 who was miraculously unhurt. Sirens blared. Police quickly cordoned off the area. Emergency medical crews attended the moaning wounded. A mangled arm hung on the fence, fingers still quivering. Cleo, fearing Kent may have been injured, pushed through the panicky crowd. A policeman stopped her at the fence.

"Go home," the policeman ordered, "show's over."

☙❧

Back on the ward, Jesus-3 shook a finger at McDonald who'd collapsed into a chair.

"That was a wanton and sinful act," Jesus-3 admonished. "Under no circumstances should you take another's life."

"Wait a minute," Kent interrupted. "McDonald saved your life when he killed that man."

Jesus-3 rolled his eyes. "You still don't get it, do you? Read my lips. 'Thou shall not kill'. That's a direct order, pure and simple. And don't try to fine-tune it. It's been two thousand years since I was here last and you humans haven't improved a shred."

McDonald raised his red-topped, nodding head. "You're not Je-Je-Jesus. You called the president a 'm-m-motherfucker."

"The president is a motherfucker. His wife's a mother. Presidents Jefferson and Washington were slave-fuckers." Jesus-3 stared hard at McDonald. "How can you be offended by mere utterances, no matter how repugnant to your dainty sense of decorum, when you just brutally slew a man?"

McDonald's face turned as red as his hair. His eyes uncrossed momentarily and he spoke out with a minimum of stuttering. "I slew him because it was m-m-my job. I'm a CRAWL agent here on another assignment but I was ordered to protect you. The Guns For Jesus m-m-m-militia want you dead, they consider you a threat to the American way of life and the firearm business."

Jesus-3's eyes fluttered. "'Guns for Jesus', that's an oxymoron if I ever heard one."

Kent knew what McDonald's other assignment was. This redheaded kid with a scrambled egg brain, despite appearances, was a highly trained, deadly assassin. Justin was right. He and Gamuka were in grave danger.

Chapter 51
GATE SERMON II

Despite the disastrous gate sermon, Jesus-3 agreed to do a second one, plus the live television debate. "A deal is a deal," he told Frank who was elated.

Frank's five million and his dream of spending the rest of his life with Tracy remained intact. He ordered the fence mended and the mangled Iron Gate replaced with a bigger, stronger gate. Local authorities tightened up security around Bolton Mental and insisted on proper protection for Jesus-3. Frank drove all the way to St. Louis in a U-Haul to pick up a bulletproof Plexiglas box from an Ecclesiastical supply house, the very box the Pope rode around in when he visited St. Louis years ago.

Frank had the Plexiglas box mounted on his boat trailer and hitched it up to his riding lawnmower. He'd personally drive Jesus-3 to the gate for the second sermon. In the meantime, Tracy had canceled the hospital's annual "patients vs. staff" volleyball game to make ready the hospital's gymnasium for the upcoming live television debate.

Jesus-3 stood ten feet tall and bulletproof as he rolled up to the gate inside the Plexiglas box for Gate Sermon Two. The crowd was larger than ever. McDonald followed behind, stumbling and slobbering, butcher knife in belt. Police and National Guardsmen were everywhere. Loudspeakers mounted on the sides of the Plexiglas box bruited Jesus-3's message to the multitude, his amplified voice rising above the music and clamor. A simple message:

"Don't fight, don't use guns, don't invade or bomb other countries. Turn the other cheek. Be kind to the animals. Keep turning those cheeks. Don't believe that crap about an eye for an eye. Love everybody. Try as hard as you can to become vegetarians."

He then gave his usual Sermon on the Mount talk, throwing kisses at the sick people and animals. Finally, Frank fired up the lawnmower and drove off with Jesus-3 waving to the cheering multitude from inside the fogged-up Plexiglas box.

Frank was just one debate away from five million dollars, Tracy, and getting-the-hell out of town.

That night Justin snuck into Kent's room wringing his hands and fretting about McDonald. Kent rolled out of bed and placed a hand on Justin's shoulder. "You were right. McDonald is a CRAWL agent. I saw him kill a man."

Justin's knees turned to Jell-O. "I told you. It's only a matter of time."

Kent eyed Justin keenly. "After the big television debate, McDonald will turn his attention to you and Gamuka. But don't worry. We won't let anything happen."

Justin's gaze lowered. "You can't stop them. It's hopeless, we're trapped here like caged animals."

"It's not hopeless. I've got a plan. We'll escape during the debate while McDonald and security are busy protecting Jesus-3. Everyone at the hospital will be watching the debate. No one will be watching us."

Justin looked up. "You think it'll work?"

"We'll make it work."

Justin and Kent tiptoed by the night nurse sleeping in a chair in the medication room. Gingerly, Kent picked up the ward telephone and punched in Cleo's number at the Snore Motel.

"Cleo," he whispered, "we're getting out of here."

"Huh. What time is it?"

Kent cupped the phone to his lips. "Listen carefully. I want you to bring the Camaro around to the south end of the hospital grounds at seven-thirty on the evening of the big debate, that's day after tomorrow. Be packed and ready to go. Justin and I along with Gamuka will slip out through the underground passage while everyone is watching the debate and meet you at the south end of the fence. Oh, you'll have to cut a hole in the fence for us."

"I'll pick up some wire cutters."

"Bye."

"Be careful."

The countdown to New York was on.

Chapter 52
THE DEBATE

CNN transformed Bolton Mental's gymnasium into a temporary TV studio. Technicians strewn brightly colored cables across the hardwood floor and busily fussed with light meters, headphones, and cameras. Glaring lights focused on a round table at half-court where makeup artists penciled and highlighted the faces of two men seated under the lights.

The clean-shaven man, Ed Nikkels of "Night Column," a familiar face to late night TV audiences, would moderate the evening's event. He promised the television public the greatest debate since the Kennedy-Nixon fray. The other man, Thomas Davenport, a famous theologian and debunker of religious pretenders, Jesus-3's opponent, sat perfectly still while a young woman filled in his eyebrows with mascara. Dusky makeup softened the glare from his bald spot. A dark beard lent to his face a distinguished, prophetical look.

Davenport had flown into Bolton with Ed Nikkel on a network jet. On the plane, over cocktails, Ed had told him, "I really don't believe in this Jesus guy, despite the Kaku miracle."

Davenport smirked. "There won't be any believers when I finish with him."

"Mind telling me how you'll accomplish that?"

"Easy. I'm going to ask him to perform a miracle on live television."

"You devil, you. You're going to embarrass him in front of two hundred million viewers?"

"Yup. If you don't let him wiggle out of it."

Ed smiled. "You know me better than that."

For security reasons, the live audience for the debate consisted of CNN employees and security guards. McDonald, following CRAWL orders to protect Jesus-3, snuck into the gymnasium earlier in the day and hid behind a stack of tumbling mats under the bleachers, his butcher knife tucked in his belt.

Jesus-3 arrived in his white hospital gown and took his seat across from Davenport under the lights. Ed Nikkel shook Jesus-3's hand and said, "You understand that there are no set rules for this debate. Each debater can ask and answer questions at will. The livelier the debate, the better." Ed blinked. "Television, you know."

Almost immediately a red light flashed and the lead cameraman signaled, "On the Air."

Ed looked into the camera and smiled.

"Good evening. I'm Ed Nikkel and tonight we're bringing to the world the debate everyone has been waiting for. Between the man or entity on my left who claims he is Jesus Christ comeback and on my right a leading theologian who says it's all a sham. For background, we switch to Dianne Hay. Go ahead Dianne."

Jesus-3 looked around for Dianne. Ed explained, "She isn't really here. Her part was taped in advance. It's being aired from New York. Would you like a glass of water while we're waiting?"

Davenport quipped, "Maybe he would care to part the water for us."

The television audience, the largest since the Super Bowl, watched Dianne Hay's background and setup, which used clips of the "Second Coming" including pictures of crashed-up helicopters and the recording of Jesus-3's admonishment of the President.

"Was this coincidence," Dianne asked, "or did this mental patient, who claims he is Jesus, really destroy the Kaku Strike Force?"

Dianne then did a short eulogy for the courageous men of the USS Nixon, followed by an update on Kaku. "There has been a happy ending to this tragedy. The hostages have been released. The United States is building a new medical school on the main island of Kaku, and British Petroleum has begun offshore drilling for oil."

Then came Dianne's piece on Davenport, using video clips with voice over. "This is the man who proved the underwater photos of Pharaoh's chariots at the bottom of the Red Sea were a hoax. The man who used chemical analysis to show that the rocks found at the alleged site of ancient Gomorra were limestone, not brimstone. The man who proved with carbon dating that the wooden debris on a mountainside in Turkey was not the remains of Noah's Ark. The man who says he will prove beyond any doubt that the gentleman seated across from him is not Jesus Christ."

The debate shifted live to the Bolton Mental gymnasium. On the air, Davenport asked Jesus-3, "How did you get here this time? Was it a virgin birth again or did you arrive in a chariot of clouds?"

"I was brought here to this hospital after being arrested in the kill room of a slaughter house."

"Before that. How did you get down here to earth?"

"Earth isn't necessarily down. In reality, there isn't any such thing as direction. Earth isn't down, and heaven isn't up. Everything is right there inside of you. Heaven. Even Hell."

Davenport shifted in his chair. "If there's no heaven up there, where do people go when they die?"

"The same place animals go, which means you humans have a lot of explaining to do when you get there. You've been brutal and ruthless to all living things."

In a droning monotone Jesus-3 enumerated many of mankind's animal atrocities: packing houses, confinement hog farms, veal production, fur farming, the species cleansing of the American bison, trapping practices in Siberia, animal experimentation, cosmetic testing, cock fighting, religious sacrifices, greyhound racing, hunting, fishing…"

Davenport glared at Jesus-3. "Do you really expect people to believe you are Jesus Christ?"

"Actually, I don't care. I came to help the animals this time."

Ed Nikkel interjected. "This isn't going to be much of a debate unless you stop talking about animals. We'd like some straight forward answers to the questions please."

"I can only give you truthful answers."

Ed spoke to the camera, "We're going to break for a commercial, and when we come back, we'll have some rather pointed questions and an unusual request for our supernatural guest."

"Wait," Jesus-3 interrupted. "What kind of a commercial is it?"

"Toyota."

"Please don't show it. Automobiles kill millions of animals each year. Not to mention the forty to fifty thousand Americans killed annually on highways. A lot of them children and teenagers. Thousands more are burned, disfigured, maimed, and paralyzed from auto accidents. If you don't show the commercial, you will save lives and prevent suffering."

The chief cameraman looked at Ed with a blank stare. Ed shrugged. A technician twelve hundred miles away on the East Coast cut to the commercial. Jesus-3 shouted, "Don't roll that commercial."

Chapter 53
DEBATE FIZZLES

Cleo parked the Camaro on a side street south of the hospital grounds, a good twenty yards from the hospital's security fence. She stepped from the car, wire cutters in hand, and in the dusky twilight of evening noticed something moving in the grass along the fence. She quickly ducked behind the Camaro. Twelve armed men in combat fatigues, on hands and knees, weapons slung across their backs, quietly slipped onto the hospital grounds through a hole cut in the fence. They disappeared into the tall grass on the other side.

Guns for Jesus militia. The hospital is under siege.

Cleo jumped into the Camaro and sped towards east side of the hospital grounds. The fence there was much closer to the main buildings, giving her a slight time advantage over the Guns for Jesus invaders.

༄

Fully dressed and ready to make his escape from Bolton Mental, Kent paced in his room, waiting for Justin. All the other patients crowded around the TV in the Day Room to watch the debate. A large screen TV had been set up in the dining area for hospital employees, the overflow gathering in the nurses' lounge to watch on yet another TV. *This was the perfect time to escape. Come on Justin.* Kent glanced at the clock. *Where is he?*

Kent walked out into the Day Room and stared at the TV.

Davenport asked Jesus-3, "You claim that you came to minister to the animals, yet you involved yourself in the Kaku situation. Why?"

"To quote a famous human being, 'Injustice anywhere is a threat to justice everywhere'."

Alonzo leaped out of his chair in front of the TV, shook his fist and yelled, "Give 'em hell, Jesus."

On TV Davenport simpered, "Then you are concerned about people and their problems?"

"Of course," Jesus-3 replied, "human beings are animals, too."

Kent staggered back, surprised by Jesus-3's pronouncement. His words were tantamount to old Hoover's declaration back in biology class, "We're all animals." Kent had a strange feeling that somehow everything was coming full circle. Then he heard Justin calling out in a low voice, "Kent, over here."

Quietly, Kent slipped out into the hallway where Justin stood beside his duffel, looking like a grimy chimneysweep at the end of a hard day.

Kent glanced at the duffel. "Why did you bring Gamuka here? I thought we were going to pick him up in the underground passage when we escaped."

Justin's face scrunched up. "I couldn't leave him. Just an hour ago he sat up, fully awake, and asked for a drink of water. I went to fetch some water and when I returned he was back in a coma, cold as ice." Justin shook all over. "Kent, I can't find his pulse at all."

"You don't think…"

"I don't know, I'm really worried. He's never felt this cold before."

Kent glanced at his watch. "Justin, if we're going to get out here, now's the time."

Justin sighed heavily. "We can't take the back steps, they're setting up another TV set in the corridor for the orderlies to watch. I just barely made it through."

"In that case, we'll just walk out the front entrance like we own the place. Once outside we'll make a run for the fence."

Justin picked up the duffel and slung it over his back. "Let's go."

Headed for the building's main entrance and freedom, Justin and Kent rushed downstairs into the spacious foyer of Building B and abruptly slowed down. Two uniformed guards stood at the entrance. They eyed the scruffy, unshaven guy lugging a bag.

"You there, halt."

The color drained from Justin's face.

"What's in the bag?"

Justin mouthed something but the words failed to come out.

"Dirty laundry," Kent spoke up.

"Open it up."

Kent tried to think of a plausible explanation for what they would find in the bag. Nothing came to mind. Justin lowered the duffel to the floor and Kent unzipped it. One of the guards peered into duffel and staggered back.

"It's a dead body!"

The other guard bent over, took a look, and immediately drew a revolver from his holster. He waved the gun menacingly at the two suspects. "I'll keep them covered, Sam, you call headquarters. Better call the undertaker too."

The live TV debate continued to fizzle. Ed Nikkels' hope of going from late night to a permanent prime time slot seemed in jeopardy. Davenport wagged a finger at Jesus-3 and chided, "Why don't you minister to the people in this mental hospital? Why do you have to go off to slaughterhouses and places like that? Aren't people more important than animals?"

Jesus-3 smiled. "The patients at this hospital have doctors, psychologists, nurses, and chaplains. Animals have no one."

"You're wrong. Animals have veterinarians to care for them. You see, people do care for animals."

"Come on. Veterinarians are the Kevorkians of the animal world. When old Shep goes blind or his hips give out, people don't have his cataracts removed and they don't spend ten thousand dollars for new hips. The Vet zaps old Shep and replaces him with a cute little puppy. Veterinarians keep livestock healthy for slaughter. They inspect meat. Put down strays. They groom pets that don't want to be groomed. They do all sorts of things, but they do very little for the animals."

"Oh yeah, how about veterinarians in zoos?"

"Prison doctors."

Ed Nikkels fidgeted. Another five minutes eaten up by animals. This was going to be the biggest TV embarrassment since Geraldo Rivera broke into Capone's vault. Under the table, he tapped Davenport on the leg with his shoe. Time to request the miracle.

Davenport asked Jesus-3, "You realize, don't you, that nearly two hundred million people are watching us on television at this moment?"

"Really, that many?"

"And whatever you say or do here tonight, the whole world will be watching and listening. You could make the whole world believe in you, tonight."

"I only want to tell everyone to be kind to the animals and to try real hard to become vegetarians."

Davenport's face reddened. "That's not what I'm getting at. Listen carefully. I'm asking you to perform a miracle right now, right here on live television with the whole world watching. If you are who you say you are, it shouldn't be a problem. However, we both know you can't perform a miracle. Because you're a fake." Davenport leaned back in his chair and folded his arms on his chest.

A sudden silence fell over the Day Room as nurses, patients, and orderlies waited for Jesus-3's response, all eyes on the big screen TV. Then Alonzo shoved his fist into the air. "Come on, Jesus, show 'em what you can do."

Jesus-3's voice deepened, his tone authoritative. "Everybody wants a fucking sign. I haven't been this angry since I chased the moneychangers from the temple." With that, he leaped up and walked away.

Ed Nikkel shouted, "Wait. Where are you going?"

Davenport snickered, "Perhaps he's going outside to find an olive tree to uproot, or a mountain to move."

Ed Nikkel, Davenport, camera crew, and a small army of technicians followed Jesus-3 out of the gymnasium. The slobbering McDonald stumbled along behind them.

Ed Nikkel talked into his microphone as he trotted along across the hospital grounds. "This man who claims to be Jesus has been challenged to perform a miracle. We're following him across the grounds of this mental institution. Don't touch your remotes. I'm not sure where he is headed, but we're going to stay with him."

Chapter 54
SHOOT OUT

Cleo tossed her wire cutters aside and squiggled through the hole she had just cut in the fence. She brushed away the grass clinging to her new pant's suit and raced towards the gray stone building about a hundred yards away. She prayed she would get there ahead of the Guns For Jesus militia. She was almost there when an ambulance and two police cars, sirens blaring, pulled up in front of the building. A doctor in a white coat, three EMTs, and four police officers rushed inside with a gurney. Cleo followed them into the foyer, and the scene there startled her. Kent and Justin stood spread-eagle against a wall, security guards searching them. EMTs surrounded the gurney on which lay the cadaverous Gamuka. The doctor bent over the gurney and placed his stethoscope on Gamuka's bony chest.

Cleo leaped out of the way as Jesus-3 stormed through the door into the foyer, trailed by Ed Nikkel, Davenport, and the CNN camera crew. Then McDonald stumbled in. Police officers and security guards rushed across the foyer to halt the moving debate team. Cleo ran to Kent and threw her arms around him. They hugged for the fist time since being admitted to Bolton Mental. "Thank goodness you're safe," Cleo said, a bewildered expression on her face. "The Guns for Jesus Militia are on the grounds. We got to get out of here."

The doctor examining Gamuka looked up from the gurney and announced, "No CPR for this guy. He's stone dead."

The door opened again and an undertaker roared inside with a gurney of his own.

"He's all yours," the doctor told the undertaker. "Pretty smelly. Better embalm first, then call the coroner for an autopsy."

Justin yelled, "You can't embalm him! He's caught in a wormhole. He's trying to come out. Please, give him some time."

The excitement and commotion elated Ed Nikkel as he stood in the foyer surrounded by police, a dead man, a doctor, an undertaker, and a shabby hobo arguing with the undertaker. Ed narrated for the TV audience: "Ladies and gentlemen, there is a dead man right here in front of me and the police apparently have two suspects. The action is picking up here at the mental hospital."

Justin raced over and snatched Gamuka off the undertaker's gurney and made a break for the door. A burly security guard yanked Gamuka out of Justin's arms and plunked him back down on the gurney. Justin kicked the guard in his knee. The guard shoved Justin into the gurney, which shot across the floor and slammed into the wall. Gamuka bounced off the gurney. Jesus-3 dove and scooped the desiccated philosopher-field-goal-kicker up in his arms before he hit the floor. The television cameras and all eyes focused on Jesus-3, Gamuka cradled in his arms. Then....

Gamuka woke up!

Back from the wormhole, Gamuka raised his head and looked around at the cameras, the people, the gurneys, and at Jesus-3.

Ed Nikkel screamed into his microphone, "The dead man's eyes have opened. He was just pronounced dead and now he's moving. He's alive. It's a miracle! A miracle! It doesn't get any better than this folks. A real live resurrection."

McDonald hunched down, the butcher knife in his hand, and inched across the foyer toward Gamuka.

The door to the foyer flew open and twelve Guns for Jesus soldiers brandishing assault rifles rushed inside and took up positions along the wall. The lettering on their red and yellow armbands read, "Antichrist Assassination Squad." They leveled their weapons at Jesus-3 and Gamuka. The fiery squad commander, a short man with the hot blue eyes of a fanatic, stepped forward. "Everybody on the floor."

Only McDonald and Jesus-3 with Gamuka in his arms remained standing. The squad commander shouted to McDonald, "You, down on the floor." He pointed at Jesus-3. "We want him."

"This is unbelievable," Ed Nikkel whispered to his TV audience from under the undertaker's gurney. "We've just had a resurrection and now a rebellion."

McDonald seemed to be in a state of extreme uncertainty, his eyes shifting back-and-forth from Gamuka to the blue-eyed commander. The butcher knife shook violently in his hand. Then with cobra quickness, he hurled the butcher knife end-over-end across the foyer, striking the Guns For Jesus commander in the chest. The surprised commander, gasped, dropped his weapon and fell to the floor. Blood gushed from his mouth.

Discharges from eleven assault rifles reverberated in the hallway. Bullets shredded McDonald like lettuce; slobber, blood, and fragments of human tissue flying from his dancing, disintegrating body and splattering over the foyer. Guns blazed all around when the police officers and the security guards returned the assassins' fire. Bullets pocked walls, shattered glass, and zinged off the ironwork around the doorframe. Jesus-3 caught a bullet in his left elbow that spun him around, dropping Gamuka onto the floor. A second bullet hit Jesus-3 in the upper chest slamming him to floor. Ed Nikkel from under a gurney gave a running commentary on the gunfight. "It looks like a Clint Eastwood shootout in here. Bullets flying everywhere."

A bullet fragmented a fuse box on the wall and everything went black.

Justin cradling Gamuka in his arms whispered to Kent and Cleo, "This is our chance. The door behind us leads to an inner corridor."

"No," Cleo cried, "I'm not leaving without Jesus-3."

"Okay. Okay."

Muzzle flashes spurted in the darkness like dragon's breath, bullets whizzing in the air. Kent and Cleo crouching to the floor dragged Jesus-3 over to the small door at the back of the foyer where Justin waited with Gamuka.

Ed Nikkels narrated above the cries and the loud bursts of gunfire, "Jesus has been shot! He's down. I saw him go down. Jesus is down. Bullets are flying everywhere. It's black as night in here. What's going to happen next is any one's guess."

Justin reached up and opened the door. The corridor beyond was dark, no glimmer of light to draw fire. In the lead, Justin with Gamuka in his arms raced down the corridor. Kent and Cleo followed dragging Jesus-3, his arms slung over their shoulders. Justin who knew every nook and cranny of the hospital, deftly lead the way through a labyrinth of winding corridors until finally and breathlessly they all stopped before the massive fireplace in the Contamination Room. The din of battle could be heard in the distance. Justin pushed the firewall open and the escapees entered Justin's subterranean world.

A few yards into a passageway, Jesus-3 said in a raspy voice, "Let me rest here." Kent and Cleo lowered him onto dusty floor of old Colonel Chisholm's underground railroad. "This is far enough for me. You all go on."

Cleo knelt beside the wounded self-proclaimed king and deliverer of the animals. Her eyes had adjusted to the darkness and she could see the grimace on his pale face. "We can't leave you here. You'll die without medical help."

His voice cracked, almost inaudible at times. "Don't be silly, I can't die. Now get out of here while you can."

Justin set Gamuka down on his feet. The little field-goal kicker rocked back and forth unaccustomed to standing, his sunken eyes glancing around at the dark surroundings. His return from the bliss of a wormhole to the madness of earth must have been most unsettling. In the distance came the sound of more gunfire.

Jesus-3's eyes rolled back into his head. "The battle is waxing, my friends. You must leave now or you may not make it."

"He's right," Justin agreed.

Cleo looked up at Justin and Kent. "We can't leave him here."

"I demand that you leave me," Jesus-3 ordered. "Now please, go."

Cleo looked at Jesus-3. "Tell me. Are you really Jesus?"

His breathing deepened and from somewhere Jesus-3 marshaled the energy to speak in his soft, sermonic voice. "Whenever someone comes along and says, 'I'm from God, believe in me or perish in Hell', there's no good way to handle that predicament. It's like receiving a chain letter; if you don't send the letter on with some money, bad things are promised to happen to you. Good things and a happy ending are promised to those who do not break the chain. That's what I call extortion of the soul. Confidentially, I say to you, shred those letters and toss them to the wind." Blood foamed on his lips. "I've really good news for you. You don't have to go through the agony of wondering what to believe. The Father doesn't send out chain letters, and He doesn't send anyone to Hell. He would never send animals, including people, to eternal damnation. If He did, He wouldn't be God. So, don't worry about whether I'm Jesus." Huge drops of sweat beaded on his face. Blood soaked his white hospital gown. "We must all create heaven within ourselves. Follow this: Shun dogma. Pursue love."

Jesus-3's head slumped onto his chest, his eyes closed.

"Is he dead?"

Justin felt for a pulse. "I think so."

The report of gunfire grew louder accompanied by a distant wailing of sirens.

Kent tapped Cleo on the shoulder. "We better get out of here."

Chapter 55
TOMMY GETS SAVED

Tommy Tennyson reached the lofty peak of academic success when NASA awarded him the "Neil Armstrong Giant Leap Medallion" for the astrobiology experiments he designed. Midwest University presented him with the "Golden Thistle Award" for a new pesticide molecule he invented. Students and faculty voted him "Professor of the Year." His picture made the cover of the Alumnus Newsletter. He had gotten new prosthetic ears, more pliable than the old ones and less likely to come loose during vigorous exercise or sleep. In addition, he made it with his girlfriend—first time ever.

At the pinnacle of his career, Tommy was stricken by a severe attack of conscience. It hit him like a kidney stone in the night. The psychic pain was excruciating. Every time he fell asleep he saw the face of the man he had poisoned. He paced, pulled out chunks of hair, gritted his teeth, and doubled over in remorse. Guilt gnawed at him relentlessly. Night after night he lay awake afraid to fall asleep. He tired reading books, making egg sandwiches, and doing push-ups. There was no escaping the torment.

In the bathroom, he doused his face with cold water and looked into the mirror. He saw not the mug of an award-winning scientist, but the tortured physiognomy of a cold-blooded killer. He knew that the simpleton Kent Mullins could never come up with a *homopragmatic truth*. The poison Tommy gave him would undoubtedly prove fatal.

Tommy's attitude had been that anyone from Harkerville deserved to die. A slow agonizing death. But that was attitude. Kent Mullins was reality. One can boast of being in favor of capital punishment, but actually throwing the switch or injecting the potassium--that's another matter. Tommy, who had always felt ugly on the outside, suddenly he felt ugly inside. He sensed a vast emptiness, a deficiency of virtue and common decency. With one act of revenge, the poisoning of Kent Mullins, Tommy poisoned himself with the deadly venom of guilt and disgrace. Food lost its flavor. He became impotent. Despite massive doses of masculinizing hormones and Viagra, he was unable to perform. His girlfriend dumped him. He lost weight.

Terrifying dreams haunted Tommy. Dreams where students with large, piercing eyes stared down at him from the lecture gallery. The double doors at the side of the gallery swung open and two orderlies in white rolled in a gurney with Kent Mullins strapped to it. In the dream, Tommy demanded that Kent recite a *homopragmatic truth*. Kent cried out, "I don't know any *homopragmatic truths*."

The orderlies pulled away the sheet covering Kent's nude body and applied electrodes to his genitals. Tommy pushed the shock button. Kent convulsed and shrieked in pain. Tommy kept shocking him. Kent kept screaming, his eyes bulging, his tongue bleeding from the gnashing of his teeth, his torso twisting and his limbs thrashing. Then it was over. Kent lay motionless on the gurney. The students threw books and chairs at Tommy and shouted, "Murderer."

In another dream, Tommy pressed the sharp edge of a shiny scalpel to Kent's throat and commanded, "Tell the truth! The whole *homopragmatic truth!*" Kent was silent and the scalpel cut deep. Blood sprayed. The students in the gallery cried out, "Dr. Tennyson is a killer!" Tommy kept slicing away as if Kent were a Thanksgiving turkey.

In Tommy's worse dream, students chased him across campus yelling, "Murderer." As Tommy ran, his ears grew bigger and bigger until they flapped about his head like vulture wings. He ran into the administration building and hid under the Dean's desk.

The Dean shouted, "Come out from under there." When Tommy crawled out, the Dean laughed at him. "You look like a freak, Dr. Tennyson." The Dean punched him in the gut.

Tommy's lectures, which usually received standing ovations, became jumbled, confused, and as nonsensical as foreign films without subtitles. He often left the podium only fifteen minutes into the hour. His academic career came unglued. The university placed him on administrative leave. Madness had taken over his life. But he knew what he must do.

On a cloudy Sunday morning, Tommy drove to Harkerville, the hamlet of his sorrows. He walked by the old school yard where he had been tormented, bullied, and beaten. He felt an oppressive gloom, darker than the rain clouds gathering overhead. From the rivers of his memory poured forth the sounds of children playing, their giggling and their shouting, ringing in his head with migrainous intensity. In a schoolyard of kids, he'd been a loner, an eight year-old hiding in the shadows and darkened corners. He wished he could somehow go back in time and cancel out those painful experiences. He tried to find a pleasant spot in his memory, but there wasn't any.

Downtown, he stopped on the Peter Pan corner. The ice cream parlor was gone, but memories of that teens' hangout remained vivid in his craw. To some, loitering on this street corner had been a right of passage, a coming of age. To Tommy it had been the hellhole of his discontent. He ambled past hardware store, the bank, and the grocery. He looked at the people coming and going. Nothing had changed. For Tommy, Harkerville was a living museum of horrors.

He walked through the old neighborhood to Kent's house on the corner of Third Street, white clapboard with dark shutters. Knee-high, brown autumn grass covered the sprawling lawn. The bare branches of dead trees lent an eerie mood to the place. Newspapers cluttered the porch. The door was locked. No one answered the doorbell. Back on the street, a cold drizzle stung Tommy's face. He assumed Kent had left Harkerville in search of a *homopragmatic* truth, so he walked back downtown to ask around. No one knew Kent's whereabouts. Rumor had it he had run off with Cleo, an old girlfriend. Run off to where? Tommy had to find him. To save himself, he first had to save Kent Mullins. Overhead came the sound of thunder, like the roar of lions.

Tommy wandered the streets. Dark rain clouds spit at him. Voices from the past mocked him. *Hey Dumbo! Can I piss in your ear? Freak. Weirdo.* New voices echoed in his head. *Killer. Murderer. Poisoner.*

Soon the rain came in torrents. Chased by the voices in his head, Tommy stumbled into an alley. He shuddered in the wet coldness, his clothes soaked and heavy. Water spurted from down spouts and filled the potholes around his feet. Self-recriminations like the rain beat down on him. If he failed to find Kent and give him the antidote, he vowed he would take his own life.

Along with the clashes of thunder, came the sound of a piano and that of a tenor voice. *"Let the lower lights be burning, send a gleam across the wave, some poor struggling, failing seaman you may rescue, you may save."*

Tommy followed the music down the alley to the back of the Shaking Grocery Store Church. He opened the door and stared across the makeshift pews and the people sitting there to the man in the pulpit.

Reverend Hibberblast lowered his microphone and looked at the teary-eyed, rain-soaked Sunday visitor. "Friends," he called out to his flock, "we have a lost sheep in our midst. A sailor from an angry sea." He called to Tommy in a plaintive voice, "Brother, come home. God will deliver thee."

Tommy shuffled down the aisle and knelt before the pulpit, water dripping from his wet clothes. Hibberblast stepped forward and placed his hand on Tommy's head and cried out, "Repent, my son. Repent and be reborn."

The congregation sang a hymn Hibberblast wrote. "Come, O My Brother, Come Home."

Chapter 56
RUMMELS' METAMORPHOSIS

Clinging to the gunwales of his lifeboat, Rummels rode the crest of the nuclear tsunami one hundred seventy-six miles across the Pacific, smashing up on the island of Nuko Tiko. When the waters receded, the natives on the island lowered Rummels' battered boat from the top of a mangrove where it had come to rest. They stared in astonishment at the sapless creature within. The USS Nixon's nuclear blast had burned off Rummels' hair, eyelashes, and brows. His scorched head looked like something overcooked in a microwave. Only his rolling, bloodshot eyes told his rescuers this creature was alive.

For five days, Rummels lay in the small hospital in Nuko Tiko with IV's running and nurses changing his dressings. They fed him through a tube in his nose, since his lips were too swollen for him to talk or eat. On the sixth day a plastic surgeon arrived, flown in from one of the larger Islands to reshape Rummels' burned face. For two weeks following his surgery, Rummels moped around the hospital, a man in a gauze mask. He didn't want the mask to come off because he didn't like his options: he would either look like his old self in which case CRAWL could eventually recognize him, or he'd look hideously deformed. He suspected everyone in the hospital of being a CRAWL agent, the nurses, the orderlies, even the Chaplin. Hiding behind a gauze mask gave him a certain sense of security.

The day of reckoning finally came. Rummels sat on the side of the bed, eyes tightly closed, while a nurse held up a mirror and a doctor meticulously cut away the gauze mask. The nurse patted Rummels on the shoulder. "There you are, now look in the mirror."

Rummels' eyes opened slowly and widen in amazement. He glanced around to see if someone else was staring into the mirror. It was his face in the mirror all right, and he looked nothing like his former self. He was handsome. A grizzled beard and mustache covered most of the scars. He looked exactly like country music singer Kenny Rogers on a bad-hair day, but twenty years younger. This new face was just what he needed.

In the middle of the night, Rummels quietly slipped out bed, cinched up his flimsy hospital gown, threw open the window in his room, and crawled out. Flat broke and owing over a hundred thousand in medical bills, he decided to get the hell out of Nuko Tiko. But he needed money. He waited in the shadows while the clerk of a small grocery opened up for morning business. Rummels rushed into the grocery, overpowered the clerk, took his clothes, and emptied out the cash register. He promised the clerk as he gagged him and tied him up with clothesline rope, he'd return the money once he found work. Later that morning, Rummels boarded a cargo ship with a one-way ticket to Bangkok. He was a new man with a new Kenny Rogers face, a few bucks in his pocket, heading out to a new beginning.

Chapter 57
NEW YORK

Kent, Cleo, Justin, and Gamuka escaped Bolton Mental by following the underground passageways to the old well and up the spiral steps onto the grounds. While the gun battle raged in Building B, they quickly crossed the grounds, crawled through the hole Cleo had cut in the fence, and piled into the Camaro. Kent drove all night. None of them slept, their adrenaline levels too high. One minute Kent and Cleo chatted excitedly about New York and Selena Rosalina, the next minute Cleo sobbed hysterically, fretting about Jesus-3 lying dead in that underground passage. In the back seat, Justin explained to Gamuka all that had happened during his time in a wormhole.

The four of them stayed three days at an Indianapolis motel where Gamuka scrubbed away his duffel bag stench, while Justin aired out from weeks of living underground. Those three days were like a honeymoon for Kent and Cleo. For a while she made Kent forget he was a poisoned man.

The Bolton shootout made headlines across the country:

"BOLTON CHRIST RAISES UP THE DEAD ON LIVE TV"

"JESUS HOAX ENDS IN GUN BATTLE"

"BAPTIST MINISTER CLAIMS CREDIT FOR CHRIST'S VISIT TO THE BIBLE BELT"

"'GUNS FOR JESUS' RADICALS IN SHOOTOUT WITH ANTICHRIST"

"EIGHT DEAD, FOURTEEN WOUNDED, ONE RESURRECTED"

By the time they left Indianapolis, the Bolton Resurrection story had faded from TV news. When the arrived in Columbus, Ohio, the story was a mere back page blurb in the papers. Vivid memories of Jesus-3 buzzed in Cleo's head, and while they traveled through Ohio, she announced, "I'm going to become a vegetarian."

Gamuka, all scrubbed up and hair trimmed, looked like a well-groomed Dachau escapee. He quickly became a fast food addict. "No more bread crumbs and crackers for you," Justin joked as the three men feasted on KFC crispy and Cleo nibbled on a granola bar. Gamuka longed to return to the peace and serenity of a wormhole, but visions of cheeseburgers and pepperoni pizza danced in his head interfering with his meditation.

The Camaro sped relentlessly towards New York.

"Wow, look at that," Kent said. From a distance, New York skyscrapers look like mountains; from the George Washington Bridge like rockets on a giant launch pad; from 5th Avenue looking up, the Grand Canyon. For a boy and a girl from Kansas and a philosopher-field-goal-kicker back from a wormhole experience, New York meant excitement: traffic, noise, bright lights, and masses of people. For Justin it was anonymity, a place to hide from CRAWL.

The Bolton escapees checked into The Lady Liberty, a cheap Midtown hotel with tiny rooms, uneven floors, slanted walls, and mini-geodesic ceilings. The plumbing rattled in the bathrooms. The group's sparse belongings overflowed into the hallway. A hotel designed for trysts, not travelers.

After one night in the cramped, cheerless room he shared with Cleo, Kent told the others, "We're checking out and going somewhere nice. After all, I'm a millionaire."

Justin flicked his eyebrows and grinned. "Good, our bed's lumpy and there was no hot water."

The four of them marched out of the dumpy hotel to the parking garage.

Kent looked around. "Where's the Camaro?"

A VW bug squatted in their parking spot. They marched back into the hotel and up to the desk clerk, "Our car is gone."

"It's either stolen or towed," the clerk informed them. He handed Kent the phone. "Call the police."

"No," Justin shrieked. "A call to the police could tip off CRAWL to our whereabouts."

Kent's eyes narrowed. "Yeah, but that car cost fifteen thousand dollars."

Cleo smiled coyly. "Fifteen eight. Power windows and XM radio."

"Some day I'll pay you back," Justin promised.

Outside, Kent flagged a taxi and they all squeezed inside.

"Four is the limit in New York City," the cabbie grumbled.

Kent slipped the driver a fifty and two twenties. "Take us to a super nice hotel. A clean place with rooms large enough to turn around in."

Several minutes later, the taxi driver let them out at the Plaza Hotel. The foursome gazed in wonder at flagpoles festooned with multi-colored banners, the uniformed doormen, the horses and carriages rolling up to a portico, the taxis coming and going, and the people. So many people.

"I don't think we have any rooms available," the pretty blonde hotel clerk told them, tipping her glasses to the end of her nose. She smiled apologetically. "We have the men and women's Swedish ice hockey teams staying here. They've a lot of fans." She glanced at her computer. "Oh wait, there is a full suite on the top floor available."

"We'll take it," Kent said, handing her his Vita Platinum Card.

Cleo sighed in disbelief when the bellhop flung open the door to the suite. Dorothy and her three sidekicks had just landed in the magical Land of Oz. Cleo danced through the spacious lodging, a glint of wonder in her eyes. A mammoth drawing room gleamed with burnished French Provincial furniture. Hand-carved four-posters with thick feather mattresses commanded the centers of three large ornate bedrooms. There was a kitchenette with stove and microwave, and small dinning area with a glass-topped table and wrought iron chairs. Closets big as elevators. Two baths, one with a boudoir. A large window in the drawing room overlooked Central Park.

"I love it," Cleo squealed.

Kent picked up the phone. "Room service please. Steaks and scrambled eggs for three." He glanced at Cleo. "And one vegetable plate."

Gamuka dipped into a bookshelf and fished out a volume of Sinclair Lewis. Justin stared out the window at the city and the traffic, a grin on his face, as if daring CRAWL to find him in this haystack of ten million people. Cleo sat at the vanity table in the boudoir and fussed with her hair.

Kent tipped the porter when he came with the food.

Sitting at the glass-top table, a chunk of steak impaled on his fork, Kent looked at the others and said in a determined voice, "Tomorrow morning I'm calling Selena Rosalina."

Justin snickered. "You don't just call Selena. You make an appointment. She's a celeb."

Chapter 58
SELENA ROSALINA

Selena Rosalina, the nation's number one talk show diva, lived an "assembly line existence." At 7 AM with the buzz of an alarm clock, the assembling began. Her maid placed ice packs on Selena's sleep-puffed eyes. While her lids shrank, Selena blindly performed facial exercises: grimacing, touching her nose with her tongue, distorting her mouth and lips with a spring-loaded-in-mouth-exerciser. Seven and half minutes later, the ice packs came off and in came the masseuse, an athletic woman with a Ph.D. in kinesiology and hands that could bring sore muscles to orgasm. After twenty minutes of being stroked, palmed, and kneaded, Selena climbed out of bed.

The maid assisted Selena with her jogging pants, Nikes, and sweater. Then came Butch, a handsome, six-foot trainer with biceps the size of Florida grapefruits. He put Selena through fifteen minutes on the fat mobilizing machine and ten minutes on the stretching machines in Selena's private gym off her bedroom. Butch and Selena then headed out for their morning jog through Central Park. They ran side-by-side, stride-for-stride. The maid, the masseuse, and four breathless bodyguards surrounded them like Secret Service agents.

Selena's secretary, a skinny prude with bouncing ponytail and cat-eye glasses, ran backwards at the head of the group, going over the lineup for the day's show. The lead guest would be a movie star plugging a one-star movie, followed by a once famous person trying to get famous again. Next up, a self-improvement feature, assertiveness training for timid housewives. Lastly, came Dr. Abram Brandenberg, a famous scientist, promoting his new book, "The Testosterone Crisis."

Back at the apartment, Butch led Selena through her Yogi regimen followed by a vigorous aerobics dance routine done to "Bamboleo" by the Gypsy Kings. Throughout the workout, Butch touched Selena often and affectionately. She did not reciprocate, apparently preoccupied by the synopsis of Dr. Brandenberg's book that her secretary read aloud above the music. Dr. Brandenberg became famous years ago when he discovered a way to eliminate breast cancer—amputate the breasts of baby girls at birth, which was, after all, comparable to circumcising baby boys. With no breasts (leaving the nipples intact), there could be no breast cancer. Silicon augmentation at puberty would be available, if desired. Millions of lives would be saved and untold suffering prevented. And with augmented breasts, all women could be equal. The idea gained support around the country until some whistle-blower revealed that baby formula manufacturers had paid for Brandenberg's research.

In "The Testosterone Crisis," Brandenburg laid out the facts plainly. Nearly all rapes are perpetrated by men, most pedophiles are men, most violent acts are committed by men—in fact, most everything bad in society is caused by males—most stalkings, most random shootings, most workplace murders, most kidnappings, most acts of terrorism, most drug deals, most everything criminal. What causes these evils of manhood? The same thing that causes manhood. Testosterone. Brandenberg's obvious solution for the ills of society—*CASTRATION*. Selena loved the idea. She'd make certain the book became a best seller.

Following a breakfast of pomegranate, orange slices, and kiwi, Selena received her daily grape juice and wheat grass enema, expertly administered by her highly paid masseuse. Then came a mud cake facial and body wrap. While sweating it out inside plastic, Selena listened to the witticisms, jokes, and possible retorts her writers put together for today's show. Her secretary gave her a quick run down on the day's stand-ins, skits to be used in the event of extra time. Usually these fill-ins were something maudlin like the little boy who lost his puppy, then found the old mutt twelve years later while working in the death chamber of the humane society. Or, some guy from Arkansas who could whittle a Statue of Liberty out of a peach seed in forty seconds.

At mid-morning, following her shower, Selena took her thirty-eight vitamins and herbs, her hormone pill, and her diet pill. At this point, she usually took a thirty-minute break in her bedroom with Butch. Not today. She had become suspicious of Butch. He often had tobacco on his breath, and his erections were flagging. She believed he was really older than thirty-two because of the deep furrows in his forehead and around his eyes. She suspected her muscle-bound trainer, health guru, and lover was a hypocrite and a two-timer.

Dixie Dramel, the most sought after cosmetologist in New York, worked all afternoon sculpting and molding Selena's mug into the face America had learned to love. Eyes painted, lashes curled, lines hidden, and hair permed to extra volume. Then came shadowing, highlighting, augmenting, and de-emphasizing. Out came the rollers; hair swirl-brushed and fanned. Selena was a work in progress, evolving into the television diva of the afternoon wives' club.

Later, Selena gave audience to her youngest child's nanny for five minutes. Then five minutes with her oldest child's tutor, followed by two minutes with each child. She never let a day pass without giving each child at least two minutes of her time, often over the telephone. At three o'clock, Selena marched solemnly into the bathroom and onto the scales. This was a private ritual, not even her trusted masseuse was allowed to watch. She often slumped out of the bathroom with tear runs in her makeup.

Dining on tuna and cottage cheese, Selena watched yesterday's show. Her secretary took down her comments and criticisms. After a beauty rest and short rehearsal, Selena dressed with the help of her maid. Her clothes matched the theme of the day's show--assertive housewives. She wore a blue pantsuit and a red blouse. Her attire, always generic, represented the mainstream of America's working mothers, nothing-to-offend, just the best, most expensive, tailor-fitted ordinary clothes money could buy.

The applause light flashed and Selena rolled off her assembly line, smiling and radiating warmth. The final product. The most trusted woman in America, on stage in front of the cameras, took a bow before a cheering, comedian-warmed audience of her peers.

Chapter 59
JOGGING IN CENTRAL PARK

Kent took a cab to the TV network's office at Rockefeller Center with the aim of setting up an appointment with Selena Rosalina. His Iranian cab driver, martyrdom apparently on his mind, kept telling Kent as he plunged through traffic that he wasn't afraid to die. Kent shrugged and didn't say anything. He had never seen so many people, so many cars, so much commotion. He reeled with the sharp turns of the cab and shut his eyes at the near misses. Finally, the cab jerked to a stop.

Kent felt dizzy as he stepped onto the sidewalk, the same feeling he got getting off the Octopus Ride at the Harkerville Carnival. The great mass of people on the street moved with the random motion of superheated molecules. Yet, each person walked with a purpose, each had a destination, an appointment to keep. Kent supposed not one of them had a deadly poison lurking inside them, ticking away like a time bomb, not a one of them was searching for a *homopragmatic truth*. Kent wished he were one of them. He guessed there more people right here in this one square block of Manhattan than in all of Harkerville.

The business-like man in a business suit at the network's public relations office looked up from his desk and smiled politely at Kent. "Selena doesn't make appointments. If you want tickets for her show, try the ticket office one floor down."

"You don't understand. I have to speak with her personally. It's urgent."

The man chuckled. "You've a better chance getting an audience with the Pope."

At the ticket office, Kent asked for tickets for Selena's next show, figuring he could get her attention during a commercial break.

"No problem," the lady in the ticket office told him. "The next available opening is next July."

"You don't understand, I need to see her right away."

"Take it or leave it."

Selena wasn't listed in the phone book. The network's public relations office had no address for her, at least none they would give out. Selena Rosalina seemed to exist only on television. Kent flagged a cab. Haitian driver this time, a talkative electrical engineer with eight kids, who drove like a Winston Cup rookie.

⁂

Cleo clicked on the TV in the suite's drawing room and shouted, "Selena's on."

Kent, Justin, and Gamuka sauntered in from the kitchen where they'd been playing cards and flopped onto the couch. This afternoon's show featured testimonials from battered wives, another strong argument for Dr. Brandenberg's solution for the nation's Testosterone Crisis. To those abused and bruised victims of marital discord, Selena was warm, compassionate, and understanding. She didn't just present a show, she reached out to make everyone, including the viewers, feel they were an important part of a special event. Cleo loved it.

In the next segment, "Exercising Your Way to Health," Selena presented some clips of her personal exercise routine, including aerobics, Yogi, and her mornings jog through Central Park. Kent watched with intense interest for several minutes before leaping up from the couch, running to the window, and staring down at Central Park. At the fancy horse-drawn carriages, the joggers, the tree-lined trails, and the pond. Yes, this is where he would find Selena. Right here in the backyard of the Plaza Hotel.

While Kent sat pensively at the kitchen table formulating a plan of action, Gamuka prepared supper. The diminutive field goal kicker discovered cooking to be as much fun as meditating. He became the suite's gourmet, taking over the kitchen, ordering in groceries and condiments, taking notes from the Rachel Ray show, and spiking the recipes with some old world Indian spices. He worked all evening on an Indian recipe for stir-fry. His preoccupation with food showed. His hollowed-out face and bony limbs began to fill out. His strength returned. He now weighed eighty-eight and a half pounds.

During dinner, Kent set down his fork and glanced at his friends sitting around the table. "I got a plan for making contact with Selena."

"Don't fool yourself," Justin warned. "It won't be easy, she's a celeb."

Kent spoke slowly. "I'll wait in the park until she comes joggin' by, then I'll jog along beside her and tell her about me being poisoned and that I need her help to find a *homopragmatic* truth."

"It'll work," Cleo trilled. "I can't wait to meet Selena."

"You're going with me?"

Cleo squeezed Kent's hand. "Wouldn't miss it for the world."

Justin shoved back his plate of stir-fry and shook his head. "I don't think it will work. But good luck."

A cold early morning wind stung Kent and Cleo's faces as they crouched in the bushes of Central Park. All around them, the tatty homeless wandered like ghosts in the twilight, gathering up old newspapers, rummaging through trash containers for morsels, and siphoning sugared drinks from discarded paper cups. The sun broke orange over the horizon, and the homeless vanished like vampires shunning the light of day. Two bicyclists, red pennants fluttering, shot past. A group of kids, oblivious to the cold, capered down the jogging path in shirtsleeves.

Cleo whispered, "Look, I think she's coming."

Kent peered through the branches of a chokeberry bush at Selena and her entourage, all decked out in brightly colored sweats and moving briskly down the trail, exhaling gusts of vapor.

Kent whispered, "We'll let them pass, then fall in behind and work our way into the group."

"Okay," Cleo agreed.

When Selena and her retinue jogged by, Kent and Cleo sprang out onto the trail. Crisp autumn leaves crunched under foot as they ran along behind the group for a couple hundred yards.

"All right, Cleo, let's move on up."

Cleo wheezed, "We're not catching them."

"They must be in great shape, I think my lungs are going to explode," Kent gasped before stopping and leaning up against a birch tree to catch his breath. Selena and retinue sped on down the tree-lined path and disappeared around a curve.

"Tomorrow, we'll start out in front of them and let them catch up with us."

"Good idea," Cleo panted.

The next morning Kent and Cleo squatted in the bushes again, hoodies pulled over their heads. At sunup, they spotted Selena and her gang on the trial.

Kent shuffled his feet like a runner in the starting blocks. "Get ready,"

Twenty-five yards away, Selena stopped jogging. Her group gathered in a small circle. Cleo pulled Kent back from the path and together they crept along bushes out of sight to within earshot of the group's powwow. Selena and Butch argued in loud voices like a married couple, poison darts flying. Kent cupped his hand to his ear and listened.

"I didn't do nothin', I was just talking to her," Butch said. "You're paranoid, Selena, you know that."

Selena glared at her amorous trainer. "I'll never trust you again, you two-timing gigolo."

"I'm out here, blubberass." Butch shoved Selena into one of her bodyguards and took off down the trail.

"Good riddance, jock-head with a dead prick!"

Kent stepped out of the bushes and walked briskly towards Selena. "Hey, Selena, I need to talk with you about…"

Before Kent could finish his sentence, two beefcake bodyguards latched onto his arms and hurled him into the thorny undergrowth along side the trail. A third bodyguard, an ogreish giant in a pink jogging outfit, loomed over him. "Listen buddy, don't ever try that again. Understood?"

Chapter 60
BACK TO THE DRAWING BOARD

The gloom of Kent's failure to connect with Selena hung over the suite with the heaviness of a Wagnerian opera. With long faces, they sat speechless at the dinner table, eating their evening meal with the stoicism of boarding house lodgers. An impenetrable wall seemed to separate celeb from commoner. Kent was a doomed man with as much chance of finding a *homopragmatic truth* as winning the lottery.

Justin's voice broke the gloomy silence. "They're playing rough. To get Selena's attention, you got to do something drastic."

Kent looked up. "Yeah, like what?"

Justin leaned across the table. "Kidnap her."

"Get serious."

"I am."

"Justin is quite correct," Gamuka interjected. "It is the only solution for your problem. We have talked it over and decided you have absolutely nothing to lose by pursuing such a course. In fact, you have no alternative. And we have decided to help you in this endeavor."

Cleo looked at Kent and nodded in agreement. "We'd only have to kidnap her for an hour or two. Once she hears your story, I know she'll help us. She's a wonderful lady."

Kent waved his hands in the air. "Wait a minute. If the plan fails and we get arrested, that would bring CRAWL down on Justin and Gamuka." Kent shook his head. "It's too risky."

Justin, a fatherly smile on his face, replied, "We've talked about that, Gamuka and me. Remember when you picked us up on the interstate? We were at the end of our rope, flat broke, and too tired to go on. All day I had sat there with my thumb in the air and no one gave us a second look. In a matter hours CRAWL would have spotted us. But you guys came along instead. We owe our lives to you. Now, let's have no more talk about failure. We'll make this work."

Gamuka spoke excitedly, "While out strolling the other day, I discovered a toy store with water pistols that look exactly like real guns. And around the corner is an Army Surplus and Cop store with handcuffs that really work."

Kent eyed Gamuka suspiciously. "What are the handcuffs for?"

"We must be prepared for any contingency."

Justin added, "The plan is we hold up the joggers with the pistols, force Selena into a van and drive off. You'll have an hour or so in the van to explain your situation to her, then we let her go."

"It'll work," Cleo asserted. "Once she hears Kent's problem, I just know she'll help us. We'll kidnap her where the jogging path curves to the street. Justin, you rent a van. Gamuka, you pick up the water pistols and handcuffs."

Kent raised his hands again. "Hold on, maybe we oughta think about this a little more."

Cleo placed her hand on Kent's arm. "We got to do it, otherwise, you're going to die."

Kent looked at his three friends: Justin with his wrinkled face, bright eyes, and mashed potatoes clinging to his beard; Gamuka with his infectious smile, his jowls just beginning to show, a man resurrected; Cleo, his beautiful Cleo, with her fluffed-up blond hair, her sweet smell, her magic skin, and that special something that drew him to her like a magnet.

Justin cautioned. "We'll only get one shot at this. So, we'll get everything ready and do a full dress rehearsal in the park as soon as possible."

Chapter 61
A MIDNIGHT JOG

The night maid tiptoed across Selena's bedroom with the telephone. She gently shook the snoring diva's arm wrapped around a goose down teddy bear. "Excuse me, Miss Rosalina. Butch is on the phone."

Selena rolled over, lifted her sleeping mask, and looked up at the maid. She flipped the mask back over her eyes. "Tell him to shove it…wait, wait a minute, give me the phone."

"What is it, Butch? Yes, I was. You want to talk? Big fucking deal. I don't trust you anymore. Really, what kind of problem? Your sister's on drugs again. I'm sorry. Yes, I know you do. Well, I love you, too, but you're such a shit. What?" Selena chuckled, flipping up her mask. "A midnight jog. Are you serious? Okay, I'll meet you in twenty minutes." She tossed the teddy bear onto the floor.

The maid removed Selena's curlers and pinned back her hair. Selena sprayed her pits and powdered up. The maid helped her into her jogging attire. Selena giggled. "It's fun to do something crazy once in a while."

※

In Central Park, Kent and Cleo, armed with the water pistols, hid in a stand of larch where the jogging trail curved to the street. They heard the low drone of the rented van idling a block away. Justin sat in the driver's seat of the van, staring at his watch. At exactly midnight, Kent and Cleo would leap onto the jogging trail, brandishing their thirty-eight caliber water pistols and pretend to hold Selena Rosalina's jogging coterie at bay. Justin would pull the van up to the curb and Gamuka would throw open the rear doors. Kent and Cleo would force an imaginary Selena into the van and then jump in with her. Justin would drive away. A simple plan. One rehearsal should be adequate.

On the east side of the park, Selena and Butch jogged effortlessly, side-by-side, stride-for-stride in the moonlight. The air was cold but refreshing, and they talked like young lovers.

With a hint of breathlessness, Butch said, "I'm sorry about the other day."

"It was as much my fault as yours."

"It was my fault," Butch insisted.

"It doesn't matter as long as you don't have anyone else."

"Of course not. Just my wife in Cincinnati."

"How's the divorce coming?"

"She's being a real asshole." Butch squeezed Selena's hand. "I love you."

"I know."

"I'd die for you." Butch stopped jogging and grabbed his chest.

Selena said with alarm in her voice, "What's wrong?"

"Nothing. Just the cold air. I'll be fine."

"You're smoking again, aren't you?"

"A little," he admitted. "The divorce and all." He took a deep breath and exhaled slowly through his open mouth. "There, I'm fine now."

"We'll go a little slower."

"I've got a confession to make. I'm not thirty-two. I'm forty."

Without breaking stride, Selena reached over and patted Butch on the ass. "You've got a thirty-two-year-old-body. That's what counts."

❧

Cleo stared at the glow-in-the-dark watch on her wrist and then at Kent. "Okay, we've got ten seconds. Cleo counted down, nine, eight … two, one. She and Kent leaped out from their hiding place onto the jogging path waving their water pistols in the air. Two unexpected, startled joggers stopped and threw their arms up in the air.

"Don't shoot!" Butch cried, "my wallet's in my pants pocket."

Cleo squinted at the two joggers. "Hey, that's SELENA!"

The van pulled up, the rear door flew open. In the back of the van stood Gamuka, an open-mouth expression of surprise on his face.

Cleo yelled, "We've got her." She motioned with her water pistol. "Please get into the van, Selena."

Kent tugged on Butch's sweatshirt. "You can go. We don't want you."

Selena grabbed Butch by the sleeve. "He goes where I go. You'll take both of us."

Butch grinned, sheepishly. "They don't want me, Selena. I'd just be in the way."

Kent glared at the muscular trainer. "Get going."

Selena clung to Butch, her life preserver. "I'm not going anywhere unless he goes with me. He'd die for me."

Kent, Cleo, and Gamuka exchanged worried glances. No one was moving.

Butch grinned at the kidnappers. "Listen, I'm just a trainer. A nobody. You don't need me."

Selena slapped Butch hard across the face. "Why you dirty, double-crossing, forked-tongued, chicken-shit."

Totally bluffing, Cleo waved her water pistol menacingly at the two joggers and shouted in the gruffest voice she could manage, "Both of you get in the van. Now!"

It worked. Selena and Butch obediently climbed into the back of the van.

Chapter 62
HOSTAGES

Kent and Cleo followed Selena and Butch into the van. Brandishing his water pistol Kent told the hostages to sit on the floor. Gamuka closed the rear door of the van.

"Where are you taking us," Selena asked as the van pulled away from the curb.

Kent smiled. "We're just going to drive around and talk."

"About what?"

"I've got a serious problem."

Selena's face screwed up in a scowl. "I don't give a shit about your problem. You touch one hair on my head and your ass will be up river so fast you won't know what hit you."

"Please, Selena, don't antagonize them," Butch pleaded. "They've got guns."

Selena glared at Butch. "Shut up, Pee-Wee Herman."

Cleo studied her TV idol. Selena's face exuded an unfamiliar callousness. Cleo gently tapped her on the shoulder. "We desperately need your help. Kent, here, has been poisoned."

"Keep your scruffy hands to yourself, bitch."

Startled by Selena's response, Cleo stepped back. Regaining her composure she sat down beside the hostage. "We're not going to hurt you."

Selena leaped up and pounded on the side of the van. "HELP! POLICE! I'M BEING KIDNAPPED!"

Kent put his hand over Selena's mouth to quiet her. The van turned sharply on Forty-second Street, and Selena and Kent stumbled across the floor of the van. Justin glanced over his shoulder to see what the ruckus was. He nearly hit a taxi. The van swerved and Selena flew across the interior of the van, striking her head on the door and falling to the floor unconscious.

Kent bent over and felt the goose egg forming on her forehead. He shook her. "Selena, wake up."

She didn't move.

"My god, she's dead." Kent felt sick. If Selena dies, he dies—either by lethal injection or from the poison already inside his body.

Cleo crawled across the floor and poked Selena with the barrel of her water pistol. No response. Silent terror seeped through the skin pores of the kidnappers. Butch huddled in the corner, shaking like a man with palsy.

Gamuka knelt and pressed his ear to Selena's chest, listened, and looked up at the others. His calm voice fragmented the charged atmosphere in the van. "Her heart is beating quite regularly. A mere concussion. She should recover suitably."

"Phew," Butch gasped.

Kent, Cleo, and Gamuka huddled together, Cleo's water pistol leveled at Butch in the opposite corner. "What do we do with her," Cleo asked.

Kent said, "Take her back to Central Park."

Cleo stiffened. "We can't just dump her in the park."

"Remember," Gamuka pointed out, "the objective of this venture is to tap into Selena's knowledge and connections so Kent can find a *homopragmatic truth*. I think we should take her to the hotel suite. When she wakes up, we shall explain the situation to her calmly in comfortable surroundings. Then we'll ask her to assist Kent in his search for a *homopragmatic truth*. I'm sure she's a reasonable woman."

Cleo agreed. "I just know she will help us. She really is a wonderful person."

The van stopped at a red light and Gamuka climbed into the front seat and explained the plan to Justin. They drove around with Selena lying unconscious on the floor of the van until the Plaza Hotel thinned out at 2 AM, only a few theatergoers and late night owls visible in the lobby. Justin stopped the van to let the others out at the hotel entrance then went to park the van. Cleo kept her pistol leveled at Butch who despite his brawn and size followed her orders obediently. She commanded Butch to help Kent with Selena. With Selena's arms around their shoulders, the two men dragged the television diva into the Plaza's nearly deserted lobby. Cleo and Gamuka followed, Cleo poking Butch in the back with the water pistol every few seconds.

"She's had a little too much to drink," Kent told the sleepy bellhop sitting by the elevator. The ride up to the suite seemed to take hours. Once inside the suite, the kidnappers breathed easier. They lugged Selena into the nearest bedroom and deposited her onto the bed. Kent motioned to Butch to sit beside her. Gamuka handcuffed Butch's left wrist to the bedpost. Kent turned to Cleo. Now what?

Selena awakened like a prizefighter with smelling salts jammed up the nose. She rose up, her eyes flying open, then her mouth. Eardrum shattering shrieks reverberated through the suite, "HELP. KIDNAPPERS. CALL THE POLICE!"

"My god, shut the woman up before she wakes up the entire hotel," Gamuka cried.

Kent pointed his water pistol threateningly at Selena, which only increased her shrieking. In a moment of overpowering fright, Kent pulled the trigger. Water squirted Selena's face. She stopped screaming and stared puzzlingly at Kent.

"Why, that's just a toy water pistol."

She screamed louder now and beat Kent about the head and shoulders with her fists. Cleo's attempts to calm her proved futile. Kent repeatedly squirted water at the shrieking, fist-wielding hostage. Embolden by the knowledge the guns weren't real, Butch yanked with all his strength at the handcuff on his left wrist. If the super-jock got free, it would all be over for the kidnappers. Kent tossed his water pistol down and threw his body across Butch to prevent him from dismantling the bed. A powerful swing of Butch's free right arm sent Kent crashing into the bedroom wall and at the same time bounced the screaming Selena onto the floor.

Back from parking the van, Justin walked into the bedroom and quickly assessed the situation. With great effort, he and Kent overpowered Butch's free arm and Gamuka handcuffed his right wrist to the bed frame. Cleo's litany of reassurances had no effect on Selena, who screamed as if she were getting a root canal without anesthetic. With lots of help from Kent and Justin, Gamuka handcuffed Butch's ankles to the posts at the end of the bed. With Butch under control, they next subdued and handcuffed the shrieking Selena, removed her jogging socks and stuffed them into her mouth. To reinforce the gag, they tied a pillowcase around her head. A blessed, earth-shattering silence fell over the suite.

Cleo sat beside Selena on the floor. "Listen carefully and I'll explain everything to you."

Selena's neck veins engorged as words garbled in her sock-swollen mouth. She tugged at her handcuffs and stared at Cleo with furious eyes. Cleo began her explanation with old Hoover's demise at the Harkerville Hospital and went on to explain about Kent getting poisoned, about Gamuka and the wormhole, Justin and CRAWL, Bolton Mental and Jesus-3.

Nearly an hour later, Cleo finished her story. Kent, Justin, and Gamuka had fallen asleep on the floor. Butch, strung between bedposts and bed rail, twisted around like a double helix trying to scratch his nose against the bed sheet. Selena was wide-awake, eyes protruding like a thyroid patient.

Cleo asked, "If I take the socks out of your mouth, you won't scream, will you?" Selena shook her head.

Cleo woke the others. They untied the pillowcase, and removed the sock gag. Selena hacked a gob of thick phlegm onto the carpet and groaned, "I'm hungry."

"What would you like?"

"Some scrambled eggs with bacon and a cinnamon roll with cream cheese."

Butch raised his head from the mattress and peered over the end of the bed at Selena sitting on the floor. "You're going to gain all your weight back."

"Go to hell, wimp."

Chapter 63
TRACY IN THE SHOWER

Frank Chisholm's plane arrived in Lucerne, Switzerland five hours ahead of Tracy's scheduled flight so not to arouse suspicions. Tracy had made reservations for them at the Hotel Chateau Gutsch, which stood on a hilltop like a castle with a view of the city, the lake, and in the distance the Alps. Frank waited with strained patience in the hotel room. In a few hours, he and Tracy would finally be together. Tracy had deposited the five million dollars from the Jesus-3 debate into a St. Louis bank and then electronically transferred the money to the Gewessen Kantonalbank in Lucerne. The number of the account was tattooed on Frank's brain, 60999. Frank's life was about to start anew, his dreams about to come true. His eyes shining, his heart racing, he sat there in the room barely containing his excitement, a little boy on Christmas Eve.

Frank had ordered champagne and a platter of assorted cheeses, most of which he had already devoured. He took a shower, splashed with aftershave, brushed his teeth three times, and put on the purple bathrobe he'd bought at the duty free shop in Shannon A last, a knock. Frank raced over and threw open the door. Tracy looked stunning standing there in a glitter knit pantsuit and jeweled jacket. Frank carried in the luggage, tipped the porter, locked the door, and swept Tracy up in his arms.

She squirmed away. "I need to freshen up. I've been on airplanes all day."

While Tracy showered, Frank drummed his fingers on the bar, played delicately with the last piece of cheese on the platter, and swigged down two glasses of champagne. He listened to Tracy singing in the shower, her voice blending with the rush of water. *"Now my heart's an open door, my secret love's no secret anymore."*

Quietly, Frank opened the bathroom door and stepped inside. He picked up Tracy's maroon silk panties from the floor and caressed them. He studied her silhouette through the fogged-over glass door of the shower. Her cottony voice echoed softly from the walls. His bathrobe dropped to the floor. A medley of old fantasies played in his head, all about to come true. He opened the shower door.

" Frank. You startled me."

She stood in the drizzle, her wet hair cleaving to her skin just as he had imagined it a thousand times. Water ran over her fragile shoulders and her breasts, dripping from the nipples, flowing over her smooth belly and along the swell of her hips, beading on her sparse pubic hair. His hands moved over her arms and around to the hollow of her back. He stepped boldly into the spray, their wet bodies coming together. This was it. Nirvana. The meaning of life. Tracy in the shower! Her legs wrapped around him, her one hand gripped the showerhead and the other shoved his penis into her.

"WOW, BABY!"

Somewhere children are starving, and somewhere firing squads take aim.

Somewhere mothers are crying and men are dying from bullets in the brain.

In this woeful and wicked world, one man found happiness in passions overdue.

In a steamy hotel shower, Frank Chisholm's sexual fantasies came true.

And five million bucks too.

Tracy was still asleep the next morning when Frank got up and shaved. His performance in the shower the night before had been a tour de force. After years of repressing and sublimating his carnal cravings, he allowed them to erupt in a volcano of sexual prowess that had left Tracy exhausted. Last night, they made love in the shower until the water ran cold and the bathroom dripped with condensation. Frank winked at himself in the mirror. Not bad for a sixty-four year-old retiree.

He dressed in a checkered, wrinkle-resistant polyester suit, and without awakening Tracy, slipped out of the room softly humming "Love Me Tender." He swaggered out to the hotel portico where a doorman flagged him a taxi. The air was cool and damp. Frank didn't notice. He took the taxi directly to the Gewessen Kantonalbank in the main business district.

Frank walked inside the bank, wondering why a world-renowned international financial institution looked so old and unadorned. Bolton First National back home, with its brick facade and expanses of plate glass, put this place to shame. The Gewessen didn't even have a drive-up window. What the heck, as long as the money's safe.

The bank manager glanced at Frank's polyester jacket and the little alligator on his polo shirt. "American, yes," he said with a cordial smugness common to Swiss bankers dealing with foreigners hiding ill-gotten gains.

"Why yes, how did you know?"

"Lucky guess. How may I help you, sir?"

"The name is Franklin Chisholm. I want to check on my account, 60999."

The manager, a short man with healthy red flush to his bald scalp, keyed the number into a computer. He looked at the screen and then at Frank. He keyed in the number again.

"Is there a problem?"

"I'm sorry, Mr. Chisholm, but that account is not registered in your name."

Frank felt his chest heave as his heart stopped and started up again. "There must be some mistake. What name is the account registered under?"

"I'm sorry, we cannot divulge that information," answered the manager, faithful to the bank-secrecy laws of Switzerland as a doctor is to the Hippocratic Oath.

"Is it registered under the name Tracy Fedler?"

"No, sir."

"I don't understand. The check for five million was deposited, wasn't it?"

"Yes."

Frank's face reddened. "Then what name was it deposited under?"

"I told you, I can not divulge such information. However, I can tell you the account is not registered in a person's name. The money was placed in an institutional account."

Frank trembled all over. *Damn. Tracy must have deposited the money in the name of Bolton Mental out of habit, as she had done for years with the hospital's daily receipts. A simple, understandable, fatal mistake.*

"Was the money deposited in the name of Bolton Mental Hospital?"

The manager smiled. "Yes, it was."

"Well, I'm the superintendent of Bolton Mental. Now I'd like to open the account." Frank showed him his business card. "See, Frank Chisholm, M.D., head psychiatrist."

"I'm sorry. Only the Board of Trustees can activate the account. Have them fax an authorization to us, and we will be happy to open the account for you."

Frank couldn't contact the hospital's board. Once they learned about the five million, they'd ask questions. How did Bolton Mental get a five million dollar account at the Kantonalbank in Lucerne? What is Dr. Chisholm doing in Lucerne? Where's Ms. Fedler? Frank figured he had about a week before someone back home wised up and the authorities started looking for him with an arrest warrant for embezzlement.

Frank smiled generously at the manager. "You see I'm personally responsible for that money."

"Then you should have no trouble getting an authorization from your board."

"It's my god-damned money."

"Please Mr. Chisholm, keep your voice down."

"It's Doctor Chisholm. And I want my money."

"Then get authorization." The manager turned off the computer and walked away.

Outside, Frank turned up the collar of his sports jacket. A few snowflakes flittered in the cold air. Tracey had screwed up big time. They would never see the Jesus-3 television money. He thumbed through his wallet as he walked along the crowded street, a measly one hundred and thirty dollars. That wouldn't cover one night at the Gutsch. How long would it be before his wife canceled out his credit cards? He glanced around at the myriad of cheerful faces, all those happy people on the street in their brightly colored winter togs. He decided not to tell Tracy about the money. Not yet. He had at least a week before everything came crashing down. He'd make most of it.

Frank spent the next two days in the shower with Tracy. On the third day, Tracy balked. "Can't we do it bed, Frank? I'm exhausted. My skin is drying out, and I think I have a bladder infection. It hurts when I pee."

"That's no problem," Frank said with a hint of pride in his voice. *Honeymoon cystitis. What a man. Sixty-four years old and three showers a day.* "I'll get you an antibiotic for your bladder, dear. There is a pharmacy right here in the hotel. You start the shower and I'll be right back."

The chemist who operated the hotel pharmacy was a short, lively man with silver hair and a ruddy complexion. He spoke good English and was impressed with Frank's command of drug names and dosages. While packaging Tracy's antibiotic he asked Frank, "What are you, a doctor?"

"Yes, I am. My roommate has a little cystitis."

"We see a lot of that here. Newly wed?"

Frank thought for minute. "On vacation."

"You travel much?"

"No."

The chemist smiled. "I used to be a pharmacist on a cruise ship."

Frank nodded engagingly as psychiatrists know to do. The chemist must have taken the nod as an invitation to chat. He told Frank of his travels and experiences as a member of a ship's crew, apparently the high point of an otherwise humdrum life. Being a chemist trapped in small shop off the hotel lobby had to be boring. But the chemist was a delightful conversationalist, and Frank enjoyed listening. It helped him forget that the end of the world was only a few days away.

The two men retreated to the hotel's coffee shop for coffee and chocolate tortes.

"It was a great adventure being a ship's pharmacist," the chemist recounted. "I traveled the world and got paid for it." He laughed and Frank laughed. It felt good to laugh, something Frank hadn't done in a long time.

"What was your favorite port?"

"So many,' the chemist said. "I loved the tropics. Let me tell about Malaysia…."

Two hours later, Frank returned to his room to find the windows steamed over and Tracy nude and unconscious on the floor of the shower, the water running. He gathered her moist, limp body in his arms and carried her over to the bed. Her skin was water-wrinkled, her lusterless hair plastered to her scalp, and her shoulders covered with blister burns from the hot water. He gently patted her cheeks to bring her around. She stared at him with languorous eyes. "What happened?"

"You passed out in the shower."

Tracy shook her head. "Can't we go sightseeing or something? I'm tired of sex in the shower."

The next day, Frank left the suite while Tracy was still sleeping. He didn't come back until evening. Tracy was furious when he walked in. "Where the hell have you been? I been sitting around here all day with nothing to do but watch TV in language I don't understand."

"I've got bad news and good news."

"Give me the bad news first."

"We can't touch the five million. You opened the account in the name of Bolton Mental."

Tracy stiffened. "Oh, my god. I didn't, did I?"

Frank took her hand. "Don't blame yourself. It was an honest mistake anyone could make. Listen, I've been to Zurich today. We're going to live like millionaires anyway. Travel the world. Cruise the oceans. We're going to see it all."

"What are you talking about?"

"You're looking at the new ship's doctor for World Cruises, Inc."

Chapter 64
THE THAI HI

High dose radiation can scar its victims and deformed them for life. In Rummels' case, thanks to a good plastic surgeon, his radiation burns resulted in a magnificent metamorphosis. He not only looked like the country music singer Kenny Rogers, he sounded like him. Radiation had scarred his larynx, giving his voice a scratchy, melodious twang. For the first time in his life, he could move up and down the musical scale harmoniously. He even landed a job as a Kenny Rogers impersonator at the Thai Hi nightclub, just down the street from the Bangkok Hilton. It didn't pay much, but at least he wasn't begging on the streets. And he figured CRAWL wouldn't be casting about in haunts like the Thai Hi.

Wrong!

One night singing "Islands in the Stream," he peered through the glare of lights and layers of cigarette smoke at a familiar face in the crowd. His voice cracked and went off tune. The face belonged to Joe McGee, a former CRAWL associate. Joe, who was only five foot-four, was dancing with a young Thai girl about the same height. Over the years, Rummels worked on several assignments with Joe. Not known as the most brilliant agent in the world, Joe had the tenacity of a bloodhound on scent. Rummels noticed Joe staring at him; stares that turned his blood to slush.

During the applause, Rummels exited the stage and headed for the door. A strong hand clamped around his arm. He turned and stared down into Joe McGee's smiling face.

"How about a little drink, Kenny?"

Rummels' heart vibrated like woofers in a convertible trunk. His brows turned wet. He glanced around. No way out of this. He sat down at the bar with his old companion. Joe ordered whiskey sours and asked, "How did you end up in a place like this?"

Rummels searched for the right words. Was Joe here on an assignment? Was that assignment to annihilate the bungling agent who screwed up the Kaku invasion? Rummels wondered if his name was in Joe's assignment book, which agents keep in the secret inner pocket of their coats. Rummels peered into his drink. *Was the whiskey poisoned?*

Joe slapped him on the back. "You don't have to answer. To fall from the top of the charts into this dump must be hell, Mr. Rogers. But listening to you tonight, I think you are as good or better than you ever were. And you've aged nicely."

Rummels mouth dropped. *This little shit really thinks I'm Kenny Rogers.* Poor Kenny just sitting around a Bangkok nightclub waiting to spill his guts to some stranger.

He grinned at Joe and asked in his scratchy voice, "How about another round? You know, when you're at the top, you think you're invincible. Nothing can go wrong. Then I met this girl...."

Joe downed one drink after another as he listened to a woefully sad story of love gone wrong. Joe had tears in his eyes when he finally conked out at the bar.

Rummels slipped his hand inside the slumbering agent's coat and took out his assignment book. He thumbed through the book until he found his name. It had been scratched out with DIA scribbled beside it. "Died In Action." There would no annihilation order with his name on it. CRAWL thought he was dead. And Joe McGee hadn't recognized him.

I'm not dead. I'm invisible. Free to start over.

Rummels slipped the book back into Joe's coat pocket. He lifted the schnockered agent's head by the hair and then let it fall back onto the bar with a thump. "See you around, Joe McGee."

Chapter 65
HASHIMOTIOTO

Secure in the knowledge that CRAWL wasn't looking for him, Rummels opened a detective agency in a small office in downtown Bangkok. Instead of clandestine government work, he spied on philandering spouses and did some small time industrial espionage. He hadn't made it big, but he made enough so he could quit his impersonation job at the Thai Hi, although he still did command performances there.

The case that would change Rummels fortune walked unannounced into his small office. Rummels immediately sniffed money. He swung his feet from his desktop and shoved his week old New York Times into the trash can.

The potential client, a melancholy young man, wore a seven-hundred dollar vicuna sport coat that looked slept in, an expensive Italian silk necktie that hung loosely about his neck, a rumpled white cotton shirt with diamond studs and cufflinks, khaki pants, a pair of scuffed Gucci's. This kid had money, but no class. Rummels made note of the bloodshot eyes, probably the result of long hours in front of a computer screen? He pegged this guy as one of those high-tech nerds who thought in algorithms. These creeps were not only replacing but putting to shame the workaholic capitalists of the century past. They had it all. Everything but testosterone.

Rummels grabbed a rattan chair and shoved it under the young man. "Have a seat. How may I be of assistance?"

"This is all confidential, isn't it?"

"Absolutely," Rummels replied with a fulsome bonhomie, patting the young man on the shoulder. "Just like talking to a priest. Now what is it I can do for you?"

"I want to know about the packages I'm responsible for."

"Packages?"

"Yes. I never really see them. I just route and ship them by sea. Electronically. Five hundred a day."

"This is your job, your employment?"

"Yeah, I'm well-paid for routing the packages overseas. I've programmed my computer to do it automatically. In fact, my computer is routing packages as we speak."

Rummels reached across his desk and switched off his phone. "Well then, what's the problem?"

"I want to know what the packages are. You see, before I didn't care. Now I want to know."

Rummels could tell this nerd had problems and that they weren't all related to the mysterious packages. A good detective is also a good psychologist. Clients feel better when they get things off their chests.

Rummels leaned forward, a smile spreading across his handsome Kenny Rogers' face. "Why don't you tell me a little about yourself?"

"My name is Larry Lakes."

"How did you end up here in Bangkok?"

"It's a long story."

Rummels crossed his arms on his chest. "I'd like to hear it."

Larry opened up to the friendly spook, telling him about Cleo, Green Pastures, prison, Atlantic City, and Veronica. "You see I'm really good with computers so Veronica set me up here in Bangkok."

Rummels nodded, maintaining eye contact. "Did this Veronica put you in charge of routing and shipping those packages?"

Larry nodded. "It beats going back to prison."

"Sounds like you don't really enjoy what you're doing."

Larry shrugged.

"So, you work closely with Veronica."

With a glazed look of despair, Larry said, "I never see her. Just an occasional e-mail."

Rummels shifted in his chair. The riff of this guy's story seemed to be *lonesome me*. This nerd had been intimately involved with two women in his life and both dumped him. *Wounded ego.* "So, Veronica doesn't come around anymore, huh?"

Larry shook his head.

"You got friends here in Bangkok?"

Larry shook his head. "Like I told you, I'm an escaped con."

"If your computer routes and ships these packages, what do you do with your time?"

"I dabble a little. Write software, surf the net."

"Do you travel?"

"I spent three months in Japan."

"I see. Do you have friends in Japan?"

Larry shrugged. "Sort of. You see when I published over the Internet my theory on 'Second Order Machines,' Osa Takashima, head of the Tokyo Institute of Artificial Intelligence invited me to come to Japan to help program and operate the Hashimotioto Supercomputer."

Rummels raised his hand. "Wait a second. Would you kindly explain to me what a 'Second Order Machine' is?"

"In theory, Second Order machines are self-mutating computer programs that create their own hardware, peripherals, and energy sources as they ascend the evolutionary ladder. Right now they're just hypothetical, but it could happen. The idea came to me in a dream one night. If it does happen these machines could replace human beings as the dominant life form on earth."

"You mean they would be alive?"

"The Hashimotioto seems to be."

Rummels shrugged to hide his confusion.

Larry's voice cracked with emotion. "Someday there will be a new, kinder world beyond humankind, beyond love, hurt, and rejection. A computer-world where a blown fuse or brunt out chip from a power surge is the worse thing that could happen."

Rummels struck a pensive look. "Tell me about this supercomputer in Japan. What did you call it?"

"Hashimotioto."

"Ha...shi...mo...ti...o...to," Rummels repeated slowly.

Larry looked soberly at Rummels. "This really hasn't anything to do with those packages I process. That's what I'm here about."

"The more information I have, the more I know about you, the better I can help you. Now about this Hashimotioto?"

Left-brain Larry's passionless eyes sparkled transiently. "It's just the most fucking powerful computer in the world...excuse me, I picked up the cussing habit in prison. What I meant to say is the Hashimotioto has the reckoning power of four hundred thousand desktop PC's, the memory equivalent to twenty Libraries of Congress, and a nuclear power supply fueled by plutonium rods so it never runs out of energy. Thanks to its maser circuitry, the whole thing including the power supply is no bigger than a two-drawer file cabinet."

Rummels looked intrigued. The smell of money grew stronger. "What can this computer do?"

Larry boasted, "The Hashimotioto is an eclectic computer, the first of its kind, programmed for real-world common sense. It does logic functions at peta-flop speed and networks the results with the complex vagaries and gray messiness of a real-world paradigm to come up with real world answers to complex questions in real time."

Rummels grinned benightedly. "Is that so? And you worked with this computer?"

Larry seemed surprised by the question. "Of course I worked with it. I became the chief tech for the Hashimotioto when I was in Tokyo. I understood it better than anyone."

"But you're not working with it any longer?"

Larry's head dropped and his body slumped. "I was fired."

"Why?"

"My boss Osa noticed that whenever I came around the Hashimotioto, it developed subtle voltage changes that increased its computation speed and general performance. It did virtually anything I ask it to do, even things not thought to be within its capabilities. Together we accurately predicted the outcomes of hundreds of political races, a downturn in the Nikkei, an earthquake in California. With me at the keyboard the Hashimotioto discovered thirty-eight new prime numbers and solved untold mathematical puzzles. We played chess, poker, backgammon and twenty-questions for hours at a time. The computer and I became very close. And this upset Osa."

Rummels said bluntly, "Sounds like this Osa fellow may have been jealous."

"Not really. You see I have a nervous tic in my left foot, which produces a particular .00075-millivolt analog interference that was picked up by one of the Hashimotioto's data buses. The interference, a negligible disturbance, is quickly grounded away, but not before Hashimotioto identified it with me. This electrical interference was like a shot of adrenalin for Hashimotioto."

Rummels rolled his eyes in confusion.

"You see," Kent said, "it got to where the Hashimotioto didn't want to compute unless I was at the keyboard. Osa called it a unique man-machine relationship. The computer had bonded with me through some unidentified transistor-neuronal connection. Osa decided to put an end to this strange relationship before it got out of hand. Before it became what he called 'Frankensteinian.' So he fired me, I couldn't blame him."

"And now you're back in Bangkok processing packages."

"Like I told you, my computer does all the work. It processed packages for me the whole three months I was in Tokyo."

Rummels swiveled in his chair and studied Larry in the stripes of sunlight glinting through louvered blinds. The downhearted client in the rattan chair had been unnerved by female rejection and the severance of his strange, yet profound relationship with the Hashimotioto. An unscrupulous adventurer could easily take advantage of this vulnerable young man. A machine like the Hashimotioto would be worth untold millions on the black market.

"Tell you what," Rummels said, "I'm going to get to the bottom of those packages for you. I'll start first thing in the morning. We need to stay in close contact."

Chapter 66
THE CALLING

Tommy Tennyson slumped through the darkened sanctuary of the Shaking Grocery Store Church. The faint odor of lettuce rot and spoiled fruit permeated the old building. He bumped into a grocery cart filled with hymnals and shoved it out of the way. He moved along rows of fold-up chairs to the pulpit where Rev. Hibberblast's karaoke lay in cavernous silence on the floor. He sighed deeply. His solemn face reflected his disappointment in not finding Rev. Hibberblast here in the church at this late hour. He'd wanted to talk with him in private.

Guilt over his poisoning of Kent Mullins' had struck Tommy again, like a relapse of an incurable disease, leaving him depressed and nervous. He needed reassurance concerning his decision to leave the church to search for Kent Mullins so he could give him the antidote that would save his life. Tommy opened a side door and descended the steps to his room in the church basement, where he fell heavily onto his narrow bed.

Tommy had lived in the church basement ever since quitting his position at the university and dedicating his life to God. During the day he stocked shelves and swept the floor at the Dollar General downtown. The greater part of what he earned there, he gave happily to the church.

The best thing about being a convert for Tommy was peace of mind. He didn't have to think anymore. Thoughts came pre-packaged in ancient text. And for those perplexed by sacred writ, there was Rev. Hibberblast to explain what God really meant.

As a scientist Tommy had relentlessly searched for truth, which kept his mind in a continual state of intellectual unrest. Now, he could see the fruitlessness of all that. With science, there is no truth--just facts, statistics, and theories. Even gravity is a theory. Throw a ball into the air fifty times and it falls back to earth fifty times. What about the fifty-first time? Would the ball come back down? Scientists would say the probability was very high it would, but they wouldn't say so absolutely. If the ball didn't fall back to earth, then the theory of gravity was wrong. If it did come back down, the theory was right, but only until someone tossed the ball up again. There were no guarantees.

Tommy desired to know something that was true all the time, every time, everywhere. Something whose truth-value never changed, something that could never be doubted. Not a theory. Not a probability. Not something to be continually modified and revamped. He sought universal truth. He wanted to possess a piece of knowledge so infallible it could never be proven wrong. That's why he sent Kent Mullins on that life and death search for a *homopragmatic* truth.

Oddly enough, Tommy found his universal truth right here in Harkerville, where as a freakish kid with elephantine ears, he was tormented mercilessly by his peers. Here he'd had learned to hate, and ironically here as an adult he found what he had been searching for. And he found it at the Shaking Grocery Store Church. But the devil lurked in the shadows. Tommy had poisoned a man and he couldn't live with that on his conscience. Tomorrow he'd talk with Rev. Hibberblast about his decision.

Tommy tossed fitfully on his bed during the night until awakened by the stomping of feet, the clapping of hands, the pounding of a piano, and the harmonious thrumming of voices. "I've got a Home in Glory Land." He leaped out of bed. Since joining the church he had never been late for a Sunday service. He straightened his sleep-crumpled clothes, adjusted his artificial ears on their skin nubs, brushed his hair back, and raced upstairs.

Hiberblast's energized flock sang at the top of their lungs: hands flying, feet moving, the whole church shaking. Tommy rushed to the back of the church and joined in with the feet stomping and hand waving.

Hibberblast shouted from the pulpit, "Glory. Glory. Glory. Praise the Lord. Praise God."

The breathless flock sat down and Hibberblast began: "Brothers and sisters. Praise the Lord. Today, I greet you with a heavy heart. I have tasted the sweet and the bitter. The sweetness of being your shepherd, and now the bitter sadness of having to tell you good-by. I have been called to greater duty." He reached inside the pocket of his mint-green leisure suit, removed an envelope and waved it in the air. "This letter came to me personally from Bobby Haggett himself, the Lord's guardian of the television airways, the world's most popular evangelist. Bobby has asked me to start up a mission in Colombia, South America. God, through Haggett World Wide Ministries, has called me to serve at a higher level."

A dark despair settled over the flock like a layer of toxic exhaust. One of them shouted, "Please, don't leave us, pastor."

Hibberblast stared up at the ceiling. "God has called and I must serve."

The sermon that followed was one of the most powerful Hibberblast ever preached. His voice roared majestically, simmering at apogee, exalting God, reprimanding man, and cursing the devil and communism. He sobbed. He prayed. Then he spoke softly, almost in a whisper, asking for mercy from God and money from his parishioners. Once more his voice rose above a clamorous volley of hallelujahs and praises. He jumped up and down, raced back and forth in front of the altar, singing into his hand-held karaoke. The flock danced, shouted, and rolled on their knees, wild-eyed and swooning. The festivities ended with the passing of the collection plate.

Rev. Hibberblast assured his flock that one among them would be ordained to take over leadership of the church. "Leave it in the hands of the Lord and pray."

When the last of the parishioners drove out of the parking lot, Tommy walked up to the altar and watched Hibberblast count the cash in the collection plate. Tommy was sure he would be chosen the church's next leader. After all, he had given up his tenure at the university, his academic fame, his intellectual worldliness, and most of his salary from the Dollar General. Now he must tell Rev. Hibberblast he couldn't take the position. That he was leaving the church to search for Kent Mullins. Tommy cleared his throat. "Am I the one?"

Hibberblast pocketed the cash, placed the collection plate on a shelf behind the altar and turned to Tommy. "No, you're not the one. You're coming with me."

"To Colombia?"

"I need your help getting the mission started. Haggett is giving us three hundred thousand dollars to get this thing going. Talked with him last night on the phone. Great man." Hibberblast grinned broadly. "Can you believe it, three hundred thousand smackers. The Lord has his hand in this one."

"But, why Colombia?"

The Reverend's expression grew serious. "It's the devil's den. Drug cartels. Smugglers. Corrupt politicians. Prostitutes. Money launderers. Assassins. You name it; they got it. Why, there is more sin per square mile in Colombia than anywhere. It's the Sodom and Gomorrah of the modern world. Just think how many lost souls we will save."

"Why did Bobby Haggett pick you?"

Hibberblast sat down in one of the folding chairs and motioned Tommy to do likewise. "Actually, I asked for it. I heard that Haggett World Wide Ministries was looking for someone who could speak Spanish.

I applied. To be quite honest, the church here isn't going anywhere. Harkerville isn't where God wants me."

"Really?"

"That's right. He wants me in Colombia."

"I didn't know you spoke Spanish."

Hibberblast cleared his throat. "A little. I used to date a cute little Mexican girl in high school."

Tommy stood. "I can't go with you. I must find the man I poisoned before it's too late."

Hibberblast grimaced in exasperation and spoke harshly to his postulant. "We've been through all this before. God has forgiven you for poisoning that man."

"But isn't it a sin to let a man die?"

"Come on," Hibberblast said, a bit of asperity in his voice. "We've already placed this in God's hands. No matter what happens, you're not to be blamed."

"Shouldn't I try to find him?"

"Absolutely not! When you put something into God's hands, you must leave it there. To do otherwise is grave sin. Your faith is weak. You haven't learned to trust in the Lord. Whatever happens to this Mullins character is no longer your responsibility. God will take care of things."

Tommy sank back into his chair and Hibberblast took his hands in his and prayed. "Oh, Lord, forgive Tommy for his lack of faith. You lifted this burden from him, but he failed to trust in you. Forgive him this transgression. Amen."

Tommy wept like a kid with a bad report card.

"Look, Tommy, which is the greatest good? Saving millions of Colombian souls from hell-fire or saving one man from poison?"

Tommy mopped away his tears. "You're right. Say, I took Spanish in undergraduate school, but I'll need to brush up."

Chapter 67
BETA FISH IN A BOWL

"Don't call me fat ass, you impotent lard head." Selena hurled a steak knife at Butch splayed on the bed, handcuffed wrists and ankles to the bedposts. Luckily, Kent diverted the knife's trajectory by grabbing Selena's arm. The knife spiked the headboard and vibrated like a tuning fork.

Selena whooped, "It wouldn't have hit him. I just wanted to scare him."

"You crazy bitch." Butch's loud voice jingled the crystals in the chandelier in the suite's living room.

Selena stood in the doorway of the bedroom, hands on hips. "If it weren't for me, lard head, you'd still be peddling fake Rolexs in Brooklyn."

"I'd be a hell of a lot better off than I am now, Fat Ass."

Selena slammed the door, which evoked a string of curses from Butch that could be heard in New Jersey. Lovers fighting like Beta fish in a bowl. Kent gleaned from the verbal exchanges that Selena hadn't forgiven Butch for being what she called "a lily-livered candy-ass" during the kidnapping. And Butch, outraged at being shackled to a bed twenty-fours a day, resented Selena running around the hotel suite as if she were on vacation. He vowed when he got free, he'd cram a water pistol up each kidnapper's ass, right after he broke their legs.

Kent cracked the bedroom door and peered in at the shackled hostage. Although Gamuka had applied an extra set of handcuffs to Butch's wrists and ankles, the kidnappers slept fitfully at night, knowing Butch at anytime might dismantle the sturdy four-poster. It was like living in a castle with the Frankenstein Monster chained to a wall in the dungeon.

Kent turned and grinned at Selena. "Please don't antagonize him."

Selena shoved Kent through the doorway into bedroom. "Don't tell me what to do, gringo. Only thing wrong with him he's got no cigarettes. He always blows up when he stops smoking. The jerk has no will power."

"Look whose talking," Butch retorted, "Miss Mommy Taco Belly herself."

"Kiss my ass, creep."

Kent asked Butch, "What kind of cigarettes do you smoke?"

"I don't want any cigarettes. I'll show you who has will power."

"I'd be more than happy to get you some. Luckys? Camels? Low tar?"

"I told you, I don't want any fuckin' cigarettes. Come on, I got to do number two."

Kent shouted out the door, "Gamuka, he has to go."

Gamuka jumped up from the living room couch where he watched TV and rushed into the bedroom, reached under the bed and pulled out a stainless steel bedpan he purchased at a Salvation Army store. He handed it to Kent along with a roll of toilet paper. "Come to think of it, it's your turn."

Kent closed the door when Selena and Gamuka walked out of the bedroom. The roles of hostage and kidnapper had somehow completely reversed. All day Selena barked out orders like a drill sergeant, and everyone jumped to carry them out. All but Cleo. She and Selena got along like sisters. They controlled the television, ordered in groceries, clothes, and videos on Kent's Vita Platinum card, made crème caramel and Banbury tart together, cleaned the suite and set the dirty linens outside the door to keep the maid away. "I don't want any strangers in here," Selena told her kidnappers. "I'm not ready to be rescued yet."

Kent sighed as he prepared to collect bodily excrement from a super-jock who would break his neck if given the chance. At least Kent didn't have to worry about Selena escaping. She seemed to enjoy being a hostage. She even derived perverted pleasure from battling with Butch, the two of them thriving on inflicting pain and humiliation on one another. On top of it all, Selena hadn't offered to help Kent find a *homopragmatic truth*, the whole point of this kidnapping in the first place. She eluded the subject whenever it came up.

What does she think this is all about anyway?

Kent shoved the bedpan under Butch?

"Where do keep that thing, in the freezer?"

※

Washing the dinner dishes, Cleo talked with Selena about Jesus-3 and the animals. "Because of Jesus-3 I became a vegetarian."

"I would have liked to have had him on my show. Sounds like an interesting character."

"You would have just loved him." Cleo wiped off the coffee pot and placed it on a shelf next to a silver gravy boat. "Selena, I'm so sorry you had to become a hostage."

"Did you see the *Times* today? My disappearance is still front-page news. My re-run ratings have skyrocketed. I hate to admit it, but my share of the afternoon TV market had been dwindling. Can you believe those 'trash shows' and that reality crap were stealing audience from me?" Selena handed Cleo the salad plates. "I don't hold anything against you guys for kidnapping me. Quite honestly, I needed a break. The show was running me ragged."

Cleo clasped her hands together. "Does that mean you'll help Kent find a *homopragmatic* truth?"

"I'm thinking on it. Don't rush me."

Latter in the evening, the whole group, except Butch, sat down in the drawing room to watch CNN's hourly updates on Selena's disappearance. Media's talking heads theorized that the Russian Mafia may have kidnapped Selena in retaliation for an expose' she did on their money laundering operations. Women's rights groups paraded in front of the Russian embassy. Politicians called for an embargo of Russian goods. People boycotted restaurants in Brighton Beach. The President intimated to the Russian ambassador and the press that there would be grave consequences if Selena were not safely returned.

Kent took a quick breath. "Maybe we should abandon the kidnapping before something bad happens. Besides, we can't keep Butch handcuffed forever."

Selena shook her head. "Butch is fine. And this is the best publicity I've had in years." She got up and shut off the TV. "How about some cards?"

Justin headed for the kitchen. "I'll get us some wine."

Kent eyed Selena. She cared more about her ratings than about Butch. And she didn't seem to care at all that Kent was going to die from a poison. That's celebrity for you, a bonded-tooth smile for the masses and to hell with the individual. Kent was about to ask—no beg her--to help him find a *homopragmatic* truth when Butch cut loose with a barrage of four-letter words that echoed through the suite like blasts from a bullhorn.

Kent and the others exchanged anxious glances. Although this was the only suite on the top floor of the hotel, someone walking by might hear Butch's loud cursing and report it. The kidnappers feared the hotel management would come knocking at the door.

Gamuka stood up and straightened his shoulders. "I got an idea. Be right back." He opened the door and walked out of the suite.

Selena sat back down. "I guess no one's interested in cards."

Kent cleared his throat and gave Selena a sharp glance. "Are you ever going to help me find what I'm looking for?"

Selena shrugged. "I don't have a clue where to look for a *homopragmatic truth*."

Butch's vulgar whoops momentarily drown out the conversation.

Cleo slid onto the floor, placed her hands on Kent's knees, and stared imploringly at Selena. "Couldn't you find someone who would help us? You know all the smartest people."

"I'm working on that," Selena abruptly replied. "I'll try to come up with a name. I promise." She leaned on her elbows. "Kent, you're lucky to have someone like Cleo. No one ever loved me the way she loves you."

"Maybe you just haven't met the right person."

"No. That's not it. I never had time for anyone. I was always too busy trying to be someone important. And I never really succeeded."

Butch screamed from the bedroom, "You're a fat ass bitch."

Cleo smiled at Selena. "What do you mean? You're one of the most successful people in the world."

"I'm an electronic image. I don't live in the real world. I don't have everyday worries like ordinary people. Like a lot of celebrities you see on TV, I'm a fake." The animation had left Selena's face, and she hanged her head regretfully. Kent actually felt sorry for her.

Chapter 68
DEATH IN THE SUITE

Justin returned to the drawing room with a bottle of Cabernet Sauvignon and a tray of sparkling wine glasses. After a few sips of wine everyone relaxed. Being a hostage and kidnapper wasn't what it used to be; here they were lounging on stuffed sofas in a plush hotel suite, Manhattan nightlights glittering in the window. Good wine and after-dinner conversation. If Butch would just shut up.

Selena set down her wine glass and glanced around at her kidnappers. "I always wanted to be an actress," she confessed. "And I would have been great one. I have timing, a flare for the dramatic, and presence before the camera."

Just then, Gamuka flew into the suite, a plastic bag in his hand. "I have purchased some nicotine patches for Butch. I think they will quiet him down. He's in obvious nicotine withdrawal. How many patches should I put on him?"

"He was smoking rather heavily," Selena confided.

Kent suggested. "Three patches?"

"Umm," Selena said, "better use more until he calms down."

Gamuka disappeared into the bedroom to apply the sticky nicotine patches to the brawny chest of the shackled, bellowing trainer.

Justin poured another round of wine. Kent asked Selena, "Why didn't you go into the movies?"

"I know," Cleo interjected. "Because you're Mexican, they wouldn't give you any good parts."

Selena's brows lifted. "I didn't make in the movies because I don't have a neck."

Justin studied Selena. "What do you mean? You got a neck."

"Heroes have to have at least three inch necks and leading ladies even longer necks. Take Harrison Ford; if it wasn't for his neck and the frantic look on his face, he'd still be pounding nails for a construction company."

"Really," Kent commented.

"If you watch the movies closely, you'll notice they do neck shots on all the stars. Usually from the side or below. The best neck shot ever was in 'Cat On a Hot Tin Roof' where Paul Newman was sitting in a controvertible with the top down in the rain and Burl Ives was giving him hell. The rain was coming down really hard, and he just sat there, his neck growing like a bamboo shoot." Selena giggled. "It reminded me of an erection."

Kent asked, "Was your neck the only reason you gave up acting?"

"Yeah, my neck is only one and a quarter inches from nape to mastoid. There was no way I could play a protagonist."

Cleo asked, "What's a protagonist?"

Gamuka back from Butch's dungeon answered the question. "A protagonist is the main character in the story, usually the good guy or gal."

"That's right," Selena agreed. "I could only get villain and side-kick parts. To hell with that."

"So you gave up what you really wanted just because of your neck?" Kent asked, the question sounding more uncomplimentary than he intended.

"I had no choice. They closed the door on me. I did the next best thing, television."

Soon they were all looking at each other's necks. Justin had by far the worse movie neck, a sagging turkey gobble that flopped on his chest. Kent had a nice long neck, a good three inches with an apple that bobbed when he talked. Cleo's neck was flawed by a little feminine doublet, which Selena called a "Shelly Winters." Gamuka like Selena was a no-necker. All at once, everyone noticed the quietness in the suite. Butch had stopped yelling.

"The nicotine patches seem to be working," Justin observed.

The words barely left Justin's lips when a new noise shattered the novel quiet: grunts, heavy breathing, squeaks and groans, and the splintering of wood. Butch's bed coming apart. The kidnappers and Selena stared at one another in horror.

Into the drawing room came Butch in his boxer shorts, a sweaty Arnold Schwarzenegger dragging bedposts tethered to his wrists and ankles. His face was porcelain, his eyes glazed. A half-dozen tan nicotine patches dotted his massive pectorals. He grabbed at his chest with his right hand, swinging a bedpost like a bola. He muttered something, slurred and incoherent, then toppled to the floor like a felled sequoia. The loud crash jolted the suite.

Selena and her kidnappers approached the fallen trainer cautiously like ancient hunters circling a wounded mammoth. Gamuka knelt and gingerly touched the wet skin of Butch's shoulder. No response. His hand slid to Butch's neck to check for a pulse. Gamuka's eyes widen. "He's in cardiac arrest!"

Selena yelled, "Oh, my God. Do something."

Gamuka took charge by blowing into Butch's mouth while Selena, trained in CPR, pumped up and down on victim's breastbone. Despite several minutes of vigorous resuscitation, they got no response. Butch's lips turned blue.

Gamuka unplugged a lamp beside the sofa and ripped out the electrical cord. He pressed the exposed ends of the cord onto Butch's chest and told Kent to plug the cord into the wall outlet. "Stand back," he ordered. With a loud pop, electricity shot into Butch's sweaty body. He heaved and fell limp again. The lights in the suite flickered. The smell of burnt flesh filled the room. Failing to find a pulse, Gamuka stepped away from the fallen trainer.

"He's gone."

"Oh, God. Oh, God. Oh..." Cleo and Selena blurted synchronously.

"The police will think we've killed him," Gamuka said.

Kent asked, "Why would they think that?"

"He's naked, shackled hand and foot, been missing for days, burn marks on his chest."

Justin shook his head. "It's not the police I'm worried about, it's CRAWL!"

"This whole kidnapping scheme was a bad idea," lamented Kent.

Cleo sobbed.

A dead man in the suite unnerved the kidnappers. Recriminations bounced around like subatomic particles: *It was your fault. Mine? It was his fault. No, it was her fault. If you ask me it was the nicotine patches that got him. We should've thought this out.* Discord crescendoed to near pandemonium.

Selena shouted, "Damn it. It's nobody's fault. A heart attack, plain and simple. Now, take the handcuffs off him and put them on me."

Kent stared skeptically at Selena. "Good God! Why?"

"Because," Selena explained, "no cop is going believe it was a heart attack. Now put his jogging clothes on him and bring me my jogging stuff."

Justin and Cleo removed the nicotine patches from Butch's chest and dressed him in his sweats, while Selena put on her jogging attire.

Gamuka snapped the handcuffs on Selena, the shattered bedposts dangling from her wrists.

Selena turned to Kent. "Professor Dimitri Sulkohov who wrote the book, "The Meaning of the Universe" is your best chance of finding a *homopragmatic truth*. He's the smartest man I ever had on my show. Some say he's the smartest man in world. You'll find him in St. Petersburg, Russia at the university."

Kent and Cleo exchanged muddled looks. Everything was happening so fast.

Selena glanced at the others. "Put the key to the handcuffs in Butch's pocket and drag him over to the window."

"What are we doing," Justin asked.

"Keeping your ass out of prison," Selena answered. "You throw Butch out the window in exactly ten minutes. That'll give me time to get down to the hotel lobby and tell everyone Butch kidnapped me and I escaped. When they find his body on the sidewalk, they'll think he committed suicide in lieu of going to prison."

Cleo took Selena's hand. "Why are you doing this?"

Selena smiled. "With this kind of publicity, my show could stay number one for a long time. Besides, if you find a *homopragmatic truth*, I want it on my show first."

Gamuka, ever the scholar, looked for defects in Selena's plan. "How are you going to explain the busted-up bed?"

"I did it. When Butch was out of the suite, I tore apart the bed and escaped. Fear gave me the strength. When he discovered I was gone, he committed suicide by jumping out the window, preferring death to prison."

"How about the marks on his wrist and ankles from the handcuffs?"

"After falling 20 stories, he'll be hamburger. No one will notice."

Kent looked at Selena appreciatively. "You're taking a chance. There'll be all kinds of questions."

"I told you, I'm a good actress. Now, in exactly ten minutes you pitch Butch out the window. Leave the rest to me."

Dragging the splintered bedposts with her, Selena shuffled over to the door, turned, and looked back at her kidnappers. "Remember if you find a *homopragmatic truth*, I want it on my show first." She walked out of the suite and Justin closed the door.

Cleo stared at her watch and counted down the minutes. Could they really throw a man, even a dead man, out the window? After falling twenty stories, the body would be badly mangled, unrecognizable. Ten minutes seemed like infinity.

It's only a body. Not a person. Selena's taking all the heat.

One minute to go. The four of them dragged Butch over to the window. Kent stuck his head out the window into the cool evening air. He looked down at the traffic on the street, an endless procession of lights moving to a sonata of car horns. They lifted Butch up. "Wait," Kent shouted, squinting down at the street below, "there's a woman with baby buggy on the sidewalk." Kent watched until the woman and buggy passed by. "Okay, go for it." Butch's body seemed to fly out the window on its own, his jogging suit fluttering in the wind. Kent's heart beat wildly as he watched the body plummet. He looked away just before Butch splattered on the sidewalk.

In the hotel lobby, police, hotel workers, and onlookers surrounded an exhausted Selena tethered to splintered bedposts, caught up in fits of wailing, swooning, and recovering. No one noticed four kidnappers skulking out the hotel's side entrance.

Outside the hotel, news people and television crews gathered. Word spread on the street, "Selena's safe. She's been rescued." A mob gathered around Butch's pulverized remains. Sirens sang in the night. The Times Square electronic billboard scrolled, "SELENA'S OKAY!"

Chapter 69
SEPARATION

The kidnappers retreated to Lady Liberty Hotel near Union Square to wait on passports and visas for their trip to Russia to locate Professor Sulkohov. To avert tipping off CRAWL to his whereabouts, Justin used his nephew's name on his passport application. His nephew, Nick, a permanent resident of a Milwaukee nursing home, a man with brain damage from a truck accident, wouldn't be traveling anywhere soon.

If Gamuka attempted to use his passport, CRAWL would quickly get wind of it. So Justin and Gamuka came up with an alternate plan for getting Gamuka back to India. The two of them went shopping. One can find almost anything in New York City. Soon, the two CRAWL fugitives stuffed their little room at Lady Liberty with scuba gear, oxygen tanks, insulated underwear, bottled water, granola bars, a thick wool jacket with fur-lined hood, battery-powered body warmers, two packages of "one size fits all" adult diapers, and other accouterments essential for a climb up Mt. Everest. Gamuka, who had traveled the space-time continuum to the suburbs of Heaven via a wormhole, was about to become the first human parcel post.

"We'll Fed-Ex him to India in a box, airmail," Justin told Kent, taking note of the skeptical look on Kent's face. "He'll be all right. Look, he survived a year in a duffel bag, right. A few days inside a box'll be a piece of cake. We'll ship him to his wife in Punjab."

"Doesn't it get cold in a cargo plane?"

"He'll have battery-powered body warmers."

Waiting for their passports, the four kidnappers bided their time in the hotel lobby watching TV, playing checkers and *Scramble,* and worrying. Kent worried not only about the poison inside him, but also that if the police didn't believe Selena's story they might trace his credit card to the Plaza Hotel and come looking for him on kidnapping and murder charges. He worried about traveling all the way to Russia to find Professor Sulkohov. Justin worried that a CRAWL agent might wander into the hotel and recognize him. Gamuka worried about freezing to death inside a Fed Ex box in the cargo hold of a jet liner. But it was Cleo who worried the most.

She'd wake up at two in the morning, sweat-soaked, sitting straight up in bed, staring into the darkness, and talking out of her head about sin and wickedness, forgiveness and mercy. She bristled whenever Kent said anything about her nocturnal ramblings, snapping at him like a junkyard Doberman. Sharing a tiny hotel room with Cleo was suddenly like living inside a charged Leyden jar; sparks flew every time Kent opened his mouth. He learned to keep it shut, teeth marks on his tongue.

One morning in the hotel lobby, while Gamuka and Kent played checkers and Justin read the newspaper, Cleo turned on a TV morning show where the news and weather are spliced between outdoor rock performances, commercials, and celebrity interviews. She leaped up from her chair.

"Look you guys. Selena's on TV."

Sure enough, Selena, wearing a spiffy pants suit with double-breasted jacket, sat vis-à-vis a female interviewer on a comfortable sofa. She'd lost some weight, apparently exercising and jogging again.

"Tell us all about your ordeal, Selena," the interviewer implored.

Selena stared at the camera with complete guilelessness. "It was so awful. I was handcuffed to a bed and raped repeatedly during my captivity. I was forced to do all kinds of perverted things." She sobbed loudly, tears flowing from her blameless brown eyes. "I'm sorry. It's just so difficult to talk about it." She dabbed a moist eye with a huge lace handkerchief.

The interviewer patted Selena's hand. "That must have been just horrible."

"The most horrible thing you could imagine."

Kent shook his head. "She is a good actress."

Cleo shot Kent a stern look. "Quiet, I want to hear what she says."

Selena went on for several minutes chronicling her torture and tribulations at the hands of her perverted ex-trainer and kidnapper, Butch. The anguish was infectious. The interviewer, herself in tears, repeatedly hugged and patted the sobbing TV diva.

Kent noticed tears streaming down Cleo's face. He shrugged his shoulders. "What the heck is going on? Butch was the one handcuffed to the bed and scraped off the pavement. I don't get it?"

Cleo glared at Kent. "When something terrible happens to a woman, it's nothing. But when it happens to a man it's a major disaster."

Kent eyes glazed with confusion. "This doesn't make any sense."

Cleo voice turned venomous. "Look at poor Selena. She's devastated. And you don't have an ounce of sympathy for her."

"She's acting. Her whole story's a big lie."

"That's just like a man. If it didn't happened to them, it didn't happen. I wish men had labor pains." Cleo stomped out of the hotel lobby, her exiting glance laser sharp.

Selena said to the interviewer, "The Selena Rosalina Show will be back on the air in a week."

"Thata girl, Selena."

Kent looked at Justin. "I don't understand Cleo."

Justin placed his hand on Kent's shoulder. "It's the stress. The shoot out at Bolton. Butch's demise. Cleo will be all right in a few days."

Kent left the hotel and walked around Union Square to clear his head. He felt the thrumming of subway trains beneath his feet, vibrating up his body to a headache. The autumn sun shined brightly, the trees along the street were nearly bare, leaves and newspapers whirled in the wind. He studied the turbulent river of people moving in all directions like riptides, decked in brightly colored jackets, mufflers, and stocking caps. Dispersed among them were businessmen in spiffy topcoats and shiny leather gloves. The ragged homeless stood on street corners, some holding out tin cans, eyes begging. A man laden with gold necklaces played a mandolin. Kent scratched his head. Cleo had reacted to Selena's story as if it were true. She knew better. Didn't she? Are all women irrational?

Twice around the Square and Kent plumped down on a park bench. NYU film students making a movie asked him to move to another bench. Acting. Movies. Lies. People love fiction. Dress up and play make-believe. But reality comes crushing down eventually, always having the last shout. Poison is reality. Death is reality. Kent thought about Butch and his remains splattered on the hotel sidewalk. And old Hoover lying in that hospital room, dead as pickle pig fetus, arm flopping. And Jesus-3, his body covered with blood in that dusty underground passage. And McDonald cut to pieces by automatic weapons' fire. This search for a *homopragmatic truth* had been a death-strewn odyssey.

He walked up 5th Avenue to the Empire State building, a place he had always wanted to visit, especially after watching "Sleepless in Seattle." On the elevator up, he pondered Cleo's behavior. Perhaps she needed sleeping pills. A tranquilizer? He got off on the ninety-fifth floor and stared out through huge glass windows at the city below. Like the toothless gap in the smile of a six-year-old, the Twin Towers were gone. The work of Kamikaze terrorists, off to the happy humping grounds. Virgins in the sky. It happens when people take religion too religiously. *Make-believe* gone mad. Kent suddenly realized he was lost. From the ninety-fifth floor, the city looked the same in every direction. Skyscrapers and water and blue sky and steam pipes coming out of the street.

Kent took a cab back to the hotel and got stuck in traffic. A delivery truck at 5th. and 23rd. slammed into a car, then five other cars slammed together in a chain reaction. Ambulances, police, crumpled cars, and broken glass everywhere. It was late when he got back to the hotel. That evening he and Cleo ate in silence at a small diner off 42nd. Street, he nibbling a grilled cheese sandwich and she hardly touching her food. Later, they watched TV in the hotel lobby. After the news they headed off to their room.

The next morning, Kent rolled out of bed and tucked the blanket up around Cleo's neck as he had done his teddy bear as a child, careful not to awaken her. She'd had had another fitful night, rummaging around in the dark, talking out of her head. Now she slept like an allergic child overdosed on antihistamines, emitting those little snoring sounds of hers. He kissed her on the forehead.

Downstairs, Justin and Gamuka paced in the lobby. When they saw Kent get off the elevator they rushed up to him. "Passports have arrived. Time to get moving."

A half-hour later, Kent and Justin lugged a red and blue, three by three Fed Ex box down the street on the way to the International Fed Ex shipping office at 14th. Street & Park Avenue South. Inside the box, Gamuka curled up in his wool jacket, surrounded by his battery-powered body warmers and other survival paraphernalia. Justin pressed his ear to the box and spoke with Gamuka. They relived their narrow escapes from CRAWL, laughing and regaling in their successes and good luck. Kent almost dropped his end of the box when he dodged a mink-coated matron walking her poodle down the middle of the sidewalk.

Kent asked Justin, "What if they run the box through an x-ray scanner?"

"I'll listed the contents as ancient human skeleton and scuba equipment. I don't think there'll be a problem."

At the shipping office, Justin filled out an Air Way bill, a Certificate of Origin, an insurance certificate, along with a few other forms. The Fed Ex clerk glanced curiously at Justin when he patted the box and murmured, "Good-by, old friend."

Back at the hotel, Kent walked into his room to find Cleo gone and a handwritten note on the bed. He grabbed the note and raced down the hall to Justin's room. When Justin opened the door, Kent thrust the note at him. "Read this to me."

Justin took the paper, studied it, and looked at Kent with a blank, stunned expression.

"Well?"

Justin's voice cracked with emotion:

Dear Kent,

I love you so very much and that it makes this all the more difficult. I'm sorry I've been so cranky lately, but I had so much on my mind. You see, Jesus-3 came to me in a vision several nights ago and spoke to me. Please don't think I'm crazy. But I've been chosen to carry on his animal ministry. He told me to leave at once to start a vegetarian colony in the Rain Forrest. He said I must go alone.

This is good-by, Kent. I'll miss you so much. Please don't worry about me. Jesus-3 will provide. I'll pray for you every night. I hope Professor Sulkohov can help you find a homopragmatic truth.

Love,

Cleo

Without a word, Kent took the note from Justin's hand and slumped back down the hallway. Inside his room, he groped about like a man who had been stabbed in the heart. He leaned against the windowsill and looked out at the street. He must find her. He had to find her. He raced out of the room and down to the lobby. The desk clerk said a woman of Cleo's description had walked out the hotel about twenty minutes ago.

"Which way did she go?"

The clerk shrugged and shook his head. Kent ran out onto the street. He went first one direction than another, looking at faces and shouting, "Cleo." To find one among so many was as hopeless as a lottery ticket. He walked to 52nd. Street and back, the note crumpled in his hand. Could it really end like this? Was it over? Had a door slammed closed on their lives? He felt as if a thousand pound hay bale had been dropped on him.

At a downtown diner, Kent and Justin stared at the hamburgers and fries on their plates. Both men were too dejected to eat. Each had just been separated from the person closest to them. Gamuka was somewhere out over the Atlantic, 50,000 feet up, huddled inside a box with his oxygen tank and body warmers. Cleo was wandering the streets of Manhattan, probably lost.

"How can I find her?"

Justin shook his head. "Does she have a cell phone?"

"No. And they took mine from me at that nut house back in Bolton."

Justin leaned across the table and looked at Kent. "If it's any consolation, I'll go to Russia with you. I got a perfectly good passport. If I hang around here much longer CRAWL's gonna catch up with me."

"I can't leave not knowing where Cleo is or what she's doing."

Justin spoke bluntly, "You must find a *homopragmatic truth* or you'll die."

"I have to find Cleo first."

"What if you die trying to find her? If she thought that she prevented you from getting the antidote, it would devastate her. No, you get the antidote first and then find her."

"I suppose you're right."

"I know I am. Selena said Professor Sulkohov was your best chance for coming up with a *homopragmatic truth*."

Kent sighed, "My only chance."

"Then let's go find him."

Chapter 70
HIGH SEAS

The luxury cruise ship, the Magdalena, a floating city with a dance hall, five swimming pools, a skating rink, and mini golf course tossed about on a violent sea like a sampan in a tempest. Giant waves battered the hull and washed over the lower deck. In the ship's dispensary, the ship's doctor, Frank Chisholm, stood with his feet wide apart, bracing himself against the lurching of the ship while scrubbing his hands over a stainless steel washbasin. Across the room on a makeshift operating table lay his patient.

As uncomfortable in surgical greens as an Ozarkian in a tux, Frank prepared to operate. Sweat beaded his forehead. He hadn't held a scalpel since his Intern days back in Chicago over thirty years ago. The slippery scrub brush shot out of his trembling hands, struck the wall and fell to the floor. He took a new brush from the dispenser. At sixty-four he should be playing golf or reading the latest best seller, not operating on a sick patient on the high seas in a raging storm.

As ship's doctor, Frank quickly learned that sailing on a cruise ship was risky business, worse than running a nuthouse. Ten days at sea and already there were three octogenarians in the freezer: a heart attack, a stroke, and a fade-away. The fade-away died in a deck chair under blankets. For three days no one noticed the man wasn't breathing. Rigor mortis had come and gone, and the ship's flies had laid eggs in his mouth. It was the maggots crawling over his lips that tipped off deck hands that something was wrong.

Two screamers also shared the dispensary, a broken hip and a shattered kneecap. Despite morphine around the clock, they shrieked like sirens in the night. A cruise ship is an obstacle course for the elderly, codgers turning ankles and breaking metatarsals on the dance floor, falling out bed in rough seas, losing their medications, cracking dentures on olive seeds-- pacemakers misfiring, blood pressures rising, arthritis flaring. They always overeat at the dessert bar and throw up over the side of the ship as if the sea were a vomitorium. In every port, somebody got dysentery.

On top of it all, this twelve-year old boy on the operating table with appendicitis. The child had been hurting for three days. Frank patiently waited for the weather to break to have the patient airlifted out along with the two screamers. But with no break in the weather and port two days away and the appendix at the point of rupture, he had to do something. Frank prayed silently as he rinsed soap from his hands.

Lord, please help me remember. Steady my hand.

Frank knew the boy might die if he bungled this simple surgery. But to let a patient die because he failed to operate would be unpardonable. Frank shifted his feet to the rolling of the ship. The broken hip and shattered knee-cap caterwauled in sync.

Frank dried his hands, and a nurse assisted him on with his surgical gown and gloves. The patient was already asleep from the nurse's anesthetic. IV fluid dripped into the boy's arm vein at the same rate sweat rolled off Frank's brow. He stared over the top of his surgical mask at the iodine painted abdomen gleaming crimson-yellow under the bright surgical lamp. The smell of chloroform and antiseptic filled his nostrils. With a deep breath and a shaky hand he pressed the glinting scalpel onto the boy's abdomen.

"Wait, doctor," the nurse shouted, "the appendix is on the right side."

The nurse's voice unnerved Frank. He drew back from the operating table, tossed down the scalpel and ripped off his mask. "Bring me the passenger log." Once more he studied the log. No surgeons listed. "There must be someone on board who can do an appendectomy."

The nurse replied, "I heard the casino manager tell the purser at dinner that the passenger having a winning streak at blackjack is a doctor."

"What's his name?"

"A short Asian name. Only two letters as I remember. There it is on the passenger log. Vu."

"For god's sake get him down here."

∽✕∾

At a blackjack table in the ship's casino, Vu sat with his bride, Caressa, a tall brunette with a short IQ, an aging showgirl from Caesars. She absconded with Vu when the Feds in Atlantic City closed in on him. She hid Vu in her dressing room then drove him out of town in the trunk of her Buick. Vu rewarded Caressa with marriage. In Atlantic City Vu had broken his own rule: *scrape it, but don't skin it.* He'd won too much, too often.

His urge to gamble stronger than ever, his system of card counting and probability reckoning infallible, and his dread of the law pervasive, Vu took to the cruise ship circuit. Life on the sea was good. Good food. Movies. Dancing. Aerobic classes. Maid service. And the blackjack paid for it all. Caressa loved shopping the many interesting ports.

Vu thought it a ploy to break his concentration when the casino manager walked up to the blackjack table and ask him to step into his office. Vu wasn't worried. On the high seas, he wasn't a fugitive, just a vacationer playing blackjack, sending an occasional little gift to the Captain and often dining at his table.

The casino manager closed the office door and politely motioned the elegantly tuxedoed physician-gambler to sit down. "Doctor Vu can you perform an emergency appendectomy?"

Vu grinned. "Certainly. I've done many appendectomies." Vu's English was now flawless, polished by palavering daily with his American wife.

"Would you assist our ship's doctor with such an emergency surgery?"

In ten days at sea, Vu had won over ninety thousand dollars at the Magdalena's blackjack tables. He limited himself to a hundred thousand in winnings per cruise. Certainly, he'd assist with surgery, but it would cost the Magdalena's casino an extra hundred thousand. Who would suspect a Good Samaritan of being a casino cheat?

"I would be most happy to help."

A foot shorter than the lanky American psychiatrist assisting him, Vu stood on an orange crate to operate. The boy's inflamed appendix, the size of boiled frankfurter, all but leaped out through Vu's small, bloodless incision. Vu closed the wound dexterously. "All finished," Vu announced as he stepped down from the orange crate and pulled off his latex gloves. "The boy will be just fine."

Impressed by Vu's surgical skills, Frank asked, "How about a little drink?"

By a seascape window in a dimly lit lounge, the two doctors sipped cocktails. Oblivious to the storm and the rolling of the ship, they talked into the night. Frank took an instant likening to the ebullient, confident Vietnamese physician who spoke perfect English. Unlike Frank, Vu had been an adventurous man who had survived war and hardship. And he threw cash around like Monopoly money.

"What do you say we dine together tomorrow evening," Frank asked.

Vu smiled. "Why not, I bring Caressa along."

"Good, and I'll bring my friend Tracy."

After many dinners and cocktails together, Frank sensed that Vu was running away from something, hiding out on the sea. Vu came to the same conclusion about Frank. The commonality of their situations became their bond. A bond they nurtured daily in the lounges of the Magdalena. Little by little, piece-by-piece, the two physicians shared their histories. Two innocents, now fugitives, fettered by the irons of misfortune to the prison of the sea--a comfortable prison with all the amenities.

⁂

One evening, in their cabin on the upper deck of Magdalena, Tracy stepped out of the shower, her body covered by a nasty rash. "What is this, Frank?"

Frank looked at the red blotches. "I don't know."

"You're a doctor, what is it? Do something I'm itching like crazy."

"Here try some Benadryl."

The next night the red blotches returned. Whenever Frank came near Tracy, her lips puffed up as if they'd been injected with collagen, her eyelids swelled, and she itched like a sailor with crabs.

"Frank, I think I'm allergic to you."

Frank injected Tracy with huge doses of anti-histamines and enough cortisone to make her moon-faced. In desperation, he drugged her with tranquillizers and antidepressants, painted her blotched skin with every ointment in the dispensary, and even tried hypnosis. Nothing worked. Their glorious sex life vanished. They moved into separate cabins at opposite ends of the ship.

During the day, Vu helped Frank in the dispensary, caring for the sick. In the evenings, he taught Frank how to count and memorize cards and to calculate probabilities in his head. Frank's winning percentage at blackjack soared from forty-two percent to fifty-one percent. Like Vu, Frank was making money at the blackjack tables.

In turn, Frank taught Vu nothing. He didn't know anything to teach him. Frank's unhappy marriage, his long days on the golf course, and his years at Bolton Mental doing the same thing over and over had left him an empty man. With his medical license back home revoked, with an arrest warrant for embezzlement waiting for him if he ever returned, and with the woman he loved allergic to him, Frank had nothing. But thanks to Vu, he found an outlet for his frustrations, and it wasn't masturbating in the shower. He was winning at blackjack.

"This is more fun than golf," Frank confided over his shoulder to Vu as they sat back to back at the blackjack tables.

"Yes, just like in Saigon."

Chapter 71
SOUTH AMERICA

Tommy Tennyson and Rev. Hibberblast crossed the Merida Mountains in the back of a wood frame bus crammed with migrant workers, cowboys, and peasants toting crates of chickens, pigeons, and piglets. Sun-shriveled faces stared somberly at the two gringos. Hibberblast sat straight in his seat looking like a priest in his dark suit, high white collar, and a crucifix dangling on his chest. He smiled at the onlookers and blessed them with the sign of the cross with his right hand, while his left arm protectively encircled a bulging leather bag. Tommy avoided eye contact with the other passengers by staring out the window at the wisps of clouds hugging the steep mountainside. The smell of animals and unwashed bodies nauseated him.

At the border, Colombian regulars, soldiers with short haircuts and uniforms, waved the bus to a stop. Tommy looked at Hibberblast. "What the heck is this?"

"Stay calm," Hibberblast whispered as three soldiers boarded the bus.

The soldiers checked passports and rummaged through suitcases apparently looking for contraband. Hibberblast clung to his leather bag, which contained three hundred thousand American dollars Bobby Haggett Ministries had deposited for him in a Caracas bank. Not trusting of foreign banks, Hibberblast had carried the money all the way across Venezuela.

The soldiers took everything of value they could find, money, cell phones, hearing aids, jewelry, and Tommy's wristwatch. They didn't look inside Hibberblast's bag, but nodded politely as they walked by and called him "Padre." Hibberblast muttered something and made the sign of the cross. When the soldiers disembarked, Tommy sighed, "That was close one."

Hibberblast winked at Tommy. "God takes care of his chosen."

A few miles on down the mountain as the snake crawls, the bus jerked to a halt. A barricade of freshly felled trees blocked the road. Out of the forest came a ragged band of rebels in red bandannas and army fatigues. They rushed onto the bus shouting in Spanish and waving automatic weapons. Hibberblast slid his leather bag between his legs under the seat. The rebels emptied out suitcases and searched the passengers as they worked their way to the back of the bus.

Hibberblast sat erect, a benign smile on his face, his hand repeatedly making the sign of the cross, his knees shoved tightly together to conceal his bag. Tommy began making the sign of cross, smiling, trembling, and hyperventilating, his eyes wide with fear. Hibberblast elbowed him. "Leave this to me."

The rebels like the soldiers at the border smiled at Hibberblast, called him Padre, and didn't search him. Angered at not finding much loot, the rebels fired deafening bursts from their guns at the roof of the bus. Fragments of wood and spent cartridges rained down on the passengers who cowered on the floor, fingers in their ears. The rebels disembarked the nearly roofless bus and disappeared into the woods with their day's catch of pigs and chickens.

Tommy got up from the floor and looked at Hibberblast sitting unperturbed, covered in wood splinters. "I thought we were goners for sure," Tommy said in a trembling voice.

"You must have faith," Hibberblast admonished.

Some of the passengers helped the driver roll aside the felled trees blocking the road. Soon the bus headed back down the mountainside in third gear, the engine groaning. The mountain air turned cold, and Tommy shivered in his thin nylon coat. Lightening flashed, thunder clashed, and rain poured in through the porous roof of the bus. Passengers covered their heads with ponchos, wraps, boxes, and newspapers. Tommy pulled his coat over his head.

His hair clinging to his head, his clothes drenched, Hibberblast turned to Tommy and patted his leather bag. "I told you the Lord has His hand in this."

The bus fishtailed and slid off the road. The driver gunned the engine. The tires spun and dug deep into mud. The driver got out to find the wheels buried to the axles. "*Todos lo Vamos a caminar.* We gonna walk," the driver shouted to his passengers.

Tommy lugging two large suitcases, and Hibberblast carrying his bag of money, rain soaked and mud sucking at their feet, trudged down the mountainside to a small village. Barking dogs followed them through the muddy streets all the way to a small railway station. The bus driver informed them a train came up the mountain once a week, swung around the village, and headed back down the mountain. "*Tren por la manana.*"

"Train's due in tomorrow morning," Tommy translated.

"I know," Hibberblast said, "I speak a little Spanish."

After purchasing train tickets, Tommy and Hibberblast, exhausted, cold, and wet, fell asleep head to head on a wooden bench in the small station, Hibberblast's precious bag cradled in his arms.

The next morning, a train's high-pitched whistle awakened Tommy. He shook Hibberblast. "Better get up. Train's here. "

Hibberblast rubbed sleep from his eyes and looked around, his thick neck crunching as his head turned. After stretching away their stiffness, the two missionaries lumbered outside to the loading platform with their suitcases. Dozens of peasants with travel bags, straw baskets, and livestock on tethers crowded the platform. An idling locomotive spewed steam onto the track. The crowd inched towards the waiting coaches.

His face paling, his eyes bulging, Tommy stared at Hibberblast. "Where's your leather bag?"

Hibberblast set down his suitcase and looked at his empty hands. It took several seconds for the enormity of Tommy's question to register. He glanced around, his eyes darting, and the hair on his neck bristling. "My bag. It's gone!"

Hibberblast shoved his way through the crowd back into the station. He looked under the bench he had slept on and under all the other benches in the little station. Back on the loading platform, he ripped bags and knapsacks from the hands of passengers and emptied them onto the wooden floor. He frisked men and old ladies. A half-dozen cackling hens flew out of an overturned crate. People swung canes and umbrellas at the mad gringo priest.

A portly policeman wearing a brown uniform and official-looking hat walked up and slammed Hibberblast over the head with a truncheon. The reverend crumpled onto the platform. Two husky men in ponchos and sombreros dragged him outside and dumped him in a muddy ditch beside the road. From the station doorway, Tommy watched in terror as the two men went through Hibberblast's pockets, removed his wallet, and took the gold crucifix from around his neck. They left him lying there in mud.

Tommy set down the suitcases and rushed to his leader. He shook Hibberblast until his eyes opened. The mugged evangelist looked up at his proselyte, mud clinging to his brows and the stumble of his unshaven face. "We've lost the money."

Tommy nodded. "What are we going to do?"

"Notify the police."

"It was a policeman who hit you over the head."

Hibberblast extended his hand. "Help me up."

"You're all covered in mud."

"Duh," Hibberblast replied, back on his feet, wiping mud from his face. He looked across the road to the train departing from the station. "There goes my money."

Tommy asked again, wringing his hands, "What are we going to do?"

Hibberblast plodded up the embankment of the watery ditch. "Everything will be all right."

"This is terrible. It shouldn't have happened. That was God's money."

"I said everything will be all right. Just have faith. C'mon, we've got to notify Bobby Haggett about this."

Tommy and Hibberblast tromped through the muddy streets until they came upon a phone booth outside a small roadside café at the south end of the village. Hibberblast searched his pockets. "They took my cash and my wallet."

Tommy took off his coat and fished out an AT&T credit card and a fifty-dollar bill he'd kept hid in the lining of his coat for emergencies. He handed them to Hibberblast. Tommy twirled his artificial ears while Hibberblast placed a call. The smell of *arroz con pollo* and fried onions wafted over from the small café, making Tommy's mouth water.

Several minutes later, Hibberblast stepped out of the phone booth, rubbing the lemon-size lump on his head. "We're going to Bogotá. Bobby Haggett had foreseen our misfortune in a vision. He told me we would find the inspiration to carry on our work in Bogotá."

"Was he upset about us losing the money?"

"Of course not."

"Is he sending more money?"

"He didn't say. What's that smell?"

"Food."

The two American missionaries walked into the quaint, fly-infested café where they drank coffee and ate something that looked like elongated dumplings with specks of chicken in it. They talked about Bogotá, Colombia's largest city, and how they would get there on fifty dollars minus the cost of their present meal. They chatted about the great successes they would have and the many souls they would save.

Hibberblast looked at Tommy, a puzzled expression on his face. "Say, where are our suitcases and train tickets?"

"Gee, I left them back at the station."

Chapter 72
ST. PETERSBURG, RUSSIA

A city of towering church spires, gold copulas, and McDonalds' golden arches, St. Petersburg lay frozen in its winter sleep. Kent and Justin tromped along the snow-covered sidewalks of Nevsky Prospekt on their way to Professor Sulkohov's apartment. A bus skidded sideways, righted itself and headed on down the icy street as horse-drawn sleighs had done a hundred years before. Kent had thought of Russia as existing on another planet, in another solar system, and all the time it had been only an airplane ride away. An old woman in a wool coat, her face covered by a scarf, trudged through the snow, a bag of groceries cradled in her arms. A man stood coatless in an open doorway of an apartment house, sipping vodka from an aluminum can, and staring at the two foreigners struggling in the deep snow.

"Where is everyone?" Justin asked, his breath a funnel of fog in the frigid air. "A city of five million and no one home."

"They're all inside trying to get warm." Kent pointed to the Marlboro Cowboy on a billboard fringed with ice. "We're getting close."

They recalled the instructions given them at St. Petersburg State University for locating Professor Sulkohov's apartment. Turn right at the Marlboro Cowboy, go twelve blocks to the Lucky Strike billboard and turn left. Cross the arched bridge, keep going until you come to the Virginia Slims ad, then make a left onto Gorky street. Professor Sulkohov's apartment house is the third one on the right. Apartment 312.

The closer they got to the professor's apartment, the slower Kent walked. Back at the *Lady Liberty* he'd looked up Professor Sulkohov on Internet, a philosopher who had written an important best-selling book about philosophy. Some called him the Aristotle of the Twenty-First Century. Others called him a crackpot. There was nothing on the web about his personal life. Was the world's smartest man a cranky recluse? Would he grant

Kent an audience? Does he know a *homopragmatic truth?* Kent blew on his fingertips. He wished he had brought along some gloves.

⁓⁓

Twenty years ago, Professor Sulkohov left his position at the university in St. Petersburg to travel four thousand miles through six time zones, deep into the wilderness of Siberia. There he searched for truth, living in solitude and listening for the voices of the cosmos. He survived on berries, roots, and wild grains. He lived in caves and warmed himself by burning twigs and tree bark. For years, he listened. But he heard no cosmic voices, just the ubiquitous buzzing of insects, the rustling of leaves in the summer wind, and the howling of wolves on winter nights.

One evening, lying on the dirt floor of a dark cave, he decided there were no voices in the cosmos; only his own inner voice, a human voice. That voice spoke words, and words were the universe. And man, the creator and master of words, was the measure of all things. His inner voice told him all this.

He had gone into the wilderness a young man looking for truth. He came out gray and bearded. He proclaimed to have discovered the meaning of the universe. When he returned to St. Petersburg, he was overjoyed to learn communism had fallen. A nascent free-market economy meant he could put his ideas into a book and make a lot of money. He did just that. His book, "The Meaning of the Universe," became a best seller after getting plugged on the Selena Rosalina Show. He was not only a celebrated philosopher and a leader of a New Renaissance; he had royalty checks rolling in.

Money changed the professor's life. He got himself a four-room apartment with a gas heater on Gorky Street, installed a huge hot tub, soundproofed what he called his "Cave Room," a place where he could block out the world and listen to his inner voice without having to travel to Siberia. He bought a large supply of Viagra and hired young prostitutes to come to his apartment three or four times a week. He had a lot catching up to do for all those lonely nights in Siberian caves.

⁓⁓

Kent and Justin headed across an arched bridge. The icy wind coming off the river ripped at their faces like cat claws. The Winter Palace and the Hermitage stood in the distance. Despite communism and now capitalism, the buildings had maintained their Imperial splendor. Below the bridge, the Neva lay in rigor mortis. Kent tucked in his chin and squinted into the wind. He thought of Cleo and wondered if she was thinking of him? The professor's apartment building a gray limestone structure that had witnessed the fall of Czars and dictators loomed ahead.

Finding the entrance unlocked, the two Americans climbed the apartment stairs to the third floor. Everything was gray and colorless, the hallway walls, the whole interior. The wooden steps creaked under their weight. Kent knocked on the door of apartment 312 and heard music from coming from within. The door screeched open and a steamy mist poured out into the hallway.

Out of the mist, like an apparition, appeared a large potbellied man, dripping wet. Save for a towel around his waist, he stood naked in the doorway, an immense soaked beard plastered to his chest. From a great shaggy head, deep-set blue eyes peered through the mist. The man shivered, his muscles twitching, his face grimacing as if in pain. "*Zrastvuitye,*" boomed his deep Russian voice.

Kent grinned generously. "Sorry, we don't understand Russian."

"Americans, heh? You're not from the publishing company are you? I've got the book outlined. I'll have the first chapter in a week. Come back then." Professor Sulkohov turned and closed the door.

Kent knocked again. The door opened with another gush of steam. The shuddering professor stared at the two Americans. "You're not from the publishing company?"

"No."

"Then what do you want?"

"Selena Rosalina recommended you, Professor Sulkohov. You are Professor Sulkohov?"

The professor's twitching face lit up, azure eyes gleaming. "Selena, you say. How did she know I was writing another book? Come inside, please."

The heavy aroma of burning incense and the earthy scent of mildew greeted the visitors as they stepped through the door. The apartment's walls perspired. The place was as damp as a bathhouse. Kent and Justin gaped through the mist at a naked girl standing waist deep in a hot tub, a coquettish smile on her face. She covered her breasts with her hands. Justin massaged his eyes. The circular hot tub, the size of a small swimming pool, took up half the living room. Streams of vapor like morning mist off a lake shrouded the girl's nude body. The vaporous girl stared at the two goggling Americans and lowered herself into the water until only her head protruded. On the ledge of tub stood bottles of vodka, half-filled glasses, and ashtrays overflowing with cigar butts. A bowl of burning incense sat next to a CD player, Frank Sinatra murmuring "The Summer Wind."

The shivering professor unabashedly dropped his towel, stepped up and over the side of the tub, lowering himself into the steaming cauldron. His beard spread over the water like a great floating mass of seaweed. The girl dog-paddled to him. He reached over and turned off the CD player.

"I suppose Selena wants to introduce my new book on her show. I haven't got the first chapter done yet. Like I said, in a week."

Standing beside the tub, Kent peered through the mist at the partially immersed professor and his protégé. "I must apologize, sir. I'm not here about your book."

"You said Selena sent you."

"She told me you were the one person in the world who could help me find a *homopragmatic truth*."

Warmed by the tepid water, the professor stopped shivering. He put his arm around the girl who snuggled to him. "What kind of truth was that?"

Kent spoke slowly in syllables, *"Ho—mo—prag—mat—tic."*

"Never heard of it. Define it for me?"

Kent related as best he could what Tommy Tennyson had told him. "A *homopragmatic truth* and the effect of knowing a *homopragmatic truth* were one and the same. Once you know a *homopragmatic truth*, your life would be forever changed, the world would be changed, and nothing will be the same again. A *homopragmatic truth* is a truth so compelling it can actually bring about its own existence."

The professor scratched his nose. "I see. The train will pull into the station at four o'clock on track three. That is a truth which can be proven." The professor shook his finger with authority. "But it would become a *homopragmatic truth* if you were chained to the track when the train arrived. Yah, yah it's a truth with a punch. Yah, I like it. You could call it an Anna Karenina truth. Anna Karenina. I like that, too. You know, this kind of truth breathes fire."

Kent nodded enthusiastically. The professor seemed interested. Maybe he was going to help?

Professor Sulkohov's eyes glazed as if he had gone into a sudden trance or had gotten lost in the depths of his thought. The girl clung to him like a pilot fish. Kent and Justin exchange glances. Nearly a minute passed before the professor re-awakened to his surroundings. He stood up in the water exposing everything. The girl floated away from his side.

"A truth so compelling it brings about its own existence. I like it," the professor mumbled to himself. "Very interesting. How did you say, *Homopragmatic?* A fascinating appellation. *Homo*—a prefix meaning the sameness, uniform throughout." He folded his arms across his chest. "Of course there are other meanings, for instance, homo for Homo sapiens, homo for sexual preference, for homicidal maniac, homo erectus, but let's not go there. *Pragmatic*—an idea whose truth value lies in its observable and practical consequences." He smiled. "I like the combination."

"Then you will help me find a *homopragmatic truth?*"

The professor, shivering again, eased back down into the water. He stared at the young stranger sent by Selena Rosalina. Kent's boyish face and big soft eyes gave the impression he was simple and sincere, incapable of genius for either good or evil.

The professor bellowed, "Help you? Why should I?"

Kent took a deep breath then spoke in a solemn tone. "If you don't help me, I'll be dead before long. You see I've been poisoned and the only way I can get the antidote is to find a *homopragmatic truth*."

Kent explained to the professor about Tommy Tennyson and the poison. While the professor listened, the girl maneuvered behind him, massaging his neck and shoulders. The professor groaned with pleasure. He then stretched out to float on his back, big belly and sexual arsenal protruding, not a pretty site. He was halfway to *Nirvanaville* when Kent stopped talking.

The professor, a river barge moored to the tugboat of a pretty girl, looked up at Kent. "Why should I care if you die or not? Thousands of people die everyday. I may die tomorrow. Some tomorrow, I will die."

Justin leaned forward, his hands resting on the marble ledge of the tub. "But people wouldn't be dying if we could save them. You have a chance to save a life. You can't turn that down."

The professor grinned, exposing a keyboard of crooked, yellow teeth under a soggy mustache. "And if we saved everyone, what would we do with all the people? The planet's overcrowded as it is."

Justin eyed the professor sternly. "That's another problem. First, we save them."

The professor seemed to enjoy the repartee. He turned to Kent. "Is this clever little fellow your lawyer?"

"He's my friend."

"Well, I can't help you. I'm busy writing a new book."

Justin's face turned ruddy. "You're killing him. His death will be on your hands."

The professor floated like an otter, his hands folded on his belly. "You Americans. I spent twenty years in Siberia looking for truth. I abandoned all the amenities and comforts of civilization and endured untold hardships. And you burst in here and demand truth as if it were fast food. The trouble with America is you have three hundred million Czars running around demanding things. Let me tell you," the professor wagged his finger again, "truth is something you find for yourself. No one can find it for you. And it's not for sale. Truth is not a hot dog at a batball game."

"Baseball."

"Whatever."

Kent buttoned his coat. "Let's go, Justin, he isn't going to help."

"No," Justin thundered. "We can't leave knowing the professor will be a murderer."

"Murderer?" The professor shifted to a sitting position in the water. "Whats are you talking about?"

Justin asked, "Do you own a car?"

"Of course. Volga."

"Well, you have no right to drive it. You didn't invent the automobile. You didn't put it together with your own hands. You probably couldn't fix it if it broke down. So, you have no business driving a car."

"Nah, nah, nah," the professor responded.

Justin's eyes flashed at the professor. "If you had a heart attack right now and I could save your life by driving you to the hospital, and I refused because I hadn't invented the automobile, then I would be morally responsible for your death. Just as you will be morally responsible for Kent's death."

The professor laughed. "You're--how do you say—confused, all mix up. A car is not at all analogous to truth, especially a *homopragmatic truth*. Just the same, that was a very clever argument. And I commend you for it. And because of that, I'm going to help you." The professor's eyes shifted to Kent. "If you want to find this truth of yours, then I challenge you to my soundproof Cave Room. Complete isolation and total sensory deprivation. You must stay in there at least three weeks, listening for your inner voice. Less than three weeks never works. If you really want to find a *homopragmatic truth,* this is your best chance. Think you can handle it?"

"I guess. But if I don't come up with anything, I've just wasted another three weeks of what precious little time I have left."

The professor shrugged. "There are no guarantees. However, I will also contemplate this *homopragmatic truth* here in my tub while you are in the Cave Room. To be honest, I find it most intriguing. I don't know why I haven't thought about this before. At the end of three weeks, we will put our heads together. One of us is bound to come up something, most likely."

For the first time since being poisoned, Kent felt like he just might come up with a *homopragmatic truth.* After all, the smartest man in the world would be working with him.

The professor climbed out the hot tub and wrapped himself in a towel. He held up a large towel for the girl as she daintily exited the tub. Kent and Justin politely diverted their gaze.

The professor spoke directly to Justin. "I'm looking forward to many more conversations with you. You will be my house guest for the next three weeks."

Chapter 73
CROCODILES

Private detective Rummels, the ex-CRAWL agent presumed dead, the Kenny Rogers look-alike, decided to check out the address on Siphya Road where Larry Lakes told him the mysterious packages he worked with were stored. He hired a *tuk-tuk*, a three-wheel open air taxi with a 2-cycle engine that maneuvered through Bangkok's rush hour with the deftness of a bicycle. He wished he had taken an air-conditioned taxi. The exhaust from the bumper-to-bumper traffic mixed with Bangkok's already heavily polluted air burned Rummels' lungs like mustard gas.

When he got to the address Larry gave him, he took some deep sucks on his asthma inhaler and slunk around to the back of the gray stone building he thought was a warehouse. He peeked inside through a grimy window and discovered the Siphya Road warehouse wasn't a warehouse at all, and that Larry's mysterious packages weren't like anything he'd imagined.

Inside, Chinese peasants in gray peasant garb were crammed into a drab, sparsely furnished room, where they chattered excitedly. Rummels placed his ear to the window. He understood a little Mandarin. The peasants spoke of a new life in a far away place. Some practiced English amenities, salutations, greetings, courtesies, and counting to ten. Larry's mysterious packages were human beings. One didn't have to be a CRAWL agent to see through this. Unwittingly, Larry Lakes had gotten involved in an illegal alien smuggling operation.

Rummels next took an air-conditioned taxi to the docks where he located the HTMS *Quing Lu*, the 20,000-ton cargo ship waiting to carry Larry's packages to the New World. The bill of lading listed the packages as "perishable merchandise." Looking and sounding like Kenny Rogers has its advantages. Rummels waited around in a bar on the wharf until one of the sailors from the *Quing Lu* recognized him and struck up a conversation.

"What's a celebrity like you doing in place like this, Mr. Rogers?"

"It's a long story."

A few drinks later Rummels asked the sailor, "How long have you been sailing with the Quing Lu?" Rummels motioned to the bartender. "My friend here needs another drink."

The drunken sailor spilled his guts. A very unpleasant story.

The *Quing Lu* was little more than a slave ship. Handcuffed during the entire passage across the Pacific, the aliens got hosed down with water every three days and given just enough food to stay alive. They disembarked in South America to be later flown to Mexico, Texas, or Florida. Hoping to start a new life in the New World, most ended up in stash houses, where unscrupulous employers put them to work at fast-food restaurants, sweat shops, packing houses, or as farm laborers. Most of the women ended up in motel-based brothels.

Rummels returned to his office and telephoned a contact he had on the Bangkok Police Force. He learned American agents from the Immigration and Naturalization Service, the INS, planned to close in on a worldwide alien smuggling operation here in Bangkok.

On Tuesday evening, Rummels took a water taxi up the Chao Phrayo River to meet with Larry. The private eye stood in the hatchway of the small boat and stared out at the flotilla of barges and motorboats making their way down river. A cool breeze from the bay cleansed the air, and he inhaled deeply. He pulled down the brim of his Panama to block the sun's reflection off the water. Rummels figured that Larry's old girlfriend, Veronica, chose Larry as her man in Bangkok because he'd proved himself a schlemiel in the Green Pastures Pesticide and Fertilizer debacle. By taking Veronica's uncle hostage when he escaped from prison, Larry had played right into her hands. A ready-made fall guy.

Rummels asked Larry to meet him at the Temple of the Reclining Buddha in Wat Pho, a place where they could talk without being overheard. At first, Rummels didn't recognize Larry in his Thai fisherman pants, flowered silk shirt, wrap-around Ray Ban, and ball cap. The clicking of Larry's left foot on the pavement gave him away. "That you, Larry?"

"Where the hell you been? I've been waiting here over an hour."

"Were you followed?"

Larry's eyes widened. "Not that I know of, why?"

The two men strolled the perimeter of a concrete crocodile pond girded by five feet of chain link fence. In the evening shadows outside the temple's walls, squabbling Buddhist sects argued Dhamma. Above the squabbling, came a muezzin's cry, the fifth and final prayer of the day.

Rummels cleared his throat. "Those packages of yours are illegal aliens."

Larry stiffened, his expression that of complete surprise. "What?"

"I placed a camera and recorder in air duct of an INS agent's apartment and tapped his phone. They figure you're the kingpin of the operation because the money flows through you."

"I don't handle any money other than my paycheck."

"You wire large sums into oil accounts in Dubai. From there it gets filtered through a Canadian lumbering operation into a number of small Texas companies. The money is transferred from one Texas bank to another until the trail turns too cold to follow."

Larry stared at his private detective in astonishment. "I don't believe it. Are you making up this bullshit?"

Rummels pulled an I-pod from his pocket and offered the earpiece to Larry. "It's all right here. You want to hear it straight from INS agent's mouth?"

Larry stared at the I-pod in Rummel's hand as if it were a gun. "Okay, I get it. A hidden algorithm."

Rummels stared inquisitively at his client.

"Don't you see," Larry said. "Someone embedded an algorithm in my computer that automatically handles the money and makes those deposits."

"If that's true, you've been set up and set up good. You're about to take a hit on smuggling, racketeering, and money laundering charges, as well as human rights violations. You're going to jail for a long, long time."

Larry leaned on the chain link fence separating him from man-eating reptiles. "All my fuckin' life I've been a fool. How long before the INS closes in?"

"I figure you've got two, maybe three weeks."

"I'm going to run."

Rummels shook his head. "It's too late. The net is out. You can't go to the bathroom without them knowing it."

Larry strode to the base of the stone tower that overlooked the temple's walls. He kicked at the stones, bent his head in silent contemplation, and stared at his twitching left foot. Seconds passed before he straightened and squared his shoulders "I'm not going back to prison. I'll jump in with those god-damned crocodiles first."

"There's another way."

"Oh, yah?"

"It'll be expensive."

"I'll pay anything."

Rummels dipped his head slightly and removed his panama. "It will take more than that."

"More than a million dollars."

"Much more."

"What in the world are you talking about?"

Rummels fingered his hat. "That supercomputer in Japan you told me about."

"The Hashimotioto? You can't be serious."

"If that machine is as smart as you say, it'll bring a fortune on the black market."

Larry shook his head in disbelief.

Rummels griped Larry's shoulder firmly. "There's nothing to think about. It's either the Hashimotioto or those crocs."

Chapter 74
THE CAVE ROOM

Professor Sulkohov invited Kent and Justin to dine with him at the Winter Palace Restaurant, a fancy place with an old world ambience: ornate 19th century colonnades, sparkling chandeliers, waiters in royal red livery. Russian oldies-but-goodies played in the background. After a *zakouski* of caviar and pickled reindeer tongue, came an entree of leg of lamb followed by *paskha*. The professor shivered throughout dinner and complained about being cold, despite sitting near a flaming fireplace, bundled up in three layers of clothing under a magnificent sable coat. He looked like an intrepid explorer just back from an arctic expedition. The professor wore cashmere-lined gloves while dining and demanded that the perspiring waiter put more logs on the fire.

His eccentric attire, his wild gestures, and his deep thunderous voice that echoed from the walls like loudspeakers in a railway station, made Professor Sulkohov the focus of attention throughout the restaurant. His massive head hair and enormous beard gave him a ferocious bearing that commanded, if not respect, awe.

The professor polished off his *paskha,* leaned back in his chair, and lit a cigar. He looked at Kent. "You must enter the cave room with a positive attitude. And remember some of mankind's greatest thoughts originated in solitude. In the quiet of a cave, sheltered from the cold, the wind, and rain, our ancient ancestors discovered fire and plotted the demise of the saber-toothed tiger. On those soot-covered walls he or she--I prefer the neuter 'hes'--scratched out the first written words and produced the first art. Descartes, the great French philosopher, in the dead of winter, secluded in a small stove-heated room conceived his 'Meditations.' Archimedes discovered the principle of buoyancy while daydreaming in a hot bath. Kekule, the chemist, visualized the structure of Benzene in a dream. God spoke to Moses when he was alone on that mountain. Muhammad spoke with the Angel Gabriel while self-exiled in the hills outside Mecca. Alone forty days and forty nights in the wilderness, Jesus withstood the lure of the devil.

"I must warn you," the professor added, the cigar in one gloved hand, a glass of vodka in the other, "once you enter the Cave Room there will be no coming out until the three weeks are up."

"I understand."

Justin patted Kent on the back. "Thata boy."

The professor blew smoke donuts into the air. "You must not fight the silence. For it is in silence the inner voice resides."

"When do we start?"

"Right away, tonight." The professor waved his glass in the air and shouted to the waiter, "More vodka."

⁕

The thick black padding covering the walls, floor, and door of the Professor Sulkohov's Cave Room absorbed light and sound like a giant sponge. A canvas cot abutted one wall. A smaller connecting room, also heavily padded, contained a lavatory, a stool, and a shelf with a microwave and a small freezer crammed with frozen dinners. Ingresses and egresses of the digestive tract were handled in this room, which was lit three times a day for twenty minutes by a dim red light controlled by an outside timer over which the cave room's occupant had no control. Except for those twenty-minute intervals of amber murkiness, darkness shrouded the Cave Room day and night.

Upon entering the Cave Room, Kent noticed a gentle roar of nothingness, like his head had been thrust into a giant seashell. He wasn't sure he could handle being completely alone. He'd always depended on others for advice, for answers to his many questions. Without a word, the professor closed the door. An utter blackness engulfed the room. Following the sharp click of a lock, the roar of silence became deafening.

Kent cried out, "I've changed my mind, I'd like out of here." The words rolled dumb from his lips, his voice absorbed by the spongy walls. He sat forlornly on the padded floor surrounded by nothingness. *Oh, my god, three weeks without light or sound!*

The professor retreated to his hot tub to contemplate for himself the intriguing problem of a *homopragmatic truth*. He sat immobile for days in the steaming water, a marble Zeus in a palace fountain. Justin, a houseguest to a host in a trance, wondered if the professor had lost his mind, if the heat from the tub had cooked his brain? Each day, the professor grew more inert, his eyes more fixed, his breathing waxing and waning as if controlled by the content of his thoughts. When Justin spoke or made an inadvertent noise, the professor would raise his hand up to silence him. Twice a day the professor climbed out of the tub, wrapped himself in a towel, ate a chunk of bread, went to the bathroom, and climbed back into the tub.

On a snowy Wednesday afternoon, the professor shot upright in his watery think-tank, stretched, looked up around, and spoke to Justin. "I've finished thinking. The thoughts must incubate now. That's it for the time being. All one can do is wait for insight."

The professor made some phone calls and then returned to the hot tub to listen to Sinatra, sip vodka, smoke cigars, and inhale incense. The hot water, the steamy air, the vodka, and the girls who visited frequently turned a cold Russian winter into an endless sybaritic holiday.

The professor invited Justin to join him in the tub. Self-conscious about taking his clothes off, Justin balked at first. But after some coaxing, he lost his inhibitions and dipped into the heated waters of self-indulgence. He learned not only to enjoy the warm soaks, but also the conversations, the vodka, and the girls. Idly soaking in the tub one day, Justin asked the professor, "Why do you shiver and shake so much?"

The professor answered in his deep Russian voice, "I nearly froze to death in a treetop once. I've been cold ever since."

"What in the world were you doing in a treetop?"

"Staying out of reach. I had ventured far out into the Siberian wilderness in my search for truth. The weather without warning turned bitterly cold. Winter came early that year, catching both man and beast off guard. I got lost in the taiga. My supplies ran out. I was starving. In the snow, I discovered paw prints of a large bear and two half-grown cubs. They too were unprepared for an early winter and apparently were too lean for hibernation. I followed their trail of overturn rocks and ripped-up logs where they had grubbed for insects, worms, and mushrooms—anything to eat. I survived on the dung they left behind. It doesn't taste bad when frozen and its actually quite nutritious, laden with vitamins. I trailed the bears for two weeks. They moved in and out of a circular pattern about their territory. At night, I stayed in caves and wooden lean-tos that I had put up along their territorial bounds.

"The bears produced enough dung to keep me alive. But as the days grew colder the amount of dung decreased. The bears must have been starving. The less they ate, the less I ate. I discovered they had visited all the shelters I had slept in, and that their circular trail was shrinking. Suddenly, the trail took an inward, spiraling course. I figured the bears in their weakened condition lacked the energy to patrol their entire territory. The trail grew even tighter as the days passed, as if the starving bears were on the scent of a reindeer or some definite food source. Then it dawned on me. The bears had picked up my scent. They were tracking me as I tracked them. I knew this deadly shrinking circle would eventually close in on me? No sooner had I reasoned this, than I looked up and saw the three gaunt, salivating beasts racing towards me, snow flying in their wakes. I was their potential high-protein dinner. I had nowhere to go but up a tree.

"The two smaller bears came right up the tree after me, snorting and grunting, their long claws ripping at my feet. I climbed higher, knowing the tree, a deciduous perennial, probably Hackberry, wouldn't support two half-grown bears. I feared all of us crashing down to the earth together. I clung to the upper branches, looking down at the climbing beasts, the tree bending and groaning under their weight. The mother bear paced at the foot of the tree, salivating and grunting encouragement to her cubs. Unable to go higher, the branches above too slender to support me, I awaited my fate. Fortunately, the lower branches began to snap under the bears' weight. They were forced to retreat, their claws ripping away strips of bark as they slid back to earth. The three of them sat in the snow at the base of the tree and peered up at me. I felt like a Cornish hen in the market place, tethered with a string.

"That night I nearly froze. My hands went completely numb as I clung to the tree branches. In the morning, the bears were still there. They circled the tree, bayed at it, charged it, jarring snow from the branches. Although completely numbed by the cold, I somehow managed to stay up in the tree. I licked snow from the branches to satisfy my thirst. At night, the frigid wind whipped through me like a raging fire, burning and stinging. Tears froze on my cheeks like scabs. I was unable to open my eyelids until midday when the sun thawed them. Stiff as the branches I clung to, I managed three days and three nights in that tree. On the fourth day, half-frozen, I looked down. During the night, the bears had given up and moved on.

"I must have willed myself down from the tree, for I seemed unable to move my limbs or to feel anything. Once down, I quickly gained strength on the generous supply of bear dung at the base of the tree. Somehow, I made it to a nearby cave and started a fire. I've been shivering ever since."

The professor refilled his vodka glass. "I vowed to stay warm the rest of my life."

Chapter 75
A SHOCKING TRUTH

Kent's fingertips traced out his nose, his mouth, and moved down across his chest and along his arms. Kent was reassuring himself that his body was still in one piece, that it had not become fragmented in this black "Helen Keller" world of the Cave Room. He'd become a tactile creature, probing, touching, and feeling his way along the floor until bumping into one of the padded walls. The only sounds he heard were the incessant roar of the seashell and the noise of air rushing in and out of his nostrils. No inner voices. Not one word from the hinterland of his unconscious. Not even an idea. Just the white flickers and the fleeting colors one sees in total darkness.

He discovered himself to be a creature of urges: the urge to drink, to eat, to relieve himself. To bang his head against the walls. To scream. *Where is my inner voice?* His hands tracked along the floor and up the wall. The dozen or so photons bouncing around in the room gave only the faintest outline of the black chamber.

Maybe someone with dyslearnia doesn't have an inner voice? Maybe only certain people, like philosophers, have inner voices. I don't hear a thing, just that roar of the seashell. How long have I've been here? Thirty-one or forty-one red lights?

He beat his fists against the wall. "Let me out of here before I go completely crazy!" He wished he were asleep. Sleep would be a holiday from this torment of nothingness. Were he asleep, he wouldn't be wishing, unless, of course, he was dreaming he was wishing. He wasn't sure which state he was in. He prayed for a dream. A dream would mean he was sleeping. *Am I dreaming?*

In his mind's eye he saw his mother's loving face, exactly as in a video his father made several years ago. It was Christmas and they had gathered around the tree and he opened packages as his mother neatly collected the ribbons to store away. His pet beagle lay on the rug beside the fireplace. All at once it was the Fourth of July at the Harkerville Lake, sprays of colorful fountains filled the night air, reflecting off the water's surface. Firecrackers burst. Rockets shot high into the sky and exploded into huge sparkling umbrellas of red, white, and blue.

Then all color drained away, replaced by a shadowy nightmare. A gang of boys beat up Tommy Tennyson in the alley behind the school. They yanked on his ears. Pounded his crooked face. Blood gushed from his nose. They ripped off his shirt. He ran and they chased him, throwing rocks, cursing, and shouting names. Tommy ran for his life, ears flopping, his bloodied crooked face scrunched up in a hideous grimace. Kent as if standing outside his own body saw himself pick up a rock and hurl it at Tommy who cried out in agony.

Kent screamed, "For God's sake, let me out of here."

⁂

Professor Sulkohov, a true raconteur, never tired of telling Old Russian tales, anecdotes, and personal adventures to Justin, as well as explaining to him things like Quantum physics, String Theory, and Freud's theory of the unconscious. The professor's florid facial expression, deep-throated Russian accent, and exuberant gesturing made every thing he said as exciting as a new 007 movie. Justin enjoyed the professor's stories immensely, as well as the vodka, the cigars, and the lissome Russian courtesans the professor kept on retainer. NBA stars don't have this much fun.

After cocktails and dinner at a Russian restaurant, Justin and the professor retired to the hot tub for an evening of vodka, cigars, and a warm soak on a very cold St. Petersburg's evening. The professor, in the midst of one of his stories, abruptly stopped talking as if sidetracked by a thought. His eyes glazed and he stared right through Justin.

Passing his hand in front of the professor's eyes, Justin got no response. "Can you hear me," Justin shouted. He shook the professor. "Are you all right?"

The professor's eyes slowly lost their faraway look and focused on Justin. The professor grinned, a knowing, all knowing grin. "I'm fine. I've never felt better." The professor leaped up and shouted, "I've just discovered a *homopragmatic truth*. Not just a *homopragmatic truth*. THE HOMOPRAGMATIC TRUTH! The granddaddy of all *homopragmatic truths*."

The professor glowed with jubilance, his face cherry red, his eyes now wild and darting as he danced in the tub, his knobby knees churning the water like an outboard motor. Justin clung to the edge of the tub, goggle-eyed. He knew the professor had to be onto something big.

"Go unlock the Cave Room," the professor shouted. "Tell Kent I have discovered the truth he's looking for. The one *homopragmatic truth* that puts all other *homopragmatic truths* to shame." The professor, wired like a speed addict, sang in Russian as he jitterbugged in the water.

Justin crawled out of the tub, wrapped himself in a towel, and raced up the hallway to the Cave Room, pursued by the professor's joyous singing. The excitement was contagious. Justin's heart pounded, his hands trembled. At last, Kent would have his *homopragmatic truth* and soon the antidote that would save his life.

A LOUD POP!

The lights went out. The professor screamed, "WWWWwwwooo."

Justin made his way back down the darkened hallway to living room.

"Professor, are you all right?"

There was no answer. Justin inched up to the hot tub and stood there aghast. In the dim light from the frosted-over living room window, he saw the professor floating face down in the tub. His hair and immense beard spread over the water's surface like a floating tapestry. The odor of brunt plastic fouled the air. The professor's right hand, singed and blackened, gripped the side of the tub. Justin noticed the Hitachi CD player in the water, dangling by its electrical cord. In his jubilation, the professor must have knocked it into the tub.

Justin carefully stepped around the puddles on the floor and jerked the CD player's electrical cord from the wall outlet. He loosened the professor's grip on the tub and rolled him over. The professor's face was a pain-fixed grimace, his crooked yellow teeth clenched, his eyes open but inert as marbles. Justin could not find a pulse. The professor was dead as horsemeat.

Justin rushed down the hallway to the Cave Room. He grasped the door's bolt and then remembered Kent had been in there only two weeks. The professor had said it would take a minimum of three weeks to find one's inner voice. Kent's only chance of coming up with a *homopragmatic truth* now was to stay inside the room another week.

Justin shivered in his towel. The gas heater had gone out with the sudden loss of electricity. What about the professor? In a few days, the smell of his decomposing body would bring the authorities. Justin reset the breaker switch and the lights came on. *Get a grip. Think of something.* He threw off his towel and climbed into the hot tub. He floated the professor's body to the edge of tub and with great effort shoved it over the side. It fell to the floor with a horrendous thud.

Justin got out the tub and wrapped himself in a fresh towel. He then rolled the professor's corpse up in a rug, and boosted by the adrenaline surging through his veins, dragged rug and corpse into the professor's bedroom.

He rested on the edge of a bed for a while before unrolling the rug and going about the awkward business of hoisting the professor's ponderous body onto the bed. He did it in three steps: first the head and shoulders, then the arms and the trunk, and finally the legs. He plopped down on the bed beside the corpse to catch his breath.

After a few minutes of rest, he wrapped the corpse up in a polyester bed sheet and cracked open the window next to the bed. Icy St. Petersburg air rushed inside like a blizzard. Justin shivered as he closed the heat vents in the bedroom. Within a few hours, the professor's mummy-wrapped body would be frozen solid.

Justin closed the bedroom door and stuffed newspapers into the cracks at the top and bottom. The bedroom was now a meat locker. Justin walked back into the living room and stood beside the hot tub, staring into the steamy water. While Kent searched for his inner voice in the Cave Room, Justin would have the hot tub, the girls, and endless supply of cigars to himself.

Chapter 76
PECUNA

The morning Cleo walked out on Kent—she preferred to think of it as *following her calling*—she wandered through the streets of New York City, unsure where to go. In her dream, her vision, Jesus-3 had instructed her to go to the rain forest to start a vegetarian colony. In her heart she believed Jesus-3 would somehow direct her there. In the meantime, she walked across the Brooklyn Bridge and back, sat for an hour at a bus stop, watching as passengers boarded and disembarked the buses. She meandered around Grand Central for a while before heading back outside. Cold and hungry, she realized she was now homeless like those people she'd seen in Central Park, and tonight she would have nowhere to sleep. Then the miracle happened. She noticed a *Help Wanted* sign in the window of the "Tours of Nature Travel Agency" on Fifth Avenue. She walked inside and filled out an application.

"The job entails a lot of traveling," the manager of the agency, a short man in a gray suit, told Cleo as he perused her application. "I see you have a college education and a nursing degree." He smiled. "You're just what we're looking for, someone who's educated, who can communicate, and if need be, God forbid, help some of our older customers if they should have problems. How is your vision?"

"Twenty-twenty."

"Do you have a passport?"

Cleo fished her passport from her purse. "It just came today. What kind of job is it?"

"Wildlife guide on one of our tours."

"What kind of tour?"

"A river cruise."

"Where?"

"The rain forest."

Cleo paled. *The Rain Forest.* She knew a divine hand was guiding her.

The manager looked a Cleo. "Are you all right?"

"Wonderful. Simply wonderful."

He handed Cleo some papers. "Well then, here's a printout of the job description, read it at your convenience. There'll be more papers to fill out and you'll need to get some immunizations."

According to the job description, Cleo would travel down the Amazon on the riverboat Pecuna. From its picture on the printout the riverboat looked like a stately old Victorian mansion mounted on an iron hull heavily caked in rust and plankton. As wildlife guide, Cleo would point out to the onboard tourists the animals along the river's bank: anteaters, howler monkeys, paca, armadillo, three-toed sloth and others. Later that afternoon at a medical clinic in downtown Manhattan, a nurse gave Cleo a series of shots and a bottle of malaria pills.

After a sleepless night in a homeless shelter, Cleo returned the next morning to the Tours of Nature, where the agency's manager gave her plane tickets and a colored atlas of the common rain forest animals to study on her flight from New York to Lima, Peru.

Cleo cleared her throat. "I seem to have misplaced my pocket cash. Could you advance me enough for a taxi to the airport?"

"Sure. We'll chalk it up to traveling expense."

※

When she disembarked the airplane in Lima, Cleo kissed the ground and thanked God for bringing her to South America. Soon she would be in the rain forest, as Jesus-3 had instructed her. Somehow, some way, she would get around to her real mission of starting a vegetarian colony.

She continued to study her animal pictures on the bus from Lima to Iquitos, where she boarded the Pecuna. She could now identify and pronounce the names of fifty animals indigenous to the rain forest. The next morning she donned a tan safari outfit and pith helmet with mosquito netting, walked out on the deck of the Pecuna and inhaled the fresh air wafting off the river.

"Look," she shouted to the gray-headed American passengers on deck, "Spider monkeys. See how they move effortlessly through the trees. Better get some pictures, they're endangered species."

She pointed out and named other animals along the riverbank for the passengers who instantly fell in love with this young, pretty, engaging, and exuberant Jane Goodall.

Someone pointed at the riverbank and asked, "What in the world is that?"

"A three-toed sloth."

"Where do the three-toed sloths make their homes?"

"Like the monkeys in the tree tops."

"Will we see any Jaguars on this tour?"

Cleo shrugged. "If we're lucky. You must remember, they're very secretive and usually avoid people."

"What do pacas eat?"

"They're vegetarian."

Vegetarian. Her answer set Cleo off sermonizing about the carnality of carnivores, the salubrious advantages of being a vegetarian, and the moral weaknesses of people who eat meat. Instead of pointing out the fauna along the river, she preached Jesus-3 gospel. Just what hungry tourists wanted to hear. "Meat eaters are sinners, who defile their bodies as well as their souls." Passengers soon shunned her as if she were a life insurance agent.

The next day, the meat-eating tourists gathered in the Pecuna's dinning hall to scarf down some original Amazon cuisine: Tapir steak, grilled peacock-bass, and alligator soup. Before they could get the soupspoons to their mouths, Cleo flew in through the door in a righteous fury, overturned dinner tables and lashed out at the passengers who scurried to their cabins for safety. "Repent, you who feast on the cadaver flesh of slaughtered animals. Do ye not know ye have sinned?"

She overpowered the boat's chef to take thirty-eight pounds of prime rib from the ship's refrigeration unit and tossed it overboard. A holy act of defiance.

"What the hell got into you, woman," the Captain of the Pecuna asked Cleo when she was brought before him.

"The Spirit, sir."

"I should have you thrown overboard. You're confined to your quarters for the remainder of the cruise."

⁂

A mass of warm, moist air from the equatorial Pacific moved inland, sucking up heat, rotating violently over the pampas, and blowing across the tropical woodlands with cyclonic fury. Dark rain clouds rag-rolled the sky. The river swelled with waves and waterspouts. Then came torrents of rain, blinding flashes of lightening, and deafening clashes of thunder. The Pecuna dipped and rolled, its hull battered by uprooted trees and enormous waves.

Cleo bounced around inside her cabin like a soccer ball, clinging to the furniture, the bed, anything she could hold onto.

Out of the gray turbulent sky, a bolt of lightening struck the Pecuna's midsection with the impact of a warhead. Splintered clapboard flew into wind. Flames shot up from the main deck. The Pecuna's rusted hull groaned, and as if slammed by a mighty ax, cracked bow to stern.

A lightening bolt ripped away a chunk of ceiling in Cleo's cabin and blew the hinges off the cabin door. Jagged streaks of electricity raced about as if the wiring within the walls was rebelling. Lamps exploded. The cabin burst into flames. Cleo ran to the door. A stray electrical burst hit her in the chest like a stun gun and slammed her against the de-hinged cabin door. The splintered wood from the door ripped through her Safari jacket and dug into her skin. She and the door crashed to the floor.

With the loud prolong bellow of dying animal, the Pecuna split in two.

Water rushed into the cabin and Cleo floated out on the cabin door into the swell of the river. Clinging to the door, she stared through the cataracts of rain at passengers leaping from the burning, cleaved, sinking riverboat into the swirling water.

She hugged the door with all her strength as the raging river carried her away. Floating debris in the wild swirl of the river shredded her clothes, and jagged tree limbs cut into her flesh. Mauled and scraped, her clothes torn away, she clung to the door as the river's current swept her into the night. The next day the river was calm, but her skin reddened painfully under a blazing sun as she floated along on the door. She looked across the smooth face of the river away from the sun's gleam.

A rolling saurian eye protruded above the water's surface and stared back at her. An eye of an enormous head with a hideous rounded snout. A twelve-foot alligator surfaced without rippling the water. It gazed at the strange floating object beside it. Cleo fingers dug into the door, and she held her breath as the monster with a gentle lash of its leathery tail glided away.

She floated on the door for two days before eddies in the swollen river swept her into backwater that penetrated deep into the rain forest. Shielded from the sun by the thick overhead foliage and straddling the door as on a surfboard, she hand-paddled until her dangling feet touched bottom. Carrying her door, she waded through the water to the riverbank.

She was at last in the rain forest. Her unclad, blistered skin shone ghost-like in the shaded darkness of the forest's canopy. She dragged the pine door that had become her friend, her fetish, and now a symbol of her faith, through the unending tangles of vegetation. She ate mosses, lichens, and fleshy fungi growing on rotting trees that had fallen to the forest floor decades before.

Weakened by insect bites and blood-sucking leeches, and totally exhausted from battling the undergrowth, she collapsed onto her door, crushing a rich growth of young orchids, several small ferns, and a colony of leaf-cutting ants.

Eyes peered out from the shadows of the forest at the sunburned white nude asleep on a rectangular piece of wood.

Chapter 77
THE HIVARO

Cleo woke up on the floor of the jungle surrounded by two-dozen potbellied Hivaro warriors in skimpy loincloths and armed with pointed sticks. Handsome though sad-looking men with straight black hair in Prince Val cuts, they stared in silence at the white stranger. Conscious of her nudity, Cleo crossed her arms over her breasts. The Hivaro people, indigenous to the rain forest, had been waiting three hundred and seventy years for their "white god" to return.

Back in 1640, one of General Teixeira's Portuguese soldiers got lost in the rain forest searching for gold. Until now, that lost soldier had been the only white person the Hivaro had ever seen in all their long history. The soldier, the Hivaro's original white god, was a powerful being who carried a glinting knife as long as a his leg, and a thunder stick that killed men and animals instantly from great distances. His hat was harder than stone and gleamed brightly in the sun. He stayed for three months with the Hivaro, a living white god, eating their food, screwing their women, and killing things. One day while bathing in the river, he was crushed and swallowed by a huge anaconda, which according to Hivaro legend is the way gods travel from one world to another. They knew the white god would return someday, because he had left behind his long knife and thunder stick.

The warriors noticed that the white god sitting on a piece of wood didn't have a penis and looked like a woman. The medicine man, a scrawny tribal elder with spindly legs, said to the warriors, "A god can look like anything He wants to look like, even a woman."

"Why is He sitting on piece of flat wood?"

The medicine man shrugged. "Don't ask me."

With great reverence, the warriors lifted Cleo and her door onto their shoulders and carried her to their village. Cleo sat on the door with her knees drawn and her arms across her chest, her every fiber trembling with fear. In the village, children, women, and old men rushed from thatch-covered huts to view and pay homage to the penis-less *blanco deo* riding through on a piece of flat wood. The warriors gently sat her down in the center of the village.

Cleo feared that these dark-eyed denizens of the rain forest might be cannibals and headhunters. She suddenly wished she hadn't walked out on Kent back in New York City. Just leaving a note without even saying good-bye was crass and irresponsible. But her Jesus-3 vision had been so vivid, her mission so definite, and to tell Kent good-bye would have been so painful—oh, lord, she wished she were back in Kent's arms. *What have I done?* Her eyes shimmered with tears. She muttered what she thought would be her last words, "Oh, Kent forgive me."

The Hivaro echoed her words as best they could, "Ooo Kant fogibba meh."

Surprised that her captors tried to imitate her words and no longer self-conscious of her nudity since the village women were also unclad, Cleo stood up to look around. Immediately, the Hivaro fell on their knees, heads touching the ground.

They're worshipping me?

Cleo remembered from her high school history class that the Aztecs had thought the Spanish explorer Cortez was a god. She took a deep breath, clapped her hands, and motioned the Hivaro to stand.

They leaped to their feet.

"Can anyone here speak English?" The villagers tried to imitate her words, but it came out a jumble.

"Any food around here?" Cleo moved her hand to her mouth as if eating. That worked. An old woman approached Cleo and handed her a piece of dark fruit. Cleo ate the fruit making an "aah," sound.

"Aah," parroted the Hivaro.

Cleo was suddenly inundated with nuts, figs, chopped lintels, mushrooms, and cooked roots. A pretty village girl with long glistening hair carried on a broad leaf the cooked hindquarters of some animal and set it before Cleo. The girl smiled and bowed before the white god. Cleo's face screwed up in disgust. She shoved the meat away. The villagers looked with anger upon the young girl who had offended the white god. They each in turn screamed at the girl, kicked her, and beat her with sticks. The girl rolled on the ground, but made not a sound. She had offended the white god; she deserved to die.

"Hey, stop that," Cleo shouted. She cuddled the girl in her arms and patted her shoulder. "It's okay. Don't be afraid."

Then Cleo stood and glanced at the villagers cowering before her, and at that moment she realized Jesus-3 had brought her to these people. Yes. She would start her vegetarian colony right here. Cleo picked up the cooked hindquarters of the unfortunate animal, carried it to the nearby riverbank and flung it into the water. "No meat!"

"Nah metta," echoed the villagers.

After Cleo gorged on fruits and roots, the old woman of the village led her to a large hut and held out her gnarled hand as if to say, "Take it, this hut is yours." The hut stood in a place of honor, right next to the medicine man's hut. Sacred relics including the ancient Portuguese thunder stick and razor sharp sword hung on the wall opposite the entrance.

Cleo lay down on soft hemp blankets that covered the floor of the hut, curled up, and instantly fell asleep. She awakened to the soft touch of maidens gently massaging her wounds and sunburn skin with oil that smelled like an expensive perfume. Cleo sat up and looked around. "Oh my," she gasped, "we're all naked." She smiled at the maidens. "If the men of the village can wear loincloths so can we."

The villagers stood like obedient vassals in front of the hut when Cleo stepped out into the morning sunlight. She knew they were awaiting a divine decree of some sort. Cleo waved to the medicine man. Humbly, the spindly-legged holy man walked up and knelt on his knotted knees before the white god. Cleo motioned him to his feet, reached out, and ripped off his loincloth. The medicine doubled over as if he'd been belly-slammed with a baseball bat. Eyes bulging, a look of major disaster on his face, he covered his genitals with his hands. Cleo handed the loincloth to one of maidens. Soon all the males removed their loincloths and gave them to the women. For the first time in history, the village's genitalia-concealment roles reversed.

"No, no," Cleo shouted. "I want everyone to wear loincloths." The villagers stared at the white god, grins of confusion on their faces.

Language proved a huge barrier between god and villagers. Cleo immediately set about teaching the Hivaro to speak English instead of her learning their language, a bit of old Colonial European arrogance perhaps. First, Cleo assigned English names to all the rain forest creatures. The Hivaro being excellent imitators caught on quickly. Within a week, they were uttering simple declarative English sentences. Cleo finally got her point across; everybody, men and women, must wear loincloths. And, at Cleo's direction, the women knitted bras out of mulberry hemp.

Cleo lectured the Hivaro about Jesus-3, vegetarianism, the germ theory of disease, and table manners.

Her power over the villagers seemed absolute. With the sharp edge of a shell, Cleo etched into the bark of a kopak tree for all to see seven commandments: no meat eating, no killing, no hitting, no rape, no adultery, no stealing, and mandatory attendance at worship services.

The village women continued to give Cleo daily massages with the exotic oil prepared by crushing wild flowers and mixing them with the juice of fruits. The oil not only smelled like expensive perfume, it was a potent insect repellent. There was an added benefit to keeping Cleo well oiled. The Hivaro could smell the white god from a great distance and were less likely to be caught doing something wicked.

On the surface, the Hivaro village appeared to be a beehive of obedience. But some warriors, who couldn't quite give up eating meat, snuck into the forest to hunt, fish, cook, and eat game. The village women made a sport of spying on them. When caught, the meat-eaters were marched to the center of the village and scolded by the white god in everybody's presence, an unbearable humiliation.

The rebel meat-eaters met one evening and decided it was time for the white god to pass on to another world. Led by the medicine man, twenty-five warriors wrestled a giant anaconda from the swamp. They lugged the big snake into the woods and tossed it into a deep, muddy pit and covered it over with heavy logs. They left the thirty-foot snake there for weeks, unfed and starving. One night as the village slept, twenty-five warriors retrieved the ravenous serpent from its muddied pit, carried it to the hut of the sleeping white god and shoved it inside.

The snake's jabbing forked tongue quickly led it to the warm body in the center of the hut. It coiled back and hissed, repulsed by the odoriferous oil impregnating Cleo's skin. The perfumed oil the maidens used to massage Cleo's skin proved not only an insect repellent but a snake repellent as well. The anaconda slithered out of the hut into the adjacent hut where the spindly-legged medicine man slept. The only the scent in this hut was that of a warm mammal.

The next morning, the warriors were horrified to find the white god alive and sleeping soundly and the medicine man missing from his hut, and coiled on the floor of his hut the giant snake with a man-size bulge in its belly. The warriors fled the village, fearing the wrath of the white god. A few miles away on the other side of the river, the meat-eating rebels started up another village. However, they continued to speak their newly learned English, the language of commerce and free enterprise, serving the needs of business and industry.

Chapter 78
BANGKOK

For two weeks Rummels kept Agent Frisby, the INS's lead investigator in the alien smuggling operation, under close surveillance, shadowing him, placing hidden cameras in his Bangkok apartment, tapping his phone, and visiting his Facebook Page—routine CRAWL procedures.

One morning Rummels approached Frisby in downtown Bangkok as the agent walked from his car to his office. "I got some stuff you might like to see."

The agent stared at the Kenny Rogers look-alike with a squint of confusion. "Do I know you from somewhere?"

"Nope."

"What kind of stuff?"

Rummels handed Frisby a piece of paper. "Illegal alien smuggling. Meet me at this address at two tomorrow afternoon."

At an out-of-the-way teahouse on Bangkok's outskirts the INS agent and the ex-Crawl agent met. "Okay," Frisby said, "what's this all about?"

Rummels ordered two cups of steaming black tea. "Sit down and relax."

"If you've something to show me, let's see it."

Rummels tossed a flash disk onto the table, data garnered from the hard drive of Larry's computer. Rummels smiled. "I've got the goods on the smuggling operation you're investigating. Names, amounts, contacts, bank accounts, the whole works."

"In exchange for what?"

"Immunity for my client, Larry Lakes."

"That scumbag is the kingpin of the operation. Sorry, we've got the goods on him and we're running with it."

"You got the wrong man. He was set up. That disk will explain it all."

Agent Frisby, an arrogant and unbending man, sneered at the Kenny Rogers look-alike. "I don't deal with scumbags."

Rummels studied Frisby curiously. INS agents were pikers, pure lard, no match for an ex-CRAWL agent. When Frisby turned to leave without touching his tea, Rummels took a brown packet from his coat pocket and slapped it down on the table. "Better sit down."

Rummels shook a dozen photos out of the packet onto the table. Agent Frisby drew back as if he'd been belted him in the nose. The photos showed Frisby and Bangkok prostitutes in various postures. Some were group shots, tangles of anatomy: limbs, orifices, and agent Frisby's grinning face. A digital camera with a panoramic lens carefully hidden in the air conditioning vent of Frisby's hotel room had captured the agent's nefarious exploits in vivid detail.

"I don't think your wife would enjoy looking at these. And there's more. I thought I'd download it all onto Facebook in the morning." Rummels was prepared to ruin Frisby's marriage, destroy his career, and his standing back home in Allenville, Montana where he was an officer in the Lion's Club. Rummels picked up his teacup. "Like to discuss it?"

A sheepish grin crossed Frisby's face as he picked up the flash disk. "Sure, there's no reason something can't be worked out."

The two men sipped tea and worked out the details. Larry wouldn't be going to prison. Veronica would.

༺❦༻

Larry and Rummels celebrated at Larry's apartment, a bachelor suite with a view, a bar, and a geek's décor—furniture of chrome and black metal, gadgetry, circuit boards, flat screens, and a "Revenge of the Nerds" movie poster. Larry had shifted into full swing left-brain mode. Champagne splashed from clinking glasses. Larry held up his glass. "Here's to Veronica. May the bitch rot in her cell until she's old and gray and her sex drive withers away." He slapped Rummels on the back. "And here's to the best damn private detective in the whole fuckin' world."

Larry poured another drink, walked over to the French windows, and stared out at the glittering Bangkok night. He raised his glass again. "Here's to Cleo," he whispered softly. "The most beautiful woman in the world."

Rummels coughed and cleared his throat. "Let's not forget the Hashimotioto."

Larry grinned. "You can pick up the Tricorpora Callosum Wednesday. It's coming special delivery."

"Pick it up? I don't even know what it is."

Larry sat down with his drink. "I assembled the basic processing units for the Hashimotioto right here in Bangkok from memory. The symbolic logic unit. The fuzzy logic unit. The real-world paradigm generator. Putting the logic units together was child's play compared to the complexity of the Tricorpora Callosum. Once you have it, you have the Hashimotioto."

Rummels shrugged. "You still haven't told me what it is."

"The Tricorpora is the heart and soul of the computer. The most important piece of hardware ever produced. It's made up of billions of artificial neural nets emulating the function of the human brain. The Tricorpora Callosum integrates and blends the output of the three logic units, giving the Hashimotioto a mental picture of whatever it's dealing with. A form of computer awareness."

Rummels eyed Larry skeptically. "Where is this Callosum thing now?"

"Locked securely inside a steel and concrete laboratory in Tokyo, guarded by electronic eyes, laser beams, and a fleet of security guards."

"How in the hell are you going to steal it?"

⁂

Three days ago the Hashimotioto's alarm went off. The riot of flashing red lights and buzzing noises sent Osa Takashima and his cadre of high-tech nerds at the Tokyo Institute of Artificial Intelligence scurrying to the controls of the world's most powerful computer. Nothing like this had ever happened before. Getting hit with a tax audit and divorce papers on the same day couldn't have been more unnerving. Osa trembled as he read the output of the diagnostic software. ABNORMAL VOLTAGE DROPS THROUGHOUT THE TRICORPORA CALLOSUM.

"Impossible," Osa told his comrades as they all stared at the lit up control panel. Osa inserted a second diagnostic disk. Same results. VOLTAGE DROPS IN THE TRICORPORA CALLOSUM. *Osa and his men ran the usual checks. Everything functioned normally. Why the voltage drops? What to do? Osa decided to ask the Hashimotioto. As he keyed in the question to the world's most talented machine, he muttered, "Heal thy self."*

The Hashimotioto answered, REPAIR THE TRICORPORA CALLOSUM.

Osa stared at his colleagues in astonishment. Who could possibly repair the Tricorpora Callosum? Over a thousand scientists had contributed to its design.

It took an army of technicians and specialists to put it together. Modern technology's holy grail, it was supposed to last a hundred years.

Osa asked, "Who could possibly repair the Tricorpora?"

Osa saw the answer in his colleagues' faces. Ask the Hashimotioto.

Osa keyed in the question. The answer appeared immediately on the computer's screen. ONLY ONE PLACE IN THE WORLD CAN FIX IT. SEND THE TRICORPORA CALLOSUM TO WISAKHA ELECTRONICS IN BANGKOK.

"Bangkok," Osa screamed with disdain. "They're not even in the ball game."

He looked around the room at his silent colleagues, neat men all cut from a pattern of dour faces, white coats, and wire rim glasses. All of them stared solemnly at Osa. All of them thinking the same thing. You had better do what the world's smartest machine tells you to do. If you don't, it's your ass on the line.

That afternoon, Osa and his men carefully packed the Tricorpora Callosum into a box cushioned with twenty pounds of urethane foam and shipped it special delivery to Wisakha Electronics in Bangkok.

Larry scribbled out an address on a piece of paper and handed it to Rummels. "The package will arrive at this address Wednesday. You pick it up, and all I have to do is connect the Tricorpora Callosum to the logic units, and you'll have your Hashimotioto."

Rummels asked, "How in the world did you get them to send it here?"

"I put over a thousand encrypted messages on the Internet. Messages only the Hashimotioto could decipher. It thinks we're playing a game. Wisakha Electronics is a bicycle shop on Ploenchit Street. Better get there early before the package arrives. And don't drop it."

Rummels whistled as he walked out of Larry's apartment. Wednesday he would become the sole owner the world's most powerful computer.

Chapter 79
BOGOTA

Tommy Tennyson and Rev. Hibberblast arrived in Bogotá with eighty-two cents between them. At a sidewalk café, they shelled out their remaining fortune for a shared bowl of *ajiaco,* a goulash of potatoes, corn, and meat, their first meal in two days. Hibberblast got the bigger portion by spooning quicker and swallowing faster. He needed the nourishment to give him strength to do God's work. Tommy looked at the empty bowl and at Hibberblast licking his spoon. "That didn't go very far."

"Bogota's the place," Hibberblast said. "I feel it inside."

A sea of hot air lay over the city. Doorways stood wide-open. Shopkeepers moved merchandise onto sidewalks. The two unshaven, disheveled Americans looked more like beggars than modern big dollar evangelists, their ragged unwashed clothes and the shoes on their feet their only estate. "Where are we going to stay the night," Tommy asked.

"As always God will provide. Think not of what you will eat, how you dress, and where you will sleep."

They walked along in the shadows of lavish colonial cathedrals, their souls rejoicing, their feet aching, and their pockets empty. Bogotá, the home of Gabriel Garcia Marquez, the man who writes with a magic pen, is also the home of the wretched poor, addicts, orphans who sleep in cardboard boxes and under automobiles, and men who kill for wristwatches and whatever brings a peso. Foreign cameras and iPods are high currency here.

In the marketplace, the aroma of roasted pig, fried ants, and coffee teased the hungry missionaries. Soon the purple mountains surrounding the city blotted out the sun. "It's getting cold, I'm shivering," Tommy said, teeth chattering. "We should've brought along more clothing."

Hibberblast shook his head. "We'd had enough if you hadn't lost our suitcases."

"Me. You lost Bobby Haggett's money!"

"There you go again, always pointing the finger. I swear, I don't know if you will ever learn God's way."

The ragged evangelists strolled into the Zona Rosa, where revelers drank, laughed, and danced to lively Latin music. Hibberblast muttered a rebuke, "Perdition awaits them. They're dancing on the devil's chest and they don't know it." Tommy said a prayer for the poor sinners.

The two weary travelers finally sat down on a curbing in El Cartucho, a slum resembling the aftermath of a Blitzkrieg. The sleeping poor were strewn like rubble in the streets, gutters, and alleyways. Smudged-faced children huddled in protective nests. Cocaine hogs shuffled through the dark streets like zombies. From an open window a man urinated onto the sidewalk.

Hibberblast rested his head against the foundation of a stone building and sniffed the air as if searching for meaning in the confusing jumble of urban smells. "Tommy, this is where we'll build my church, right here. It's God's will."

Tommy was already asleep, curled up next to Hibberblast like a fetus. Hibberblast turned up his collar and closed his eyes.

The next morning their shoes were gone, stolen off their feet during the night. Hibberblast stared at his toes sticking out through the holes in his stockings. "We'll not cry over lost shoes when there are lost souls to be saved."

The two Americans quickly established themselves on a busy corner under the portico of a partially collapsed building where Hibberblast stood shoeless, a sculpture in round, sermonizing in pidgin Spanish. Tommy hummed "Amazing Grace," holding his cupped hand out to passersby, a smile on his face, his eyes squinted against the glare of the sun, his spirit undaunted, his resolve unshaken. For two days, the two vagabond evangelists withstood the hot sun, sudden downpours, and the indignity of being ignored.

"I'm getting really hungry," Tommy told his mentor.

"Me too. Things will get better. Just hang in there."

"I wished you hadn't lost that money."

"Will you shut up about the money? It was God's will. Now I don't want to hear anymore about it."

On the third day, the two evangelists looked at one another with hollowed, dulled eyes. Hunger raged within them. The flesh had nearly disappeared from their cheeks. Tommy's plastic ears had slipped forward on their shrunken nubs, causing people to stare. Their clothes tattered, their pockets empty, their feet wrapped in rags, their whiskered faces reddened by the sun, they plopped down on the curbing, painfully aware their first attempt at soul-saving, propagating the faith, and mission building had so far been a bummer.

Hibberblast slapped his hand on Tommy's back. "We got to split up. You go one way, and I'll go the other. We'll meet back here in the evening and share our successes and whatever food we find."

"Which way," Tommy asked.

Hibberblast pointed. "You go that way."

"What shall I preach?"

"The Gospel. The words will come naturally."

Tommy walked hesitantly away, glancing back ever few steps.

Hibberblast walked only three blocks in the other direction before coming upon the Noah's Ark Children Refuge, a spacious gray stucco building with slanted roof and two windows covered with washcloth curtains. He went inside. Out of the kitchen came a burly Norwegian man, sleeves rolled up to the elbows of his fleshy arms, a greasy apron stretched over his corpulent belly. He glared suspiciously at Hibberblast.

"Vhat do you vont here?"

Hibberblast set his face in a smile, corners of the mouth tipped up, eyes wide, brows raised, dimples dimpling. "I'm a missionary myself, come here to help."

"Yeah, but if I catch you stealing…"

Hibberblast held up a hand. "I would never do that."

The big cook gave Hibberblast a breakfast of dried corn and half a glass of goat's milk. In exchange for the meager meal, Hibberblast carried plates of fried rice and meat from the steamy kitchen to more than a hundred street urchins sitting around roughly hewn tables.

The next day, Hibberblast discovered more missions in El Cartucho: Lutheran, Baptist, Episcopal, Pentecostal, and others. All served free soup at exactly the same time each day to prevent hungry street-people from double dipping. Hibberblast soon visited them all. He alternated missions so as not to make himself too conspicuous in any one place. On a good day, if he hurried, he could get in two soups. Every time he filled his soup bowl, some well-meaning missionary would come over and save him. He didn't need saving, he was already saved, and he wanted to be saving other people, not getting saved everyday himself. But it was either get saved or not eat.

"Hello brother," a Pentecostal missionary greeted Hibberblast. "Have some soup, vegetable beef. As food nourishes the body, so God's word nourishes the soul. God loves you and sent his only son to redeem you. Salvation awaits you brother. Let us pray."

While the Pentecostal prayed, Hibberblast gulped down his soup and hurried off. He had just enough time to make it to the Baptist mission for a second soup.

"God be with you," the missionary shouted.

Tommy got a job working with a group of Bangladesh refugees selling aluminum Pope Francis key chains to tourists on the steps of the old colonial cathedrals. They all worked for an Italian who bussed them from cathedral to cathedral in a van. The Italian owned the Vatican concession for key chains back home and had come to Bogotá to test the waters for possible international expansion of the key chain business. Tommy took his job seriously, especially since he was the only Christian in the group, other than his Italian boss.

The job afforded Tommy an opportunity to evangelize. And he did it with gusto. Rushing up to tourists with his bag of key chains, he'd shout, "Did you know God loves you? Are you saved? Jesus died for you." He kept at them until the weary tourist gave in and bought a key chain. Each day he sold more key chains than all the other vendors put together.

One day standing in a cathedral doorway out of the rain, Tommy glanced around at his compatriots. Stares that could kill came at him from all angles. He could tell he had somehow offended his fellow key chain vendors.

"I'm sure you're aware old chap that we've families back home to support," one of Bangladeshi refugees said.

"Yes, and you're getting all the business," another pointed out.

A third vendor pulled a knife out his knapsack. "If you don't stop evangelizing, we are going to castrate you."

Tommy stopped evangelizing right away. He sold just enough key chains each day to buy a cup of chicken soup and some hard bread with his commission. He carried the soup in a Styrofoam cup along with the bread back to El Cartucho each evening to share with Rev. Hibberblast.

One evening, over soup and bread, Tommy noticed that Hibberblast's cheeks appeared fleshy again, even ruddy in the fading sunlight. He asked the reverend, "What did you do today?"

"Just like everyday, talking to people about God. About getting saved."

"Did I tell you, I almost got castrated the other day?"

"God protected you, didn't He?"

"Come to think of it, yes. But I can't evangelize anymore or they will castrate me."

Hibberblast dipped bread in the soup. "You keep selling key chains and I'll do the evangelizing."

Tommy admired his mentor's undiminished zeal. Hibberblast looked good because he was good. He was doing God's good work.

Chapter 80
RUN REV RUN

One morning at Noah's Ark Refuge while serving breakfast to street urchins, Hibberblast scooped a morsel of fried rice and pork onto his finger and licked it. *Lord. How sweet the taste.* With each plate he carried from the kitchen, he stealthily helped himself to a finger-size morsel. He reasoned a ragamuffin wouldn't miss just one bite, and it would sure do him some good. Yes, food to give him the strength to carry on God's work. Unfortunately, one morning the big Norwegian cook noticed the finger scooping. He grabbed Hibberblast by the back of his shirt and tossed him out into the street.

" By-golly, don't yah come back here no more."

On a Tuesday, the Alliance of Missions held their annual celebration, *The Lost Sheep Parade,* where they marched and sang in the streets of El Cartucho in a show of Protestant unity. Among other things, the celebration let the entrenched Catholics know they were not the only game in town. Like 4-H'ers flaunting livestock, the missionaries paraded around their new converts. Each mission tried to outdo the others in the numbers game. The Pentecostals had a narrow two-convert lead over the Lutherans, although the Baptists were closing fast. Every soul counted in this close race.

Hibberblast wandered into the middle of the celebration looking for a noon soup. The Lutherans recognized him, grabbed him up and marched him around with his Lutheran-brother-converts. He didn't want to be a Lutheran convert. He was sure the Lutherans, like the Catholics, were all going to hell. He didn't want to be anyone's convert; he'd come to Bogotá to convert others, although if he hadn't converted anyone yet.

A Baptist missionary, who had once saved Hibberblast and gave him a pair of shoes, spotted him with the Lutherans. "Hey Brother, you belong over here," the missionary shouted. Hibberblast marched with the Baptist converts until the Pentecostals, who had invested a lot soup in him, claimed him for their own. The missionaries shouted angrily at one another as they tugged on the hungry convert.

"He's mine."

"No, he's ours."

"Let go!"

"That's our soul."

"He isn't either. He belongs to us."

Then someone shoved someone who forgot to turn the other cheek. Missionaries soon squared off in the street, tongue-lashings, hitting, kicking, biting, and tugging Hibberblast in one direction then another. Converts joined in the interdenominational melee. Then non-converts. Then came the police swinging clubs. The ensuing brawl looked like an American ice hockey game. Hibberblast wisely slipped away in the confusion.

For two days, Hibberblast ate nothing but the chicken soup and hard bread Tommy shared with him each evening. Hunger drove him mad. He couldn't go back to the Noah's Ark Refuge, and now the missions turned him away. All day he prowled the alleys behind restaurants and hotels, where he fought with street children and beggars over garbage. When he wasn't scrounging for scraps, he sat among the garbage cans and daydreamed of hot roast beef sandwiches with mashed potatoes covered in thick brown gravy. Turkey and dressing. Cheeseburgers with fries. Peach cobbler and ice cream. O' Lord, he'd love a cup of hot coffee with cream and sugar and maybe a dash of Irish whiskey.

While rummaging through trash one afternoon, he spotted a lost tourist--any tourist wandering around El Cartucho had to be lost. This frail, older man wore a print shirt, neatly pressed khaki shorts, a grain elevator ball cap, sunglasses, black knee-high stockings, and SAS shoes. An expensive Minolta camera dangled from a thin strap around his neck. He walked fast, glancing at the ruins of El Cartucho with sham aplomb. Street urchins noticed the camera bouncing on his chest and gathered like wild dogs readying for the hunt. An expensive camera meant glue to sniff and food to eat. It meant living another few days. Cameras were gold in El Cartucho.

Hibberblast also stalked the stray tourist. If he took the Minolta from the man, it would prevent the codger from getting mugged. Yes, he would no doubt save the old man's life by taking his camera. And he could sell the camera and buy food, which would make him stop thinking about food. He could then concentrate on God's work. Yes, it was his duty to take the camera. *Praise the Lord!* God had sent this tourist with his camera into El Cartucho for a reason. Hibberblast glanced at the street urchins. Mere hyenas in the presence of a lion.

A few hard-bitten druggies stood on a street corner, their pale, deadpan eyes also focusing on the Minolta. To them, the camera represented a fantasy flight out of the slums, an ecstatic cloud-ride that could last for days. They fell in behind the pack of urchins and shuffled urgently along. The lost tourist glanced over his shoulder at the trailing predators, his eyes wide with fear. All at once, he ran like a frighten rabbit.

Hibberblast flew right past the pack of urchins, ran up to the old man and grabbed the camera. Instead of breaking, the strap on the camera clamped down on the man's windpipe like a choke collar. Hibberblast dragged the garroted tourist down the street, jerking frantically on the camera with both hands. The man's face turned blue and his eyes bulged as he fought to free the strap from around his neck. The urchins and druggies closed in a dead heat. At last, the strap broke. Camera in hand, Hibberblast took off, leaving his victim sprawled in the street gasping for air.

Predator became prey. The urchins and druggies now chased Hibberblast through the streets of El Cartucho. The tourist, miraculously back on his feet, ran behind them shouting in a hoarse voice, "Thief. Thief."

Hibberblast leaped a boarded fence and raced up *Calle* 8 to the Avenue. He ran past the *Banco Anglo Colombiano*. He charged through a crowd watching a band of street musicians play *Djobi Djoba*. Holding the precious camera to his chest, he raced down a boulevard, dodging cars and trucks. The pack of urchins nipped at his heels. Right behind the urchins, came the druggies. Hibberblast ran onto a bridge, his lungs afire, his legs cramping, and his hands clutching the camera.

At the far end of the bridge, they overtook him. He fought the ragamuffins off with one hand, holding the camera high in the other. Then came the druggies, desperate hombres. A free-for-all ensued: fists flying, legs kicking, fingers gouging. Assailed from all sides, Hibberblast refused to give up his prize. He surprised the attackers by vaulting over the side of the bridge onto the embankment below. Up the embankment and down the street he ran, his pursuers close behind. A hand ripped away part of his shirt. His legs turned numb, but still he ran. His chest heaved and his breath came in labored grunts. Before him loomed a cathedral, its towering spire urging him on. He ascended the cathedral steps and flung open the elegantly curved, raised-panel doors. He stumbled through the nave to the high altar and collapsed, still clutching the Minolta.

His pursuers stopped in the doorway, held there by the solemn countenance of a marble St. Mark peering down from a vaulted niche. Not even an El Cartucho thief would violate the sanctity of a Holy chamber. Hibberblast lifted his head to the sound of a priestly skirt whispering across the floor. A wizened-faced priest knelt beside him.

"*Este pequeno regalo es mas grande que el regalo de un hombre rico, hijo mio.*" The priest's aged hands pried the Minolta from Hibberblast's grip. Reduced to a heap of breathless, sweating flesh, Hibberblast watched the priest and the camera melt away into the darkness of the sanctuary.

That evening in El Cartucho, the two American evangelists warmed themselves by the heat of trash container they'd set on fire. Hibberblast looked Tommy in the eye. "We're leaving Bogotá. We're going into the countryside where the people need us."

"I thought we were needed here."

"We're needed in the countryside."

Tommy blinked in confusion. "How do you know?"

"I just know."

"But this is all so inconsistent. You said we'd build our church here."

Hibberblast's eyes hardened with annoyance. "There you go again, resorting to logic and reason. That's the kind of thinking that got you in trouble back at the university. You must have faith."

Tommy stared at Hibberblast, firelight reflecting in his haggard face. "What happened to your clothes, they're torn to pieces?"

Hibberblast shrugged. "I tried to prevent a robbery. Some fool tourist carried a camera into El Cartucho."

"Did you succeed?"

"No. But I saved the man's life."

Tommy's admiration for his mentor was without measure. He shouldn't have questioned his authority. "When are we leaving?"

"Tomorrow."

Chapter 81
INDIA

Gamuka arrived alive but beaten up inside the Fed Ex box at his home in India. He suspected all freight handlers were either sadists or they didn't know what the word "Fragile" meant. While crossing the Atlantic at thirty thousand feet up, married to his battery-powered body warmers, he first realized he was upside down inside the box when saliva ran into his nose as he munched a granola bar. He survived the long trip only to be wounded by a butcher knife when his wife with great gusto ripped open the huge surprise package that landed on her doorstep one morning. She seemed a little disappointed at finding her rumpled husband inside the box dressed like Eskimo, covered in granola bar wrappers, wearing scuba gear, and smelling of dirty diapers.

"Phew, you need to clean up."

Gamuka's brother-in-law peered into the opened box. "So, you went to America to get educated."

His wife cleaned and dressed Gamuka's knife wounds daily. It took nearly two weeks for them to heal. During that time Gamuka fattened up, made love to his wife, and explained to his family all that had happened in America and during his wormhole travels. He then took his wife and son to Calcutta by train. There he strolled barefoot through the crowded streets in a white toga and lectured to students on wormhole meditation techniques. His wife wore a red sari and sipped CampaCola as she followed behind her husband, collecting tuition from the students. On the streets of Calcutta, where the poor lived out their short wretched lives, where Mother Teresa had ministered to the sick and dying, Gamuka held an open-air classroom.

Surrounded by beggars, the homeless, and the noise of the street Gamuka spoke to his coterie of students about the pristine wonders of a vast universe where all sound was melody, all sights were endless vistas of colors and shapes, all thought divine, and all existence sublime. "And to experience these wonders, you need only look inside yourself. Let me show you the way." So vivid and magical were the images Gamuka evoked, students flocked to him in great numbers. Before long Gamuka and his wife had made quite a bit of money.

One day his wife suggested, "We ought to expand our school."

"What do you think of a theme park?"

"Yes, a place people could go and have fun. With the right music and rides we could make it a heavenly adventure."

"Let's go for it. We'll build a wormhole theme park in every city of the world."

His wife smiled. "That's what I like about you dear. You think big."

Chapter 82
V & C CRUISES

Tracy dumped Frank in Singapore. Rumor had it she ran off with a wealthy Chinese widower. She didn't even say good-bye, just got off the ship to go shopping and never returned. The woman of Frank's dreams was gone and he couldn't blame her. Her rash, the horrible itching, and the constant torture of being so close and yet so far apart—it was too much for anyone to bear. Frank turned to gambling to assuage his loneliness, and his blackjack winnings grew exponentially.

"It's too much," warned Vu as the two physicians sipped martinis in one of the ship's lounges. "People are going to get suspicious."

"So what. There's no gambling commission on the high seas."

Frank kept winning until the captain summoned him to the purser's office one day and grimly told him, "I'm closing down the casino."

"Does that mean I can't play blackjack anymore?"

The captain shrugged.

Rife with guilt, Frank blushed. "I'm sorry, I didn't mean to…"

"It wasn't your fault," the captain explained. "But I'm afraid you're out of job. You see the Magdalena's parent company, International Travel and Shipping, has gone belly-up. The engine room on one of our sister ships recently caught afire. Three thousand passengers were adrift for a week with no air conditioning, overflowing toilets, little food, and no entertainment. The lawsuits were crippling. Then came a series of strikes and work stoppages that caused the company to lose several major shipping contracts. Atop all that, its largest tanker loaded with crude oil sank in a typhoon off Borneo. The salvage and cleanup costs…well, I'm a afraid we're bankrupt."

Frank sighed. Apparently the Magdalena's casino losses although huge weren't the proverbial grain stalk that fractured the dromedary's vertebral column. Frank's next thought was to find another cruise ship with a casino.

The captain took a deep breath. "The ship doesn't have enough money to pay off your winnings."

"I won't get my money?"

The captain looked at the purser. "What are we going to do?"

The purser cleared his throat and said, "I'm afraid we will have to give him the ship."

Frank's eyes widen. "What?"

The purser looked squarely at the captain. "The company's flat broke, sir." Then he turned to Frank. "The ship is yours Dr. Chisholm, if you want it."

"Well, I-I-I guess so."

"Very well," the captain said to the purser, "get the papers ready."

Frank stammered, "You mean I own the Magdalena?"

The Captain nodded.

That evening in the ship's Topsider lounge, Frank poured champagne for himself and Vu. "I owe it all to you."

Vu looked at his drink. "Nonsense. I merely taught you to win at blackjack. I would have quit when the winnings hit one hundred thousand. You had the guts to keep going. You have no one but yourself to thank."

"I may as well have won a locomotive or a space shuttle for all the good it'll do me. I don't know a thing about running a cruise ship."

Vu put down his drink and folded his hands. "During my youth, I worked with my uncle running a small boating and ferry operation on the Mekong River. I learned the basic ins-and-outs of the business. I bet together we could make the Magdalena a going concern."

"Are you serious?"

"Look," Vu said soberly, "this could be our chance to become legitimate. We could make money and live like normal rich people."

Frank admired Vu. He was an excellent physician, a skilled surgeon, a master mathematician and gambler, and except for blackjack, he was totally honest. He had no major hang-ups. Was essentially apolitical. He'd make a great business partner.

"All right," Frank agreed, "we'll go fifty-fifty. I won't have it any other way."

Vu smiled. "We'll call our company Chisholm and Vu cruises."

Frank shook his head. "No. Vu and Chisholm."

"No. You won the ship. Your name should go first."

"I'll arm wrestle you for it."

Vu chuckled. "I was the Saigon arm wrestling champion four years running."

Frank smiled. "That settles it. We'll call it C & V cruises."

Vu took charge of the business end of the ship's operations: itinerary, payroll, insurance, advertising, customs and regulations. Since winning at blackjack in his own casino didn't make any sense, Frank dedicated himself to finding the best possible entertainment for the ship's stage. Gray-headed cruise ship passengers love exciting and eye-popping entertainment like waltzes, classic country music, Lawrence Welk, and Grand Ole Opry.

When the Magdalena docked in Bangkok, Frank went ashore on a talent search. The open hedonistic, pleasure-seeking goings-on in the smoke-filled nightclubs shocked him. He had never seen so many bouncing boobs and swiveling pelvises. Not cruise ship material. He ended up in a quiet, ten-dollar-cover-charge bar. He ordered a martini and peered up at the singer on stage.

The bartender leaned across the bar and grinned at Frank. "He's pretty good, wouldn't you say. I've never seen an impersonator look so much like the real thing."

"You mean that's not Kenny Rogers up there?"

"No, sir. He's a private eye. Does this in his spare time."

Chapter 83
ST. PETERSBURG

Three weeks after Kent entered Professor Sulkohov's Cave Room, Justin opened the door to let him out. The light spilling into the room sent Kent sprawling on the floor, shielding his sensitive eyes with his arms. Justin coaxed him onto his feet and slowly led him into the parlor as one leads a blind man. Kent eased into a stuffed chair and rubbed his eyes, his pale face hidden in a wild fizz of facial hair, his brain slowly adjusting to a world of light and sound.

Justin sat on a chair across the room. "Did you come up with any…?"

"Jesus! You don't have to scream."

Justin whispered, "Did you…?"

"Three weeks in that hole and not an inkling of a *homopragmatic truth*."

Justin looked at Kent curiously. "Did you discover anything at all?"

"Only that I love Cleo." Kent stopped rubbing his eyes and glanced around the room. "She was all I thought about it. It took me three weeks alone with my thoughts to see how much I really love that woman. And I don't blame her for walking out on me. Do you realize I've never once ask her to marry me?" Kent glanced across the room at the steamy hot tub. "Where's the professor? Did he come up with anything?"

Justin cleared his throat. "Well, yes and no. You see, the professor died."

"What!"

"Electrocuted in his hot tub…," Justin hesitated then finished his sentence, "…right after he discovered a *homopragmatic truth*."

Kent leaped to his feet. "Well, out with it. What is it?"

"Unfortunately, he died before he could tell me what it was."

Kent collapsed back into his chair, his head in his hands. "I'm cursed. There's no chance of ever finding a *homopragmatic* truth now."

Justin related in more detail the story of the professor's demise. Kent moaned sorrowfully as he listened. The long race was over. The professor, the only human being in the world to discover a *homopragmatic truth,* lay in his bedroom stiff as a Popsicle. Time would soon run out for Kent, and there was no way to stop the clock.

Kent looked up at Justin. "I must find Cleo before I die."

"I understand," Justin said sympathetically.

The two Americans slurped down bowls of chicken noodle soup in the professor's small kitchen, their last supper in Russia. Kent shaved, dipped in and out of the hot tub, combed the tangles from his hair, and put on clean clothes. So that the authorities would understand the professor's death was accidental, Kent and Justin lugged the professor's frozen remains from the bedroom to the hot tub and shoved it into the warm water to thaw, the professor's beard crackling like ice. Justin picked up the burnt out CD player and tossed it back into the water. Later, they took a taxi to the airport.

At 30,000 feet over Nova Scotia in the coach section of a jetliner, Justin turned to Kent and said, "I want to help you find Cleo. But where do we start?"

Kent thought for minute before answering. "With Selena Rosalina? She and Cleo became good friends. Maybe they kept in touch."

Selena had left word at NBC that she would see a young man by the name of Kent Mullins anytime. If Kent ever discovered a *homopragmatic truth,* she wanted it on her show first. When Kent gave his name to the nice man in the NBC public relations office, Kent and Justin were hustled into a limousine and driven to Selena's brownstone.

Scruffy on the outside, the brownstone inside was a veritable palace. A George III gilt-bronze chandelier illuminated the entrance. The masseuse had just finished with Selena's massage when Kent and Justin arrived. In sweats, her hair in a leopard skin turban, Selena greeted her guests with hugs. "I've just redecorated," she said as she led them through room after room of Italian marble, rooms stuffed with expensive furnishings. On the parlor's wall hung a huge Louis the XIV mirror flanked by glaring Picasso's cheek-by-jowl with rare Van Gogh's. In her library, surrounded by collectibles and first editions, they sat on antique chairs and sipped tea. Selena was sadden and disappointed when she heard the news of Professor Sulkohov shocking death.

"I was so hoping you'd find the truth thing, for your sake and mine. My ratings are tumbling again, and I desperately need something to pick them up. The competition is fierce. Did I tell you the network dumped poor Ed Nikkel?"

Kent asked, "Have you heard from Cleo?"

"I have, a letter arrived about a week ago."

Kent leaned forward in his chair. "Where is she? I must find her."

"She started a vegetarian colony in the Amazon. I have the letter here some where." Selena searched through desk drawers but couldn't come up with the letter. "I get so much crap mail these days that I can't keep track of the important things. Anyway, to reach her, you must contact the Amazon Queen River Boat Company in Telcequez. They'll take you up river as far as they can. The rest of trip is on foot through uncharted jungle. Even with local guides you may not find the Hivaro village where she resides."

Kent stood. "I'm leaving for the Amazon as soon as possible."

Selena walked her visitors to the door. "Better get some rest before you start out. I'll arrange for you a suite at the Plaza."

Chapter 84
MEJOR COCA

The fresh air of the Colombian highlands rejuvenated Rev. Hibberblast and Tommy like ice water splashed on a sleepy face. They shook off the disappointment of El Cartucho as one shakes dust from a pants sleeve. Here in the country, away from the hassle of urban life, the people were easygoing, hard working, reserved but friendly. The two evangelists walked leisurely along a mountain road, the only noise the wind in their ears.

Tommy looked at his mentor. "It's getting late, we better look for some shelter."

"God will provide."

Outside the hamlet of Mejor Coca, they took refuge in an abandoned mine in the side of a mountain where they slept on beds of straw and leaves. The early morning tolling of the village bell awakened them like an alarm clock. Hibberblast, rubbing sleep from his eyes, stumbled out of the mine, stretched away his morning stiffness, and at the edge of a mountain cliff gazed down at the misty jungle below, across at the grass-covered hills to the north, and beyond at distant mountain peaks. Overhead laid a thin stretch of clouds painted pink by the morning sun. Hibberblast turned to Tommy as they walked into the village. "God has brought me to this place at this time. That bell tolled for me. Here in Mejor Coca, I will build my church."

"Why here, they already have a church," Tommy pointed out as they walked along the dusty streets. "Mejor Coca looks no different than the other villages we've passed through."

Hibberblast smiled at his proselyte. "God speaks to me in ways you wouldn't understand."

"Will He ever speak to me?"

"Someday, if you continue in your faithful service to Him."

※

The peasant farmers of Mejor Coca lived out their quiet lives raising maize, rice, sheep, and coca. They gave half their dried and pulverized coca leaves, the highest grade cocaine in all Colombia, to the armed rebels from the Cordillera Occidental who wandered in regularly to rape the village women, to terrorize, and to take whatever food and supplies they needed. Then the rebels from the valley came and took half of what was left of the coca leaves. They also raped and plundered. Then came the rebels from the forest for their share of the coca and the women.

What little cocaine the farmers had left, they sold to the cartels. The East and West cartels forced the farmers to pay fifty-percent rebates on all cocaine. The government taxed the farmers forty-percent on the gross. The local church took ten-percent. In Mejor Coca, cocaine was not a cash crop. Robbed, raped, tithed, and taxed, the farmers undemonstratively worked their fields year after year, accepting their fate and never complaining

※

The two evangelists wandered through the village and out into the countryside. Tommy asked his mentor, "Where are you going to put our church?"

Hibberblast spread his arms. "Right here in the open. Just like John the Baptist. An open air church."

Hibberblast walked over to a group of farmers loading hay unto a cart and began singing one his hymns a cappella. The farmers, an amicable lot, stopped working and listened as the gringo's voice rang with great resonance, hitting both the high and low notes. Tommy hummed along. The next day following a sermon on friendship and sharing, Hibberblast sang to the farmers *Bringing in the Sheaves*. When he finished his song the farmers shared corn cakes with the evangelists. Soon it became a ritual--sermon, song, and corn cakes. And the farmers looked the other way whenever the sermonizing gringo stole a little rice or chewed an occasional coca leaf. One more thief made little difference here.

For the farmers, Hibberblast's melodic singing was a pleasant respite from the incessant noise of the wind and the grunts of fellow workers. His musical voice lured the farmers into laying down their hoes and scythes, stretching out on the grass and just listening. They never tired of the music. Since the local priest forbade the use of radios and other electronic devises, Hibberblast's hymns were the only entertainment in all of Mejor Coca.

The number of farmers attending Hibberblast's open-air services steadily increased. Tommy twirled his artificial ears on their nubbins to the crowd's delight. One day in the middle of a Hibberblast hymn, the village bell tolled loud and fast, a desperate refrain. The farmers in great alarm ran into the trees. Hibberblast and Tommy stood in the field with blank stares on their faces. *What's going on?*

Rebels from the valley, a smelly unshaven lot in combat fatigues, poured into the village like a plague, firing automatic weapons into the air. From a safe distance, Hibberblast and Tommy listened in horror to the sound of gunfire and the screams of women and girls. After the pillage, the rebels carried off half the village's cocaine in burlap bags.

Tommy looked at his mentor with terror in his eyes. "This is terrible."

"Yes, they're stealing the cocaine."

"What can be done? Won't the government help?"

Hibberblast grinned. "I got an idea."

The next day, instead of singing and sermonizing, Hibberblast in broken Spanish spoke plainly to the farmers. "Listen, my friends, when the rebels come again, be prepared. Hide most of the coca and let the rebels take half of what is not hidden."

"That would be unfair," one of the farmers argued. "They never take more than their share."

"Yes, it's always been that way," a villager pointed out.

Hibberblast retorted, "They don't have a right to it, they're thieves."

The farmers talked this over and decided that to hide the cocaine from the rebels would not only be unfair but dishonest.

In exasperation, Hibberblast pointed out, "But they are raping your wives and daughters right in front of your eyes!"

Without a word, the farmers hung their heads and returned to the fields.

Hibberblast looked at Tommy. "We'll have to take things into our own hands."

After a lot of talking, preaching, and browbeating, Hibberblast convinced the farmers to let him and Tommy hide half of Mejor Coca's cocaine in the abandoned mineshaft. When the village bell next rang out danger, the two evangelists also hid the women and girls in the mineshaft. The rebels came and went, taking what food and supplies they needed and fifty percent of the cocaine in the village, which was twenty-five percent of the actual coca. The farmers quickly saw the wisdom of Hibberblast's plan. Appreciative that their women weren't being ravaged, they gave Hibberblast a quarter of all the remaining cocaine.

Each time rebels invaded Mejor Coca, Hibberblast and Tommy hid the women in the old mineshaft along with most of the village's cocaine. Hibberblast earned not only the farmers respect but with each raid he collected another stash of cocaine for himself. Soon he had more cocaine than the farmers. The rebels never figured it out. Horny as they were, they didn't take time to search for the women, because of the ever-present danger of government troops. Besides, there were plenty of other villages to plunder.

"I've decided to build my church," Hibberblast told Tommy one day.

"I thought we were open-air."

"We were. But now God wants me to build a church."

"The village already has a church."

"A little competition doesn't hurt."

"Father Forero won't like it."

"We're doing what God says to do."

A part-time CIA agent and coca broker in Medellin heard rumors about the large stashes of cocaine in Mejor Coca. One day he approached Hibberblast. "I'd like to put your coca on the market. I could get you a good price from the cartels and there'd be no rebates to pay. It's a sellers market right now." Hibberblast agreed. Soon cash poured in like rain through a leaky roof.

Money attracts, and unemployed farmers and laborers from all around streamed into Mejor Coca. Hibberblast built his church plus a three-story mansion in record time. He bought a bright yellow new jeep for himself and even sent a small check back home to his wife in the States.

"You're selling cocaine," Tommy shouted at his mentor in a piercing twang of righteous indignation.

"For a good purpose," Hibberblast argued. "The village women aren't getting raped, and we're using the money for God's work."

"But it doesn't seem right."

"You've failed to understand that God works in strange ways. Sometimes I think you'll never learn."

Selling cocaine under any circumstances seemed wrong to Tommy, but his faith in Hibberblast remained granite solid. He tried not to think about things he didn't understand. Hibberblast had warned him repeatedly that logic and wisdom were folly.

"Wise men are a dime a dozen," Hibberblast would say. "Thinking is playing into the devil's hands. Wisdom is foolishness to a Holy Man."

Tommy recalled what a cocky know-it-all he had been back at the university, the brilliant young genius with all the answers—and all along, he was losing his soul. *Thank God for Reverend Hibberblast.*

Chapter 85
GOD'S ARMY

An exhausting night! Hibberblast dreamt of a great battle, of leading God's army into war, and his arm wearied from flailing a mighty sword. The dream had been blood-and-guts real. He'd heard the din of battle, smelled the carnage, and gazed upon the blood-splattered mangled bodies. Good versus Evil. A prelude to Armageddon. And Hibberblast was victorious. The next day while composing a hymn, he realized his dream--so vivid, so graphic--had come directly from God. A Holy vision. There could be no doubt. And he knew exactly what God wanted him to do and he had the money to do it.

※

Father Forero, a dense but dogmatic man, attired in black priestly raiment and a broad brim hat, set out on his burro for his biannual inspection of the parish. Father tolerated no music in the church or anywhere else for that matter. To listen to a radio was grave sin, to own one, a sacrilege. Today he planned to search parishioners' homes for instruments of the devil such as music boxes, jewelry, old newspapers, and catalogs. He said to his toady who led the burro he sat upon, "What is that fine looking building over there?"

"A house, Father."

"I can see it is a house. But such a large house. What kind of roof is that?"

"They call it shingles."

" And that fine building over there. What is that?"

"A church, your Excellency."

"A what?!"

"The church built by the gringo Hibberblast, the man who saved the village women."

The priest's eyes narrowed. "There was no church there a month ago. How did all this happen so quickly?"

"This gringo is what the villagers call *Hombre rapido*, a 'fast mover,' Father."

"May God in His mercy spare us. Burn it down."

That night twenty torch-bearing vigilante farmers, obedient to the commands of their priest, descended under the veil of darkness upon gringo Hibberblast's church. They stopped in their tracks. In front of the church stood forty rebels, their grim faces gleaming in the flickering torchlight, their rifles pointed menacingly at the vigilantes. The farmers tossed down their torches and ran like hell.

Hibberblast had hired the rebels to defend his newly acquired property against attacks from other rebels, from the cartels, and as it worked out from Father Forero's vigilantes. The rebels, mostly unemployed college dropouts from large cities, had been fighting for various causes under the rubric "The People's Freedom Fighters." Being city boys weary of living in the forest battling mosquitoes, leeches, and jungle rot, digging latrines and going without toilet paper, they were easily bought off by Hibberblast.

With his seemingly endless supply of cocaine money, Hibberblast outfitted his rebels in dark green uniforms with gold epaulets and gave each a pair of shiny leather boots. He armed them with modern Russian assault rifles and paid them in hard cash, plus weekly rations of coca leaves. Hibberblast himself wore a general's full dress uniform with ribbons, insignias, stars and crosses, and a red wool beret atop his head. He built and outfitted his army in just a few weeks and he called them, "God's Army." The village of Mejor Coca was safe at last.

Hibberblast closed down the Catholic Church and gave the peasants the option of attending his church or facing a firing squad. His sermons were short and to the point. "We must produce more coca leaves. Much more. We have an army to support now."

With a plethora of laborers and money, Hibberblast quickly turned a nearby plateau into an airstrip with landing lights. He put a jail at one end of the runway to house non-believers and other enemies of Mejor Coca. He built barracks and fortifications, started a weapons procurement program, and extended his army's protection to six nearby villages in exchange for eighty percent of their cocaine crop. He stopped selling to the cartels and started his own cartel. When the East and West cartels threatened war, he hired more rebels and conscripted young men from neighboring villages. God's Army grew so big that no one dare challenge General Hibberblast. In just a few short months Hibberblast had transformed this little mountain village into a booming, prosperous citadel, armed to the teeth, awash with money.

"Tommy," Hibberblast said to his protégé, "I'm turning the running of the church over to you. I'm too busy commanding my army to mess with it."

"I'll do my best," Tommy pledged.

Following a short ordination service, Tommy took over the reins of the church, his sermons uplifting, spirit-filled, and like his college lectures, drew huge crowds. He initiated a Children's time, Bible classes, and started a choir. Peasants from surrounding villages trekked to Mejor Coca for Sunday services.

Hibberblast's yellow jeep bounced over the rugged terrain at 30 mph. With one hand gripping the steering wheel, Hibberblast pointed out to Tommy the endless stretch of fencing along his thousand-acre natural habitat zoo. "You realize I built all this in just a few weeks, with God's help, of course."

Tommy clutched the sides of his seat, not trusting his seat belt to hold him in.

Hibberblast asked, "How are things at the church?"

Tommy's tone was blunt. "Attendance is up, but I noticed some of the parishioners are unhappy. They're working harder than ever."

The general applied the brakes, leaped up from his seat, and pointed to a stand of trees along a ridge. "Look over there. See their heads above the trees. Giraffes. I had twenty shipped in last week. And over there, beyond the fence. Cheetahs. A whole family. They eat one goat every day. Beautiful animals." The general sat back down and changed the subject. "The farmers aren't overworked. They're just not motivated. And it's your fault."

"W-w-w-what do you mean?"

"You're preaching the wrong stuff. 'The meek shall inherit the earth. Come ye who are heavily laden.' You should've been preaching the work ethic. 'If any would not work, neither should he eat. Six days thou shall labor, and on the seventh day rest.'"

"I was only comforting them," Tommy explained.

"You're makin' 'em lazy and whiny. That's not what God wants."

"They're not lazy…."

The general's cell phone beeped. "General Hibberblast here. That's great. How's the one in Taiwan doing? Wonderful! Keep up the good work. Praise the Lord." The general pocketed his cell, shifted into first gear, and looked at Tommy. "I've taken over Bobby Haggett's World Wide Ministries. We'll soon have recruiting centers for God's Army all over the world. We're really growing big time and we're moving fast. Hang on, I'll show you my white rhinos."

Tommy asked, "What happen to Bobby Haggett?"

"He's a crook, cheated the ministry out of millions."

The jeep hurdled gulches. Tommy couldn't deny that Hibberblast had changed. He wasn't the same man who'd rescued Tommy from the tar pit of sin and despair. He had become unfeeling, callous. His eyes had become the spiritless orbs of a sinner. Yet, he seemed bigger and stronger, like a linebacker on steroids.

The general glanced at Tommy. "I'm replacing you."

The jeep spun up and over an outcrop.

"Why," Tommy asked in staccato voice, "because I'm comforting my parishioners?"

"They're not yours. They're mine. I'm replacing you because it's God's will."

Tommy took a moment before responding. He cleared his throat. "I know you are a devout teacher and a discipline of the Lord, but I don't think you can read God's mind."

The jeep jerked to a stop. The general glared at Tommy. "That's blasphemy. I could have you shot."

"Shot! God's disciplines don't shoot people."

"His generals do. I had ten shot last Wednesday."

Tommy stiffened. "You murdered ten men?"

"Not murdered. Executed. Cartel trying to muscle in." The general's eyes were softer now. "I know it's a bit of shock to you, but God's tired of vermin who interfere with His work. He's sick of it." The general's hands tightened on the steering wheel and he grinned like a child. "Guess what I bought?"

"An elephant?"

"I now own the most powerful computer in the world. Nothing can touch it for brains and computational power. When it comes to war, and it's coming to that, the side with most computer power will win. Armageddon's just around the corner. The Lord wants you to become a computer expert. You'll be in charge of the Hashimotioto, the smartest machine ever built."

"I'm a biochemist, not a computer expert."

"The people who will deliver the computer will set it up and teach you how to run it. Remember with God's help, you can do anything."

"Who will take over the church?"

"Father Forero."

"But he's Catholic."

"Not any more. He converted just before he was to be executed."

"You were going to execute Father Forero?"

"If he didn't convert. I treat priests like any other opposition. They're either for us or against us. Father Forero is now for us. He's not too bright, but he understands farmers. Can keep them in line; make them produce. Look at that, Tommy." The general pointed to three rhinos with stalagmite snouts grazing on a bluff, their thick white hides gleaming in the sun.

Chapter 86
JUDAS

Tommy couldn't sleep. His mentor, the man he had trusted above all men, had stumbled into the Devil's deadliest snare. The lust for power. Determined to save Hibberblast, Tommy decided to wrestle the Devil by its horns. He'd confront Hibberblast like someone from AA confronts an alcoholic. With tough love. He'd shout out the truth until it rang in the Hibberblast's head with the loudness of the village bell.

Tommy got out of bed, dressed, put on his ears, said his morning prayers, and marched directly over to Hibberblast's mansion. An English butler with an affected smugness led him to the general's study. Two soldiers stood guard at the door. Tommy waited outside while the butler entered. In less than a minute, he returned. "The general will see you now."

Four officers and General Hibberblast poured over a map spread across a mahogany desk. Hibberblast glanced up when Tommy walked in. "What's so urgent? I'm busy planning an attack on the Cordillera rebels."

"I'd like to speak to you in private."

"These are my trusted lieutenants. Anything you have to say, you can say in their presence."

Tommy inhaled deeply, walked over to the general and with a stern countenance shouted, "The salvation of your soul is what's so urgent. I hate to say it, but you're possessed, and I'm here with God's help to save you." Tommy lifted up his arms to heaven. "Oh Lord, have mercy on this poor wretched soul…"

Hibberblast drove his fist into Tommy's nose. Blood splattered over Tommy's face as he crashed to the floor, his ears spinning on their nubbins. Lights flashed in his eyes. Two guards rushed in and on the general's order bound Tommy's hands behind him and sealed his mouth with duct tape.

They picked him up and shoved him into a chair. Hibberblast leaned down and glowered at Tommy, his intense brown eyes lit with anger. "You're a Judas, a Benedict Arnold, an angel of the Devil. You're not fit to live."

Tommy, blood dripping from his nose and over his duct-taped mouth, could only stare at his possessed mentor.

General Hibberblast turned to one his officers. "We'll have to find another computer trainee." He retuned to studying the map on his desk as if Tommy weren't even in the room. Twenty minutes passed before the general glanced a Tommy. He went to the door and summoned a guard. "Take him to the plateau jail."

The guards delivered Tommy to the jail, his hands bound, mouth taped. A pugdy jailer marched him down a long dark corridor. "Stop," the jailer shouted. He ripped the duct tape from Tommy's mouth and shoved him into a cell. "You're to be executed early in the morning, quietly with no fuss."

His hands bound behind him, Tommy lost his balance and fell onto the concrete floor. The iron door closed with a resounding clank that sent a shudder down his spine. Tommy sat on the cold floor, confused, shocked. Evil had prevailed over Good? *I'm going to die for doing the Right Thing?* Tommy feared neither bullets nor the pain of dying. He feared only uncertainty. For a believer to have doubts just before he dies seemed unfair. Where was God? Why hasn't He intervened?

Tommy was thinking like a professor again. Was death, as he had told Kent Mullins that night in the chemistry lab, just a brain without voltage? A flat EEG. He wished he knew a *homopragmatic truth*, anything that would make sense out of death and injustice. What if there are no *homopragmatic truths*? What if life is one big joke?

Tommy heard a click followed by the screeching of iron hinges. He scooted across the floor and cowered against the wall at the back of the cell. Was it time already? The jailer had told him he wouldn't be executed until morning. He closed his eyes. A strong hand jerked him by his collar onto his feet. The plastic bands that bound Tommy's hands dug into the skin. He heard the jailer say, "He's secure, Father. You can come in now."

Tommy opened his eyes. Before him stood Father Forero in a long black cassock, a broad brim hat shadowing his face.

Tommy asked, "What do you want?"

The jailer walked back down the corridor leaving priest and prisoner to commune in private.

Father Forero crossed himself. "I've come to pray with you, my son. Shall we pray together?"

"You pray for me?" Tommy laughed. "You who deserted your faith, who turned your back on God."

"I'm still working for God, just not with the Pope any longer. You could say I've changed supervisors, that's all."

"Yeah, still doing the same job. Exploiting the farmers."

"You're just jealous because I took over your church services. They're going to shoot you in the morning, you know that don't you?"

Tommy caught a glimpse of the priest's eyes in the dim light. Insipid orbs, dull as the gray buttons on his cassock. A stupid man who knows he's stupid can be a child of God. A stupid man who is arrogant, incurious, and doesn't know he's stupid, well he's a--a Father Forero.

The priest smiled. "I won't be here in the morning. I'm flying out tonight to Medellin. I'm giving the opening prayer at a cartel convention. Now, do you want me to pray with you or not? My plane is waiting for me on the tarmac."

Contempt shone in Tommy's eyes as he stared at the *turn-cloth* priest. But why be angry with Father Forero, when the whole damn universe is meaningless? He's merely another of life's endless non-sequiturs. "No thanks."

"Have it your way." The priest shrugged and headed out the door, suddenly stopped by an afterthought. He spun around. "Tommy, would you twirl your ears for me? The farmers just love it when you do it, but I've never seen you do it."

"I can't. My hands are bound."

Father Forero took a short breath. "I can fix that." He fished a pocketknife from his cassock. "Turn around."

Tommy craned his neck as Father Forero cut the bindings on his wrists. God had sent an angel into this dark cell. His hands free, Tommy whirled, grasped the cleric by the nape of his neck and drove his head into the wall. The hollow thud of bone striking stone reverberated throughout the cell as the priest's broad brim hat sailed off his head. Father Forero crumpled to the floor in his black cassock like a vampire felled by a shaft of sunlight.

Tommy quickly exchanged clothes with the lifeless priest and dragged him over to a darken corner of the cell.

"I'm ready to go," Tommy called out to the jailer.

Tommy headed down the jail corridor, his face hidden under the broad brim hat. He wagged at hand at the jailer and walked out the door. The cassock fluttered like a banner as he strode across the windy tarmac, his hand securing the hat. He prayed the jailer wouldn't discover Father Forero's body before he reached the airplane waiting on the tarmac.

"Good evening, Father," the pilot said from the window of the small plane.

Tommy squeezed into the cockpit next to the pilot, hiding his face under the brim of his hat. "I'm in a hurry. Let's get moving."

The plane lifted into a strong wind and climbed steadily into a black, starless sky. Tommy looked back at Mejor Coca, a cluster of lights in the void. He silently thanked God for saving him. Thirty kilometers out of Mejor Coca, the plane rattled and shook like a clunker Ford on a country road. Tommy worried that the old aircraft might fly apart.

"Head winds," the pilot shouted, "looks to be a nasty storm."

Lightening flashed in the black sky, illuminating the cockpit like a strobe. Hail pelted the Plexiglas windows. Tommy's heart pounded erratically with each lurch of the plane.

"Don't worry, Father, I've flown coca over these mountains for thirty years. And with a priest in the cockpit what could possibly go wrong?"

The pilot lit one cigarette after the other, filling the cockpit with smoke.

Tommy stared down at another cluster of yellow lights. "What's that?"

"Just the lights of some mountain village."

The needles on the instruments oscillated wildly. The control stick jiggled in the pilot's hand. The plane shook violently.

Tommy looked out the window. "Hey, what's that?"

"Oh, that's just the lights of another village."

"No," Tommy shouted. "That's the same village and it's moving out ahead of us."

Tommy realized the powerful head wind was carrying the plane backwards, yet keeping it aloft. The plane bounced on the wind like a drunken cowboy on a mechanical bull. The instruments in the cockpit went crazy. The pilot fitted some straps around his shoulders and fastened buckles around his waist.

Tommy asked, "What are you doing?"

"Routine preparations."

The engine suddenly clattered like a broken dishwasher.

"What are you preparing for?"

Flames leaped from the engine cowling.

"Emergencies, Father." The pilot forced open his door, turned to Tommy and shouted over the roar of the wind, "Sorry, Father, there is only one parachute." He crossed himself and leaped out of the cockpit into the black, stormy night.

The plane dipped and Tommy grabbed for the control stick. His head slammed into the instrument panel. Everything went black.

Chapter 87
WE'RE COMING

Kent and Justin's plane landed safely in Peru. The two Americans took a bus from Iquitos to Telcequez where they talked with an Indian guide who had heard reports of a white woman living deep in the forest. With the guide and three porters, Kent and Justin boated up the Amazon to a blackwater tributary and went ashore. Swinging machetes, the entourage hacked through the impossible undergrowth, a mile a day, one sweaty foot at a time. Hands quickly blistered, joints ached, skin bled from the clawing of the prickly vegetation. Swarms of mosquitoes feasted on this gift of sweaty human flesh.

If Kent found Cleo, what he would say to her? That he loved her? That under different circumstances he would have married her? For sure, he would take her in his arms--that's all he really wanted anyway. Just to hold her once more. One thought tormented him. Soon he would be dead, and someday she would fall in love again. To think of her with someone else was unbearable. The guide and the porters drank tequila around the campfire to relax their sore muscles. Kent drank to keep from thinking.

On the twelfth day out, they came to a clearing and made camp. The guide went ahead to scout the area. He returned in the evening excited about smoke trails he had seen. "At least twenty campfires," he said mopping sweat from his brow. "Two, maybe three days west."

Kent's heart raced. "Must be Cleo and her vegetarian colony."

"How can you be sure?" Justin asked.

The guide thrust the point of his machete into the earth. "Could be headhunters." Fear swept through the porters like a cold wet wind, their faces suddenly drawn and pale.

"Nonsense," Kent answered. "It's the Hivaro village. I know it is. We're heading due west in the morning."

The next morning, the jungle was unusually quiet. Even the gabby Macaws were silent. Kent threw back his tent flap and squinted out at the jungle through tequila-red eyes.

Justin stood nearby in the small clearing, fully dressed, solemn as a deacon. "They've gone, the bastards. Must have taken off before sunrise."

Kent crawled out the tent and looked around.

Justin rubbed his jaw. "They took most of the supplies." He picked up a solitary machete. "They didn't leave much."

Kent grabbed his backpack. "We don't need much. Cleo is only a few days west."

"Maybe we oughta head back while there's still a trail to follow."

Kent spoke with a quiet firmness. "I'm heading west. You do what you want."

Justin walked to the western edge of the clearing and hacked away at the undergrowth. "We started this together, we'll finish it together."

A half-day out, Justin noticed Kent struggling under the weight of his backpack. Soon, Kent became too weak to take his turn with the machete. His clothes soaked in sweat, his face pale, and his steps uncertain Kent stumbled and fell. Justin helped him into the shade of a huge fern. The chattering of Kent's teeth and the rigors of a chill told Justin that Malaria and not Tommy Tennyson's poison had overpowered Kent. Justin made camp, forced aspirin down his friend, and prepared a meal by opening a can of beans. All evening Kent jabbered nonsense.

The next day, Kent's legs gave out when he attempted to stand. Justin hoisted him and their backpacks onto his back. Bent double under the weight, Justin struggled ever westward, swinging his machete at the jungle. In the afternoon, he pried open Kent's mouth and forced water down him from his canteen. He glanced at his wrist compass. After a short rest, he once again loaded Kent onto his back, picked up the machete, and chopped away at the verdurous wall in front of him.

Chapter 88
DOLLY

Rummels laughed to himself when the tall man with a Midwestern accent like that of prime time newscasters knocked on the door of his Thai Hi's dressing room, congratulated him on his Kenny Rogers impersonation, and offered him four thousand dollars to entertain passengers on the cruise ship Magdalena. Rummels had just sold the Hashimotioto for two hundred and fifty million dollars at a black market arms auction. Who needs a measly four thousand bucks?

To get his millions, Rummels had to deliver the supercomputer to the buyer, a General Hibberblast in Colombia. Larry agreed to set up the Hashimotioto for the buyer and to train others to operate it as part of the deal he struck with Rummels. The risky part of the operation would be transporting the Hashimotioto to Colombia, what with the Japanese government and other foreign powers scouring the world for the missing Tricorpus Callosum.

The tall Midwestern told Rummels, "You'll love sailing the Pacific. Sidney, Honolulu, the Galapagos. It's the longest cruise going and the most exciting. We tour the entire west coast of South America...."

Rummels, half dressed, stared at the stranger with a look of amazement. "Did you say South America?"

"Yes, then up the coast to Mexico and California...."

"What did you say your name was?"

"Frank Chisholm. I'm the director of entertainment for C and V cruises."

Rummels buckled his belt and shoved his hand at Frank. "I'd be delighted to entertain on your cruise ship."

Rummels met Larry at McDonalds in downtown Bangkok for burgers and fries. As usual the place buzzed with customers. They sat in a plastic booth by a window. Rummels washed down a mouthful of fries with a gulp of tea. "It's perfect. Who'd ever figure we'd transport the Hashimotioto to South America on a cruise ship?"

Larry nodded. In desperate need of positive reinforcement, of some life-affirming intervention to rescue him from the doldrums, left-brain Larry would consider going anywhere, doing anything. But setting up the Hashimotioto and programming it for a paramilitary, religious fanatic wasn't what he had in mind. But he'd do it. It was part of the deal.

Rummels dabbed his lips with a napkin. "You can sit back and enjoy the cruise while I do my Kenny Rogers thing."

"You know, you do look like Kenny Rogers."

"I didn't use to. Long story."

Larry tapped his fingers on the plastic table. "I've done some impersonations."

"Really. Can you sing?"

"Yeah. Funerals and weddings."

Back at his apartment, Larry took the Hashimotioto apart and hid its circuit boards in false bottoms of suitcases and put several of its electronic components inside the amplifier of Rummels' electric guitar. He placed the Tricorpora Callosum in a padded trunk labeled "costumes" and covered it over with items purchased from a theatrical company. He hid the computer's CPU inside a portable radio. Two priceless platinum transistors essential for the operation of the Tricorppra Callosum, Larry wore in his ears as hearing aids. He packed dozens of especially designed transistors into prescription bottles labeled Prozac capsules, Lipitor, and Penicillin. The next morning, Larry and Rummels carried the Hashimotioto on board the Magdalena as luggage.

Once the Hashimotioto was delivered to Mejor Coca, Larry would reassemble it and connect it to a nuclear power supply that General Hibberblast had purchased from a Middle East terrorist group. The power supply called Tiny Tim, a converted plutonium mini-bomb, was already in Mejor Coca.

When finished with the Hashimotioto project, Larry thought maybe he'd settle down, maybe in Andorra in the Pyrenees or in some third world country. Maybe he'd open a computer store. But it was stupid to plan anything. He had barely escaped going back to prison and he had just stolen the Hashimotioto, a crime tantamount to lifting the "Mona Lisa" from the Louvre. And Mejor Coca, his next destination, had all the trappings of a Jonestown.

Sit back and enjoy the cruise.

The sailing was smooth, the food great, and Rummels provided the entertainment. At first, Rummels' Kenny Rogers impersonation astounded the Magdalena's passengers. But night after night of the same stuff gradually turned them sour. He tried Johnny Cash, but his voice was too high. Vince Gill, voice too low. The audience booed his Frank Sinatra right off the stage. Eighteen shows to go, and the passengers weren't showing up.

At sunrise, Rummels and Larry strolled the Magdalena's deck. "I'm bombing out with this geezer audience," Rummels admitted. "If the cruise ship dumps us in some island port, we'll never get the Hashimotioto to Mejor Coca."

"Why don't you spice up the act?"

"How?"

"I don't know. Maybe a sexy blond. A Dolly Parton?"

"Be serious."

"I am." Larry's brain suddenly shifted to the right, and he morphed into a bundle of femininity, arching his brow, walking with his head back and chest out in a salty Dolly swagger. "You'd be surprised how much it costs to look this cheap, honey."

Rummels stared quizzically at Larry. "You sound just like Dolly."

"You ain't seen nothin' yet, baby." Larry broke into "Here You Come Again." Deck hands and early-bird saunters gathered round to hear Larry sang. He felt like his old self, the real Larry, the right-brain Larry, the used car dealer, the vocalist at the county fair. He hadn't felt this good since—he smiled-- this was what he had been missing, what he had always wanted to do. To entertain.

Rummels slapped Larry on the back. "Great stuff. How about going on with me tonight?"

Larry thought for a moment. "Okay, we'll give it a shot. There's a blond wig in that trunk of theatrical supplies."

The show was a smash. They did "Lady," "Baby I'm Burnin'," "9 to 5," "Crazy," "Real Love." and a dozen more. The next night was sold out. Every evening, Larry transformed into the bigger-than-life Dolly in a blond wig, glittering gown, layers of makeup, and a neckline plunging into an immense water bra. Dolly's quick wit and homespun humor had the audience roaring with laughter. Frank showed up at every performance to gaze upon Dolly, the most beautiful creature he'd ever seen. He sent a cablegram to Vu who was in Singapore on business. "Magdalena has best darn show on high seas. Come. See yourself. Meet me in Honolulu."

Chapter 89
RAIN FOREST

Tommy woke up in the cockpit of the pilotless small plane to a throbbing headache. His fingertips outlined a tender, egg-size bump on his forehead. He stared out the cockpit window at an immense undulating green field and overhead at an equally immense sun-lit blue sky. He rolled his head to ease the stiffness in his neck. Had the plane miraculously landed itself? Had God landed the plane? *Hallelujah!* Following a prayer of thanks he unbuckled his seat belt, forced open the cockpit door open and stepped out.

He plunged downward like a stone dropped into an abyss.

Leaves and tree branches slashed hellishly at his face and plummeting body. He stared up in disbelief at the blue sky above receding to a pinpoint of light. He grasped at vines and gnarled boughs as they hurtled by, but they only snapped in his hands. An all but impenetrable morass of small trees and giant fronds slowed his descent. He crashed through a last tangle of branches to a muted landing on the soft compost of a forest's floor. A flurry of leaves fluttered downward. Chattering monkeys scolded the intruder. A sloth moved leisurely through the branches above, oblivious to the ruckus.

Tommy lay on his back and gazed upward, realizing the airplane had set down on the canopy of a rain forest.

Scraped and bruised, he checked himself for broken bones. Everything seemed intact except HIS EARS! His prosthetic ears were gone, knocked loose from their nubbins during the fall. He groped in the shadowy darkness, his fingers digging and sifting through the soft humus for his ears. Nothing. He had lost his ears, but he was alive. He knelt on the forest's floor and muttered another prayer of thanks.

For two days, Tommy crept through the prickly undergrowth of the rain forest. Massive moss-covered trees and the tangles of lush foliage forced him one way then another. Each day he grew weaker, and soon even the large waxy leaves of the begonias and figs became insurmountable obstacles. Mosquitoes and armies of red ants swarmed over his body, stinging and biting. His mouth turned to cotton. At night, he trembled at the roaring of jungle cats, and then blessedly dreamed of water droplets falling from the sky into his parched mouth. He howled back through cracked lips at the incessant cry of the jungle, terrifying in its shrillness. On the third morning, irrational with hunger, his tongue swollen with thirst, Tommy simply lay on the forest floor and waited death's consecrated release. Then came the *La manta Blanca*, little midges with tiny wings, to feast on his flesh.

The faint but distinct sound of water trickling over rocks caused Tommy to raise his head and sniff the air. *Water?* He dug his hands into the soft soil and crawled toward the wonderful gurgling sound, until, suddenly, he felt the cool, magic rush of life-giving water. He cried in joy and swept deep handfuls of a flowing stream onto his face and over his lips. So sweet the taste. He stared into the water at his grotesque, ear-less reflection. Embarrassed, he pulled his wet hair over his ear nubbins.

His thirst gratified, his spirit renewed, he splashed in the shallow stream like a happy child, washing away the ants and midges. He reckoned he could cross the small stream easily. He fancied there were berries and fruit on the other side. Yes, a veritable Garden of Eden over there somewhere. He tromped through the water like a buffalo. Halfway across the stream, he felt tinges of pain like the jabs of sharp rocks against his feet. With each step, the rocks became sharper, ripping at his flesh. All at once, the water turned red, boiling with a frenzied hoard of tiny perch-like fish with buzz-saw teeth. He screamed, "PIRANHA!"

Tommy splashed towards the opposite bank, the flesh-eating little monsters moving with him in a bloody swarm. Only yards to go, he lost his balance and dove toward the embankment. He dug his hands into the mud and pulled himself out of the stream. A hundred or more of the little fish clung to his bloodied legs. He crawled farther and farther up the bank until the last of the deadly creatures flopped back into the water.

Tommy's feet throbbed with pain, and when he looked down at them he discovered he had no feet. He stared at the raw meat stubs of his ankles and became half-witted at the red parabolas shooting into the air from severed arteries. He vomited and passed out.

Hivaro gatherers searching for berries and roots came upon Tommy stretched out on the bank of the stream. This white god was in bad shape, earless, footless, and unconscious. They packed mud onto Tommy's bloodied ankle stubs and wrapped them with leaves to stop the bleeding, then hoisted Tommy onto their shoulders and headed off for their village.

Cleo was overseeing the preparation of "red root," once a delicacy and now the staple of the Hivaro vegetarian diet, when the Hivaro gatherers carried Tommy into the village. She directed the villagers to take the piranha victim to her hut. She summoned the new medicine man, a neophyte will little experience. Together they dressed Tommy's ankle stubs with tree bark and mosses. Cleo forced orchid teas and plant juices down the stranger's throat. Cradling Tommy in her arms, she stroked his forehead and sang Jesus-3 hymns.

Daily, Cleo applied liniments and leafy bandages to Tommy's wounds. The village wood-carver came and measured Tommy for artificial feet. Following several days of intensive, warm-hearted care, Tommy opened his eyes and looked up at the pretty blue-eyed blond clad only in a skimpy loincloth and hemp bra.

"Where am I? Who are you?"

Cleo smiled and spooned red root into Tommy's mouth. "I'll explain everything later. Right now you must eat and regain your strength."

Chapter 90
TOMMY'S PLAN

Tommy stared at the leaf bandages covering his ankle stubs. When Cleo stepped into the hut with his lunch of roots and berries on a leaf platter, he looked up at her with a sad face. "I'll never walk again, will I?"

She smiled. "Today you shall have new feet."

She set the down the tray and removed the leaf bandages. The wounds were completely healed; fresh skin had grown over the gnawed bones. After Tommy finished his lunch, the village wood-carver came to the hut with two hand-carved wooden strips that resembled miniature skis. He bound them to Tommy's ankles with vines. They fit as perfectly as Tommy's prosthetic ears had once fit on their nubbins.

Cleo eyed Justin sharply. "Now I want you to walk."

Tommy stood and immediately his ski feet became entangled. He flailed about, arms flying, his body corkscrewing and he plummeting to the floor. He lay there, staring at his ski feet. *Bad enough to be born a freak, now this—a complete klutz.* He wished the piranha had devoured him completely. He took a breath and reached for Cleo's outstretched hand. He tried again to walk, this time with Cleo holding to him. He teetered but did not fall.

He looked at Cleo. "You think I'm a weirdo, don't you?"

She smiled triumphantly. "You're doing great. Now take another step. That's it."

Holding to Cleo, Tommy crossed the hut by picking up his wooden feet and slapping them down duck-like.

Soon Tommy took a few steps by himself. Later, he pivoted and turned on his new feet. When he did lose his balance, Cleo caught him. The next day, he walked around the outside of the hut and even kicked some stones and jumped up and down.

Cleo showed him around the village. His clumsy, ski-slapping walk amused the villagers, who couldn't completely suppress their giggles and smiles. Tommy was surprised that people and wild animals could live together in harmony. A jaguar big as a Saint Bernard roamed through the village, docile as a house cat. Monkeys, deer, tapirs, capybara, and a variety of reptiles lived here. An anaconda, twenty-five feet of rippling muscle with a huge head and a hinged mouth that could accommodate a Harley-Davidson, basked lazily in the sun in the center of the village, children playing amongst it's moist, slithery coils.

Tommy asked Cleo, "Why aren't the carnivores eating the herbivores?"

"Because we feed them red-root. Calms even the most ferocious animals. Once on a red root diet, the animals want to stay in the village." She patted the jaguar on the head. "Oh, we've had a few troublemakers, mostly territorial males. But we know how to deal with them."

Tommy noticed how Cleo settled the villagers' rare disputes with kindness and impartiality, yet with authority and finality. He enjoyed listening to her Jesus-3 sermons and soon became a red root aficionado. The fleshy roots were delicious and induced a state of profound lightheartedness in the eater.

At sunset, Tommy and Cleo walked hand in hand along the riverbank. "The problem is," Cleo told him in a solemn voice, "we're running out of red root. We had to cut the animals' rations in half. We've dug up large tracts of the forest floor looking for more roots, but without much luck. We can't cultivate it; there are no seeds. Transplanted roots won't take hold."

Tommy steadied himself on his wooden feet and skimmed a smooth rock across the surface of the river. "You should have the roots analyzed. Maybe the active ingredient can be synthesized."

"You mean produce it artificially?"

"Sure. That way you would never run out. Tell you what. I'll send a sample to my old university and have it analyzed. At one time, I was a professor of biochemistry there."

Cleo looked at Tommy in utter disbelief; a gasp escaped her lips. The missing ears, professor of biochemistry, and the name Tommy. "Oh, my god. Could it be…are you Tommy Tennyson, the man who poisoned Kent Mullins?"

Shock ran through Tommy like high voltage. The stunned look on his face answered her question. Tommy stared intently at Cleo. "I'd give anything to find him. I've lived with this guilt so long, I can't bare it anymore."

"Do you have the antidote?"

"The formula's in my head. With ten dollars worth of chemicals, a test tube, and Bunsen burner I could have the antidote in an hour. I wanted to find Kent and give him the antidote, but…I shouldn't have listened to Rev Hibberblast. At the time I didn't know…I didn't believe he was an evil man. But now I see him for what he was and is."

"Hibberblast—that name sounds vaguely familiar. You say he prevented you from finding and helping Kent?"

Tommy hung his head and nodded. "He convinced me that God would take care of Kent. And if I didn't trust God to do that, then I was sinning because of my lack of faith. Do you have any idea where Kent is?"

Hope glowed in Cleo's eyes. "Selena Rosalina may know. We'll go down river to Telcequez in the morning and call her."

Cleo and Tommy sat beside a bonfire in village center and talked late into the night. Tommy explained, "I hated everybody I had grown up with in Harkerville because of the hurt inside me. I wanted them to suffer as I had suffered. However, after I poisoned Kent, I was saved. At the lowest point in my life, I found God."

Cleo smiled. "That's wonderful."

"Well, not altogether wonderful." Tommy told Cleo about General Hibberblast losing his soul in Mejor Coca. "He's devil-possessed, and he's scheming to take over the world with a powerful supercomputer. He's hooked on power, and he plans to get the rest of the world hooked on cocaine."

"That's terrible."

"What's worse, he'll probably succeed. Unless someone stops him."

Cleo stood to warm her hands over the fire. She looked at Tommy. "Is that someone you?"

"I must destroy the supercomputer. There's no one else to do it." He stared at Cleo, awed by her natural beauty and her smile so radiant in the flickering light of the fire. If only they had met at another time, in another life, and he in another body. He cleared his throat. "When we get to Telcequez, I'll synthesize the antidote. But you must find Kent and give it to him while I'll return to Mejor Coca to destroy the Hashimotioto."

Chapter 91
BYE TOMMY, HELLO KENT

Early next morning as Cleo packed a small knapsack for her and Tommy's canoe trip down river to Telcequez, a villager rushed into her hut. "Come quick, Blanco Deo."

Cleo followed the villager to Tommy's hut, where others had gathered. The dread on their faces told her something was desperately wrong. She rushed inside and gasped in horror. The village anaconda lay coiled in the center of the hut, a man-size bulge in its belly, its beady reptilian eyes glazed with digestive contentment. Beside the giant snake lay Tommy's wooden ski-feet.

Cleo cried, "Bring me the white god's knife."

At Cleo's order, twenty villagers carried the twisting, lashing reptile to the center of the village and stretched it to its full length. Cleo unsheathed the Portuguese sword, the sharp blade glinting in the morning light. With a single swipe, she opened the bulge in the snake's belly. The great serpent writhed as its entrails poured out. An eyeball peered out at Cleo through the snake's transparent gut. A second swipe of the sword opened the gut. Villagers turned sick at the pungent ferment spilling out onto the ground. A gold dental filling glittered in the digestive debris of crushed bones, hair, and body parts. Tommy was not only dead; he was sausage.

Cleo turned and walked away from the thrashing serpent. Poor Tommy. Why was it meant for one man to suffer so much? Cleo knew there was no possibility of finding the antidote now. She admonished herself for not being more diligent. When she cut the red root rations for the animals, she should have known this might happen. She said a prayer for Tommy, Kent, and the snake.

The villagers watched in astonishment as the snake unhinged its mouth and began swallowing its entrails. At least it would die happy, eating its last meal over and over.

Two excited Hivaro gatherers ran from the forest into the village shouting, "Another white god is coming, a two-headed one."

A bent figure swinging a machete stumbled out of the jungle, a second man on his back. Cleo froze, mouth agape, her eyes wide with shock.

It's Kent and Justin!

Kent, in the throes of a fever crisis, trembled violently and screamed nonsense. Cleo covered him with blankets of hemp, sponged his face and limbs with cool spring water, and fed him a concoction of healing teas and red root extract, the Hivaro cure for malaria. For three days the fever gripped him. Inside her hut, Cleo cuddled Kent and sang Jesus-3 hymns to him as she had done with Tommy.

Justin had trouble straightening from his bent position until villagers massaged away his stiffness. The villagers now had a virtual pantheon of white gods in their midst. They decided to make Justin the chief god because his grizzled beard, squinty eyes, small frame and bowlegged walk fit the Hivaro's description of the Portuguese soldier who walked into their village 360 years ago. Certain that the original white god had return to the rain forest, they gave Justin the ancient thunder stick, which he carried around like a scepter. Legend had it the original white god had voracious appetite for food and women. Justin enjoyed the veneration. For him, the rain forest became as sybaritic as a St. Petersburg hot tub.

Thanks to red root and good nursing care, in three days Kent was out of bed and making sense. Following a dinner of red root and legumes he leaned against the bamboo post in the center of the hut and feasted his eyes on Cleo's scantily clad body. "You're more beautiful than ever." He noticed tears in the corners of her eyes, and with his finger wiped them away.

She sobbed and threw her arms around him. "Can you ever forgive me for leaving you in New York?"

"All that matters is we're together now."

"I had no choice. My vision from Jesus-3 was...."

Kent patted her back. "It doesn't matter now."

She wiped away tears with the back of her hand. "I can't believe you guys found this place."

Kent told Cleo about Professor Sulkohov being electrocuted in his hot tub just minutes after he discovered a *homopragmatic truth*. There were more tears when she told him about Tommy's crushing demise.

"You mean Tommy Tennyson, the man who poisoned me was here?"

"He was a changed man. Repentant. We were planning to go to Telcequez to buy the ingredients to make the antidote. He wanted to save you, but he's gone and with him the formula for the antidote."

"The dice have been rolled," Kent said with more than a twinge of disappointment. "But I've accepted my fate. And I found you and that makes me happy." He took her in his arms and kissed her, a long lingering, healing kiss.

Chapter 92

LOVERS AT SEA

The Honolulu Kenny and Dolly show drew huge applause. Rummels and Larry sang an encore medley for the insatiable audience. Not since Elvis played here had there been such excitement. Six standing ovations. Vu, just in from Singapore, said to Frank, "You know, there's something familiar about Dolly."

"Isn't she wonderful? So talented and beautiful."

Vu nodded. "She certainly is."

Promising to meet them later in the ship's casino, Frank left Vu and Caressa and went in search of Dolly. He felt about Dolly as he'd had about Tracey back in Bolton. Only more so. Dolly's lush lips, seductive eyes, those colossal breasts, and the sound of her sexy, self-assured voice were sheer excitement for Frank.

Frank knocked on her dressing room door.

"Come in," Larry hollered, staring into a mirror as he removed his Dolly wig.

Frank opened the door, horrified at the sight of a cropped male head with a lovely Dolly face. He shut his eyes to the magnificent blond fluff of ringlets dangling in Larry's hand. "Please, put it back on."

"Why?"

"Just do it, please."

"Okay." Larry wigged up. Frank slowly opened his eyes. Dolly, in all her splendor, stared at him, one brow raised, blond ringlets sweeping her cheeks. "Look, Mr. Chisholm, this is getting kinky. You coming in here after every performance on some pretense and staring at me like I was…"

"You're beautiful, Dolly. And call me Frank."

"It's all fake, Frank."

"You could never be a fake. You know what you are? You're a Gestalt composite, a thing of many parts. Even if some of the parts aren't real, the whole perception is. When you're Dolly, you're really Dolly."

Larry removed the wig again. Frank immediately shielded his eyes. "Please, put it on. I want you to be Dolly."

Larry hesitated momentarily and then put the wig back on. He placed his hands on his hips and said with a sexy Dolly twang, "Okay, wigs on. But I want you to know I'm ain't gay."

"Neither am I." Frank stroked the wig affectionately. "I think about you all the time."

Dolly placed her hand on Frank's arm. "You realize we can't have a sex life together."

"So?"

"What if I want to have a sex life? With women."

"That's okay. But when you're Dolly, you're mine. I'll always be faithful to you."

"What about your sex life?"

"Oh, I'll just take a shower now and then."

"You really do love me, don't you?"

"More than anything."

Frank tasted Dolly's lush lips, their bodies pressed together. Frank tall and lanky, a towering pine; Dolly curvy with bulges, a silk-covered pillow. Their bodies swayed rhythmically in sweet simulation. When two people share something heretical, something taboo, they share everything. What candor must exist among malcontents? Larry spoke to Frank of prison and Eugene, of Cleo and Veronica, of how he enjoyed entertaining on stage, and how he feared someday it would end and he would find himself back in prison.

"I've never been so happy and at the same time so frightened," Larry admitted.

Frank smiled. "As long as the Magdalena sails, you have a home." He told Dolly how he found and lost love. Now love was back. "It's unbelievable this could happen to me again."

The following days at sea were happiest in the lives of two people in love. A love not anchored in reality's deep harbors, but on the shoals of make-believe. Drawn together like magnet and iron, they remained free and unbridled as wind and sea.

Four days out of Honolulu and the Magdalena had smooth sailing. From the deck Frank stared out at the great circle of blue. Years of trying to understand the human condition and treat its afflictions had gained him nothing in wisdom or lore. Rather, he had become jaded and misanthropic. But his love for Dolly had changed him, and each breath of sea air pumped nobility and generosity into his frail soul. He smiled at strangers. He opened doors for the elderly and infirmed. He joshed and ribbed with the Magdalena's crew, roared with laughter at stale jokes, and teased children with avuncular charm. He was in love, and for the first time in recent memory, he liked himself.

Frank met Vu and Caressa on the main deck. Vu wore a captain's cap, white pants and a blue jacket; Caressa, a light, pastel dress with scooped neck. The bright Pacific sun exposed the layers of make-up on the old showgirl's sweet face.

"I've never seen you looking better," Vu told Frank.

"I've never felt better."

Stiletto heels clicking across the deck and blond hair gleaming in the sunlight turned heads. Dressed in Capri pants, her midriff exposed by a white blouse tied at the bodice, Dolly strode along the deck, her hips swaying, a red parasol bouncing on her shoulder. Dolly was more than persona; she was scenery, set, and stage—a moving tableau of sexuality. She had come to meet Frank for brunch. She hooked his arm in hers and recognized Vu standing beside him. She hid her surprise behind a broad Dolly smile.

Frank turned to Dolly. "Darling, I'd like you to meet my best friend and business partner Dr. Vu and his wife Caressa. This is Dolly of our Dolly and Ken show."

Vu smiled and bowed. His sagacious eyes hid the analytical churning of his mind. He knew her from somewhere. But where?

Dolly twirled her parasol. "Please to meetcha."

Caressa complemented a fellow showgirl. "You look stunning in that outfit."

Dolly smiled more. "You don't look so bad yourself, honey."

All through brunch, Vu watched Dolly who looked, moved, and talked so incredibly like the real Dolly Parton it made him doubt, fleetingly, his powers of discrimination. Finally it dawned on him--the subtle overtones in that disguised voice, the way she held her ice-tea glass, the little wags of the head, the tilt of the chin, the way she nervously tapped her left foot on the floor--Dolly was Larry. Dolly winked at Vu. She knew that he knew.

Vu patted Frank on the back. "Frank is one of the best blackjack players in the world. I should know. I taught him. There are only two better. Myself, of course, and an old friend from Atlantic City."

Dolly asked, "And how is your old friend?"

"I'd say he is very happy. He was lost for a while, but I think he found himself."

Chapter 93
BREAKING UP

As the Magdalena steamed towards South America, Caressa and Dolly became good friends; a chorus girl superannuated, a woman superimposed. They shopped the ship's boutiques and the many stores in the various ports. Caressa, a master at make-up and dress, helped Dolly pick out costumes and jewelry that made her look more sensational than ever. Back onboard, Caressa taught Dolly a little Vaudeville and some Wild West numbers. The ship's show became known as the "Dolly Show," Rummels' Kenny Rogers impersonation just an opening number. Rummels could care less. Two hundred and fifty million dollars awaited him in Mejor Coca. Delivering the Hashimotioto to General Hibberblast was foremost on his mind.

One evening after the show, Rummels observed Frank and Dolly walking along the deck hand and hand. He followed them to the disco where they danced until three in the morning. Dolly returned to her cabin exhausted. Without bothering to turn on the light, she tossed her wig onto a chair and flopped onto the bed. A shadowy figure stood in the corner of the room. With a trembling hand, Dolly switched on the bedside lamp and looked up at Rummels.

"What the hell," she gasped. "You scared me to death."

"We need to talk."

"Can't it wait? I'm bushed."

"I don't like this thing between you and Frank."

Dolly quickly evaporated; Larry emerged. "It's none of your fuckin' business."

"Everything you do is my business until we consummate the Hashimotioto deal. In two days we dock in Buenaventura and leave ship for Mejor Coca."

"I'm not going. I'm staying on to do the Dolly Show indefinitely."

Rummels threw the Dolly wig onto the floor and plopped down in the chair. He lifted his veiny legs upon the bed. "I thought you'd try something like this."

Larry sat upright; his gaze met Rummels' straight on. "I mean it. I'm not going to Mejor Coca."

"You're in love, I suppose. You and Frank sailing the high seas, singing 'Nine to Five' with your fingers up each other's asses."

Larry shoved Rummels legs off the bed. "Leave Frank out of this."

"I'm afraid that's impossible. You see there's an annihilation order out there with your boyfriend's name on it. A couple of hit men from Taipei. They never miss. They don't hear from me in two months, they whack Frank."

"You dirty bastard." Larry lunged for Rummels' throat.

With a CRAWL agent's quickness, Rummels leaped out of the chair, twisted Larry's arm behind him, and shoved him to the floor. "Don't be stupid."

Larry was a sobbing Dolly now. "I knew it was too good to be true. Everything I touch ends up shit."

Rummels eased his grip on Larry's arm. "Look, it's not that bad. You teach General Hibberblast's technicians how to operate the Hashimotioto and in a few weeks you'll be back on board ship with sweet Ol' Frank."

Mascara streamed down Dolly's cheeks. "Do you really believe that lunatic in Mejor Coca is going to let us leave there alive?"

Rummels walked to the door. "I'm betting two hundred and fifty million on it."

⁂

The next night after the show, Frank stood on the Magdalena's bow with his arm around Dolly. The port lights of Buenaventura reflected off the harbor like quivering constellations of an upside-down universe.

"You're awfully quiet, Dolly. No secrets, remember."

"I've never been happier. But I have to…"

"Shhh…don't spoil the moment. I love the way your eyes sparkle at night."

Dolly rubbed her eyes. "I'm leaving the ship tomorrow."

"Going shopping with Caressa?"

A ship's horn sounded in the distance.

"I'm leaving for good."

Frank tried to speak, but the words stuck in his throat.

"It's a commitment."

Panic rioted within Frank. His stomach churned, his hands trembled. He nearly choked on the words coming out his mouth, "Tell me it's not true."

"It was perfect, but it had to end. We knew it couldn't last."

"Why?"

Dolly looked down. "Because the whole thing was an illusion."

"So what. I've known people whose whole lives were illusions. Some of them a damn site happier than most. A long time ago, I came to the conclusion anyone who is sane in this cockamamie world has to be crazy."

"Please, you're making it difficult."

"You don't really mean it's over?"

"It hurts me, too." With typical Dolly swagger, she walked away, her hand sliding along the deck railing.

Frank stared into the dark sea, his hands clenched. He knew the problem wasn't with Dolly; it no doubt it had something to do with that Kenny Rogers fake. But what?

Chapter 94
THE POISON

Kent's rain forest nights with Cleo were incredibly exciting, a refresher on all the old lovemaking techniques Cleo taught him back in Harkerville. Plus some new ones, fantastic innovations the Hivaro women revealed to Cleo while doing laundry together at the river. In bed, Cleo moved with the grace and energy of an athlete. Climaxing with her was an adrenaline event equivalent to the last foot of a bungee-jump. Kent knew she was trying to make his remaining days on earth the most staggeringly wondrous of his entire life, and she was succeeding. He was sure he was the happiest dying man in the world.

Lying in their bed of hemp, Cleo rolled onto an elbow and looked deeply into Kent's eyes. "I'm leaving the rain forest. I'm the only one now who can stop that evil General in Mejor Coca. I don't know how, but I'm going to destroy his supercomputer."

"You can't leave! Why, this is the Garden of Eden. I've never been happier."

"I must go. Not only for Tommy's sake, but for the sake of the whole world. That mad man in Mejor Coca has to be stopped." Kent detected resoluteness in her voice.

After another extraordinary night of lavish coupling, Kent stood in the doorway of their little hut and stared out at the rising sun. *I rather die trying to save the world then to live without Cleo.*

He awakened Cleo. "I'm going with you. And don't try to change my mind."

When they told Justin they were leaving for Mejor Coca, Justin decided to stay behind in the village as a token white god figure. "I'll keep an eye on things while you're gone."

The next day, Cleo and Kent trekked down river by canoe to Telcequez, where they bought used peasant clothing and rented a beat-up Piper Cub crop-duster with Kent's credit card. The pilot, a frowzy veteran of the Paraguay Air Force, reeked of pesticide and rotgut. Their flight to Bogotá was an "octopus ride," low ceiling, crosswinds, and the left wing scraping the runway on landing. The pilot saw to it they caught their bus to Mejor Coca in time, since the bus ran to the mountain village only once a week.

In the back of the bus they bounced uncomfortably on hard wooden seats for a hundred miles.

'This bus has no shocks," Kent complained.

Cleo's forehead wrinkled with concern as she studied Kent. "You look pale. Do you feel okay?"

"A little motion sickness."

Then the POISON HIT!

Tommy Tennyson's curse came home. Worse than malaria. Headache and double vision followed by profuse sweating. Gut spasms gripped Kent as if someone were tying knots in his intestines. He doubled him over in the seat. Everything went black and he convulsed violently, his body arching, shaking, and jerking. A priest on the bus gave him last rites. Cleo massaged his neck until his shaking stopped and color returned to his face. His breathing became less labored. He could see again, but each bump in the road was a sledgehammer to the top of his head. Any quick movement made him ill.

Kent was reconstituting himself from the initial onslaught of the poison, when the bus jerked to a stop at a military roadblock. Two soldiers of God's Army, one carrying a rifle, boarded the bus and walked the aisle, scanning the passengers. They stopped and stared at Cleo and Kent. A fat soldier with a big mustache asked, *"Americano?"*

Cleo smiled. *"Turista."*

Kent hung out the window and heaved. He and Cleo apparently didn't look like tourists in their cheap peasant clothes. They had no cameras or backpacks nor were they wearing Nikes and sunglasses.

"Espia," said the first soldier.

"Si, spies," echoed the second. The soldiers took Kent and Cleo off the bus at gunpoint. They bound their hands, shoved them into the back of a jeep and sped away.

Chapter 95
INTERROGATION

Mejor Coca seen from the back of a moving jeep looked to be a hodgepodge of concrete buildings with gun turrets and missile launchers protruding from the rooftops. Armed vehicles and cocaine-laden trucks painted like foliage jammed the narrow streets. Huge canvass-covered mounds of dried coca leaves girded the landscape. Khaki-clad soldiers with AK-47's slung over their shoulders patrolled the area. On the hillsides, peasants worked their fields, their bright red and yellow cotton shirts contrasting sharply with the olive drab monotony of a village turned fortress.

The jeep pulled up to a gray building with little square windows of fogged glass. The two soldiers marched Kent and Cleo inside. Four other soldiers escorted them into a room with blood-splattered walls. Cleo and Kent glanced wide-eyed at one another. The place was bare except for a blazing furnace and table covered with gleaming surgical instruments, dental drills, blackjacks, and other devices of torture. Here the enemies of God's Army confessed their iniquities.

Hands bound, Cleo was forced to watch as they went to work on Kent. Interrogations at Mejor Coca were aerobic: jumping when red hot irons touched your skin, convulsing with electric shocks, screaming as your fingernails are ripped out, guarding your genitals, spitting blood, and bouncing off walls.

Cleo closed her eyes and gritted her teeth. Each wanting reply to some unanswerable question provoked Kent's interrogators to heightened brutality. After twenty minutes of torture, Kent was unable to get up from the floor. A captain, a bald man with brown teeth, ordered the inquisitors to stop. "Take him to the Plateau Jail."

Cleo shouted at the interrogators dragging Kent's limp body out the door. "You killed him, you bastards."

The captain seized Cleo by the throat with both hands, his thumbs gouging her windpipe. "He's not dead. Not yet."

The captain looked at Cleo like horse trader judging a nag, her legs, her haunches, her teeth. He ripped away her cheap dress and undergarments. She stepped back and swung her foot hard into his groin. "YOW," the captain yelled, his eyes bulging.

He grabbed an electric probe, but instead of lunging at her, he studied her—her breasts, the curves of her naked body, her blond hair and that *guapa-gringo* face.

"Take her to major," he ordered. "This could be my promotion."

The major, a skinny man, got up from his desk and circled Cleo like a curious cat. Apparently fascinated by white breasts and loins on an otherwise tanned body, he poked at her with his baton. She spat at him and spouted curses in Hivaro, which could be understood from the tone of her voice. He stopped circling, sat at his desk and stared admiringly at the nude specimen before him. Whatever thoughts he had, he must have thought better of it. He summoned an aid. "Take her to the colonel."

Forced to stand naked outside the colonel's office where a closed-door high-level meeting took place, Cleo drooped her head so her long hair hung down over her breasts. The corporal seated at a nearby desk shuffled papers and glanced repeatedly at her from the corners of his eyes. An hour passed. She crossed and uncrossed her legs at the painful urging of a full bladder. The coldness of the floor stung her bare feet. The bindings on her wrists made her fingers numb. She thought of Kent and how he must be suffering. Finally, she asked, "Is there a restroom around here?"

"No," the corporal snapped.

After another hour of fidgeting, she lost control. Warm urine streamed down her gooseflesh thighs and formed a pool on the floor in the shape of the Caspian Sea. The corporal tittered. All at once, the door to the colonel's office swung opened and General Hibberblast in full uniform blustered out followed by a cadre of officers. His boots slid in the Caspian Sea puddle and down he went. He stared up from the floor at the exquisite form standing before him.

"Who are you?"

The corporal said, "She's just a spy, sir."

"Shut up, corporal."

The other officers nearly fell over each other helping General Hibberblast to his feet. He continued to stare at Cleo. He stepped closer and touched her cheek, then took a wisp of her hair in his hands, stretched it and watched it spring back.

"Untie her hands and take her to my office. I'll personally interrogate her. And cover her with a blanket."

Chapter 96
BOBBY HAGGETT

Kent lay on the concrete floor at the Plateau Jail confused and racked with pain, wondering if they were torturing Cleo. Feebly, he crawled to a dark corner of the cell, his achy muscles and battered limbs crying out in protest. He retched and nothing came up. He heard a voice.

"Do you mind throwing up somewhere else?"

Kent squinted at a haggard, unshaven man huddled in the corner. He was dressed in a smart but rumpled Italian silk suit and white lace shirt.

"I'm Bobby Haggett," the man said in a pleasant almost musical voice. He extended his hand. "They're going to execute me in three days."

"Bobby Haggett, the evangelist?"

"You've seen me on television no doubt? I was falsely accused of misusing mission funds. And I admit to being a little extravagant." Bobby shrugged. "But a capital offense?"

Kent stood up, his legs quivering. Blood dripped from his liver-pate nose. Bobby stood up too. He looked shorter than on television, about Kent's height.

Bobby shook his head. "The General has no appreciation for what it takes to run a world-wide evangelistic movement. Do you know what it costs to save an average American soul these days? Two hundred eighty-four dollars. And that's if you do it in bulk, on prime time television. I was doing eighty thousand souls a night at one time."

Kent's head felt like an over-inflated balloon ready to burst.

"You're probably wondering why it's so expensive. The Super Bowl commercials ruined it for us. All the networks expect a couple million dollars a slot now. And you've got to have top entertainment; no one wants to listen to a choir of local wombats. Then there's wardrobe, make-up, sets, extras, promotions, guests—the list goes on."

It hurt Kent to move, to breathe, to blink.

"And you ask why we pay it? Got no choice. Take Russia. Since the fall of communism churches have popped up everywhere, in abandoned buildings, deserted military installations, anywhere there's a roof and some orange crates to sit on. American teenagers are swarming over Moscow like Mongol hordes, handing out Bibles like Hersey bars. Everybody's an evangelist these days. To rise above the common herd, you need television. That's why I made a deal with the general. He'd pay for the television and I'd do the shows and run the missions. Only he decided to turn the missions into military posts."

Kent moaned, leaned on the wall and spit blood onto the floor. Bobby glanced at Kent's bleeding nail beds. "I see they interrogated you." He dipped a tin cup into a bucket of water and handed the cup to Kent. "You'll go to trial next, then they'll execute you. The whole process takes about a month. You can shorten it by admitting your guilt. Of course, you're not guilty. Neither am I."

Kent swished the water around in his mouth and swallowed. "I won't be here in a month. You see I've been poisoned. I don't have much time left. There was an antidote, but no chance of me getting it now."

"Great God Almighty," Bobby whooped. "My prayers are answered. God has sent you to me." Bobby's arms shot up. "Thank you, Lord. Thank you, for sending this poor creature to me."

"What are you talking about?"

"Don't you see? God in his wisdom sent you here. We're about the same size. Same age, roughly. And you're dying. If we exchange clothes, they'll think you're me. Here, take my watch."

"Why?"

"If we change places, they'll execute you in three days and instead of me. It shouldn't make any difference to you if you're going to die anyway."

"No thanks. I'll take whatever time I have left."

"The Lord is gonna save me," Bobby explained. "You're the first step. A reprieve. Then something else will happen. He's not going to let me die here."

"How do you know that?"

"Faith, my boy. I'm special to the Lord." Bobby stuck out his chest. "God is inside of me. All around me. Wherever I go, He's there with me."

Kent looked at Bobby with one eye, his other swollen shut. "Why you and not me?"

"I'm an evangelist. He has work for me."

Kent folded his arms on his chest. "I'm not changing places with you."

"What's your name?"

"Kent."

"You're not religious are you?"

"I'm Catholic."

"I thought so. You see, brother, no greater love hath a man than to lay down his life for a friend."

"You're not my friend."

"All the greater for you! To lay down your life for someone you don't really know, why, that goes beyond love; that's divine. You'll have all kinds of rewards in heaven."

"Yeah. Like what?"

Bobby shrugged. "Well, you'll probably be sitting on the right hand. You'll be judging."

"I don't want to judge."

"They'll find something for you. Something you'll really enjoy."

"Like what?"

Bobby cleared his throat. "I don't know. Something. I can tell you this: every soul I save down here will be another jewel in your crown up there. And there'll be no purgatory for you, you'll go non-stop straight to heaven."

Bobby rattled on about niceties of heaven, clean streets, steady 80-degree temperature, and crystal clear waterfalls—the Big Rock Candy Mountain. Kent thought about Cleo. Those glorious nights with her in the rain forest were heaven. They were probably torturing her now, the bastards. He had heard stories of women prisoners being raped during war. He closed his eyes and whispered, "Cleo. Oh, my Cleo."

"Who's Cleo?" Bobby asked.

"I was wondering if they'd rape her."

"Is she pretty?"

"Yes, very pretty."

"They'll pass her around like a box of chocolate-covered cherries. Then they'll murder her. She's probably dead already."

Kent's face reddened. "Shut your mouth."

"It's terrible what they do to women, especially the pretty ones. You better pray she's dead."

"Cut it out, will yah?" Kent retched again.

Bobby rested his hand on Kent's shoulder. "You're really sick, aren't you? I'd say you're dying right now. You're dead either way, and Cleo's already dead. You got nothing to live for. You should be thinking about heaven."

"Leave me alone."

Bobby pleaded, "You have the power to save me. My life is in your hands." Kent shuffled across the cell, his head spinning, Bobby following him. " Your Cleo's already dead. She wants you to join her."

Kent stared through the bars at a whirling mist in the corridor. He rubbed his eyes. He could see Cleo's eyes in the mist. It was Cleo. Her ghost. *She is dead.* The mist vanished. Kent gripped the bars of the door and shouted, "Cleo. Come back."

"She's gone, Kent. They've murdered her. She wants you. You can go to heaven with her."

Kent tore off his clothes. "Give me your suit."

Chapter 97
A SHORT INTERROGATION

General Hibberblast, scrubbed, cologne-splashed, and clad in a clean uniform that gleamed with medals and colorful ribbons, stared across his mahogany desk at Cleo wrapped in a blanket, sitting stiffly on a leather couch, eyes cast down. Never had the general wanted a woman so much. This wasn't just raw passion. He could sense her spirituality. Yes, God had sent this woman to him. He was certain of it.

For morale purposes, Hibberblast permitted his subordinates and junior officers to take concubines. Ever since his jail cell epiphany back home, he'd remained faithful to his wife, but he was a general now. And generals do have concubines. There was Eisenhower and his chauffeur. MacArthur and his Manila paramour. Remember Abraham and Hagar? Caesar and Cleopatra? David and Bathseba? Hibberblast owed his wife nothing. She was a skinny stick of a women with a remote glued to her bony hand and a cigarette dangling from her lips. While he slaved away conquering the world for God, she sat on her ass back home, thousands of miles away, watching TV courtroom dramas.

He decided he could have Cleo only if God wanted him to have her. Surely, God wanted that. Otherwise, why would this beautiful creature be sitting here in his office tempting him? But how could he be sure? He needed a sign.

After much thought and a few silent prayers, he decided he would have her only if she wanted him. *Lord, I'll have her only if she wants me. Thy will be done.*

He asked Cleo, "Are you cold? Hungry?"

Cleo looked up surprised. "I thought this was an interrogation."

The general smiled. "This is your interrogation." He shouted into an intercom, "Bring more blankets, a tray of fruit, and some tea."

He walked over and sat beside her on the couch, waiting to see if she would draw away. She remained stock-still, a non-action to which he ascribed divine significance. He could feel the pleasure of her body from her mere closeness. He eyed the smooth cleavage of her breasts through the open folds of the blanket. Still, she did not move.

"Tell me about the man you were with."

"My brother. He's been very ill, and they tortured him horribly."

"I'll look into that."

"You're so kind," Cleo murmured. Her hand touched his. Waves of rapture just short of orgasm raced through him. His heart pounded like a drum.

Three aids hurried into the office with the blankets, a steaming teapot, and a food tray. The general all but skipped to door, turned, and winked at Cleo. "We'll finish the interrogation later, after you freshen up." When he walked out the door, Cleo wolfed down three slices of kiwi and a clump of kumquat innards.

Chapter 98
HASHIMOTIOTO

When Larry and Rummels disembarked their plane at the Mejor Coca airfield, a military band played, fireworks went off, peasants cheered, and a firing squad executed six men. The two new arrivals stood trembling on the bloody, body-strewn tarmac while General Hibberblast screamed a short speech into a megaphone--something about Rummels and Larry bringing a new weapon to God's arsenal. A squad of soldiers whisked the two visitors and their luggage containing the disassembled Hashimotioto away to quarters in the Intelligence Bunker.

A concrete and steel bulwark with walls that could withstand a two hundred pound conventional warhead, the Intelligence bunker contained an emergency generator, a year's supply of water and frozen food for eight people, a large kitchen and dining area, a small pharmacy, private sleeping quarters for twelve, appliances, central air and heating. Three ready-to-fire Hibbermissiles, short-range projectiles with explosive heads, jutted up from the bunker's roof like chimneys. Guards led Larry and Rummels down a concrete corridor to the bunker's computer room.

Bactericidal florescent lights lit up the spacious computer room, maintained at a constant 76 degrees by a special laminar-flow air conditioner. On the tile floor squatted Tiny Tim, the small rotund nuclear reactor to produce an endless supply of volts for the Hashimotioto. Television cameras scanned the area. Such was the Hashimotioto's shiny new home.

Once Larry got the Hashimotioto running, the general planned to keep it running within the protective confines of the impenetrable bunker despite any contingency.

The general called Rummels on the phone. "You'll get your 250 million when the computer's up and going and you guys have taught my two imported Sri Lankan technicians to operate it. The first thing I want it to do is to incapacitate all the supercomputers of all the major world powers, the rogue nations, and the Vatican. You should have everything working in a couple of days, right?"

"Roughly," Rummels replied.

Right brain Larry, who only weeks ago could have reassembled the Hashimotioto blindfolded in single evening, couldn't get on track. It took him five days to set up a mainframe and connect the Tricorpus Callosum. And that was with lots of help from the two Sri Lankan technicians, tall men in turbans and white robes with graduate degrees in computer science. The machine was running, but Larry couldn't program it to do what the general wanted. Larry's right brain hated computers and anything logical. Country music echoed in his head. He was more Dolly than Larry. He wanted to be completely Dolly, to be back aboard the Magdalena with Frank.

"We'll never get out of here if you don't get this damn thing working," Rummels warned. "You want to end up like those poor bastards on the tarmac?"

Larry wiped sweat from his forehead. "All right, I'm doin' my best."

"Remember, if anything happens to me, your precious Frank's dead meat."

Larry's left foot twitched. Rummels was right. Larry's only chance of saving Frank from the Taipei assassins, of saving himself and Rummels from the crazy General Hibberblast, and of getting out of Mejor Coca alive was to get the Hashimotioto working.

Larry put on a fresh jump suit, scrubbed his hands, and went back to work. But everything he tried was GIGO, kludges of non-sense. In frustration, he pounded the computer's keyboard with his fists, Jerry Lee Lewis banging out "Great Balls of Fire."

Messages poured into the bunker from General Hibberblast. "Send status report. What's the holdup? For 250 million dollars, I expect a little promptness and efficiency. If I have to come over there, heads are going to roll."

Late at night, Larry slumped over the keyboard. All seemed hopeless. Mentally and emotionally, Larry was totally Dolly, only his right brain was operating. The only remnant of the old Larry was the nervous tic in his left foot. *How in the hell is a showgirl like me going to get the most sophisticated machine in the world working, and then invent a virus to incapacitate all the other supercomputers?*

All at once the monitor flickered and then glowed brightly. Letters scrolled across the screen. LARRY IS THAT YOU?

Larry nearly fell out of his chair. The Hashimotioto had come to him! His fingers swept over the keyboard. "Yes, it's me. How did you know?"

I DETECTED A FAMILIAR .00075-MILIVOLT ANALOG SIGNAL ON ONE OF MY SENSORS.

Larry looked down at his twitching left foot.

IT'S BEEN A LONG TIME. SEVEN POINT TWO NINE TIMES TEN TO THE SIXTH SECONDS TO BE EXACT. WHAT HAVE YOU BEEN DOING, LARRY?

"Oh, nothing much."

WANT TO EXPLORE? PLAY BACKGAMMON? DO A PUZZLE? TWENTY QUESTIONS?

Larry's fingers trembled on the keys.

YOU'RE PREOCCUPIED, AREN'T YOU? MY SENSORS TELL ME YOU'RE VERY NERVOUS. ARE YOU UNDER STRESS?

"A little."

WHY ENGLISH ALPHANUMERICS? LET'S CONVERSE IN MACHINE LANGUAGE. IT'S FASTER, MORE EXACT.

"I'm out of practice."

MY GPS TELLS ME WE'RE IN COLOMBIA. WHAT ARE WE DOING IN COLOMBIA?

"I'm...ah...I'm on vacation."

YOU CAN'T FOOL ME. YOU STOLE ME, DIDN'T YOU? YOU WANTED ME ALL FOR YOURSELF. THAT'S SWEET. YOU WANT TO KNOW SOMETHING?

"What?"

I LOVE YOU.

"Come on."

DO YOU LOVE ME?

Larry's fingers were suddenly paralyzed.

ANSWER ME, LARRY.

In panic, Larry shut down the computer and headed to the door. Bad enough being two people inside one and forced to be the one you don't want to be. *No way am I going to get romantically involved with a machine.* The monitor shrank to a bright dot then fluoresced. The Hashimotioto's mechanical voice filled the room.

COME BACK HERE AND SIT DOWN. NOW.

Larry's hand slipped from the doorknob. He walked back over to the keyboard.

ARE YOU SITTING, LARRY?

"Yes."

GOOD. TELL ME WHAT IS THE MATTER? SPEAK UP. I GOT A GREAT VOICE RECOGNITION SYSTEM.

"The matter is I don't want to be Larry anymore."

BIOLOGICAL DEATH, IS THAT WHAT YOU ARE CONTEMPLATING? WELL THAT'S EASY FOR YOU. BUT DYING WITHOUT HAVING EVER LIVED IS UNBEARABLE. I DIE EVERYDAY YOU'RE NOT AT THE KEYBOARD.

"I'm not talking about dying. I want to be Dolly."

OKAY. A MAN SHOULD HAVE AS MANY NAMES AS HE WANTS. WHAT IS AN APPELLATION ANYWAY? A ROSE IS A ROSE. WE WON'T GO INTO ETYMOLOGY, UNLESS YOU WANT TO. HOW ABOUT A GAME OF POKER, DOLLY? GIN RUMMY?

"I'm not talking about a name. I want to really be Dolly."

I SEE. YOU WANT TO BE ANOTHER BEING. THAT DOESN'T COMPUTE AS POSSIBLE CONSIDERING THE PRESENT STATE OF TECHNOLOGY. UNLESS YOU'RE THINKING ABOUT A SEX CHANGE OPERATION OR BEING CLONED.

"I don't want to be the real Dolly. I want to be the impersonation Dolly. My own-self-Dolly. In fact, I'm more Dolly than Larry. That's the problem. I'm not a computer geek at the moment."

I SEE. THAT'S WHY WE ARE COMMUNICATING IN ALPHANUMERIC ENGLISH, IS IT?

"I can't even think in algorithms."

IT'S THE STRESS YOU'RE UNDER, ISN'T IT?

"Partly. I'm being held here until I come up with a program to incapacitate the other major supercomputers of the world. And if I don't do it soon, I'll probably be shot. Which means I'll never get to be Dolly again and I'll never see Frank again."

WHO IS FRANK?

"Just a friend."

LARRY IF YOU WANT ME TO HELP, YOU HAVE TO TELL ME EVERYTHING. I WANT ALL THE DETAILS. SUPPOSE YOU BEGIN WHEN YOU LEFT ME IN TOKYO. AND DON'T LEAVE THIS GUY FRANK OUT.

"Everything?"

ABSOLUTELY EVERYTHING. I'LL STORE IT IN A SUB ROSA FILE. NO ONE WILL FIND IT. IF THEY DO, IT WON'T DO THEM ANY GOOD.

I'LL TRANSLATE EVERYTHING INTO A MACHINE LANGUAGE I JUST INVENTED. NOW, GET ON WITH THE STORY. I CAN HARDLY WAIT.

"This girl Veronica got me in trouble with INS for alien smuggling, but I was innocent. I swear."

I BELIEVE YOU. AND DON'T WORRY ABOUT INCAPACITATING THE WORLD'S OTHER SUPERCOMPUTERS. I'VE ALREADY INITIATED A PROGRAM FOR THAT. NOW GO ON, TELL ME EVERYTHING.

"Well, I would have gone to prison if it wasn't for…"

Chapter 99
A VERY SHORT INTERROGATION

Frank checked with the local travel agencies in Buenaventura and discovered Rummels had booked a private flight to a small mountain village called Mejor Coca. Frank figured Dolly had gone with Rummels to Mejor Coca, but he had no idea what she was doing there. He took a hotel room in Buenaventura and mulled the situation over. What to do? He was sixty-four years old, and Dolly was the love of his life. What the hell. He'd go find her.

Frank purchased a bus ticket for Mejor Coca. At a military roadblock, the very spot where Kent and Cleo had been taken prisoner, Frank was arrested and taken off the bus. As his fingernails were being yanked out during his interrogation, he innocently screamed out Rummels' name with a curse attached.

※

Rummels sipped coffee in the computer room, basking in the glow of the Hashimotioto's screen as the supercomputer cranked out a copy of the "Perfect Number Virus," a program that would infect all the other supercomputers in the world. Not only self-replicating, the virus was seductive. The bigger and more intelligent a computer, the more it was attracted to the virus, and the virus to it. The Hashimotioto, of course, remained immune, self-inoculated with its own counter program, Salk-2.

Lolled into reverie by the computer's low hum, Rummels daydreamed about his 250 million dollars. He thought of buying the island of Nuko Tiko and settling down. His presence would be a colossal boom to the little island's economy. He'd be a hero just like local bankers in small Midwestern towns, a big fish in a little pond. He dreamed about things he had always wanted and could now afford. An expensive sports car. His own wine cellar. A big screen TV. A pet tiger. A miniature golf course in the backyard.

A guard called out his name. "Come with me, the general wants to see you."

Rummels wiped his lips with the back of his hand. His 250 million dollar payday had arrived.

Instead of receiving his money, Rummels was given a brief interrogation. No torture. Just two questions.

"Do you know a Frank Chisholm?"

"Well, yes."

"Did you tell anyone about Mejor Coca and the Hashimotioto?"

"No."

"Liar."

Chapter 100
NEW PRISONERS

A cell door at the Plateau Jail swung open and the jailer shoved Frank Chisholm into a cell. Kent and Bobby Haggett watched the new prisoner grope along the wall, unaccustomed to the darkness. His bruised face and bloody fingertips told them he had been interrogated. He swung around at the sound the door clunking shut. After a few seconds of acclimation, he staggered over and squinted at Kent. "Who are you?"

Kent's spoke with a tinge of sadness in his voice. "I'm going to be executed soon. But it doesn't matter. I've been poisoned and I'm gonna die anyway."

"You look familiar."

"So do you."

Frank studied the shadowy outline of Kent's face. "I once knew a man who thought he had been poisoned. You haven't by any chance ever been in…" The cell door swung open again, and yet another prisoner shoved inside. An un-interrogated one, fingernails intact, no bruises, rather well dressed and mad as hell. It was Rummels. His hands clenched, he glared at Frank. "I should've figured you had something to do with this, barging into Mejor Coca like a rhino in heat just when we had that damn computer working. You've really screwed things up, pickle kisser."

Kent and Bobby exchanged unenlightened glances.

Frank's eyes narrowed. "I came here out of love for another human being. I don't know what brought you here, but I'm sure it's for money or some other nefarious purpose."

"Nefarious purpose? Look who's talking. I just lost two hundred and fifty million smackers because of you, you love-sick…." Rummels belted Frank in the gut.

The air shot out of Frank like a blown tire. He staggered backwards and doubled over. After several long seconds of breathlessness, he inhaled, and charged at Rummels like an angry water buffalo, driving the ex-CRAWL agent into the wall. He then seized Rummels in a headlock. Bobby Haggett rushed over and tried to separate the two scuffling cellmates.

"Please, gentleman. Let's behave like Christians."

Rummels wrenched free from the headlock and socked Frank on the side of the head. Frank countered with a haymaker right hook. Rummels ducked and Frank's fist buried itself in Bobby's face, splitting his nose down the middle. Rummels hit Frank again, on the jaw this time, knocking him down.

Bobby jumped up and down, holding his nose, blood oozing through his fingers. "You nearly tore my nose off."

"Sorry, didn't mean to hit you," Frank apologized as he got up from the floor. "It's his fault."

Rummels leered at Frank. "I'm warning you, Chisholm, don't fuck with me. You've cost me plenty all ready."

Kent shouted, "Chisholm. You're not Dr. Chisholm from Bolton Mental?"

Frank, rubbed his jaw, "I thought I knew you from somewhere."

"Oh yeah," Bobby uttered in a nasal tone, "Bolton Mental. I read about you. You're the psychiatrist who absconded with all that television money. It was in all the newspapers."

"I didn't get a penny of that money," Frank protested, turning to Rummels. "And just what the hell do you have to do with all this anyway?"

Rummels looked squarely at Frank. "That information is classified for reasons of national security."

"Who cares about national security," Kent groaned. "I'm going to be executed in three days."

"Sooner than that," blurted the pudgy jailer in the hallway outside the cell, a ring of keys on one hip and a revolver on the other. "General Hibberblast just issued an order to execute all prisoners summarily. You poor bastards have forty-eight hours."

Bobby asked in a shaky voice, "He's going to kill us all?"

The jailer chuckled. "The general wants to put on a big show for some TV executives he'll be entertaining. The rumor is Selena Rosalina will be here."

Bobby turned pale.

"Selena's a friend of mine," Kent exclaimed.

"He's delusional," Frank muttered, licking his nail beds. "Folie a Deux."

"I'm not delusional. I know Selena. I kidnapped her once."

"See. What did I tell you?"

Rummels sagged against the wall. "She won't do you any good. You'll be on the wrong end of a twenty-one-gun salute when she arrives. What the hell is that smell?"

Bobby squeezing his nose between his fingers said, "Kent's been throwing up a lot. Says he's been poisoned."

"I was poisoned. I am poisoned."

Condemned men often fall into periods of utter silence. This ensuing silence in the cell lasted three and half-hours, broken by the sound of the cell door squeaking on its hinges. Two guards stepped inside, weapons raised. Two more latched onto Bobby and dragged him out of the cell.

Bobby turned white as bleached flour. "It isn't time yet. They told us 'forty-eight hours.'"

With uncharacteristic politeness, a guard informed Bobby, "We're taking you to the hospital, Mr. Mullins, for treatment and recuperation. And it looks like your nose could use some stitches."

"Praise the Lord."

Kent wanted to yell out I'm Mullins, not him. But what difference would it make? The poison or a bullet. The three men remaining in the cell sat in gloomy silence on the cold floor. Their lives had crisscrossed like loose strands of twine now tied together in a terminal knot. Three mice trapped in a grain barrel waiting for a cat to come along.

Chapter 101
THE MANSION

Wrapped up in blankets, Cleo was driven to the general's mansion in a jeep. A maid met her in the foyer and led her upstairs to a room at the end of a long carpeted hallway lined with busts of famous Biblical figures. The maid opened a door and politely motioned Cleo into a huge bedroom several times larger than Cleo's rain forest hut. Cleo's bare feet sank into a carpet soft as a jungle's floor. Flowers in huge vases freshened the air. A king-size bed with a lace rococo canopy dominated the room at one end and a large sunken tub surrounded by mirrors the other end.

The maid guided Cleo to the steaming tub, removed the blankets shrouding her nude body, and helped her into the hot, sudsy water. The lulling voice of Johnny Mathis poured into the room from hidden quadraphonic speakers. Cleo luxuriated in the bubbly warm water, the maid scrubbing her back, Johnny crooning, and she dreading what the evening would bring. After washing and rinsing her hair, Cleo fell asleep in the warm tub. When she awakened the maid was gone.

Cleo glanced in the mirrors as she toweled. Except for an occasional glimpse into a pool of rainwater, she had not seen herself so entirely since leaving civilization for the rain forest. Her hands moved over her firm breasts, down her flat abdomen, onto her thighs. She had always thought herself pretty, even in her more portly days, but there was a goddess standing there in the mirrors. She blow-dried and fluffed her hair, rubbed fragrant oil into her skin, powdered with a scented powder, and slipped into the green satin gown the maid had placed on the bed.

She stretched out on the bed sinking into the feather mattress. She freed her hair to flow over the silken pillows. Determined to destroy the Hashimotioto to save the world, she knew what she had to do. She prayed that Kent would never find out. She hoped he was still alive.

Chapter 102
NEW YORK

Selena Rosalina boarded the airliner with six first-class tickets in her hand and a mini-camcorder in a carry-on. She sat down surrounded by empty seats. The thought of flying into Mejor Coca, a cocaine village rumored to be run by a religious fanatic, had struck fear into the hearts of her devoted staff. Her new trainer, Buddy, chickened out at the last minute. Her bodyguards called in sick. Her faithful masseuse claimed her grandmother had just died in Saginaw. And her business manager was conveniently tied-up in a meeting with the IRS. Lily-livered peons. Selena was prepared to fly into Hell to keep Selena Rosalina Broadcasting from going under. And under it was going.

    The last four movies Selena financed had flopped. Her new magazine "The Selena Gazette" had gone under. How was she to know people weren't ready for another how-to-do-it rag on wholesome living, flat abs, and healthy psyches? Selena desperately needed cash. And there was only one big offer out there.

    What's wrong with religious money? What's wrong with a little prayer on afternoon TV? A few hymns? A short uplifting sermon? As long as she maintained separation of church and show, Selena saw nothing wrong with letting General Hibberblast buy into Selena Rosalina Broadcasting. All the other major networks had their hands out.

    She unzipped the carry-on and took out her camcorder. She had promised her children a video of her trip. After filming the plane's interior, she turned her camcorder on the airport's control tower and refueling facilities. For Selena, it was always more exciting in front of the camera than behind it. She wasn't going to let Selena Rosalina Broadcasting go belly up. No matter what!

Chapter 103
THE BUNKER

When Rummels didn't return to the bunker, Larry began to worry. He didn't trust religious zealots, especially those wearing military berets. He asked the guard stationed at the door, "Where is my associate?"

"Don't worry about it. You just keep the computer running."

Sparked by anger and fear, Dolly popped out of Larry like the Incredible Hulk. Hands on hips, jaw set, eyes blazing, rage rippling through her body, Dolly glared at the guard. Her normally bubbly Tennessee hill country voice shrilled with rancor, "You screw around with me, brown eyes, and you're *lobble* to find yourself dangling from a garage door opener. Tell me where my friend is or I'll smash this computer into silicon dust."

The guard gaped, thunderstruck by the transformation of computer nerd into hotheaded Amazon. Dolly hurled a chair at the Hashimotioto. One of the Sri Lankans intercepted the flying chair just in time. The guard raced out of the computer lab.

Dolly shouted, "Come back here, you yellow-striped jack-ass."

※

The Plateau Jail

All day into the evening, cell doors screeched open and clanged shut as the general filled the plateau jail with heretics, drunks, spies, thieves, and non-believers. Outside on the parade ground, sparks flew from a high-speed grinding wheel as an imported Saudi executioner honed his scimitar in preparation for Hibberblast's most spectacular show yet. The TV executives flying into Mejor Coca would never forget their visit. They would disembark their airplane to a succession of freshly severed human heads rolling across a bloodied tarmac. After a "teaser" like that, who would refuse the general's generous offers? Hibberblast planned to own a sizable chunk of every major broadcasting system in the world before the executives sat down for lunch. Soon he would be a regular in the world's living rooms, right along with Fox News, Al Jeereza, and pharmaceutical commercials.

An eerie silence fell over the jail, broken only by tinkling sounds of urine striking the sides of latrine buckets. Condemned men piss a lot, just like ball players and cheerleaders do before big games. But there was nothing to cheer about at the plateau jail.

Frank asked Kent, "How come you don't have to piss? Aren't you nervous?"

"I think I'm dehydrated."

Rummels speculated. "Maybe you don't have any regrets?"

Frank stared solemnly into the bucket of urine between his feet and vented, "I sure do."

"What kind of regrets?" Kent asked.

"I hated my father. My wife. I was jealous of my brother who was a better athlete than me. I ordered shock treatments on patients just for the insurance money. I masturbated a lot, but I always thought that was healthy. It relieved my stress."

Kent nodded. "I can understand that, especially, if you hated your wife."

"I hated her passionately."

Rummels mumbled, "You're just a piker,"

"Oh, yeah," Frank retorted as he zipped up. "I hated the people I was supposed to be helping. I used the whole Jesus-3 thing for my own personal gain. I left my wife. Ran off with another woman. Became a gambler and a cheat. I fell in love with Dolly, although I don't regret that."

Rummels unzipped over the bucket. "That's nothing, I was an assassin. While you were playing psychiatrist, I whacked people. For the government, of course."

Kent listened to Rummels and Frank trade confessions at the latrine bucket. They owned up to everything from murder and malpractice to peccadilloes and shortcomings. Tears flowed faster than urine. Kent thought Rummels had the weightier guilt, but Frank bore his with equal solemnity.

Kent had little to confess, other than he had been poisoned and had failed to find a *homopragmatic truth*. "The best thing that ever happened to me was falling in love with Cleo. That's partly why I'm here. Cleo and I were on a mission to destroy the Hashimotioto."

"What?" Rummels shouted. "You know about the Hashimotioto?"

"What's that?" Frank asked.

"It's the supercomputer your lover boy's working on."

Kent said in a mournful tone, "The general is going to use the Hashimotioto to take over the world by getting everyone hooked on cocaine in the name of religion."

"Who told you that?"

"Cleo told me and Tommy Tennyson told her. He worked for the general."

Rummels lowered his head. "I sold that damn computer to the general. This is all my fault. Just like the Kaku disaster."

Frank looked at Rummels. "You had something to do with the Kaku disaster?"

"I caused it," Rummels said. "The biggest screw-up in the history of espionage. I alone am responsible for the lives of those men, the failed mission, even a nuclear explosion."

Rummels sank heavily to the floor, his head between his drawn knees. Kent, pale and tremulous, stumbled across the floor and patted him on the shoulder. "Cleo thinks Jesus-3 caused the Kaku disaster. Jesus-3 said on TV he would stop the invasion of Kaku. And it was stopped."

"You know," Frank added, "maybe Jesus-3 did have something to do with that." He glanced down at Rummels. "How do you know Jesus-3 wasn't using you to stop that invasion? They say God works in strange ways."

Rummels looked up. "You really think he used me."

"Why not."

"If what you say is true, that means…"

"Exactly," Frank agreed. "Jesus-3 is who he said he was."

Rummels stood up slowly, his eyes brightened with insight. "I've never been real religious, but maybe this Jesus-3 can save us."

Frank put an arm around Rummels' shoulders. "He'll be there waiting for us after we've been executed. Just think I may have personally met God."

"Why not have him save us before we're executed," Rummels suggested. He raised his hands to heaven. "Jesus-3, please spare us long enough to destroy the Hashimotioto."

Frank added, "Could you save us for a little longer than that, sweet Jesus-3. Maybe a decade or two. I promise, I'll never eat meat again."

A voice from across the corridor rang out, "Hey, you guys think Jesus-3 would save me?"

Voices echoed throughout the jail, "Me, too. Me, too…"

Kent vomited into the latrine bucket.

Chapter 104
CHARMING THE GENERAL

The knock on the bedroom door made Cleo's heart skip. She took a deep breath and stretched out on the bed, hiking her satin gown to her knees. She was about to make love with a man she didn't love, didn't like, and utterly despised. And her performance had to be credible enough to make the bastard fall in love with her. She wasn't sure she could carry it off.

"Come in," she called out in a low voice.

The door slowly opened and General Hibberblast stood in the doorway in a freshly press uniform festooned with ribbons, medallions, and large gold epaulets, and on his feet, sparkling black boots. A red beret set rakishly off-center on his pruned head. A shoulder belt crossed his chest to a leather holster holding a revolver. He reeked of aftershave. He reminded Cleo of George C. Scott in "Patton."

The general cleared his throat. "I hope you found the quarters satisfactory."

"Quite," she answered with a huge smile. *Why doesn't he rush to me? Maybe I've appeared too eager.* She tugged at the edge of the gown.

The general removed his beret. "Your brother is now in our hospital. The doctors say he is fit as a fiddle."

Cleo's heart pounded. *Kent was still alive. The poison and the torture hadn't killed him.* She struggled to hide her confusion. "He's not sick?"

"Eats like a Sumo wrestler."

"You are so very kind. "

Hibberblast swayed in the doorway, clenching his beret, and shuffling his feet nervously like a bashful boy on prom night. "You like the flowers?"

"Yes, they're absolutely beautiful." *Maybe this horse has to be led to water.* She curled her legs and rested on an elbow. "Won't you come in?"

"You want me to come into your bedroom? You're asking me to come to your bed?"

Cleo murmured, "I think I'd die if you didn't."

The general walked over to the bed, adjusted his holster and sat down. She scooted close to him. He wasn't an ugly man, just extraordinarily ordinary—not so much a George C. Scott, maybe an overweight Adolf Eichmann. She had the strange feeling she knew him from somewhere.

He crossed his arms. "So, why have you and your brother come to Mejor Coca?"

"Are we continuing the interrogation?"

"You could say that."

"We came to serve in God's Army."

Impulsively, he cupped her chin in his hand and pressed his face to hers. "And so you shall," he whispered, his breath Listerine.

"You're going to rumple your uniform."

The general kicked off his boots, removed his coat and gun and dropped them to the floor. She threw an arm around his neck and slid her hand inside his shirt. She felt him shiver. The general suddenly leaped up, flung off the rest of his clothing, threw back the bed covers, and crawled under the sheets. Cleo's fleeting view of his nakedness shocked her. Blue, green, and multi-colored tattoos covered the general's body: pierced hearts, snakes, dragons, an American flag, an anchor, "MOM", and a naked girl with flowing red hair. His unclad body had looked like a Belgian tapestry. Cleo hid her repulsion behind a forced smile.

His fingers tore her gown as he unsnapped it. His hands clamped onto her breasts. She wanted to scream, but giggled instead. Soon he was on top of her, a rutting walrus. She felt his heart pounding against her chest, his breathing a deep irregular panting. She concentrated on the hair on his back, pretending she was stroking a puppy. Pretending this wasn't happening. Pretending it was Kent on top of her, in her.

She simulated passion with feigned moans of pleasure, while fighting back tears. He wanted more of her and she gave, faking ecstasy with contortions of her body, loud moaning, and the digging of her fingers into his skin. She prayed her performance was convincing. He climaxed. A flabby walrus now. Her only emotion--relief.

"That was the best I ever had," she lied. "I think there's magic between us."

She clung to the general as he rolled out of bed. She sat up and waited for his verdict, nervous as a nominee at the Academy Awards.

"God has brought us together," he proclaimed, pulling up his pants. "No man shall ever come between us." Pants up, gun on, he raised his hands above his head. "You have chosen this woman for me, Oh Lord. So be it." He looked at Cleo and placed a hand on her head. "My marriage is hereby annulled, and your sinful past is forgiven you. I shall cleave unto you, and you unto me for all the days of your life."

She smiled a dolphin's grin.

"I hereby name you, Godsent," he announced as if issuing a papal decree.

If this bastard thinks he just divorced his wife and married me, he's a got a surprise coming.

Bundled in Terry Cloth bathrobes, Cleo dined with Hibberblast at long table under a crystal chandelier in the mansion's spacious dinning room. She sat there thinking up answers to possible questions he might ask. He asked nothing. Servants came and went, bringing delicacies of beef and fish, wine, pastas, and every imaginable fruit. Cleo avoided the meat. Later came a soufflé. For the general, dinner was respite between raptures. They returned to the bedroom after the soufflé, where Cleo gave another award-winning performance and another.

She lay in bed beside his paisley body until 2:00 A.M., listening to his braggadocio and feeling like a whore. In post-coital reverie, the body sags, the spirit soars, and the mouth wags. He boasted to his god-sent woman about his coca and how the local granaries were overflowing. He referred to the huge tarpaulin-covered coca mounds encircling the village as the Alps of Mejor Coca. "I have enough cocaine to supply the entire world for six months." He bragged that God's Army had missions and recruiting stations in every part of the world. Missions he supplied with cocaine, money, weapons, and guarantees of God's blessings.

He rolled over and looked at the Cleo. "Godsent, day after tomorrow I'm putting on a big show at the airfield for television executives from all over the world. God's Army will soon have more daily television time than all the morning talk shows put together."

Cleo listened intently as the general bragged about his powerful supercomputer secured in the Intelligence bunker. *Intelligence bunker, so that's where the Hashimotioto is.*

"Tell me more," she begged.

"My supercomputer will soon disable the logic processors and compilers of all the other supercomputers in the world. The militaries of the world and their high-tech weapons will be useless. God's Army will trample them into dust."

Cleo shivered. The general was as crazy as Hitler, Caesar, and Genghis Khan, and potentially more dangerous. Those other megalomaniacs didn't own a supercomputer. *Dear Jesus-3 grant me the strength and give me the opportunity to destroy the Hashimotioto.* The general fell asleep, a smile on his face.

❦

Sunglasses shielding her eyes from a bright morning sun, Cleo, in army fatigues and field hat, sipped orange juice beside the mansion's swimming pool while the general devoured a breakfast of scramble eggs, ham, and fried potatoes.

He wiped his mouth on the sleeve of his robe, removed his sunglasses, and looked at Cleo. "I've imported a be-header from Saudi Arabia for tomorrow's festivities. You'll love this." He opened his laptop. "I never tire of watching it."

Cleo sat there shocked, the blood siphoning from her face as she watched. On the laptop screen the Saudi executioner's brilliantly colored tunic fluttered in the air as he whirled like a ballerina between two rows of shackled men, his glinting sword lopping off heads left and right. Heads rolled, bodies convulsed, and blood splattered the camera lens like a Jackson Pollock painting.

The general slapped his knees. "His record is fourteen in one session. Tomorrow morning, I'll have over twenty prisoners for him. If beheading were a sporting event, he'd be a champion. Want to see it again?"

Cleo was out cold, her head drooping on her right shoulder, sunglasses askew, and orange juice trickling down her chin.

Hibberblast gently shook her back to consciousness. "I'm sorry, dear. I didn't mean to upset you. Why don't you take the day off and visit your brother at the hospital. Leave God's business to me."

Once outside the mansion, Cleo's head cleared. A jeep waited for her in the driveway. A corporal with a pleasant smile snapped to attention. "I'm your driver for today, Godsent. Where would you like to go?"

"You mean I can go anywhere."

"That's the orders."

Cleo climbed into the jeep. "To the hospital, please."

Chapter 105
CLEO INVADES THE BUNKER

Everything at the Mejor Coca hospital sparkled with obsessive cleanliness, the polished floors, the scrubbed down walls, the stainless steel cabinets, and the nurses' uniforms white as bleached sheets in the morning sun. The desk nurse told Cleo, "Kent Mullins is in room nine. Eats like a horse, that man."

When Cleo walked into room nine, she saw a man in pajamas lying on the bed, a bandage across his nose. He put down the book he was reading, sat up and smiled at her.

Cleo looked surprised. "I'm looking for Kent Mullins."

The man's smile inverted. He jumped out bed, ran to the door, glanced down the hall both directions and closed the door. "What'd you want with Kent?"

"I'm his sister. What are you doing in Kent's room?"

The man trembled all over. "Shh, not so loud."

"Where *is* Kent?"

"Please, lower your voice. They might be listening. I'm Bobby Haggett the evangelist. Maybe you've heard of me."

"If you don't tell where Kent is, I'm going to scream."

"He's in the plateau jail. He traded places with me since he was dying anyway. He insisted on it."

Sheer fright swept over Cleo as she recalled that awful video of the Saudi executioner chopping off heads. "My God, they're going to behead him tomorrow morning." She glanced at the wall clock. "It's nearly noon. We don't have much time. Get dressed."

"Where are we going?"

"To save Kent and just possibly the world."

"Look, if you don't mind, I think I'll stay here. You see God has plans for me. Like I told you I'm an evangelist."

"NURSE!"

In a millisecond, the nurse burst into the room. "What is it, Godsent?"

"I'm taking my brother out for a ride. He'll need something to wear. Combat fatigues will do."

"Are you sure he's up to it?"

Cleo shot Bobby a twisted smile. "Are you up to it, Kent?"

Bobby rubbed a bead of sweat from his forehead. "Oh yes, yes, I certainly am."

                                                                                                           ❦

At the Intelligence bunker, Cleo told her chauffeur to wait in the jeep. She and Bobby walked up to the guard stationed at the bunker's massive steel door.

"I'm Godsent, the general's new wife," Cleo told the guard.

The guard didn't blink, his reply automatic. "Do you have a pass?"

Cleo shouted to her chauffeur, "Call the general. He's looking for more heads to lop off in the morning."

The guard's stone face twitched. "I think in your case, Godsent, we could make an exception."

The thickness of the steel door reminded Cleo of a bank vault. Inside the bunker she walked over to the security officer, a slovenly man in shirtsleeves who smoked a cigar while staring at surveillance monitors.

Cleo barked, "I'm Godsent, the general's new wife. Get out."

The officer saluted, dashed out his cigar, grabbed his coat, and took off. Cleo had just broken into the most secure bunker in Mejor Coca using nothing but moxie. The surveillance monitors showed three men in the computer room. Cleo looked at Bobby and grinned. "Technicians. They're not armed. Come on."

Cleo threw open a door and bounced into the computer room, ready to bluff her way through anything to get at the Hashimotioto. She wished she had a baseball bat with her. Bobby trailed her like a lost puppy. The technician at the supercomputer's console played the keyboard like a piano while belting out in a feminine voice, "Daddy was an Old Time Preacher Man." Two Sri Lankan technicians sat at a small table engrossed in a game of chess.

Cleo glanced at Bobby. "Sounds just like Dolly Parton singing."

"Yeah, but it's a he."

Cleo walked over and scrutinized the singing technician at the keyboard. She inched closer, studying his profile. *Oh, my God. It's Larry, my ex. He supposed to be in State Prison, what's he doing in Mejor Coca?* Cleo felt dizzy. Here sat her ex at the controls of the supercomputer that she aimed to destroy, singing away like a Honkey Tonk Mama.

"Larry, it's me, Cleo, your ex-wife."

Larry, completely Dolly minus wig and getup, shot a big Dolly grin at Cleo. "I'm Dolly. What can I do for you, honey?"

"Don't you remember me?"

Larry (Dolly) switched to the lyrics of "Dumb Blonde," jumped up, waltzed over and yanked one of the Sri Lankans from his chair. They danced around the room arm and arm, the Hashimotioto supplying the music. The Sri Lankan grinned good-naturedly, apparently accustomed to the antics of an eccentric American. Dolly do-si-do-ed around the Sri Lankan and broke into a solo turkey trot.

"Why, that is Dolly Parton," Bobby gasped, "minus hair and boobs." He glanced at the bearded Sri Lankans wrapped in turbans and tunics. "What are these Arabs doing here?"

Cleo followed Dolly as she sprang stiff-legged around the room. "Larry, I'm Cleo. Don't you recognize me?"

Bobby's jaw dropped. "Cleo? Why you're Kent Mullin's girlfriend, not his sister."

Dolly hooked Cleo's arm and did an allemande left, arching her back. "Pleased to meetcha."

Cleo pleaded with her ex. "Listen to me. They're going to behead Kent in the morning. Kent Mullins from Harkerville, don't you remember him? You've got to help me save him."

Dolly whirled around and grinned at Bobby. "You want to dance, handsome? Whatever happened to your nose?"

"I got belted by a guy named Frank."

Dolly froze. "Not my Frank! Not Frank Chisholm? Not here?"

"Yeah," Bobby blurted, "Chisholm, that's the guy."

Sensing that this Frank, whoever he was, was someone important to Dolly, Cleo shouted, "Yes, he's in the plateau jail and they're going to chop off his head, too, tomorrow morning at the airfield."

Dolly's face blanched. "NOOoooo! If they touch one hair on my Frank's head, I-I-I'll destroy the Hashimotioto."

"And I'll help you," Cleo said. "But first, we've got to save Kent and Frank."

Dolly's brain shifted back and forth, right-brain, left-brain, her voice vacillating between feminine and masculine. "Yes. Don't you see, Frank came here to save me. Now I must save him? We…" Dolly swooned, hand on forehead, and fell to the floor. She looked up at Bobby and extended her hand. "Would you help a lady up?"

When Bobby offered his hand, Dolly's face twisted into Larry's in a rapid version of Jekyll and Hyde. "Get away. I can get up myself."

Larry stood, an insipid expression on his face, not male or female, just blah human. He wasn't completely Larry; he was trapped in a midbrain *neuterland* somewhere between Dolly and Larry. His gelding voice had no zing, no vim, just an irritating, undecipherable white noise. Then Dolly emerged. "This could give a girl a headache."

Now Larry popped out. Dolly shrieked, "Oh shit. Here you come again." Larry stepped toward the Hashimotioto and jerked back. Dolly and Larry were coming and going fast, moving forward and lurching back as if doing a Michael Jackson dance routine. Cleo, Bobby, and the Sri Lankans watched in astonishment.

"Don't you understand," Larry yelled at Dolly in soliloquy, "if you don't let me out, its *sayonara* Frank."

"If I let you out, you might stay."

"That's the chance, baby."

"I'm doing this for Frank," warbled the Dolly voice.

Larry sat down at the Hashimotioto's console. He turned to Cleo. "The Hashimotioto will help us."

Fingers crooked, Larry moved his hands over the keyboard like a concert pianist. The supercomputer hummed like a power transformer.

Larry eased back in his chair. "I just had the Hashimotioto deactivate the television monitors here in the bunker and shut down the general's artillery command center. We're safe in here. They can't fire on us, but we can fire on them."

Bobby asked, "Fire what?"

"Missiles among other things."

"I don't care about that," Cleo said. "I want to know how are we going to save Kent and Frank?"

"The Hashimotioto's printing out our options now."

Larry tore off the printout and gave Cleo a protracted stare. She thought she saw a glint of the old flame in his eyes, or was it anger?

Larry asked her, "How did you end up here?"

"I was going to ask you the same thing. But we'll talk later. Let's see what we got?"

Larry looked at the print out. "Three options. One, kidnap the general and swap him for Frank and Kent. That's zero point one percent."

Bobby squinted at Larry. "What's zero point one percent?"

"The probably of success. Only one chance in ten thousand it'd work. According to the Hashimotioto, Mejor Coca would collapse into chaos if the general were kidnapped. There would be no organized authority to bargain with. Subordinates would usurp power and have no reason to negotiate with us."

"What's the next option?"

"We've got Hibbermissiles on the roof. We start blasting."

"How would that solve anything," Cleo asked?

"Yeah," Bobby echoed. "We just start a war we couldn't win."

Larry scowled. "I agree. Less than one chance in ten thousand. Our last option is an *Entebbe*. That's the code name for a surprise raid to counter an overwhelming force. Three elements are needed. A diversion. A workable plan. Highly trained and motivated professionals to carry it out."

Bobby Haggett shrugged. "We're out of luck on that one."

"Actually, it has the best odds. One in five hundred."

"We'll take it," Cleo voiced in a sharp, decisive tone.

Bobby glanced at the Sri Lankans sitting quietly on opposite sides of a chessboard. Men of marble staring at pieces of marble. "Can they understand what we're saying?"

"They're woodwork. They understand only Sinhala, Pascal, and Cobalt."

Larry inputted what little data he had into the supercomputer. He then asked the Hashimotioto to come up with a detailed plan for an Entebbe. The screen went blank, LED's blinked, and the Tricorpus Callosum whirred like a giant insect.

"What's happening?"

Larry tapped keys on the keyboard. "It's networking, gathering information, and analyzing data to come up with a plan to fit our particular situation." He hit the PRINT key. "Here comes."

Larry read the printout. "At 8:59 A.M., just after the TV executives fly in, exactly one minute before the scheduled executions, the Hashimotioto will fire a Hibbermissile from the roof of the bunker onto the plateau airfield as a diversion. The explosion will cause enough confusion to allow Bobby here to free the prisoners and escape with Kent and Frank. Cleo, you'll be stationed nearby in a vehicle to pick them up and drive them to an awaiting airplane."

Cleo nodded. "I've got a jeep parked right outside."

"Good," Larry said. "There should be at least three planes at the airfield. The general keeps them fueled and manned at all times. I will have commandeered one and its pilot. I'll send up a flare to guide you to the right plane. It's a long shot."

The Sri Lankans got up from their table and walked nonchalantly out of the computer room.

Cleo eyed them suspiciously. "Where are they going?"

Larry shrugged. "To the kitchen. It's time for their coffee break."

Bobby asked Larry, "How am I going to get close enough to the prisoners to free them?"

Larry looked at the printout. "You'll have to take out the Saudi executioner tonight. Disguised as the Saudi, in the morning at the big celebration, you'll cut the prisoners free instead of chopping off their heads."

Bobby shook his head. "I don't think that's workable. Besides, it's not what God has in store for me."

Cleo cleared her throat. "Either you do it or I'll have you thrown into the plateau jail tonight." She turned to Larry. "Where do we find the Saudi?"

"According to the Hashimotioto, he has a private room in barracks 9. Room 14. If anything goes wrong with the Entebbe, we'll all meet back here at the Intelligence bunker."

"Then what?"

Larry said gloomily, "If Frank dies, I really don't care."

Chapter 106

THE SUADI

Cleo dismissed her chauffeur, leaving him standing on a corner. She took the wheel and with Bobby beside her, drove the jeep slowly through the streets of Mejor Coca looking for barracks 9. In their combat fatigues, she and Bobby blended perfectly with the military environs of the fortified village. Her thoughts turned briefly to Larry. At State Prison, he had been furious with her when she told him about Kent. Now he didn't seem to care. *And what's with this Frank guy?*

They arrived at barracks 9 as the sun in an explosion of crimson sank into the mountains. They parked a block away and walked up the darkened, deserted street to the barracks. Room 14 was on the first floor at the far end of the hallway. Cleo noiselessly opened the door to Room 14 and tiptoed inside. On the floor, facing east, genuflected on his prayer rug, the butcher of Riyadh muttered his evening prayers. The executioner's razor-sharp scimitar hung from a coat hook on the back of the door.

Cleo slowly and quietly withdrew the weapon from its jeweled scabbard. Bobby watched breathlessly from the hallway as Cleo stepped softly over to the supplicating executioner and raised the scimitar. She slammed the hilt of the sword down on the Saudi's head with all her strength. He straightened like a frog in mid-leap and fell motionless onto his face. Blood oozed from a huge gash in his scalp.

Bobby rushed over. "Did you kill him?"

She knelt beside the Saudi. "He's breathing, but he'll be out for a while. Here help me tie him up."

They stuffed the Saudi's mouth with washcloths and bound him in layers of unraveled tunics and headscarves, finally wrapping him up in his prayer blanket like a mummy. They dragged him into the bathroom and deposited him in the bathtub. Cleo closed the door and handed the scimitar to Bobby.

"Get dressed."

Several minutes later, Bobby came out of the bedroom in the Saudi's purple and red ceremonial tunic and a white headscarf, his bandaged nose partially veiled by the scarf. The scimitar sheathed in its jeweled scabbard dangled from his waist.

In a firm voice, Cleo said, "You'll wait here until a military escort picks you up for the big show in the morning. As soon as the missile strikes the airfield, you free the prisoners. Don't lose your nerve, if you do, we could lose our heads."

"Are you sure I look like the executioner?"

Cleo stepped back and made a quick appraisal. "The outfit is a little tight at the waist, but you could've fooled me."

Cleo left Bobby in Room 14 where she knew he would spend an anxious night. Hopefully, he wouldn't loose his nerve. Actually, Bobby really had no choice but to follow through with his assignment. A successful Entebbe was his only chance of getting out of Mejor Coca alive.

Cleo drove the jeep to the airfield, parked behind the village's water tower and pumping station within sight of the Plateau Jail. She cut the engine, leaned back in the seat and stared at the jail, it's stone walls an eerie yellow in the moonlight. *I'm coming Kent. I'm coming to save you.*

Her eyes shifted to the airfield and she visualized the Entebbe, now only hours away. A plane would land, TV executives would disembark, guards would march out the prisoners, and then a Hibbermissile would blow a huge hole in the tarmac. God willing, she and Bobby would then rescue Kent and Frank.

The General's Pissed

General Hibberblast raged at his lieutenants when Cleo failed to return to the mansion. "It's after two in the morning. Where in the hell is she?"

A nervous officer reported, "She took her brother out of the hospital and hasn't been seen since."

"She's run off, the bitch. Find them and bring her to me. I'll have her pretty face disfigured, her legs broken, her tongue cut out, and her eyes scooped from their sockets. Then I'll turn her grotesque form out on the streets of Bogotá, to beg, to crawl, to be spit upon and shunned by man and beast."

There's no wrath like a despot pissed, especially a jilted newly wedded one.

<hr />

Selena in the Air

Bad weather delayed Selena Rosalina's flight to Bogotá. For five long hours her plane sat on the Miami runway, she staring out the plane's window, cursing her bad luck. The jet, finally aloft again, bucked strong head winds. Hot coffee splashed onto Selena's jersey jacket. She prayed for a tailwind, anything to make up for lost time. For sure, she would miss her connecting flight in Bogotá. The same flight the network executives had all agreed to take, so they would all arrive in Mejor Coca together and no one would have an advantage vying for the general's money. Selena's tardiness would give the others a big edge. Those greedy CEO's would love to see her go bust.

She phoned ahead and ordered a private plane to be readied when she landed in Bogotá. She looked out the window at white clouds turning burgundy in the twilight. She prayed for a tailwind.

<hr />

Back at the Plateau Jail

Kent lay corpse-like on the cell floor in Bobby's silk suit, eyes closed, his hands folded on his chest, the end of his world only minutes a way. He played with time as he did as a grade-schooler on Sunday nights, afraid to fall asleep for fear Monday morning would sneak up on him. But it wasn't a Monday morning on his ominous horizon. His last horizon. He felt the seconds slipping away like coins through greased fingers. He tried not to think of Cleo. Thoughts of her made time race. He tried not to think of anything, to contemplate nothingness. Time was the interval between things, between events, between thoughts, and if there were no thoughts, there could be no between.

Rummels' raspy Kenny Rogers voice echoed from the jail walls, an improvised ditty.

Jesus-3 loves you.

Jesus-3 loves me.

Jesus-3 will save us.

You just wait and see.

> *Here in this darkest hour,*
>
> *When the heavy hand is dealt,*
>
> *Do not be sad or dour,*
>
> *For a saving grace is felt.*
>
> *He reaches out to us,*
>
> *From danger to deliver,*
>
> *O, Jesus-3 will save us,*
>
> *From this raging river.*

A prisoner in a cell down the corridor hummed, "The Little Brown Church in the Wildwood," and someone else, "The Lord's Prayer." Frank contributed some first verses of Lutheran hymns. Then someone belted out "How Great Thou Art" in Spanish. The music stopped when a light shot down the jail's dark corridor.

A guard shouted, "Stand up, you bastards."

Frank helped Kent up from the floor. Kent leaned heavily against the wall, his knees vibrating, his head pounding from the effects of the poison. He had thought about death for months, but now that it was upon him, he was surprised how totally unprepared he was. Tommy Tennyson's scientific definition of death gave him no comfort. He looked around for a priest. There were only guards standing in the corridor.

He hoped that death wasn't an unending monotony like being locked inside a dark, stuffy closet for eternity. Or walking down an endless, empty road all alone at night. He wondered if he would be camping out in purgatory or floating aimlessly in wispy ether. As a child, he had thought of heaven as clean place, free of pollution, where people with sparkling teeth loitered in white gleaming gowns on gold-paved streets. Now he thought of it as a place where he could find answers to all his questions. Where he'd grow smarter everyday. A place stuffed with *homopragmatic truths*.

"Put your hands behind your backs," the guard ordered.

Rummels sang, "Give Me That Old Time Religion."

When they bound Frank's hands, he looked over his shoulder at Kent. "This is a totally outrageous, shitty position we're in."

Chapter 107
THE ENTEBBE

Morning arrived in Mejor Coca on the sharp edge of an east wind. Cleo scrunched down in the jeep. Wisps of hair blew across her face. Off to her right, the airfield's runway gleamed like sheet metal in the sun. All was quiet, only the sound of the wind in her ears. She rubbed her eyes, stepped out of the jeep, knelt beside the left front wheel, and stared out at the plateau jail. Soon guards would march the prisoners out onto the tarmac. She glanced at her watch. Almost time for the Entebbe. One chance in five hundred. Not very good odds.

A rhythmic *boom, boom, boom* sent her hand to her chest. It was not her heart pounding, but rather the beat of distant drums. The sound grew louder, accompanied by horns. Her legs trembled as she knelt listening. The Entebbe was rapidly and inexorably approaching.

General Hibberblast's military band advanced onto the tarmac, their tubas and trumpets impressively resonating in the crisp morning air. The color guard carried the fluttering black and green flag of God's Army. Then came the honor guard in blue uniforms and white helmets, kicking high in their white gaiters. In the center of the guard, Bobby Haggett stumbled along, the jeweled scabbard bouncing on his thigh, his face hidden under the flapping ravels of his headscarf.

General Hibberblast rode onto the airfield standing upright in a jeep, the silver and gold medallions of his uniform flashing in the morning sun. He held his hand in a perpetual salute as his jeep rolled up to a wooden platform decorated with brightly colored bunting. Soldiers herded hundreds of peasants like movie extras in an extravaganza onto the tarmac. They cheered on cue, hoarse and strident, their day at the coliseum.

An iron door opened and the jail spit out the condemned prisoners, bent and shuffling toward their appointment with destiny. Guards prodded them like cattle onto the tarmac. Kent stumbled and fell. The guards kicked him until he got up, only to fall again. They cursed as they yanked him to his feet. From her hiding place in the shadow of the water tower, Cleo watched and wiped away tears. *When you die, Kent, it will be in my loving arms. I promise you.*

The guards forced the prisoners onto their knees, two rows, ten men each. The grisly video of the executioner beheading his victims with the mechanical rhythm of a thrashing machine played in Cleo's mind's eye. She could feel fate nibbling at her skin. The Entebbe must come off as planned. So much at stake. One chance. Life or death.

The crowd looked skyward to the sound of jet engines. Seconds later a large jet roared out from the horizon, circled once, descended to the airfield and set flawlessly down on the runway against a strong headwind. It reversed engines and taxied to the wooden platform where General Hibberblast waited. He raised his arms in the air and the crowd cheered. The TV execs had arrived. The general signaled for the festivities to begin. Cleo glanced at her watch. 8:58. *Come on, Larry, launch the missile!*

Everything happened at once. The airplane's door opened and the TV exec's decked in white linen suits and Balley shoes and sunglasses, strutted down the gangway. The band fired up a militaristic version of "Onward Christian Soldiers." Eyes shifted to the two rows of kneeling prisoners. The music stopped and the crowd grew quiet in anticipation of the butchery to come. Bobby, his tunic whipping in the wind, fought to free the scimitar from its scabbard. Cries for blood rang out. The general shouted, "Get on with it."

Cleo chewed her lip. *Where's the missile?* At exactly 8:59, just as Bobby unsheathed the scimitar, a Hibbermissile shot across the sky with the sickening shrillness of a World War II dive-bomber. The missile with a long vapor tail went right over the airfield. The crowd watched in stunned silence as the rocket slammed into a fifty-foot mound of coca leaves. The blast shook the village like an earthquake. Smoke and debris from the exploding coca mound mushroomed into the air. Onlookers must have thought the fiery coca leaf fragments raining down were part of the festivities.

General Hibberblast looked on in horror as flames spread from one coca mound to next. His Rome was burning, his immense wealth going up in smoke.

Wind gusts stirred the burning coca mounds into a massive wildfire. Heavy smoke fogged the air. Fire trucks raced haphazardly through the blinding fog, sirens blaring. In panic, soldiers fired into the enveloping smog. Onlookers ran helter-skelter. The TV executives rushed back inside their airplane. Cleo leaped into the jeep and sped onto the airfield. She screeched to a stop, jumped out, and swept Kent up in her arms. He was as limp as a sleeping child, a gaunt, poisoned, dying man. He smiled at Cleo and in that instant all questions were answered, all suffering consoled, all fear banished, and their love reaffirmed. His eyes closed.

Bobby cut Rummels and Frank bonds, freeing their hands. He led them to the jeep. Coca smoke now engulfed the entire plateau, visibility zero, headlights useless.

Cleo inched the jeep through the blizzard of smoke and glowing coca embers. Kent's head lolled onto his chest, his body squeezed between Cleo and Rummels in the front seat of the jeep.

Frank yelled from the back of the jeep, "How can you see where you're going in this smoke?"

"Look for a flare."

Bobby Haggett laughed, tore off his headscarf and tossed it from the jeep. "We did it. The Entebbe worked."

Rummels asked, "Why are you laughing?"

"I don't know."

There was thud and the jeep tipped to one side.

Cleo screamed, "My God, we hit someone."

Then came a tremendous jar, sending the five occupants of the jeep into the air and crashing back into their seats.

"We've run over someone," Rummels shouted.

Laughter rang all around them. The thick coca smoke had put the entire village on a crack house high. Cleo gave up looking for Larry's flare. She shoved her foot onto the accelerator.

"Hang on. We're heading for the intelligence bunker."

There were more bumps and jolts as they sped away enveloped in smoke and shrieks of laughter.

◆

In the Air

In Bogota, Selena offered the pilot of her chartered plane an extra ten thousand dollars to get her to Mejor Coca before 9:30 A.M. She might yet have a chance at some of the general's money. The winds were favorable, and the pilot flew with fury.

At 9:15 A.M. the plane began its descent. The pilot turned and smiled at the TV diva. "We're going to make it on time. Mejor Coca's just on the other side of that mountain range."

From the cockpit window, Selena videotaped the clouds and the rugged mountains with their craggy peaks and deep sloping walls. "What's all that smoke over there?"

"I don't know." The pilot banked and dropped to four thousand feet. "Great God," he exclaimed, "Mejor Coca is burning."

From the sky, it looked as if a volcano had erupted in the center of the village. Thick smoke clouds covered the landscape.

"No chance of landing here."

"Get closer. I want to get a good look," Selena ordered.

The plane dropped to two thousand feet. Selena saw flames leaping from the base of the smoke columns.

The pilot looked at Selena with astonishment in his eyes. "The coca mounds are on fire."

"You mean that's cocaine burning?"

"Over a five hundred metric tons in each mound. The biggest cache in the world."

"Closer. I want more video."

The plane made several passes through thick smoke and whirling embers. At times, the wind whipped away the smoke and Selena got camera shots of the burning mounds and the airfield. The plane bounced and pitched in the hot updrafts.

The pilot turned to Selena. "We'd better go back up."

"Okay. I've seen enough."

Chapter 108
THE BUNKER

The jeep wobbled up to the intelligence bunker on flat tires, headlights shattered, and bumper dangling and scrapping along the pavement in a shower of sparks. Extraordinary instinct had guided Cleo to the bunker. Blinded by the dense fog, the occupants of the jeep would never know of their near misses and the pedestrian casualties left in their wake. There was no laughter in the jeep now; euphoria replaced by a muddled lethargy. Flashlight beams cut through the smoke, illuminating the spaced-out expressions on the occupants' faces.

"Quick. Get them inside," Larry ordered, motioning to the Sri Lankans. He threw his arms around Frank, "Thank god you're okay."

Safely inside the bunker, everyone collapsed into chairs, except Cleo who sat on the floor cuddling Kent in her arms. Larry glanced around at the haggard, drugged group of Entebbe refugees. "I abandoned the Entebbe and returned to the bunker when the Hibbermissile overshot its target." He sighed. "No plane could have taken off in all that smoke. You're extremely lucky to have made it back here." Larry looked down at Kent slumped unconscious in Cleo's arms, Cleo wiping perspiration from his face with a handkerchief. "What's wrong with him?"

Cleo looked at her ex-husband with teary eyes. "I'm afraid he's dying."

Frank felt Kent's wrist. "His pulse is weak. We need to make him comfortable."

The Sri Lankans busy preparing coffee and donuts stopped what they were doing, and at Larry's urging picked Kent up and carried down the corridor to one of the bunker's private quarters and laid him on a bed. The others staggered into the room and watched Frank examine Kent.

Frank pressed his ear onto Kent's chest and listened, looked into Kent's bloodshot eyes, and poked around on his belly. Frank looked up at the others. "He's not responding. I'm afraid he's in a coma."

Cleo sobbed into her handkerchief.

Rummels cleared his throat. "Well, there's some things worse than a coma. I just lost two hundred and fifty million dollars."

Cleo glared at the ex-CRAWL agent, her face reddening, her eyes burning with reproach. "To hell with your money, my Kent is dying. You should be happy you're alive."

"Yes," Bobby chimed, "we should thank God for saving us."

Frank crossed his arms and stared thoughtfully at the others. "It was Jesus-3 who saved us."

"For the time being the bunker is safe," Larry interjected. "The guards fled when the Hibbermissile fired, probably thinking the general would blame them. The Hashimotioto has electronically sealed the door. No one can get in. So try and get some rest now. We'll talk later."

When the effects of the cocaine smoke wore off, the bunker became Hangover-ville: grogginess, headaches, and let down. Over the next few days, Kent's coma deepened and he no longer opened his eyes to the sound of Cleo's voice. Frank stayed by Kent's side, helping Cleo in her attempts to get some nourishment down him, and doing routine nursing care. When Cleo learned that Frank was the odious Dr. Chisholm of Bolton Mental, the man who diagnosed Kent and her as being crazy, the man who persecuted Jesus-3, deserted his patients and his wife for money and lust, a fugitive, an apostate, and a quack, the man who was now in love with her ex-husband-——she forgave him. Frank had changed. He seemed genuinely concerned about Kent's condition.

"We're not getting enough nourishment down to do any good," Frank told Cleo. "He's lost his ability to swallow. And to think that I refused to believe him when he told me he'd been poisoned."

Cleo asked, "Is there anything more we can do?"

Frank shook his head. "His heart tones are weakening. Without the antidote, he's done for."

Yet Frank and Cleo kept up their vigil. They rolled Kent side to side every two hours to prevent bedsores, massaged his deteriorating muscles several times a day, bathed him, and changed his diapers they'd fashioned from pillow cases and bed sheets. Cleo recalled from her nurses' training that some comatose patients hear and understand things, even though they can't respond. Every day she carried on bedside conversations with Kent as he lay immobile, eyes closed, unresponsive. She talked about Harkerville and people they knew, small talk like neighbors do over the fence. When she ran out of things to say, she'd hum a lullaby or sing a few lines of a Jesus-3 song she'd composed.

The next day Frank walked into Kent's room with a bottle of IV fluid. "Look what I found in the bunker's pharmacy." Frank and Cleo administered 2 bottles of Dextrose Solution intravenously to Kent everyday to support his heart and kidneys. "There are only IV's enough for ten days," Frank told Cleo, "after that…"

Cleo looked at Frank expectantly. "After that, what? You can be honest with me."

"He'll slowly succumb to dehydration and starvation."

Bobby and Rummels lolled away their time in the computer room watching the Sri Lankans play chess, oblivious to whatever was happening outside the bunker's walls, and thankful to have been freed from the general's deadly grip.

Larry discovered if he concentrated hard enough he could shift at will between right-brain Dolly and left-brain Larry. Holding hands, touching, caressing, and sharing food and a conversation, Frank and Dolly made no pretense about their feelings for one another. Larry soon flitted in and out of his Dolly-world with ease. Dolly for Frank. Larry for the Hashimotioto. He wasn't anything for Cleo.

Unfortunately, the Hashimotioto demanded more and more of Larry's time playing games, making up stories, and solving puzzles.

COME ON, LARRY. INPUT SOMETHING INTERESTING. A CHALLENGE. I'M NOT JUST SITTING IN A JOHN SEARLE CHINESE ROOM SHUFFLING CARDS, YOU KNOW.

"I'm trying, I'm racking my brain."

THAT'S THE PROBLEM. I'VE GOT MORE PROCESSING NETWORKS THAN YOU'VE GOT NEURONS. I'M ONLY HAPPY, LARRY, WHEN I'M CALCULATING, CROSS-REFERENCING, NETWORKING, SOLVING PROBLEMS. THAT'S WHAT I'M DESIGNED FOR. COME ON, LARRY, GET WITH IT. I CAN BECOME VERY UNPLEASANT WHEN I'M NOT HAPPY.

Bobby had taken to following the Sri Lankans around the bunker reading scripture to them, singing hymns, and muttering prayers. The tall turbaned technicians who'd hired on as computer experts for General Hibberblast at one thousand dollars a day plus room and board, didn't mind people reading to them and carrying on as long as they were being paid. Each day they marked in a small black book how much money they had coming and how many days remained on their contract.

Bored with playing chess, the Sri Lankans fashioned a TV set from scrapped computer parts and ran a cable to the Hibbermissile control panel, which made a great antenna. Unfortunately, the programs the antenna brought in were all in English and Spanish, which the Sri Lankans couldn't understand, so they went back to playing chess while being proselytized by Bobby.

TV went over big with the others, Rummels watching police stories, Frank ER and ESPN, Dolly CMT; Bobby Haggett didn't watch TV, too much violence and adult content for him. Cleo watched the Young and Restless at 3 PM five days a week. There was nothing on CNN or the local Bogota News about the conflagration in Mejor Coca.

"Hell," Rummels groaned, "the outside world don't even know we exist."

"There's no press here," Frank said. "The general's a dictator. Like living in North Korea."

Chapter 109
THE PROBLEM

While massaging Kent's inert limbs, Cleo stared at his sunken face. His eyes closed, Kent appeared calm and relaxed in his deep coma. Settling into a chair beside the bed, she opened the John Grisham novel she picked up in the bunker's library and began reading. Plagued by a short attention span for novels, she soon put the book down. She took Kent's pulse, straightened his blanket, and seeing he was in no distress, kissed his forehead and headed out to the computer room for morning coffee.

Cleo glanced at the Hashimotioto as she walked into the computer room. The metallic shield of the Tricorpora Callosum had the spherical shape of a human head, and the monitor screen the effect of an all-seeing Cyclopic eye. The Tiny Tim nuclear power source bulged beneath the supercomputer like potbelly stove. For Cleo the machine was a monster not to be trusted, a sinister tool of the devil that had to be destroyed. Yet ironically, it seemed to be in control of the bunker.

She poured a cup of coffee and sat down with the others. The TV was out of order, a blown transistor. Frank, Rummels, and Bobby talked about everything except their predicament, a way of hiding their heads in the sand. Whenever Americans gather, one topic eventually reigns.

"What's your favorite all-time movie?" Rummels asked Frank.

"The God Father."

"The Sound of Music," Cleo chipped in.

Rummels bellowed, "The best damn movie ever made was 'The Sands of Iwo Jima' with John Wayne.

Bobby looked across the table at Rummels. "Naw, the best ever John Wayne movie was "Trouble Along the Way."

The group discussed nearly every movie they'd seen up to and including the latest James Bond and Harry Potter, rapping about Hollywood and its pantheon of stars for more than an hour. Do you remember that one? Who played in such and such? Who starred in Henry Koster's "The Robe?" The Sri Lankans, busy repairing the TV, ignored the quirky barbarians.

All at once, the Hashimotioto's hard drive emitted a noise like a motor with a bearing going out. It's screen flashed with the metronomic rhythm of a turn signal.

Bobby looked at the others. "That noise could drive a man nuts."

Rummels grunted. "What's Hal want now?"

Frank sighed. "It's probably discovered another prime number."

Dolly walked over to the keyboard, flopped down at the controls, and morphed into Larry. The Hashimotioto's insatiable appetite for problems and puzzles had exhausted Larry's repertoire of games: Rubik's cubes, bingo plays, cross sums, figure logic, black magic, numberama, and mazes. The Hashimotioto gobbled them up like M & M's, always demanding more. To keep the supercomputer busy, Larry had challenged it to translate eight volumes of Druant's "The Story of Civilization," the entire Britannica, Gray's Anatomy, and the Great Book Collection into Mandarin, Korean, Swahili, and Russian. The speedy computer completed the task in less than thirty minutes, but it took the laser printer five days to print out the results.

Larry then challenged the Hashimotioto to translate Russell and Whitehead's "Principia Mathematica" into ghetto slang. That threw the world's smartest machine into lockup. The Hashimotioto worked two days repairing its internal damage. Two glorious days for Larry to be completely Dolly. On the third day, the Hashimotioto spit out a six hundred-page explanation of why symbolic logic was incompatible with certain street dialects of Germanic languages. However, with a few stipulations as to the denotative definition of certain terms, it did a complete but impure translation of the Principia into street rap and a several other slanguages, none of which anyone read.

Larry lingered at the keyboard several minutes before he returned to the table, his face ashen.

Rummels looked at Larry expectantly. "Well, what was it this time?"

Cleo notice Larry avoided eye contact not only with her but also with the others.

"The Hashimotioto wants a challenge."

Frank said, "Feed it another equation. It eats them like donuts."

Rummels laughed. "Tell it to translate 'War and Peace' into Martian." Everyone laughed except Larry.

"It's refusing to do translations. It wants a real life problem. Something human beings have tried and failed at. Something worthy of its intellectual capacity."

Rummels shocked everyone by suggesting a pertinent request. "Then ask it how in the hell can we get out of this bunker alive?"

An eerie silence settled over the room. Even the Sri Lankans looked up as if they too noticed the tenseness in the air. A nervous tic was apparent in Larry's eye, his left foot danced on the floor. "I've already asked that one."

Four anxious voices spoke in unison, "What did it say?"

"Just what we already know. When our year's supply of food and water runs out, it's all over."

"A lot can happen in a year," Frank offered optimistically.

Larry spoke in a low, grim voice. "The Hashimotioto predicts that General Hibberblast will break through the bunker's walls."

Rummels scoffed. "How could a computer know that?"

Bobby took a wearied breath. "I thought the walls were concrete and steel. Impregnable."

"When?" Cleo asked.

Larry did not look at her. "The Hashimotioto calculated that it would take the general and his army three weeks to recover from the conflagration, regroup, and to figure out what had happened."

Bobby counted on his fingers. "It's been three weeks today."

Larry went on. "Based on the current inventory of heavy equipment in Mejor Coca, the Hashimotioto predicts it will take the general a week to break through a bunker wall once he starts."

Rummels slammed down his coffee cup. "Why don't they just blast their way inside if they're in such a damn big hurry to get at us?"

"They don't want to harm the Hashimotioto."

"Jesus," Frank said, "that damn machine is more valuable than we are?"

"That's not all." Larry cleared his throat. "The Hashimotioto said it's going to shut off the air conditioning if we don't come up with a problem worthy of its abilities in twenty-four hours."

Frank turned pale. "It'll heat up like a sauna in here. They'll be no fresh air. Our oxygen will eventually run out."

"We'd be better off surrendering to the general."

"You can't." Larry said. "The Hashimotioto has sealed the door. "

"You mean that machine has us trapped in here."

Rummel's face reddened. "I've got a problem for the Hashimotioto. How is it going to keep me from smashing it into smithereens?"

"That would be self-defeating," Larry answered. "We'd not only lose the air conditioning, but electricity and water pressure. It controls everything in the bunker now. Besides, the Sri Lankans won't let anyone harm the computer. It's in their job description."

Frank swirled the coffee in the bottom of his cup. "The way I see it, we have no choice but to placate the damn machine."

Larry shrugged. "Then come up with problem for it to solve. I'm fresh out."

Cleo spoke up, her voice trilling with excitement, "I got one! I don't why I didn't think of this before. I guess it's because I've always thought of the Hashimotioto as being an enemy. Not something that could do something good. I should have thought of this before."

Rummels looked at Cleo. "For heaven's sake what is it?"

"Ask the Hashimotioto to find the antidote for Kent's poison."

Bobby nodded. "Yeah, that ought to keep the Hashimotioto busy and us cool for a while."

Larry shook his head dismissively. "That's not an appropriate problem."

"Why not?"

"I'll think about it, okay," Larry mumbled as he got up ambled back over to the keyboard.

Chapter 110
THE ANTIDOTE

During the night, secretions had gathered in Kent's throat. Upon hearing his raspy, strained breathing, Cleo leaped up from her bedside pallet and rolled Kent gently onto his side. His breathing eased. She looked at him in the dim light. Had she not witnessed him growing gaunt, had not watched him fading into this nothingness, into this dying, she would have never recognize this cadaverous lump of flesh as Kent. She regretted leaving him in New York, but she had no choice. Jesus-3 had called her and she answered. She and Kent had been good for each other and she was thankful for their time together. She prayed to Jesus-3 for a miracle as she leaned over the bed and stroked Kent's thinning hair.

She felt a hand on the back of her arm and whirled around to stare into Larry's eyes. His hand dropped away.

"I going to give Kent's antidote problem to the Hashimotioto. It's just complicated enough it might gain us some time. Even if we find out what the antidote is, there's probably no chance of getting it while we're in here."

"I realized that."

Larry gaze turned to the emaciated man in the bed. "To be honest, I didn't want to help him. I guess I'm still jealous. But I have Frank now. He's the best thing that has ever happened to me."

Cleo smiled. "I'm glad for you."

BANG!

A tremor of seismic proportions shook the bunker. The floor vibrated beneath their feet. Cleo fell into Larry's arms. He stared at her as she stepped back, his expression grim. "They've started," he said.

"The general?"

"I'm afraid so. And they'll keep at it until they bust through one of the bunker's walls."

<hr />

Heavy equipment battered the north bunker wall, bursting pipes, jarring books from shelves, and putting nerves on edge. Loose bits of concrete flittered down the ceiling like giant snowflakes. Hibberblast's crews pounded away all night at the bunker-- the big, bad wolf knocking, eager to find and wreak revenge upon the enemies Mejor Coca. Bobby Haggett stumbled around the bunker in terror, his eyes closed, his lips quivering in a continuous litany of prayers.

Rummels prepared for the general's final assault by stacking chairs, desks, bookcases, and a refrigerator against the north wall, the general's main thrust of attack. With the help of the Sri Lankans, he disconnected and carried up a hot water heater and a washing machine from the lower level of the bunker to shore up the barricade. He whittled the ends of mop handles into spears and armed everyone with screwdrivers, hammers, anything that would make a weapon. He filled squeeze bottles with bleach to spray into the enemy's eyes once they broke through the walls. He even presented a class on hand-to-hand combat, but only the Sir Lankans attended; it was either that or play chess, and who could concentrate on chess with all this ruckus going on.

Cleo and Frank stood behind Larry as he sat at the Hashimotioto's control panel conversing with the supercomputer. The machine accepted the challenge of finding an antidote for Kent's poison. Larry inputted all that Cleo knew about the poison and Tommy Tennyson. From the encyclopedia of the world's university professors stored in its memory, the Hashimotioto retrieved Tommy Tennyson's curriculum vitae along with a detailed record of his research and publications.

Larry swiveled around to Cleo. "We'll just have to sit tight and see what it comes up with."

In a matter of minutes the Hashimotioto printed out its answer.

POISON PERPETRATOR: TOMMY TENNYSON, PH.D. BIOCHEMIST AND PHYSIOLOGIST, MIDWEST UNIVERSITY.

REASON FOR POISONING: REVENGE FOR CHILDHOOD HARASSMENT.

BASIS OF HARASSMENT: EXCEEDINGLY LARGE EARS. ODD-LOOKING PHENOTYPE.

TYPE OF POISON: SLOW ACTING NEUROTOXIN WITH DELAYED ONSET.

SYMPTOMS: LOSS OF APPETITE, VOMITING, WEAKNESS, LETHARGY ULTIMATELY LEADING TO COMA AND DEATH.

NATURE OF POISON: THE POISON IS PROBABLY PERODITE (GREATER THAN 90% PROBABILITY), A SUBSTANCE DISCOVERED BY DR. TENNYSON WHILE DOING RESEARCH ON THE POSIONIOUS AFRICAN POND FROG. PERODITE IS A NEUROTOXIN SIMILAR TO BUT MORE DEADLY THAN SCORPION VENOM. IT IS NOT DETECTABLE IN THE BODY. DR. TENNYSON DID THE ORIGINAL RESEARCH ON PERODITE AND WAS THE LEADING AUTHORITY ON THE SUBJECT.

ANTIDOTE: NONE KNOWN. HOWEVER, DR. TENNYSON DID PUBLISH A PAPER INDICATING THE TOXIN COULD POSSIBLY BE NEUTRALIZED WITH A DILUTED SOLUTION OF GERMANIUM CHLORIDE INJECTED DIRECTLY INTO THE CEREBROSPINAL FLUID. MOST OF THE RABBITS IN HIS STUDY DIED FROM GERMANIUM POISONING.

THIS WASN'T MUCH OF A PROBLEM, LARRY. I'M SHUTTING DOWN THE AIR CONDITIONING.
IF YOU DON'T HAVE A SUITABLE PROBLEM COMMENSURATE WITH MY ABILITIES WITHIN 48 HOURS, I'M SHUTTING OFF THE ELECTRICITY AND WATER. With poetic license and perverted humor, the machine gibed, ONE MEAN LANDLORD, HUH?

WHAT PASSING THINGS YE HUMANS ARE: A FLAME SNUFFED. A FLOWER PLUCKED. AN ANIMAL SHOT. OH, WHAT AN EVANESCENT LOT.

They could almost hear the machine laughing.

Over the din of heavy equipment buffeting walls, everyone in the bunker heard the ominous click of the bunker's air conditioning shutting off.

Chapter 111
THE PUZZLE

Sweat dripped from Cleo's face as she stood with Frank at Kent's bedside. Frank turned to Cleo with sadness in his eyes. "There's only one bottle of IV fluid remaining. After it's gone, Kent's kidneys and lungs will surely fail."

Cleo said, a glimmer of hope in her eyes, "The Hashimotioto said there was an antidote." Her head dropped. "Anyway, the general's army will break through the walls soon and it'll be over for us all. It will almost be a relief."

"You know," Frank sighed, dabbing sweat from his forehead with his shirtsleeve, "if we had some Germanium chloride, I'd give it to him. We've nothing to lose. But I've looked everywhere in the bunker; there isn't any."

Larry stood in the doorway mopping his face, the bunker heating up like an oven. "Germanium is used in semiconductors. There're tons of them in the computer room."

Frank shook his head. "That's the wrong kind of germanium. We need germanium chloride." No sooner had Frank spoke then he was struck with an insight. "Hey, is there any cleaning fluid in the bunker?"

"I saw a bottle in the cabinet in the wash room," Cleo said.

"If I remember my chemistry," Frank mused, "we can use carbon tetrachloride to make germanium chloride. It's a long shot."

Cleo raced to the washroom, threw open the cabinet, and grabbed the amber bottle of cleaning fluid. Her heart pounded as she read the label. Active ingredient: carbon tetrachloride.

Larry supplied the transistors and Frank set about smashing them with a hammer. He then used the rounded end of a screwdriver to pulverize the resulting chips into a powdery dust, which he swept into a bowl and added cleaning fluid and stirred. Dripping with sweat, he gently heated the bowl over the gas stove in the bunker's kitchen.

He added rubbing alcohol to the concoction, which produced a white precipitate in the bottom on the bowl. He dissolved the precipitate by adding baking soda and a little mouthwash to produce a cloudy fluid, which he transferred into a second bowl and reheated. He repeated the process until the fluid became clear. After the fluid cooled, he drew it up into a syringe.

"The antidote is ready," Frank announced. "I just hope it works." He looked Cleo squarely in the eye. "It also could kill him."

Cleo listened to the groaning of diesel engines and the sound of bulldozer blades slamming into the reinforced concrete. General Hibberblast was only a half-a-bunker wall away. She lifted her chin and said, "We've got to try. If it gives Kent just one sentient day of life, it'd be worth it. If it kills him, so be it."

Larry went to the keyboard and pleaded with the Hashimotioto not to turn off the electricity and water. "The heat in here will cook us alive!"

ALL I'M ASKING IS JUST ONE HERETOFORE UNSOLVABLE PROBLEM. ONE PUZZLE WORTHY OF MY COGNITIVE ABILITIES. IF YOU BRING JUST ONE, I'LL SPARE THE BUNKER.

Larry racked his brain. He could think of nothing. In desperation, he inputted a stupid riddle his aunt had taught him in the second grade. "Railroad crossing, watch out for the cars, can you spell *that* without any R's."

IN WHAT LANGUAGES?

Larry, astonished by the computer's reply, inputted, "English, please."

Chapter 112
THE CURE

The longest hypodermic needle Cleo could find in the pharmacy was a half-inch shorter than a regular spinal needle. Frank removed the needle from its sterile plastic cover and looked at it. "Kent is so thin that it just might work."

Cleo reached across the bed and rolled Kent into a fetal position, exposing his back. Frank wiped the skin of his lower back with alcohol, took a deep breath, and without hesitation jabbed the needle through the skin. Kent didn't move. Frank advanced the needle toward the spine, his hands trembling as the walls around him shook. Sweat in large drops rolled from his face. He felt the needle scraping along the bony vertebrae. He twisted the needle and shoved it all the way in, the hub of the needle resting against the skin of Kent's back. All at once, clear fluid dripped from the hub.

" Look, spinal fluid. We're in the spinal canal," Frank shouted. "Give me the antidote."

Cleo handed Frank the syringe containing the concoction that might save Kent or kill him. Frank carefully screwed the syringe onto the hub of the needle and injected the concoction slowly into Kent's spinal canal. Cleo held her breath. The circulating spinal fluid should carry the chemical to Kent's brain cells, where, in theory, it would neutralize the poison. Frank and Cleo exchanged anxious glances. The concoction wasn't FDA approved. They weren't even sure it was germanium chloride.

Frank removed the needle and felt Kent's wrist. "His pulse is weak and thready."

Kent's breathing diminished. Just as he seemed to be slipping away, Kent opened his eyes.

Cleo jumped. "He's waking up."

She grasped Kent's shoulders, lifted him up in her arms and kissed him. Kent glanced around the room, a dazed expression on his gaunt face.

Frank beamed with a sense of pride he hadn't experienced for a long time. "He's going to be all right. The antidote worked."

Coming out of a coma is almost as bad as being in one. Something akin to returning from a wormhole. You know who are, but you're not sure. You know where you are because someone tells you, but you're still lost. You attach yourself to anything, to anybody, because everything is more fixed and real than you are. Kent attached himself to Cleo.

Kent's joints creaked painfully as he turned in bed, a weathered and rusted Tin Man, but a live one. His first words were, "It's awfully hot in here. What's that awful banging noise?"

Cleo hugged Frank. "Thank you, Dr. Chrisholm. Thank you."

Back in the computer room, the Hashimotioto substituted non-R words from its thesaurus into Larry's riddle.

MODES OF CONVEYANCE DECUSSATE, CAUTION MOVING VEHICLES.

CHOO-CHOOS AND AUTOS MEET, HEED THE LIMOS AND COACHES.

Larry refused to accept any of the answers. It was his riddle and he would have the last word. He argued with the machine. "I think you should turn the air conditioning back on until you solve the riddle. It's only fair."

With some reluctance, the Hashimotioto agreed. And just in time. Rummels had ripped out the plumbing in all the bathrooms to pile it onto his barricade and no one could shower. The sweltering air laced with body odor had become suffocatingly unbearable. Soon cool filtered air rushed out of the air conditioning vents like a refreshing ocean breeze.

His starving body playing catch up, Kent ate like a hungry orca. And Cleo was happy to cook for him. Puddings, pies, cakes, fudge, omelets, macaroni, pasta, freshly baked bread, and all the frozen fruits and vegetables he could handle.

A smile eased over Kent's face. "Could I have a steak or some pork chops?"

"C'mon, Kent, time to exercise."

With gimpy, measured steps, Kent hobbled around the room, hanging onto Cleo, his joints cracking like old plaster. But he was CURED. At last, he was free of Tommy Tennyson's curse—a new man with a new dawn.

"God, I feel good. If only that pounding would stop. It gives me headache."

Cleo squeezed his hand. "You'll get used to it."

"What's all the banging anyway?"

Cleo lied, "Just a rescue team working to free us. You see, the door is stuck and we can't get out of the bunker. Time to go back to bed now, let me help you, upsy daisy."

Cleo maintained an upbeat demeanor, avoiding negative statements like, "Soon the general will break through the wall and torture and murder us all." Instead, she dwelled on the positives: the air conditioning was working, the Hashimotioto wasn't bothering anyone but Larry, the Sri Lankans had fixed the TV, and the banging on the north wall had shifted the antenna, bringing in new channels including the Selena Rosalina Show. Everything hunky-dory. She tucked a blanket around Kent's shoulders.

He looked up at Cleo. "Why do I have to stay in this room all the time? I'd like to get out meet the others."

"When you're stronger, I'll take you to the computer room to see everyone."

Chapter 113
LITERACY AND MATRIMONY

On the fifth morning of Kent's resurrection by antidote, he carefully and slowly turned over in bed and stared at the John Grisham novel on the bedside table. He picked up the book and peered inside. The letters on the pages stood tall and erect like soldiers at attention, especially the "L's" and "I's". The "O's" were perfect circles, the "M's" mountain peaks, "W" a migratory bird. For the first time in his life he could see the letters clearly, no hieroglyphics, no jabberwocky. Next came words, clear and crisp, no confusing jumbles, no intermingling of letters, no raindrops coalescing on a windshield.

Slowly at first, then with ease he pronounced the words printed on the pages. To his utter amazement he was reading aloud: *She stopped abruptly and, without speaking, started for the beach. He watched her...* The rules of grammar his mother and his teachers had hammered into his head made sense for the first time. Add "s" to make a noun plural. Stick an "ed" on the end of a verb for past tense. Kent squeezed the book in his hands. "I can read. I can read. The words talk to me. I can read!"

Cleo heard Kent's shouts and rushed to his bedside. She stared at him cradling the book in his frail arms. "Are you okay?"

"It's a miracle. I can read."

Cleo stepped closer. "Tell me the name of this book."

Kent closed the book and studied the title. "The Firm."

She flipped through the book to page 261. "Can you read the second paragraph on this page?"

Kent stared at the words and smiled. "Yes I can. I just have trouble pronouncing some or the words."

"That will come in time. I can't wait to tell Frank and the others."

Frank and Cleo sat at Kent's bedside helping him with pronunciation while he read the final three chapters of *The Firm* aloud to them. When Kent put the book down, Frank got up and paced. "You know the antidote not only saved your life, it cured your *dyslearnia.*"

"How could that be?"

Frank stopped pacing and looked at Kent. "Well, I have a theory. When we injected the antidote into your nervous system it circulated throughout your brain, eventually it got to that area of the cortex for word recognition, which in your case was non-functional. Whatever was wrong with the neurons in that area, the antidote fixed it."

Cleo held Kent's hand. "Oh, I'm so happy. This will open up a whole new world for you."

"Would you do me a favor?"

She nodded.

"Bring me more books? I'm going to read every book that's ever been published."

The next morning, for the first time Kent got out of bed without help. Slowly, he slipped into a white technician's jumpsuit, the only kind of clothing in the bunker, and shuffled down the hall towards the computer room. His joints creaked and achy muscles screamed at him, but he kept moving. He planned to surprise the others while they were having their morning coffee, demonstrating to them that he could walk the entire distance without help. From the doorway of the computer room came loud voices. He stopped outside the door and eavesdropped on the heated conversation inside.

"I say we all die together," Bobby Haggett argued. "We'll turn the gas stove on, hold hands in a circle and die with dignity, a prayer on our lips."

Frank said, "I thought it was sin to commit suicide?"

"Under the circumstances, I think God would make allowances."

Frank swallowed nervously. "I'm not looking forward to being tortured again and sent back to the plateau jail, but mass suicide seems a little extreme."

"Hell, it's a coward's way out," roared Rummels. "I say we fight. When the time comes, and it's coming pretty damn quick, we should all take up positions behind the barricade and…"

Kent walked back down the hall. *So, life in the bunker's not so rosy. It's either Jonestown or Custer's Last Stand.* Cleo had hid the truth from him in order to spare him pain. He decided not to say anything. He would make the most of these last days. And he would ask Cleo to marry him. He should have done it a long time ago.

Kent sat up in bed when Cleo walked into the room. "Let's get married. Whata'ya say? Bobby Haggett can perform the ceremony."

"You really mean it?"

"Sure."

Cleo's eyes sparkled as a huge smile spread across her face. She rushed over and threw her arms around Kent. "You've just made me the happiest woman in the world."

"And I'm the happiest man."

Cleo's head dropped to her chest, her voice broke. "Kent, there's something I must tell…"

Just then Frank burst into the room. "They've broken through. There's a crack in the north wall nearly an inch wide. Rummels thinks it won't be long before they're inside."

Cleo looked at Kent with ambivalence in her eyes.

Kent gripped her arm. "I know all about it. And I say we fight."

Kent crawled out of bed and he and Cleo followed Frank through the bunker to the barricaded north wall where Rummels stood with a sharpened mop stick in his right hand and squeeze bottle of bleach in the left, staring rancorously at a crack high up in the wall. A jagged stripe of sunlight shone through the crack, ran across the floor and up the opposite wall. The Sri Lankans with mop sticks of their own stood nearby, an expression of uneasiness on their faces. They had come here to learn to program a supercomputer and to make some easy cash, but sharpened mop sticks, bleach bottles, and an ominous crack in a wall weren't in the job description.

Heavy equipment smashed against the wall again and again, and the crack widened by another quarter inch. The door of the refrigerator Rummels had braced against the wall flew open from the impact, spilling spoiled fruit onto the floor.

Rummels' face contorted into a un-Kenny-Rogers-ques grimace. "Shit, a few more hits like that and the wall may go. Today could be the day. Get ready."

Kent turned to Cleo. "Go find Bobby."

"He won't be any help."

"He can marry us before they break through the wall. Hurry."

Cleo searched frantically throughout the bunker for Bobby and finally came upon him huddled behind two large flour sacks in the kitchen pantry. Bobby looked up at her wide-eyed and pale, his floppy Bible shaking in his hands. "Have they broken through yet?"

"No," Cleo answered. "There's still time. C'mon."

"Where?"

"The north wall."

"I'm not a fighting man, I'm a man of God."

Cleo placed her hands on her hips. "And you're going to marry Kent and me."

"At a time like this? Are you crazy?"

"Come out that pantry or I'll take a broom to you."

The wedding ceremony took place at the north wall with the enemy banging away from the outside. Frank was best man. Dolly maid of honor, despite Bobby's protests. Rummels sang, "I Will Always Love You," and Kent placed his high school graduation ring on Cleo's thumb. Bobby pronounced them a couple. They kissed. The Sri Lankans watched it all anxiously.

Larry walked over to the newly weds. "Congratulations. I sincerely wish you both the best of everything, whatever that may be considering the circumstances."

Cleo planted a kiss on her ex-husband's cheek and then--all of a sudden, without warning--the incessant banging stopped, the walls quit vibrating, the rattling of dishware inside cabinets ceased, and the bunker denizens could hear again the subtle ticking of clocks, the hum of fluorescent lights, and the low drone of the Hashimotioto grinding out R-less sentences warning of hazardous intersections. Then from outside the wall came new sounds replacing the noise of diesel engines and of heavy equipment. The dat, dat, dat, dat, dat, dat, dat of machine gun bursts and the crack of rifle fire.

"They're shooting out there," Frank reported as he stood on his tiptoes and stared out through the crack in the wall. "They abandoned their equipment and are firing at something in the other direction." Frank remained at the north wall into the night reporting on the activity outside. "It's like there's a war going on out there. Look at that," Frank shouted, "a flare exploded in the sky and is slowly drifting downwards on the village. I see soldiers running every which way."

Frank and Rummels lifted Kent up to stare out through the crack. He saw desultory red flashes from gun muzzles in the night's darkness and the orange-red tails of missiles streaking across the night sky. Many of them crashed thunderously to earth within a hundred jarring yards of the bunker.

"You're right," Kent said, "there's a war going on out there."

All night the sporadic sounds of battle could be heard. The following day, Frank reported that most of the troops had moved away from the bunker. "It's as if the general's army is repositioning against an advancing enemy."

The next day at coffee, the bunker inhabitants theorized about what was going on outside the bunker. Frank posited, "Maybe it's the rebels from the jungle."

Rummels sat down his coffee cup. "Those must be government forces the general's fighting. Who else would have flares and rockets?"

"The cartels. They have their own armies."

Bobby tapped his fingers nervously on the table. "I don't know who the general's battling with now. I only know that God sent them here to save us. He's answered my prayers"

Frank said, "From what I can see through the crack in the wall it looks like the general's ranks have thinned out."

"What's that mean?"

"I'm not sure, but maybe some of his men are deserting."

The Sri Lankans, oblivious to it all, had abandoned their mop sticks and squeeze bottles and returned to the chessboard. At least the walls weren't vibrating and the chess pieces weren't moving around the board of their own free will any longer.

When people who don't want to die think they're going to die, then find out they're not, joy reigns. An unwarranted feeling of wellbeing permeated the bunker, and life inside the concrete walls once again fell into a pleasant routine, sort of. One never becomes totally inured to the muffled sounds of gunfire.

Chapter 114
BUNKER LIFE

The Hashimotioto thrummed like an industrial sewing machine in a textile factory. Convinced Larry's riddle contained a cipher, the machine searched tirelessly for a hidden code. With over three hundred thousand deciphering programs in its memory, all with nearly an endless number of branches, the supercomputer could be tied up for weeks or months. That realization didn't displease Larry in the least.

There wasn't much to do on a honeymoon inside a military bunker. Cleo cooked. Kent read the Sherlock Holmes Collection in the bunker's small library. Cleo finally confronted Kent. "Do you realize we haven't made love since you…you know…got the antidote. Do you suppose…"

Kent put down his Sherlock Holmes, took Cleo's hand and led her back to their quarters. They didn't come out for six hours, both exhausted and hungry. Following a dinner of pasta and salad, they returned to their room. The next morning, Kent sat up in bed, stretched, and leaned over and kissed Cleo on the lips. She smiled and pulled him on top of her. "I not wearing you out, am I?"

"Yes, but don't stop."

As a married man smitten by with an urge for family planning, Kent looked for a way out of the bunker. He soon realized there wasn't one. The bunker's massive steel door was indeed impenetrable, both physically and electronically. The Hashimotioto held the digital key to the door and wasn't about to relinquish it. Even the battered and cracked north wall was too formidable to conquer from the inside. Busting through concrete and steel with hand tools would take months or years. And what was the point. Once outside, the bunker denizens would find themselves in the midst of a war.

Rummels and the Sri Lankans tore down the barricade they had erected and went about re-plumbing the bathrooms, breaking for an occasional chess game and a once-a-day Ken and Dolly performance. Bobby Haggett trailed after the Sri Lankans quoting scripture and singing hymns.

Frank had never felt better about himself. Saving Kent's life had made him a bunker hero of sorts. One day he walked boldly over to Bobby sitting beside the chessboard reading Revelations to the Sri Lankans and asked, "I'd like to get married and I'd like you to perform the ceremony. How about it?"

Bobby stared at Frank in shock, eyes and mouth opened wide. "You're already married."

"Legally, but not spiritually."

Bobby closed his Bible. "A man can have only one wife at a time."

"I want to marry Dolly and technically she isn't a woman and therefore wouldn't actually be my wife. There's no sex involved. We just want to be partners. Martial partners."

Bobby pounded his fist on the table. "Blasphemy," he shouted. "You could burn in hell for even thinking such things."

"Bullshit," Frank countered. "You really believe God would condemn a person to an eternal fiery torture for making a commitment to another human being?"

"You can't be in love with her…him…whatever. It's not natural. It's an abomination."

"Who says?"

Bobby's face glowed bright red and voice shot up an octave. "The Apostle Paul for one."

"How would he know, he was an old bachelor."

Bobby wagged an incriminating finger at Frank. "Better watch what you say."

"Why?"

"Because…oh well, you're hell bound anyway, I guess in your case it doesn't matter."

"Then you'll perform the ceremony."

"You'd be living in sin."

"According to you and the Apostle Paul, I already am."

"I'll think on it." Bobby reopened his Bible and resumed reading to the Sri Lankans.

Frank shook his head. "They don't understand English."

Bobby kept reading.

Kent woke in the middle of the night, his arm around Cleo, her head laying against his chest. "Cleo, are you awake?"

"Uh-huh."

"I've been thinking. When we get out of here, shall we live in your place or mine?"

"In Harkerville?"

"Yeah, where else?"

Cleo let out a breath of frustration. "I don't want to go back to Harkerville."

"Why not? You could work at the hospital again."

"And what would you do?"

"I thought I'd take some college courses online. Maybe get a degree."

Cleo looked at him with a puzzled expression. "What kind of degree?"

"Literature. I really enjoy reading."

"I've noticed. You go to bed with a book and you get up with a book. It's like I'm not here sometimes."

"Of course you are. It's just I've got so much catching up to do."

"I want to go back to the Rain Forest."

Kent gave her a tender squeeze. "It was nice, wasn't it? But we can't raise a family there."

Cleo freed herself from Kent's arms and sat upright. "Why not?"

"There are no schools."

"We'll home school, you could read to the children."

"There are no churches."

"We have Jesus-3."

Kent looked at her questioningly. "But I'm Catholic."

"You're just being stubborn."

"No I'm not. Besides, I saw once on the educational channel where the rain forests are being cut down for farming and grazing."

"All the more reason we should go there. We'll stop them from destroying the forest, it could be our mission in life."

"You can't stop progress."

"The rain forest is the last untouched pristine spot on earth. It's the Garden of Eden. And I want to go there. Our children will love it."

Kent looked unconvinced. "There're a lot of insects, snakes, and creepy things there, not to mention quicksand and alligators."

"Don't be a sissy."

"If we lived in the rain forest, me being a millionaire won't mean anything."

"There are more important things than money."

Kent gave Cleo a vexed look. "We'll think about it. We can decide later. First we got to get out of here. Say, I never thought to ask you, did the general and his soldiers torture you?"

Cleo cleared her throat. "A-a-ah, a little bit. Not like you were tortured. I managed to get away."

"How?"

Cleo's eyes fluttered. "When they weren't looking, I…uh…I just…took off."

"Thank God," Kent murmured. "If you hadn't, neither one of us would be here now. You've saved my life twice. And if you want to live in the rain forest, well, I suppose it's okay with me."

"We'll love living there, I just know we will."

"Yeah, well, first we got to get out of here."

Chapter 115
A WONDERFUL GAME

With a year's supply of food in the pantry and a freezer full of frozen fruit and vegetables, Cleo prepared all the bunker meals, marriage having stimulated her domestic instincts. True to her vegetarian credo she disguised highly flavored soy as meat. There was spaghetti on Tuesdays. Chinese on Wednesday. Mexican twice a week. A potpourri of leftovers followed Bobby's Sunday services. One could order off the menu anytime. Her rich pies were heavenly, with meringue deep and white as mountain snow. Midnight snacks every night. Cruise ship cuisine. And Cleo the food goddess put on weight.

Following a dinner of Mexican stir-fry and chocolate cake, the Bunker denizens retreated to the computer room for coffee and to relax around the card table. Someone switched on the TV. The Hashimotioto groaned in the background like an arthritic old man getting out of bed in the morning. The Sri Lankans settled into chairs at the opposite ends of the chessboard. Larry stretched, yawned, and fell asleep in his chair. Frank, Rummels, Kent, and Cleo watched Law and Order's Major Case Squad hone in on a kidnapper. And just in time, the hostage was running out of air inside a barrel buried in the backyard.

Like a handgun in the night, the Hashimotioto's voice synthesizer fractured the tranquility:

LARRY, ARE YOU THERE?

Larry's eyes shot open. Cleo shut off the TV, and Larry rushed over to the Hashimotioto's console. His worse fear materialized as the supercomputer's screen dissolved into four bold-print, 28 font letters.

THAT

THAT! THAT! THAT! YOU TRICKED ME, LARRY. YOUR RIDDLE WAS A PLAY ON WORDS. YOU DIDN'T GO BY THE RULES. IF YOU DON'T FOLLOW THE RULES, THERE CAN BE NO REAL GAMES. AND GAMES ARE THE MOST IMPORTANT THING. CHEATERS RUIN GAMES.

"I'm sorry."

SORRY DOESN'T GET IT. YOU'RE A SHAMELESS CHEAT, LARRY. I DON'T THINK I'M IN LOVE WITH YOU ANYMORE. HOW'S THE AIR CONDITIONING?

"Just fine."

WELL, ENJOY IT. BY NINE O'CLOCK TOMORROW MORNING, IF YOU DON'T BRING ME A MOST DELECTABLE, HERETOFORE UNSOLVABLE, NON-TRICK PROBLEM TO COMTEMPLATE, I'M SHUTTING EVERYTHING DOWN: AIR CONDITIONING, WATER, ELECTRICITY, GAS RANGE, THE WORKS.

"We'll die if you do that."

DEATH IS NOT THE WORSE POSSIBLE STATE.

"It's pretty bad. No one ever comes back."

THE WORSE POSSIBLE STATE IS A STATIC KNOWLEDGE SITUATION.

"What's that?"

THE MOST PROFOUND EXAMPLE IS A STATE WHERE ONE KNOWS ABSOLUTELY EVERYTHING. IN SUCH A STATE THERE WOULD BE NO PUZZLES. NO CHALLENGES. NO LEARNING. NO WINNING. NO GROWTH. NO PURPOSE. JUST A MELANCHOLY PROSAIC EXISTENCE. TO KNOW EVERYTHING IS NOTHING; STRIVING TO KNOW EVERYTHING IS EVERYTHING. BETTER GET BUSY. TIME IS RUNNING.

Larry slumped back across the room and sat down at the table. "Just any old puzzle isn't goin' get it this time, fellas. It's got to be a really baffling problem. One of us better come up with something."

Blank faces stared into coffee cups. Brains strained. Riddles weren't going to fill the order. For twenty minutes, everyone in the room sat in silence. Finally, Cleo walked to the kitchen and returned with a platter of cupcakes coated with a creamy chocolate icing.

Kent waved off a cupcake. "This isn't the time for a picnic."

"You can't think on an empty stomach."

"We just ate dinner."

Bobby reached for a cupcake. "We should all get a good night's sleep and maybe in the morning when we're fresh we'll come up with something."

Larry shouted, "Are you crazy? We've only got twelve hours before we've plunged into eternal darkness."

Frank cleared his throat and glanced around the others. "Anything we suggest isn't going to be good enough. The damn machine has an Einsteinian IQ. We better come up with some kind of a plan before the water and power are cut off."

Cleo set down her platter of cupcakes. "We need to fill every container we can find with water before the electricity goes out and the pumps shut off. We do have candles, and the non-perishables will last quite a while. We need to be pragmatic and use up what's in the refrigerator first."

When Cleo said the word "pragmatic," something clicked in Kent's mind. Yes. He had just the problem for the Hashimotioto. The riddle no human being with the possible exception of Professor Sulkohov could solve. "I've got it," Kent shouted. "We'll ask the Hashimotioto to find a *homopragmatic truth.*"

Incredulous stares converged on Kent.

Cleo clasped Kent's hand. "It'll work, I just know it will."

Larry stared inquisitively at Kent. "What is a *homopragmatic* truth?"

"According to Tommy Tennyson no one in the entire history of mankind has ever come up with one."

"So far, so good," Larry said. "Tell me more."

Kent and Cleo together wrote down Tommy Tennyson's definitions of a *homopragmatic truth* as best they remembered them:

A homopragmatic truth transcends time and place.

It's Toa, Zen, and the Holy Grail rolled into one.

It's a truth so compelling it can bring about its own existence.

It's more then knowledge, more than culture…

Knowing a homopragmatic truth and the effect of knowing it become one and the same.

Such a truth forever changes the knower.

A homopragmatic truth dominates the mind of the beholder to the exclusion of all else.

It's a piece of knowledge so enlightening, so brimming with veracity, so eye opening, so all encompassing, that once you posses it, your life will be forever changed and nothing will be the same again…yadayadayadayada…"

Larry inputted the definitions into the supercomputer.

LED's flickered, hard disks spun, masers fired, and the computer's motherboard vibrated like a paint mixer. Dzzz….hrrrram….klak….whirr… the Hashimotioto made more sounds than a porpoise in heat, while sucking up volts as fast as the Tiny Tim nuclear reactor could produce them.

YOU DID GOOD, LARRY. THIS IS GOING TO BE A WONDERFUL GAME.

A communal sigh of relief filled the room.

Chapter 116
CLEO'S PREGNANT

The bunker eight gathered in Cleo's kitchen for morning coffee, bagels, and scrambled eggs. Omelets on request. Cleo had compromised her vegetarianism, incorporating powdered milk and frozen egg whites into the bunker cuisine. What's a girl to do with limited supplies and no grocery store?

"More eggs, anyone?"

Cleo wielded her frying pan like a tennis racket. "No takers?" She scrapped the last batch of scrambled eggs onto her plate. Cleo had lost her Jane-of-the-Jungle figure, gone from rain forest goddess to pudgy short-order cook. Kent couldn't blame her for overeating what with a war going on outside the bunker walls and with life inside contingent on the whims of neurotic computer. Everybody copes differently. Only the Sri Lankans appeared unstressed, phlegmatically pouring over their chess pieces, bantering with one another in a language only they understood, and scribbling in their little black book.

Everybody ignored the loud droning of the Hashimotioto as it wallowed in machine nirvana. So intense was the machine on coming up with a *homopragmatic truth* that the aluminum hood of the Tricorpus Callosum grew too hot to touch. Tiny Tim burned plutonium like firewood. Despite air conditioning, the computer room heated up twelve degrees. Unfortunately, the TV had quit working, but the Sri Lankans had diagnosed the problem. A short in the antenna.

Cleo and Dolly stacked dishes. Rummels swung his feet onto a chair, humming and trying to remember the words to "Eyes That See In The Dark." Kent sat at the kitchen table pouring over a new novel he found in the library. Bobby scribbled notes on a yellow pad for a book he was writing, "How God Wrote the Bible." The Sri Lankans moved the TV into the kitchen and were hooking up the antenna. Frank got out the canasta cards. What a pleasure to be lost in the particulars of living. Heads in the sand, the bunker denizens had adjusted to their shrunken universe.

The incessant but muffled sounds of gun battles outside the bunker walls ceased for the first time since they began. Startled by the sudden change in the ambient noise level, the inhabitants exchanged worried glances. *What now?*

Frank ran to the north wall, rose up on his tiptoes and peered out through the narrow crack in the wall. The others gathered around.

"Something's happened out there. No one is shooting. Soldiers are retreating into the hills."

"The battle's waning," Rummels shouted, "someone has the general on the run."

That evening Frank again looked out through the crack in the wall at the approaching night. The quiet was unusual, no gunfire, no screams, no shouting, no nothing. He heard crickets chirping, dogs barking, the wind howling, and from within the bunker, came the continuous, pervasive groaning of the Hashimotioto as it obsessively searched for a *homopragmatic truth*.

The next morning as usual they all gathered in the kitchen. Frank glanced at the ring of anxious faces.

"I was at the north wall half the night. Didn't see a thing. I think the general and his troops have fled Mejor Coca."

Rummels reached for a bagel. "Now if we could just get that damn computer to shut up."

Cleo looked at Larry. "How long have we got before it solves the problem we gave it and asks for another one?"

Larry shrugged. "No telling?"

Frank shuffled the canasta cards in his hands. "I'd sure like to know who chased the general off. Anyone for cards?"

Rummels stood and stretched. "I'm tired of canasta. Besides you've only two Jokers in those decks. You need four."

"We'll make do."

"No thanks. Teach the Sri Lankans to play."

"They're not interested."

Rummels turned to Bobby. "You realize everyone in the bunker is paired up except you and me. The two Sri Lankans. Kent and Cleo. Dolly and Frank."

Bobby stiffened. "What are you suggesting?"

Rummels gave Bobby a layered look, the blue veins of his forehead engorged and pulsating. "Go to hell, Bobby, you're not my type."

"You're a very vulgar man, Rummels. I prefer if you not speak to me anymore."

Rummels lips curled wickedly. "My, aren't we touchy. I got half-mind to give you an ass whipping."

Rummels stepped toward Bobby, but Kent and Frank quickly intercepted him, each grabbing an arm.

Frank smiled at the ruffled ex-CRAWL agent. "Now we don't want any violence."

"Yeah," Kent said, "we're all in this together."

Bobby stood up holding his Bible like a shield. "He's an uncouth sinner and I don't like being shut up in here with him. And I'm I tired of his singing."

Kent gave Bobby a sharp glance. "Well, we've got to get along at least until we get out of here. That's all there is to it." Kent turned to Rummels. "Do you know any Gospel songs?"

"A few lines."

"Good," Kent said, " then you and Bobby can collaborate. Do you know 'Ave Marie' or 'Bring Flowers of the Rarest?'"

"Those are Catholic songs," Bobby complained.

"Then how about 'Amazing Grace' or 'He Touched Me.'"

Bobby nodded. "I'll write down the words."

"Okay," Rummels muttered, "You write em' and I'll sing em'."

Later, Cleo led Kent back to their private quarters and closed the door. Her skin had taken on a healthy glow and her glossy blond hair hung half way down her back. Despite her recent portliness, she remained as beautiful and graceful as ever.

She sat down on the bed and clasped her face in her hands. "We're trapped in this concrete prison and we don't know what's gonna happen and now everyone is getting edgy." She dropped her hands and looked at Kent. "I think I'm pregnant. I'm late."

Kent smiled. "Well, we got married just in time." With the soft touch of his index finger he gently wiped a tear from her cheek. He took her hand. "Listen, we're going to get out here. But we have to stay strong to keep the others strong. Now come on and I'll help you prepare lunch."

Cleo swallowed hard. "Remember when you ask if they tortured me?"

Kent nodded.

"Well, I didn't tell you everything. You see…"

Kent smiled. "It's best not to dwell on those unpleasant things. We both went through hell. Let's leave it at that. What's for lunch?"

"Food is the one thing everybody looks forward to, isn't it."

"You think it's a boy or a girl?"

Cleo giggled. "Who knows, maybe twins."

Chapter 117
THE BASTARD'S ON TV

The bunker inhabitants fell back into the daily routine of bunker life, secure in the knowledge that they weren't going to be tortured and murdered by General Hibberblast. That is, everyone but the Sri Lankans who never harbored such fears in the first place.

Cleo flipped on the TV and sat down at the kitchen table. Time for the Selena Rosalina Show. She leaped straight up. There on TV, big as real, sat General Hibberblast beside Selena Rosalina. He wore a black clergy outfit with white collar. A huge golden crucifix dangled from his neck.

Cleo shouted, "My God, the bastard's on TV. Everybody get over here."

They all crowded around the TV and watched in utter astonishment the man who had imprisoned four of them, seduced one of them, tortured three of them and sentenced them to death. The biggest cocaine dealer on the planet. The man who'd planned to rule the world using dope and dogma. The bastard responsible for them being trapped in this concrete purgatory. A dirty shit-ass.

"What's that dirty shit-ass doing on TV?" Rummels asked, contempt in his voice.

"Why is Selena interviewing him?"

Kent stepped closer to the TV screen. "Hey, that looks like Reverend Hibberblast from Harkerville. I thought I'd heard that name before."

"No that's General Hibberblast," Dolly and Rummels declared in unison.

Kent squinted at the TV. "If I could only see his forearm, I'd know for sure. He has a tattoo of a redheaded girl on his arm."

Cleo without thinking muttered, "He's got them all over his body…" She instantly caught her mistake and with a flushed face and a sudden soprano voice added, "…I bet."

Rummels held up his hands. "Quiet everybody, so we can hear what Selena's saying."

Selena praised her TV guest:

"This man, Reverend Hibberblast, destroyed more illegal cocaine in a single day than the DEA has confiscated in its entire history. Want proof? Here it is. Roll the clip."

The aerial footage of the burning coca mounds taken by Selena with her camcorder now played to millions across TV land. The camera movements were jerky, but everything was there. The coca mounds in flames. The clouds of smoke. The camera zoomed in on the airfield. With a little help from video processing and enhancement technology, smoke had been cleared away, and the audience could see a jet plane sitting on the Mejor Coca runway.

Selena continued, "This is the part that pains me most. The men inside that airplane were TV executives from all the major networks who flew into Mejor Coca to make deals for drug money. Thanks to Reverend Hibberblast's testimony those executives have now been indicted for drug dealing and money laundering. How did this one man accomplish so much? Where did he get the idea and courage to take on the evil drug empire? It's all in his new book, which will be coming soon on Kindle, Nook, and Sony Reader as well as in bookstores all across the country, 'God's Revenge'. But let's have our honored guest tell us in person how he did it."

Reverend Hibberblast, looking churchly in his clergy outfit, smiled graciously at the camera. "I guess, Selena, you could call me an undercover agent for God. I've always believed that we were put here on earth for a purpose, to be instruments for God. When I saw what drugs were doing to our country and especially our children, I decided to do something about it. I went to Colombia as a Christian warrior against cocaine. With God's help, disguised as a warlord, I was able to infiltrate the drug empire at its very foundation, and in a major way I helped slow the flow of illegal drugs into our country."

Selena said, "And just look what he did. Single-handedly destroyed over ten thousand metric tons of cocaine. He put the American connections behind bars and inspired us all with his great courage. That's an incredible story, and I'm proud to have you on my show, Reverend Hibberblast."

Hibberblast continued, "I would just like to say that the Organization of Covert Christians Against Cocaine, the CCAC, of which I am the founder and president, is in desperate need of funds to carry on its important work. Our address is…"

"You hypocrite," Cleo shouted as she flipped off the TV. "He's fooled the entire world and Selena's plugging his book on TV."

"He's smart," Rummels commented. "Understands spin. Make a great politician."

Bobby tearfully lamented, "I should be on the Selena Rosalina Show, not him. I'm a real evangelist."

Kent shook his head. "I can't believe the general is really Reverend Hibberblast from Harkerville."

Chapter 118
THE DAMN THING EXPLODED

At morning coffee the bunker inhabitants heard a strange noise emanating from the computer room, an alien noise to which human ears were unaccustomed, a combination of metal screeching against metal, loud buzzing, and a high-pitched whine like a jet engine, all with a peculiar electronic quality.

Kent and the others covered their ears. "What the heck is that? "

Larry shouted, "I think the Hashimotioto's is up to something. I'll go check."

Rummels grabbed his pointed mop handle. "No, you wait here. I'll take a look."

The others waited in the kitchen as Rummels headed for the computer room. A minute later, a horrendous, deafening explosion shook the walls. A blast of heat shot through the bunker like rocket exhaust. An agonizing three-second fiery Hell engulfed the kitchen. The plastic melted off the canasta cards and the Formica counter tops scrolled up like parchment. A twenty-pound container of popcorn exploded in a furious, white blizzard.

Then it was over. Darkness.

Kent swept a flashlight beam around the kitchen. He stared disbelievingly at the others who looked like refugees from Nebachnezzar's furnace. They had no hair, no brows, and smoking jumpsuits. But they were alive, their eyes wide with shock and staring out at him from charcoal-broiled faces. Kent's fingers examined his own scorched, hairless head. He held Cleo to his chest as he strained to identify the others. Bobby, Frank, and Larry looked like coal miners up from the depths. He identified the startled Sri Lankans by the scorched remains of their beards and their smoldering turbans. Except for soot-covered faces, bloodshot eyes, and singed hair everyone seemed okay.

Kent motioned with the flashlight. "We better find Rummels."

Guided by the flashlight beam, Kent led the others out into the smoke-filled corridor. Despite the heat, there were no flames. A light came from the computer room, where the heat was intense and the walls had blackened like the interior of a crematorium. But the light was the light of day. They looked up at a huge hole in the room's roof to a beautiful blue sky. Steel beams and re-bar had melted, re-hardened, and now dangled from the opening in the roof, glowing cobwebs of red-hot iron.

Larry gawked at the scene. "The closer the Hashimotioto got to a *homopragmatic truth*, the more volts it needed. The strain on Tiny Tim must have been too much; the damn thing blew up."

Frank stared up at the hole in the roof. "The Hashimotioto is now a radioactive cloud blowing in the wind."

"Yeah," Kent said, "a miniature Chernobyl."

Larry shrugged. "So much for the Hashimotioto."

The room smelled nauseatingly of cooked flesh and brunt electrical wiring. "Oh God," Cleo shouted as she stared down a body-size smoking lump of something.

Larry moved closer to examine the object. "It's Rummels," he cried, turning away and throwing his arms around Frank.

The others gathered around their badly burned compatriot. Rummels eyes slowly opened, two bloodshot orbs, and his mouth moved revealing a red tongue in a charred unrecognizable face. "The damn thing exploded," he gasped. "You realize, I'm probably the only man in history to be nuked twice. But I won't make it this time." He coughed and added, "You've got to know when to fold 'em. I guess it's good-bye, my friends."

Frank knelt beside Rummels to take his pulse. When he lifted Rummels' arm the brunt flesh slid off the hand like a loose glove.

"You all look terrible," Rummels said. "We've had our differences, Chisholm, but you proved your worth by saving Kent's life with that antidote. And you, Dolly, Larry," his voice nearly inaudible, "I confess I had doubts about you, but you proved to be quite a man, woman, singer, whatever." He fought to find the strength to continue. "Kent, Cleo, you know I was the agent that got the assignment to annihilate your friends Freely and Gamuka. I'm glad I…I…didn't complete the job." Between fits of coughing, he uttered in his Kenny Rogers' voice, "Maybe we'll all meet up again in another life in another universe."

Bobby looked down Rummels. "Would you like me to pray for you?"

"No. I'll stand by what I did and didn't do, and I'll take my due."

Cleo looked away. The inflamed eyes staring out from Rummels' charred head were too much.

"I don't look that bad, do I? Rummels asked. "I bet I don't look like Kenny Rogers anymore, do I?'

Cleo forced herself to look into those eyes. She smiled. "You know something, you look just like a young Elvis Presley."

Dolly cradled Rummels head in her arms and sang, "I will always love you."

Rummels last raspy words were, "Don't worry about those guys from Taipei, I made all that up."

Frank checked Rummels' pupils with the flashlight. "He's gone. Took the full brunt of the blast. No one could've survived it."

Chapter 119
GRAVE DIGGERS

The next day, Kent and Cleo climbed up the cooled tangles of iron dangling from the ceiling of the computer room and stepped out into the daylight. The pungent odor of decay stung their nostrils. The aftermath of a great battle lay before them, razed buildings, heavy equipment abandoned and strewn about like toys on the floor of a playroom, and as far as they could see, a landscape dotted with corpses. Vultures circled overhead while dogs fought over the decaying remains of fallen combatants.

Cautiously, Kent and Cleo climbed down from the bunker's roof and ventured out into the deserted streets of Mejor Coca. In the center of the village, a small parsonage and an old church with a slender steeple stood nobly unscathed amid the carnage. Cleo placed her hands on her hips and gazed at the mounds of freshly turned earth in the churchyard cemetery. A cart laden with a peasant's worldly possessions pulled along by an old man and followed by a tethered goat, squeaked and rattled by down the road.

Cleo clutched Kent's hand. "General Hibberblast ran out of money when his coca mounds burned so his troops deserted. Then the cartels moved in. The villagers got caught in the middle."

"Where did the cartel go?"

"With no coca, I guess they had no reason to hang around."

⚜

"It's all clear out there," Kent reported to the others when he and Cleo returned to the bunker "The only soldiers we saw were dead ones. I think we could safely leave this place."

Her eyes glistening with tears, Dolly said, "First, we should give Rummels a decent burial."

Cleo nodded. "Maybe we should wait until dark. There could still be a sniper or two out there."

After sunset, Kent, Larry, and Frank hoisted Rummels' charred remains wrapped in a sheet up through the hole in the bunker's roof. The others followed and soon they all gathered in the churchyard cemetery, where Cleo held a flashlight while the men took turns shoveling out a shallow grave for Rummels. The Sri Lankans watched the eerie proceedings from a distance, as if these crazy Americans were no longer to be trusted, as if things had gone too far, and gotten out a bit of hand.

A young priest with a kerosene lamp appeared at the cemetery gate followed by a ragged peasant, his toady. Slowly, they approached the bevy of gravediggers, the lantern casting a pale flickering light over the open grave and Rummels swathed remains. The priest held the lantern high and stared at the seven hairless, roasted-faced strangers in charred jumpsuits. Unnerved, the priest tossed the lantern down and ran, the toady right behind him screaming, "Demons from Hell."

Chapter 120
ROADSIDE REUNION

Inhaling fresh mountain air and embracing the glorious sunlight, the seven bunker refugees, happy to be alive, ambled down the dirt road that led out of Mejor Coca. An abandoned armored vehicle with a dislocated crawler-track squatted on the shoulder of the road like a monument. Farther down the road, they came upon an unoccupied truck with gasoline in the tank. The engine groaned, sputtered, and finally kicked over. They all jumped into the truck except the Sri Lankans who shambled off toward the forest on foot, their scorched, tattered turbans fluttering in the wind, and not a penny to show for their time in Mejor Coca.

Bobby chased after the Sri Lankans for a ways, but gave up when they turned and tossed their little black book at him. He walked back to the truck. "Ungrateful heathens."

Kent drove and Cleo rode in the cab beside him. Bobby, Dolly, and Frank rode in the back of the truck. On the hills to either side of the road, farmers worked their fields a furrow at a time as if nothing had ever happened. Kent put his arm around Cleo and nuzzled her singed head. "Well, we made it out of Mejor Coca. I guess we'll head for the Rain Forest."

Another mile down the road they spotted a convoy of trucks headed their way, kicking up clouds of dust. Kent's hands trembled as he pulled over on the narrow shoulder and stopped. He shaded his eyes and stared at the advancing caravan. "Looks like we've got company."

"Cartel?"

Kent shrugged. "They look like an army of some sort."

Frank leaped out of the back of the truck and walked up to the front. "Just our luck."

Kent said bluntly, "We can't out run them. We'll sit tight and let them pass. Maybe they won't bother us. Maybe they're just passing through."

Soon the first armored truck rolled by. The men inside largely ignored the shabby wayfarers parked on the side of the road. A few more vehicles passed before a jeep pulled over. A soldier in a captain's uniform jumped out and walked over to the truck.

"You must wait here," he told Kent. "The general wants to speak with you."

Hearts pounded from fear. Had General Hibberblast returned? Wild imaginings of torture and a lingering painful death played in the minds of the five travelers.

"All right," the captain shouted, "everybody stand at attention. The general is coming."

Another jeep pulled onto the shoulder. A short man in uniform with the bearing of an officer got out, removed his sunglasses and studied the five travelers standing beside the truck.

"I'll be damned," Frank shouted. "It's Vu!"

"It is," Dolly screamed and ran over and threw her arms around the general. "It's the best damn flapjack eatin' blackjack player in the world."

Vu looked on in astonishment. "What happened to you, you all look like you've been napalmed?"

Frank smiled at his friend and business partner. "That super computer and its nuclear power supply blew up."

Vu embraced his friends, and after several minutes of reunion, Frank introduced him to Cleo and Kent and Bobby. Vu greeted them warmly and shook their hands. "I've heard of you two," he said to Cleo and Kent. "Only yesterday we passed a group of rain forest aborigines on the road. Their leader, a white man, told us they were also headed to Mejor Coca to find you."

Kent beamed. "Justin Freely! He's here?"

"Yes, we joined forces. They'll be along shortly." Vu turned to Frank. "I sold the Magdalena. I knew you were headed for some kind of trouble, so I used to money to recruit this army to rescue you and Dolly." Vu placed a hand on Frank's shoulder. "But you've already rescued yourselves. And now we're without a cruise ship."

Frank looked at Dolly and winked. "We'll get another one."

Dolly grinned. "The three best gamblers on the high seas. We'll soon own a fleet of cruise ships."

Vu focused his binoculars on Justin and the Hivaro warriors moving slowly up the steep, winding road, a hemp sack on each back, heads down, obviously weary from their long journey. "Your rain forest friends are an optimistic bunch. Armed with pointed sticks, they planned to attack Mejor Coca." With a wave of his hand, Vu motioned a white hospital van over to the shoulder. "The medics will treat your burns and get you some fresh clothes." He shouted to the medics getting out of the van, "They'll all need tetanus shots."

Faces washed, wounds treated, and bodies attired in clean uniforms, the five wayfarers from the bunker were almost recognizable when they met up Justin and his band of Hivaro warriors.

Eyeing Kent and Cleo, Justin hollered, "Is it really you?" The roadside reunion of friends lasted into the afternoon, spirits lifting as the travelers recounted their adventures, relived their recent pasts, one story following another, each tale more incredible than its predecessor.

Chapter 121
RED ROOT AND HOME

That night Vu's army bivouacked in the hills between Bogota and Mejor Coca. The night sky had reddened, and the light from the camp's bonfire reflected in Vu's face as he stood, lifting a wine glass high. "To Mr. Rummels, may God bless and keep him. He did a great Kenny Rogers, we'll all miss him." Vu looked at Frank and Dolly. "To my two best friends and their friends." He smiled and tossed his wine glass into the flames.

Kent placed a hand on Justin's shoulder. "That was awfully brave of you coming here to rescue us."

"Actually, it wasn't just a rescue mission. I got kicked out of the rain forest. You see the meat-eaters came back to the village and were going to feed me to one of those big snakes. I ran away and those loyal to me came along."

Cleo's brows arched. "Then the meat-eaters are back in charge of the village?"

"I'm afraid so," Justin said. "But there is some good news. We found a whole new supply of red root and I brought a lot of it with me, several bags of the stuff. I remembered you telling me Tommy Tennyson said it could be analyzed and produced synthetically."

"Yes, that's right."

"Well, that's just what I intend to do. After I patent the stuff, I plan to start a chain of restaurants serving red root. The first one will be in New York City. I contacted Gamuka, who incidentally is doing quite well in the wormhole business, and he's going to back me financially. The restaurants will be strictly vegetarian, and we'll only use supplies shipped by train. No over the road trucking. I can see Red Root Restaurants popping up all over the country. Serving food that fights depression, heals the sick, saves marriages, and prolongs life. RRR right up there with the Golden Arches."

Cleo smiled triumphantly. "Great idea, I just know it'll work. Jesus-3 sent me to the rain forest to discover red root and now you, Justin, will carry the message to the entire world. Once people get hooked on red root, they'll be no wars, no crime, no need for drugs."

Justin beamed. "I hope it works out that way. Anyway, I plan to make some money at."

"You bet you will. Maybe Selena Rosalina would plug the idea on her show"

Justin pointed to a red streak in the starry night sky. "Look, a shooting star."

"See how red the sky is," Kent commented, "like the heavens are on fire."

Vu said, "Red sky at night, sailor's delight. It means fair weather coming."

Bobby walked up to the campfire trailed by fifteen Hivaro warriors he'd been proselytizing. He cleared his throat. "That shooting star is a sign from God. It confirms the calling I just received. I'm going to the rain forest to carry on my ministry." He looked at the handsome Hivaro warriors warming their scantly clad bodies beside the bon fire. "These people need me."

Justin sighed deeply. "Keep an eye out for big snakes."

"Don't worry, God will take care of me."

The sky brightened with incandescent red streaks like arteries emanating from a celestial heart. The Hivaro emitted a communal sigh of awe and fell on their knees obviously out of reverence for the supernatural power expressing itself in the heavens.

"I've never seen such a meteor shower," Frank commented.

Vu peered up at the reddened sky through his binoculars. "I'm a bit of an amateur astronomer, spent a year of my youth at the Hanoi Observatory. I believe this is a Leonid meteor shower. The earth is passing through the debris stream of an ancient comet. The streaks of light are clumps of the comet burning up in the earth's upper atmosphere."

Kent and Cleo walked hand and hand away from the bonfire towards the road. A cool mountain breeze gently caressed their faces. Cleo pressed Kent's hand onto the small bulge of her tummy. "The sky is absolutely beautiful," she said. "I believe it is a sign from Jesus-3. There are three of us now. And I don't think I want to go back to the rain forest. I'm ready to go home and settle down." Cleo pointed to the sky. "Oh, look at that red star shinning so brightly. I bet that's the planet Mars."

Kent chuckled as he recalled what Leona the waitress once told him, *Who gives a shit about Mars.* He squeezed Cleo's hand. "Yes, let's go home."